TIMOTHY BAINES

ALSO BY JOHN H. CULP

A Whistle in the Wind
The Bright Feathers

Timothy Baines

A NOVEL BY

John H. Culp

HOLT, RINEHART AND WINSTON
New York   Chicago
San Francisco

Copyright © 1969 by John H. Culp
All rights reserved, including the right to reproduce
this book or portions thereof in any form.
Published simultaneously in Canada by Holt, Rinehart
and Winston of Canada, Limited.

Library of Congress Catalog Card Number: 79-80338

First Edition

Designer: Ernst Reichl
SBN: 03-081843-5
Printed in the United States of America

TO LOUISE

ONE

Denna Cart had always thought of Connecticut from what her father had told her.

But she sat now with her bare feet in a Texas stream, watching black thunderheads slide above, then lowering her eyes to follow their racing shadows across the brown rock.

Her father had told her of the autumn colors of beech and aspen and maple in Connecticut, the green pines and hemlocks, and wisps of feathery clouds trailing seaward, of stout stone fences enclosing neat parcels of land, of mountains and rugged rockbound coasts, and the tangy smell of sea salt that tickled the nostrils.

Beside the Texas creek a horned toad in serrated armor crept from beneath a ledge; when it saw Denna, it became motionless. Once she had tried to make a pet of a horned toad, but it had died from something she fed it.

At other times of the year in Connecticut there would be work with the cattle; and the flowering azaleas or honeysuckle would blossom, and the white wild cherry; the dogwood petals would come in June. Here in Texas there was nothing but mesquite, spiny cactus, and black chaparral and yucca. The miles of growth did not color as vividly as they did in Connecticut.

Last week there had been rain on the plateau—that was why the narrow creek held water, three feet of dancing water. But even with the promise of more rain, the day was sticky and hot.

Denna stood and took her clothes off. She slipped from the rocky bank into the water like a sleek snake, slithering into it, feeling the current shove against her body, feeling its coolness. She laughed—the current felt like fingers caressing her. She shoved the palms of her hands forward, splashing a shower of spray on the horned toad.

A large Negress came from the chaparral. Her head was bound in a red bandanna, and she held a long machete in her hand. She wore gold earrings.

"Child, what are you doing here like this? There're rattlesnakes and scorpions around these rocks. Get dressed and come home with me. Right now, I say, right now."

Denna pleaded, splashing the cool water about her. "Amy, just a little while." In defiance, she slapped the water, palms down.

"Right now, I say."

"No. I don't like you!"

"You are uppity, little missy. You knew your daddy would be at the courthouse in Victory today—that's why you ran off. You are headstrong and willful."

"I think you are mean."

"With water driving the rattlesnakes out of these creeks, you'd think me meaner if one bit you. That's why I brought this machete."

"I hate you, Amy," Denna said, her eyes flashing, "I hate you."

Nearly one thousand miles away, and on the same day—across the Mississippi River—near Nanih Wayia, the sacred mound of the Choctaw Indians in the Tallahaga Valley of Mississippi, and not too far from a prong of the Natchez Trace in the days of the Indian removals, a white boy with a dour expression on his face sat beside another creek, wearing only a loincloth. A fishing pole extended before him.

Dorch McIntyre was dark, with bushy black hair; he was lank, but with good shoulders, and ten years older than the girl who sat beside the stream in Texas. He was one-fourth Chickasaw, the nation which lay half a day's trot to the north. His father was a Scotch trader, friendly to both tribes.

Dorch was tired of fishing; he hadn't caught anything. A moss-backed turtle he had seen yesterday crept through fringy ferns, its neck out. Now he could do what he had wanted to do for a long time. He leaped from the bank and took his knife and cut the turtle's head off.

Impatience in his face, he cut and hacked the body from the shell and trimmed the flesh, to expose the heart. He had often wondered why things and persons so alive one moment could be so dead the next. Old Dr. Bainbridge, who always hung around the Indian villages, had told him the same thing.

Dorch thought, squatting over the turtle, if I had some salt I could make the heart beat or jerk again—for a moment, that is. It would be like putting salt on frog legs, although there wouldn't be as much jerking as comes with the legs.

He heard the swish of wings; a blue heron swung from the leafy gloom, to land in the creek shallows; for a moment it stood and watched the scowling boy, then indifferently raised one wing and extended its long neck to peck its side with its bill.

Hunkered beside the turtle, Dorch watched the heron. It had the longest legs of any he had seen.

Dissatisfied and sullen, leaving the fishing pole on the ground, and sticking the bloody knife in the string of his breechclout, he turned from the creek and walked under the heavy trees toward his father's store.

As he moved along the village path, he saw two Choctaw men squatting beside a brook, washing their hands. They rose, shaking water from their fingers. One, Chimney Katchee, was tall, and the other, Dead Man Joiner, was chubby with a round face. Both wore burlap sacking like shawls about their shoulders.

Chimney Katchee and Dead Man were bonepickers. The Choctaw dead were placed on platforms; when the flesh was decomposed, it was stripped from the bones by the fingernails, and the litter was burned with the platform. The skeleton was placed in a coffin and moved to the bone house.

"Have you finished picking Chief Chilly and Molly?" Dorch asked.

"Yes," said Chimney Katchee. "The friends and relatives have carried the skeletons to the bone house."

Old Chief Chilly Black and his wife, Molly, had died on their Trail of Tears to the new lands across the Mississippi. Months ago, Dorch's father had equipped their party for its trip to the West.

The two bonepickers fell in beside Dorch and walked onward toward the store.

Dorch said, his words rushing furiously, "The government killed Chief Chilly and Molly by not having a steamboat where it promised. They were too old to make the trip overland." Rubbing his fingers through his unruly hair, he added, the stench of the bonepickers thick in his nostrils, "The big migration was over before my grandfather died. My father has always tried to get the Choctaws and Chickasaws who stayed to leave in small groups so he could equip them well that they would not die in travel."

"Yes," said Dead Man, the burlap flapping over his shoulders, his waddle like a duck's, "those deaths were the government's fault. If the steamboat had met Chilly Black's band at the mouth of the Arkansas—at Napoleon—babies and old people would not have wandered in swamps and died of chills and fever. Chief Chilly asked to be buried in his own country; he was floated down the Mississippi on a raft, and was rotten when he got here."

"I know," said Dorch. "I smelled him. Everybody smelled him."

Chimney Katchee said, "It is bad when Indians are torn from their land by the government. It is like taking a tooth from a jaw."

Years before, Dorch's father had sent two trusted helpers, Tom Adkins and Boyce Townley, into the new Territory to open trading stores at Doaksville and at Boggy Depot, where government suppliers were distributed. He would remain at the old post near Nanih Wayia until the last Indians were ready to leave, then he would follow, still to trade with both tribes, as he had always done.

He made no excuses for his opinions or intervention.

Standing outside his log store with his black beard blowing above his white scarf, he would say to some government agent or commissioner who thought he interposed himself too much in Indian affairs, "My Indians have been good to me and to my father. They will be good to my son. Why shouldn't I help them? Why shouldn't I see them off safely? They give me profit, but I return it full value. The best names of two tribes are on my books."

As Dorch and the bonepickers came from the valley, he could see the store now, but it was not built like a store. It was more a series of adjacent cabins grouped about a larger one, the general headquarters of sauntering or trading Indians, some in white man's clothes, others in breechclouts or leggings.

Once within the store with the bonepickers, Dorch saw his father standing at the back counter between the shelves of blankets and sugar and knives and trinkets and beads and hatchets, talking with Dr. Bainbridge.

The doctor was a slight man; he wore a string tie, a long coat, and a gray stovepipe hat; with his drunken, ferret eyes and bristle of white beard, he looked like a weasel. Dorch's father was tall and broad-shouldered. He wore his jacket and the white scarf and leggings.

As Dorch moved toward him with the bonepickers, the trader asked, "Where have you been?"

"Fishing."

"I want you to take some groceries out. They are for Chilly Black's feast."

From beneath his black shock of hair, Dorch said defiantly, "I caught a turtle. I cut around the heart, but I didn't have any salt. I couldn't make it keep beating."

Clutching his whiskey bottle unsteadily, while his other hand supported him against the counter, Dr. Bainbridge said, "If you would stop wearing loincloths and put a pair of trousers on, you could carry salt in your pockets."

The doctor raised his bottle. He hiccuped, belching the foulness of his breath about the counter. "What makes you want to be a doctor, anyway?"

Scowling, Dorch pulled his loincloth higher with his forefingers. "I don't know. I just want to learn how things work in people."

The doctor, his reddened eyes twitching, said, "After you deliver the groceries for Chilly Black's feast, bring the turtle to me. If the heart's still moist, I'll show you something."

The black-bearded trader took two bars of soap from a shelf, placing them on the counter before Chimney Katchee and Dead Man. "Go to the washing hole and clean up," he said. "When you come back, we'll talk about Chilly Black's ceremony."

Dorch flung the heavy sack over his shoulder; he would go to the village, then return to the creek for the turtle, which he would take to Dr. Bainbridge's cabin.

The bearded trader followed his moody and scowling son to the doorway and stood there, watching him depart for the Choctaw village.

In New Orleans a hunchbacked urchin who carried a shoeshine box under his arm walked through the dusky drizzle of Canal Street, the light of the streetlamps striking his face.

It was a thin face, a tired face, a streak of shoeblack on one cheek, but even in the drizzle the bright eyes twinkled.

The boy's eyes twinkled because under his other arm he carried a stick of lumber. This makes four, he thought, stopping on a corner beneath overhanging iron grillwork to let a handsome cabriolet pass, its lamps aglow. If I have some more luck, he continued to think, I'll soon have enough lumber to build a big sit-down stand so folks won't have to stand to put their feet on my box. While he waited on the corner, the rain dripped from a ragged sweater, which dropped grotesquely from his hump. In spite of the lamps along the curb, the murk was making everything even harder to see.

After the cabriolet passed, the boy continued his walk to a side street, the drizzle increasing; then he turned toward an unlighted alley. It would be good to save this lumber, he thought. Three times I've been ready to build that sit-down stand, but each time somebody has stolen all I saved. These alley boxes I sleep in aren't safe.

A bulky policeman in a belted blue raincoat and a rounded hat stood in the mouth of the alley. The boy thought, he's here because of all this gang mischief that's going on. The policeman carried a billy club.

"Timothy Baines," the policeman said.

The boy stopped. "Yes, sir, Mr. MacMurphy." Now he saw him clearer. The big officer was broad-faced and smiling.

"Come here," MacMurphy said. "I haven't had my luck today."

"Yes, sir," Timothy said.

He stepped forward, and MacMurphy rubbed his thick knuckles over Timothy's hump. "Now I've got enough luck to last me for a week. You always come back to this alley—maybe you were born in it. And you've got more lumber." MacMurphy wiped the rain from his heavy neck. He went on, "I can't imagine grown people leaving a newborn babe in a garbage can."

"My hump, sir," said Timothy.

"The orphanage let you out for adoption, but why did you run away?"

"They weren't people to stay with, sir, but I've always made out. I've got my sleeping boxes, and sometimes I use the porches. But I want that sit-down stand."

"You've been a good boy for an alley rat." MacMurphy wanted a toothpick. He always carried one in his teeth, whether he had eaten or not. He had some in his inside coat pocket now, but because of the rain he didn't want to unbelt his raincoat to get to them.

"Pat Muldoon and his saloon owe me something," MacMurphy said. "He's been keeping open after hours. Yes, sir, you're a pretty good kid, Timothy."

"I'll be all right when I get my new stand built."

"Give me your board," MacMurphy said. "Come on, let's go down the alley to the back door and see Pat."

They left the mouth of the alley and walked into the darkness, the drum of rain beating on the roofs.

MacMurphy said, swinging his billy club with his free hand, "Most of the boys take their payoffs in money. I've got my own way."

They passed a large packing crate set against a wall of the alley. "That's your sleeping box, isn't it?" MacMurphy said.

Two eyes gleamed from the box, reflected by the dim light at the alley mouth.

"Some animal," MacMurphy said, wanting to open his raincoat for a toothpick.

"That's old Star, my cat. Sometimes he stays here."

Once within the crowded back room where Pat Muldoon swung his big and shady deals, MacMurphy walked straight to the bar. He said to Pat, "Gimme some toothpicks, Pat."

Pat had snapping black eyes and a long pallid face with black sideburns which came down to his jawbones. He slid a glass of large round sharp-pointed toothpicks across the bar. MacMurphy put one in his teeth, a dozen in his raincoat pocket.

"What's the board you carry?" Pat asked suspiciously, scrubbing the bar.

"To beat the daylights out of you."

Pat jerked his head toward the end of the crowded bar. When he and MacMurphy had moved there, Pat asked, frowning, "What's your payoff?"

"You can relax," MacMurphy said. "It's not money. See this kid with me? With all the remodeling you're doing here, this place will be full of drunk carpenters tomorrow. This shine kid wants a new stand. By tomorrow night, I want a big shoeshine stand built from the painted lumber you're tearing out—a two-seater stand with arm supports, and send someone out to get the shoe rests. Tomorrow night I'll pass Pierre's Shrimp Restaurant at seven o'clock. If that stand isn't in place between the restaurant and the bank corner, you will get a payoff. Another thing—let the kid, Timothy Baines, sweep your place out before he goes to work. Give him a blanket, and he can sleep on the floor."

Pat's black eyes snapped. "What the hell?" he said.

"I've told you," MacMurphy said, chewing his toothpick. "And if it's not done my way, I'll really get you. This back-room crowd, you know." He turned to Timothy. "Here's your plank, kid. Put it on the floor. Pat will give you a sandwich and a blanket. It's wet outside."

"Thank you, Mr. MacMurphy."

MacMurphy said, "Give me my luck again, kid." His rough knuckles raked Timothy's hump. His wide face under his rain hat smiled benignly in munificence.

With tears in his usually merry eyes, Timothy submitted among the laughter of the barflies to this final mortification as he stood with his feet in the sawdust.

TWO

1

Abel Cart had left Connecticut because of a row with his neighbors. It had been the same thing all the time, at church and at town meetings, his always talking about Texas, until he had become a laughingstock.

Folks in their dry New England way had begun to say that if Abel suddenly died, they'd send their wreaths to Texas, since that was where Abel's soul would be.

Even though menfolk thought they knew Abel well, and talked with him and joked with him and drank with him on occasion, they had never known the real flint in his hide. He ran twenty cows within his stone fence lines. In those days before the Civil War, whenever he thought of Texas, he knew more than ever that he wanted ten thousand cattle, twenty thousand cattle, a million cattle to run instead of twenty.

One day he strode into the office of his old friend and attorney, Zebulon Peake. "Zeb," he said, "in spite of war talk, I'm moving to Texas. I've got money to go on, and I'm leaving my place for you to sell."

With long fingers, Zebulon scratched the back of his bald head and leaned back in a squeaking swivel chair. "I'm not surprised, Abel," he said. "It's what you've thought for years."

His gray eyes searched Abel's face keenly. He saw a thin, tall man standing before him; middle-aged, an aristocrat with a trim goatee and mustache, still wearing an old Quaker-style black hat and suit.

"What about your wife?" said Zebulon. "How will she stand that hot country?"

A shadow crossed Abel's face. "The doctors say Denna won't get well here; she's still childless. They say she will be no worse in Texas."

Abel might have liked Texas, had things gone right, but he was soured against it from the beginning.

He had left his wife at a hotel in Houston. He knew horses, and he bought a good one and a saddle. Then he rode deeper into his new home. He rode miles and miles into mesquite and shriveled live oak and chaparral, camping when sundown caught him, or staying at some white settler's dugout or within a Mexican's lean-to.

One afternoon in the heat of the day, far beyond San Antonio, he tied up at a hitchrack in a parched town built precariously on the brink of a canyon. A sign at the post office read "Victory." Victory, Abel thought. It should be Purgatory. He beat the dust from his trousers with his gauntlets and entered the swinging doors of a saloon.

"A beer," he said to the bartender, placing his foot on the rail and leaning his weary elbows on the bar. Everything in the saloon was plank, pure unvarnished plank; the tables where card players dealt their hands were plank. Cowhands in batwing chaps idling at the bar laughed and argued.

Beside Abel stood a weak-kneed little Texan, his beer before him, his face as irresolute as a rabbit's. He shook his head at a well-dressed man who had placed an open file on the bar. "Yes, my name is Waldo Smidgens," he said, "but I don't pay any bills for the house at all. That's my wife's business."

"She said I would find you here," the collector said. "That you'd be playing dominoes, or standing with one foot on the rail."

Smidgens raised his eyes from his drink. "Who are you from?" he asked.

"Liggetts from San Antone. You bought a houseful, or a cabinful, of furniture. You've made one payment on it."

Smidgens raised the glass mug to his mouth. "My wife pays the bills. I give her every check."

"She says she hasn't seen a check in months."

"She's mistaken," the little man said positively, nodding with self-assurance. "She just doesn't remember."

Abel had no wish to overhear the conversation, and at that moment the bartender put down his beer. He raised the mug to his lips, and the placid-voiced collector continued.

"We have a chattel mortgage on the furniture. If I'm not paid today, we'll bring suit. You are never where you are supposed to work, but everyone directs me to this saloon."

"Hell," Smidgens said, "you ain't the first to dun me, and you won't be the last." He raised his mug. "A dozen people are suing me. One more won't make no difference." He whined. "But I've got a wife and four children to support."

"You'll know by four o'clock," the collector said, moving with his portfolio through the swinging doors.

What Abel had just learned of Texas gave him no desire to stay there.

It was not only that he was an aristocrat; he was honest, and he loved work; he had built his own fences in Connecticut; he had plowed the soil; he had milked his own cows and had carried the milk himself to the town creamery, with his wife, Denna, seated beside him in the carriage.

Smidgens' indifference to an honest debt came as a shock.

As Abel took his second drink of beer, the laughter of cowhands down the bar becoming louder, he turned to the little man.

"This black growth along the road," he said. "What is it? I know the mesquite and cactus, but not it."

Smidgens made no effort to look toward Abel Cart. Instead, he turned to the man on his right, a supercilious smirk on his face. He said, jerking the back of his head toward Abel, "A stranger in town."

A stranger in town!

The remark tore Abel's insides. He had crossed half a nation to a land he loved, to Victory, and this was his reception. In less than a minute, one little man had made him hate Texas.

If it hadn't been for Abel's fear of meeting his old neighbors in Connecticut again before Zeb sold his property, he would have returned to Houston for Denna immediately and gone home.

He paid the bartender, and within a month he bought the bankrupt property of Smidgens and sent for Denna.

In later years he owned the town and bank, all out of hatred.

Like those who live in Rome and do as Romans do, Abel,

although strongly opposed to slavery, had bought Amy and Big Jim at an auction in San Antonio.

They were not married, as such, but it made no difference.

Big Jim, although laughing and sincere, had been suddenly shot and killed by a sheepherder who had found him where the sheep were red up to their ears from eating the tuna of the prickly pear.

Amy admitted to Abel that Jim had been a bit on the rustling side; meanwhile, she had brought forth a black baby.

At the same time, within weeks, Denna had birthed and died. Amy became young Denna's wetnurse. Jimmie became her playmate.

And amid talk of slavery and secession, Abel bought land and land and more land, and rebuilt Smidgens' cabin into a hacienda surrounded by the chaparral which, with Smidgens, had caused him to hate Texas, and the years rushed on to the inevitable climax.

But Denna was a Texan, and not a girl from Connecticut.

When the Civil War began, Abel would have no part of it.

His antislavery beliefs as strong as ever, he sold Amy's Jimmie to a neighbor and packed sixteen-year-old Denna and Amy on horses and rode for Indian Territory, hoping to reach the North.

It was a tortuous path he chose, but the fact that he had Amy with him helped. Among the Choctaws, where some of the rich owned up to five hundred slaves, and poorer Indians owned one or two, although most owned none at all, there were still black faces to be seen in the fields and woods or in the clearings about their quarters.

While Abel remained hidden in trees or brush with Denna, he sent Amy on foraging expeditions; she could pass unknown among other Negroes unless seen directly by some plantation or slave owner. The scant provisions she brought back, wrapped in a piece of cloth or in her own folded bandanna, supplied their only food, Abel being afraid to hunt game, since the sound of his rifle might attract too much attention.

Amy, on her return from the Negro cabins, also reported skirmishes between the opposing forces, both white and Indian, for the three tribes north of the Chickasaws and Choctaws—the Cherokees, the Creeks, and the Seminoles—were sharply divided.

Abel feared the troops of both sides, since one would have attracted the other; had he been captured by Union troops, he would have welcomed it, but he feared the Confederates, who would be close, and he was sometimes awed but not daunted by the solitary Confederate scouts vaguely seen in the distance.

But Amy, too, had her problems. One night while they huddled beside a miserable little fire in a dry creek bed, she burst into tears. "Jimmie, my little Jimmie," she moaned.

"Amy," Abel Cart said sternly, "let this be the last I ever hear of Jimmie."

"Yes, sir, Massa Cart."

Then from the north swept driving rain, more than Denna had ever seen before, a continuous deluge, until its steady drumming baffled her; she was battered and wet to the skin. Night after night their horses swam dark, swollen creeks and rivers, or Abel hacked beneath the wet bark of old logs with his hatchet to supply drier wood to start a spluttering campfire. He didn't like the fires, but they were necessary for warmth and drying out.

When they rode through these dismal nights, the stubborn girl felt the rain as a personal thing directed against her; she set her chin against the blow and did not whimper.

Sometimes Abel thought of the fencerows in Connecticut, but mostly he thought of release, only release. He would defeat and subdue this alien land with its slavery, and return to it only as conqueror.

When he was quit of the warring Civilized Tribes of the Territory, he led Denna and Amy to Kansas and farther north. He became a colonel in the Union Army and placed Denna in the East in Lady Burroughs' ivy-clad School for Young Ladies.

Amy, of course, went with her.

It was ten years before Denna saw Texas again, but at first she was too busy at Lady Burroughs' to think of her home state.

She immediately became a favorite among the girls. They all wore middy blouses with red borders on their square white collars, and bloomers.

Denna was alert, agreeable and independent. But it amazed her that so many girls of fine families knew so little about their studies. She reached the conclusion that these elegant families had not sent their daughters to Lady Burroughs' to learn, but only to say they had been there.

In Connecticut, Abel Cart had owned thousands of books, he

had ordered these shipped to his Texas hacienda, where a whole room was lined with them. To Denna, reading a book had been as natural as breathing; in fact, on dusty and windy days, when sand and gravel beat against the windows and the landscape was obscured, she had often read with a wet towel tied about her face so not to breathe the choking dust, only her brown eyes showing above the towel.

At the end of her first month at Lady Burroughs', she won the Geisler Scholarship Medal.

But it was not long before she learned the real reason for her popularity. The regulations at Lady Burroughs' were strict; only on three nights a week were the girls permitted to visit the rooms of the others for an hour. Denna's room was always filled with bloomered girls and secret bonbons and candy.

"Denna," someone would say, "tell us another Texas story—a real one, where people shoot each other."

Denna, in her soft drawl, which was so different from Abel's sharp incisiveness, would accommodate.

"One of the prettiest Indian stories," Denna said, crossing her legs on the bed, "is about two Indian sweethearts. They died for each other, and the boy became the moon and the girl became the sun." Then she went on and amplified the tale.

"Oh, a real story," another girl said, reaching toward a box of red-and-white-striped candy, "a story where they shoot or cut the throat with a knife. How do Indians really scalp people?"

"I don't know. The Indians are far north of where I live. I know more about Mexicans."

A fragile girl, Anthracite Bevins, leaned forward and said, "Denna, tell another sweetheart story." When the girls left, Denna stood at the door while they kissed her good night. She had never thought of popularity; it meant nothing.

But one day she learned why she was popular. She was in the library, and across the stacks she heard two girls laughing.

"Denna Cart," one was saying, "she just kills me. She seems to take what she thinks is popularity for granted. The only reason we ever go to her room is to hear that ridiculous drawl—brogue, I call it."

"Does she really believe those absurd stories she tells us? Does she think we go there to listen to them, or to laugh at her?"

Denna, standing with a book in her hand, was stunned. She

had not sought popularity; she thought she had only been friendly, as she had been to everyone in the dusty school at Victory.

"That brogue—you'd think she was brought up where no one knew how to talk. Did you hear her say 'Boston' last night? She pronounced it Baws-ton, instead of Bahs-ton."

"The most ridiculous girl in school."

Denna replaced the book and went back to her room. She lay on her bed, thinking.

Of course she didn't speak like the other girls—why should she? No one spoke as they did in Texas, far southwest Texas, where the sun came up like an emblazoned emblem each morning, in spite of cut throats and a dead Mexican now and then.

She was tired already of the exquisitely and elegantly gowned women and their mustached and impeccable husbands with their diamond studs and great vests who came to see their daughters on visiting days.

"Oh," a railroad magnate would say, his cigar pointed toward the ornate ceiling of the vast dining room, "the greatest honor of all would be for Anthracite to win the Geisler Scholarship Medal, if only once. We come from an old and scholastic family—Anthracite should really have the award next month."

Lady Burroughs waved her lace-edged handkerchief at the cigar smoke and said, "I quite agree." Her scent of jasmine was overpowering. "But, you know, for the second month a girl from Texas has won the award. Anthracite must indeed apply herself."

She led the way to the dinning table, where other elegantly dressed parents waited behind their chairs.

A year later, Colonel Abel Cart, bivouacked in the Shenandoah Valley and expecting a momentary strike by General Lee, received a letter from Lady Burroughs.

> I do not understand your daughter. For the fourteenth consecutive month she has won the coveted Geisler Scholarship Medal, but appears quite indifferent to the honor. She is aloof and consumed by a fierce inward pride, but I cannot reconcile this with the signal honor she has achieved. No one in the history of our school has attained this accomplishment.

Seated one evening with his aides before a battle, his weary troopers beside their fires looking to their rifles and singing

"Tenting on the Old Camp Ground"—a favorite of Northern and Southern troops alike—the aging colonel scribbled a reply to Lady Burroughs, his aides writing their own last letters home.

> Neither have I ever understood Denna. She has many excellent qualities, but there is an odd streak of independence in her nature which bars her from conventionality. It is my hope that before she graduates she will have achieved some balance in her life.

Long later, during the girls' visiting hours, a timid knock sounded at Denna's door. She opened it; frail Anthracite stood there.

"Come in," Denna said indifferently. It had been months and years since she had encouraged a visitor at her door.

Anthracite entered the room; she stood at the edge of the green rug, wringing her hands, her lank face above her middy blouse miserable.

"Denna," she said, "I want to be married."

"But why tell me?"

"Denna, I know what you really are. You are the only one I can turn to."

"Sit down," Denna said, motioning to a chair. She went to the closet and brought out a forbidden alcohol-burning percolator. "I'll make you a cup of coffee."

Anthracite sat in the chair, her eyes set distantly. "See how I look," she said. "I love him. I can't help it. I can't even think anymore."

"Who is he? And how could you have met him in this prison?"

"His name is Brian Doyle. It was the last visiting day for parents, and we dined at the Maple Inn. Brian is a waiter, working his way through the law school at the men's university. It happened that night as soon as we saw each other."

"Have you been to bed with him?"

"No, he won't let me. I slip out and see him every night, but he won't let me."

"Why?"

"Brian says he won't marry my money and all those railroads."

Denna handed Anthracite a coffeecup. Only a few months more, and she would be finished with these eternal bloomers and middy shirts.

"Marry him," Denna said.
Gratification shone in Anthracite's eyes.
"How old are you?" Denna said.
"Eighteen."
"You are of legal age. No one could stop you."
"Do you think my father's millions couldn't stop me? And his big vest with the diamonds and embroidered flowers all over it?"
"Do you have money?"
"Not a penny."
"Does Brian have any?"
"No, he barely makes his way."
"If you marry, you would have to quit school."
Anthracite placed her cup on the coffee table. "I'm not smart like you, Denna. I've never won the Geisler Scholarship Medal, and you've won it every month since you've been here. But I know what I want and how I can help Brian. School doesn't matter."
"If you were married now, where would you stay?"
"I don't know—we don't know. And we'd have no money."
Denna moved to her writing desk; she sat and wrote a check for one thousand dollars to Brian Doyle.
She gave it to Anthracite, saying, "My Negro maid has a little house with an extra room. You and Brian could stay there as long as no one saw you."
"Denna!" Anthracite sobbed. "I could never expect you to do this."
Denna looked about her small room. Once many girls had been here, as Anthracite tonight, reveling in her Texas brogue.
"Get married tomorrow," she said, "and leave this place forever. Amy will be waiting for you and Brian."
Anthracite stopped at the door. "The girls used to laugh at you because of the way you talked. But I never did, I swear it. I thought those were the sweetest words I ever heard."
"Good night," Denna said.
She stretched out on her bed. In a few months she would be rid of these damnable bloomers. Poor Anthracite—or perhaps fortunate Anthracite.
Several days later, Denna had a letter from her father:

>This detestable Lee. I have met him in three separate battles,

or with his detachments, and have been defeated each time. There is something unholy about that man and those who fight with him. Your old horse, Collins, is still with me. I let an aide ride him. I still remember the days you took him out alone in Texas.

I fear I am getting older, due to the constant campaigning, but there is nothing to do but try everlastingly for victory. I understand from Lady Burroughs that you are the only student who has won the Geisler Scholarship Medal for thirty-five consecutive months; one more to go, and you will have set a record never to be surpassed. I have made arrangements for you to enter an exclusive female college in the East. That will be four years more, and by then I hope the war will be over. Meanwhile, we fight for what we believe.

That night, Denna slipped out of Lady Burroughs' School for Young Ladies and trudged a grubby and unpaved street beyond the spired churches and mansions to Amy's little house. She wore a long heavy coat to hide her bloomers.

They all four of them, Amy and Denna and Brian and Anthracite, laughed and talked at the small kitchen table with a light breeze blowing the red curtains in the windows. In her association with Eastern Negroes, Amy had acquired a few social graces she had not known in Texas. She was still large and strong, and quite at home with Brian, whose eyebrows met over his nose.

Denna sent Brian out for a bottle of wine, then two bottles.

"Oh, Denna," cried Anthracite, her eyes misty, "I am so happy. Brian will graduate next year, and we will be on our own. Father has the Pinkerton Agency searching for me, but they will never find me here."

When Denna graduated from Lady Burroughs' school, she had, as her father predicted, won the Giesler Scholarship Medal for thirty-six consecutive months, a record never equaled in the school's history. Before the graduation ceremony, she had attached only one to her middy blouse.

"I've shown the bitches," she said, pinning it on before her dresser mirror, "and I've shown their parents. A Texas brogue—they can choke it down their throats."

On that same night, Lady Burroughs gave her a letter from her father:

At last, I have won a victory over Lee, or as I usually say, one of his detachments. I had sequestered my men behind a hill, deploying a few outward to defend a key road. Lee's detachment fell into the trap; after our advance guard pretended to be defeated and withdrew, we charged from around the hill. The victory was complete; Lee's force was annihilated.

My old horse, the one I rode through the Territory and was so faithful through all the years, was shot from under me. I took old Collins, the horse of your Texas days, from my aide and continued to lead the charge. But Collins, too, met his gallant fate and died at my feet. It seemed some part of my life had gone, remembering the Texas days when you rode him so much.

Denna turned from the mirror and walked down the hall.

Old Collins! How much land they had traveled together, how many times had she fed him oats, how many times had she hugged his great neck in the affection one could feel for a horse.

She accepted her final award and diploma on the stage before the crowded audience and applause, then marched stolidly off. As she left, the one thing she remembered most in her life was standing naked in a lonely stream, where Amy had pulled her out, a little horned toad watching her inscrutably.

She thought, reaching the foot of the steps from the stage, that she had done what she had set out to do, and now it mattered nothing. She had set a little record at Lady Burroughs' School for Young Ladies; well, they'd remember that, the socialites and railroad builders.

In her room, she slipped into her long coat, and left Lady Burroughs' by the front door she had entered three years ago, the dark night ivy still clinging above it.

On the grubby street to Amy's she walked into a late-closing second-hand store, two yellow gas lights burning above the door.

She said to a mustached saleswoman, "I want a skirt and a blouse. Can I change here?"

At an Italian tavern a few buildings down the street, she bought four bottles of wine and walked on to Amy's cottage. There were the shadows of roses about the doorway, and laughter within. While she sat at the kitchen table drinking with Brian and Anthracite, she thought of Collins.

It was the first time she wanted to be drunk.

"Honey child," Amy said, "ain't you drinking too much?"

Denna laughed back to Anthracite and Brian. "Yes, it's the first time I ever wanted to."

Her father had just won a victory over Lee, but Amy was still her slave, a slave who had never been freed by her father and who had won freedom by the Emancipation Proclamation.

2

Wormsley College would always be only the memory of a continuing steeplechase to Denna.

She was taller now, her figure Junoesque, but at Wormsley she evinced the same contempt for awards and honors that she had expressed at Lady Burroughs'.

During her first semester, she won the Most Sociably Acceptable Award. The correct young ladies of Wormsley were aghast at her indifference.

She was called to the carpet by Miss Agatha Hornaby, the president, who from a mahogany and antiseptic desk eyed her sternly through thick-lensed spectacles.

"I don't think you fit at Wormsley," said Miss Hornaby.

"I don't," said Denna.

As a result of the interview, she received a tirade from Colonel Cart.

> I can only say that you are willful with perverse pride. These awards are given for merit; when you threaten to refuse the most sought after of these, you do injury not only to yourself but to those who attempt to honor you.

Denna replied:

> If you think my being able to go through the formalities of greeting a group of simpering college boys from Yale or Harvard or Princeton properly entitles me to an award, you are

"No. Jennifer is afraid."

"Then why sacrifice me to Charibdes?"

Wiggins stared guiltily at the grass. "I will tell you something," he said. "When Charibdes was a colt, a careless workman who repaired the stalls nailed a board across Charibdes' to keep the upright posts parallel. When Charibdes was put up that night, he ran into the plank—an old one, and full of nails—not watching and not expecting it to be there. Charibdes jumped and somehow straddled the plank. As he turned over and fell, the nails ripped his shoulder and neck for some two feet."

"Then that's the cause of the scar."

"Yes."

"Thank you for telling me," Denna said sweetly. "Your conscience is clear now."

"Remember," Wiggins repeated, "the proper thing is form."

The day was windy, the grandstand filled with top hats and colored parasols; the judges' pavilion was gaily decorated, and the bright ribbons of the four colleges were bunched in their various sections. On the far straightaway Charibdes had taken the early barriers and water jumps well, and now his hooves thudded into the wide bend which would take him into the last stretch past the grandstand to the finish line.

That morning Denna had walked around the entire course, inspecting every yard of it. It was shaped like a hairpin—one long arm running beyond the girls' playing field, the circle, or bend, as it was called, and then the final stretch. It was lined with ditches, fences, hedges, and other obstacles.

Denna disliked most the Irish barricade located in the center of the bend; it was a high mound of brushwood with a ditch beyond. The horses could not see the ditch; it would be necessary to clear both in a single leap, or both horse and rider could be killed or injured.

Neither did she like the last obstacle, a wide and deep water jump, then a high plank fence crossing the course before the final stretch to the finish. Unless horse and rider cleared the water jump perfectly, the horse keeping stride, only disaster could follow at the high fence.

The course was marked by the fluttering flags of the four schools, beyond which no horse could turn.

I wonder, Denna thought, as Charibdes plummeted into the bend toward the barricade, if I am riding in good form today. Two girls from each college have already taken their spills.

Of the five jumps at the start—two water barriers, two fences, and a high privet hedge which had been removed from another area of Wormsley and set upright in a foot-wide trough, Denna had held Charibdes in.

Only two riders were beside her now—a square-faced, determined, and bespectacled girl from Wellsport College, and Jennifer Sloane, up on Diana.

As Charibdes thundered into the bend, Denna giving him his head for the barricade, his neck and glistening shoulders beginning to show before Diana and the gaunt chestnut from Wellsport, Denna glanced momentarily toward Jennifer Sloane.

Jennifer rode well, but she was pale; with her eyes fixed on the Irish barricade, she was terrified. But Diana was courageous; she had regained a neck from Charibdes. The Wellsport girl was still there, less than a yard from Charibdes' nose. The rider's square face behind its spectacles was like a gargoyle mask, determined, devoid of fear.

As Charibdes approached the barricade, Denna felt the great rhythm beneath her. A scream of anticipation rose from the grandstand.

Denna leaned forward in the saddle, her mouth close to Charibdes' ear. "I love you, Charibdes," she murmured. She wanted to extend her hand and caress his neck, to rub it across his driving flesh.

No, that would not be good form, she thought, and I have already transgressed by bending to whisper. She was a length ahead of the field now, Charibdes' driving hooves pounding like drumbeats.

Once over the barricade, there would remain the last barriers —a water jump of no consequence, a fence, another hedge, then the last barriers, the last wide water jump and the high fence. All of these before the long grandstand.

Denna did not know how it happened, but suddenly Jennifer Sloane was again beside her. Charibdes had not decreased his pace; if anything, he drove even faster, but Diana with a burst of speed was now first in the race. Had Jennifer lost control of Diana? The thought flashed through Denna's mind, but she

29

felt the sureness of Charibdes and made no effort to increase his speed.

At the barricade Denna saw Diana, half a length ahead, rise as gracefully as a bird and soar upward. Then, at the apex of the leap, the sight of the raw ditch loomed before Jennifer. Appealingly, stricken, she turned white-faced to glance at Denna, almost tightening the reins.

"No!" Denna screamed. "Let your horse go!"

Charibdes was rising behind Diana. Denna felt his power, the perfect coordination; she was not afraid. Now she, too, from the height of the barricade, saw the ragged ditch.

The fleet Diana, in spite of Jennifer's panic, had cleared both barricade and ditch, all but a hind hoof, which had crumbled the far side of the bank. Diana, her footing and stride lost, was going down on her left foreleg, like a ship sinking prow-first, momentum still carrying her, but leaning left and her shoulders lowering. Had Diana fallen, it would have meant a somersault and the horse's body over Jennifer, who still leaned forward.

"Back and right," Denna screamed. "Lean back and over."

To Denna, that split second was an hour, a day, a year.

As Diana staggered to her plunge earthward, she seemed to pause, so closely was she balanced between Jennifer and the hard earth; except for her driving legs, she seemed to hang motionless, as if suspended in an old illusion of no movement at all.

"Lean more!" screamed Denna.

Diana slowly straightened; the balance had been intricate; a finger touch could have pressed Diana either way, up or down. It had all happened so suddenly, and was so soon over, that Diana caught stride and raced on, swinging into the straightaway for the next obstacle, the easy water jump.

But now Charibdes was the contending horse. The uproar from the grandstand was deafening.

Between the water ditch and the fence Charibdes passed Diana; before he reached the green hedge he was out by a length and a half. Then from the right Denna heard another thunder—the gaunt chestnut of the girl from Wellsport.

She knew Diana was spent; one suicidal burst of speed had carried her well; now it was over. Diana was gallant, but the wet flesh would not respond to the challenge.

Denna leaned over Charibdes' neck. "Go, darling, go!"

The sound of the Wellsport horse and its determined rider was not so close now, and as Charibdes approached the last wide water jump before the high fence, Denna saw a gyrating sheet of newspaper swirl from the judges' pavilion into the wind.

She saw it before the horse did.

Charibdes had taken the water jump in stride, and now Denna felt the gathering of the great strength, the preparation for the dangerous high hurdle.

She felt the beginning of the leap, the horse shoving her upward, then she saw the twisting newspaper coming closer and closer and blowing before Charibdes' eyes; before he was well off the ground, he became another horse.

He flinched; his strength ebbed; his head twisted, as if he watched a strange plank which had suddenly been nailed across his eyes; his stride broken at the instant of his leap, he rose and crashed upon the top of the barrier and down.

Denna was thrown to the ground on her face and shoulder, her habit ripped and torn, her face and shoulder covered with blood.

The horse from Wellsport flashed by, then Diana.

She rose unsteadily and walked to where the horse lay, its neck broken.

She knelt and placed a hand on the hot, wet, beautiful black head, unmindful of the awestricken roars from the grandstand. Wiggins stood beside her in his red cap.

"Oh, Charibdes!" She wept uncontrollably, touching the beautiful head, its eyes rolling.

It was the only time anyone at Lady Burroughs' or at Wormsley ever saw Denna Cart weep.

Ignoring the doctors who rushed toward her and two men in white who carried a stretcher, she rose and walked across the playing field toward her dormitory.

When Denna left Wormsley, and while Colonel Cart was back in Texas having trouble with cows and his Confederate neighbors, she took a year in Europe.

She spent a month in London; then, tiring of its warehouselike buildings, she moved on to Paris. After a month she was weary of its decadence and returned to England, not even going to Rome.

Is there something wrong with me, she thought, because I can't go into an ecstasy over some portrait even in the Louvre, or swoon when I hear a symphony orchestra tuning up?

She was tired, too, of the always present tourist guides, their set little patterns of speech, repeating the same things over and over.

Then, in England again, she discovered the Lake District. It was rugged and mountainous and placid, with horizons one could see to, rugged in the sense that a child might have made its bold mountains in miniature. And the mirroring lakes were clear pools among the peaks and moors.

It was not Texas—there was no mesquite or prickly pear on the lonely moors, only time and space, and their inclination forever to share one's thoughts.

Thoughts, she said to herself one day after returning to the little slate-roofed town of Keswick after a tramp around Derwentwater and its tree-topped islands, thoughts—I haven't had a thought since I left college, and even there very few. Here, where I see distance, I feel myself again.

On a hill just out of town was a circle of old stones—the Druids' Circle—not so pretentious as Stonehenge, but in miniature. The hill was surrounded by a distant ring of mountains.

She and Amy had taken three rooms on a side street near Crosthwaite Churchyard; each afternoon she and Amy would leave the cobbled streets, the storefronts, and the slate roofs and climb the ascent to the sun circle. A pub, the Twa Dogs, stood at the edge of town; here Denna would buy a few bottles of ale for her rucksack, and she and Amy would follow the long road upward.

Then, sitting among the heavy stones, or on Old Meg, the largest, surrounded by the perfect ring of distant mountains, she and Amy would talk and drink their ale. At last Amy would curl on the ground and sleep. Denna was left with old imaginings and her thoughts.

She had found a similarity in people she met to those she had known in Texas, a quietness and independence. She had been impressed by this even down in the Lancashire country. Keeping their rooms in Keswick, they spent two weeks in Kendal, an old sheep and slate town where winds chased madly through tunneled streets and alleys, where fleece was dried.

It was late spring, and in both towns old women hawked bundles of yellow daffodils about the streets.

Life is all so simple here, Denna thought, so uncomplicated.

The rooms she had rented were near the swift-flowing Greta and the churchyard; she spent much time at both places, hardly wanting to move. However, there was one petty annoyance—a deceased poet laureate had lived in Greta Hall, and before him a greater poet who had written a sea poem; Denna was constantly stopped by both American and British tourists and asked where they had lived; they then looked up at the stone hall as if expecting to see the graybeard loon of the poem gazing at them from a window.

If the author of the Roast Pig essay had lived in the hall, it still would have been the same.

The one year turned into two. Denna was a familiar sight now, known by everyone in her red tam-o'-shanter and leather jacket. In time she was seen in nearly every small town or village of the district, or tramping on faraway moors or fells, always in her red cap and warmly dressed, with her rucksack filled with breads and tinned goods.

Although she thought she had come to know the land, she was puzzled that she could never know it. It could be bright, or in winter biting. It could be clear, or foggy, or solidly cloud-covered, the clouds sweeping in on sea winds. The tops of Skiddaw and other mountains or fells could be white with snow.

And always the rocky, rushing streams, the green grass winter or summer.

But she had found something here, although not knowing how she had found it. Distance decreased her antipathy to the continent; she even went to London and Paris and Berlin to hear a few symphonies.

Upon her return she left Amy for a few months and made a walking tour of the district, going from hamlet to hamlet—stone walls, hawthorn hedges, splotches of white sheep and black tarns set among distant hills and moors.

For two weeks she wandered near Hawkshead and Coniston, seeing the perfect view of Coniston Water and the fells beyond the height of Burnt Riggs; at times she was in sight of the sea.

There was the rocky and dominant mountain of Ald Maen—the Old Man—and the brutal desolation which surrounded Gaits Water. She had heard of this treeless spot, this volcanic wilderness, something relentless about it in the otherwise garden spot of the Lake District, alone in its savagery.

Yet she was part of it, and it of her.

Sometimes she blanketed down at night along some gnarled hedgerow or beneath a single tree, or stayed on the earthen floor of some farmer's isolated thatched stone hut, at home with his one-dress wife and red-cheeked children, loving each moment of it.

But there was a weirdness in this savage place, as if she had known the land before, that she had walked these very paths to see solitary slate or copper diggers at work in disused mines, even as she saw them now, or as she had once felt at Keswick, that she walked in some forgotten and mystic ceremony to become a timeless sacrifice in the sun circle.

One day from a rocky fell lined with miners' paths she decided to walk into Coniston.

The evening was late, the long English evening of spent spring and deepening summer. From somewhere along the road to which a path had led, a road flanked always by hedgerow and stone fences, she heard the late tolling of a church bell.

The sky was half-luminous; a young farm lad and a girl came from behind a stone wall, their arms about each other, limpid as two fishes.

Again, again, the timeless feeling came; she was walking with her hands bound behind her back, walking on some distant road from the east to a sun circle, irresistibly drawn to sacrifice.

At a stone hut she passed, an old woman with a nose bent to her chin crept toward her. She wore a gray shawl and carried yellow daffodils through a golden yard.

"Daffodils, madam? Daffodils?"

"Yes," said Denna. She gave the woman a shilling.

As she approached Coniston, hearing a cuckoo's song combining a mellow nearness and distance, she saw the mountain which lay beyond a stream. The village appeared unpretentious, and this she liked.

A stone hostelry and public house lay to the left, and beyond spread stone and thatched houses. She saw circular duck ponds, more public houses, chickens running free, the ruins of an old stocks and pillory, all protected by the circle of thatched roofs and flower gardens.

Turning from the road, she crossed the cobblestones. The sign above the hostelry read the "Partridge and Pigeon." The walk lay close to the stone walls; there was a heavily hinged wooden door, and she opened it.

A bell jangled above her head.

Denna glanced about; the bar was to one side of the room in the corner, old swords and coats of arms and pistols clung to the walls, and the heavy-beamed ceiling seemed low enough to touch.

At the sound of the jangling bell, a chubby-cheeked little man who sat head bent at a desk across from the bar and its beer pumps looked up.

Denna asked, "May I have a room?" She placed her rucksack on the floor, the flowers on the desk.

"Of course," the chubby man said, rising. "You are rather late, but tonight there is no one here. My name is Cocklebloom."

She noticed the white apron tied about his pumpkin waist. He removed it; she saw an ample belly which protruded above and below the belt line of his trousers, as two hills might be separated by a valley.

"You must sign the book," Cocklebloom said, turning it toward her.

Denna signed her name, adding, "Keswick, Cumberland."

Cocklebloom's blue eyes widened. "But aren't you American?"

Denna laughed. "I used to be, but I like it so well among the lakes I may never go back."

She had struck the responsive chord.

Cocklebloom drew himself up regally, a bulky and slightly ridiculous figure. He said, his eyes pleading, his fat jowls and stomach quivering as if a minor earthquake were in motion, "My friend, if you come from afar and love our green little island, there is nothing we would not do for you."

"I have learned that before," Denna said, embarrassed by Cocklebloom's emotion. He stood as if in another world, having delivered a royal proclamation with fanfare and trumpets from the Queen herself.

"Your flowers," he said, pointing to the daffodils, "we must put them in water." He poured it from a carafe into a large bowl, then placed the bowl on the desk.

"Thank you," Denna said, taking her red tam-o'-shanter off and shaking her hair.

"I say," said Cocklebloom suddenly, "you must stay more than one night. Tomorrow we have a fox hunt. It will be great sport. You would be welcome. Why don't you stay?"

"I should begin my return to Keswick."

She was not in the habit of making sudden decisions with strangers, but at that moment a woman who could have been only Cocklebloom's wife or sister entered the room from the kitchen, a woman also as plump as a pumpkin, wearing a white apron, her stomach bulging above and below its string, as had Cocklebloom's. Denna studied the candid eyes.

"I'd like to go," she said, her decision almost made by this new appearance, "but tomorrow I must start back."

Yes, she would like to go on the hunt. For the first time since leaving Wormsley she could use the riding graces she had learned from Wiggins; she would ride to the sound of hunting horns with red-coated lords and gentlefolk and beautifully habited ladies, the lean and frantic hunting dogs running before the galloping horses.

"Where do you start, and when?" she asked.

"From the mountain you saw across the sleekit," Cocklebloom said. Sleekit—the rocky little stream she had seen beneath the stone-covered fell as she reached the hamlet.

"And when?"

"We breakfast at six; then we meet in the common and look after the dogs, get our stores for the day, and gather to climb the hill. Once on top, we loose the dogs. Here is my pride," Cocklebloom said, leading her to an oil painting on a wall; "it is the great hunter John Peel chasing a fox across a moor."

"It is beautiful," Denna said, although the fox looked more like a rabbit, and Peel's red coat was a few shades off-color, and one leg of the horse hung askew.

Cocklebloom became conscious of his wife's presence. "Mistress Cocklebloom, this is Miss Cart." He nodded to the woman, who still stood in the kitchen doorway as stolidly as a lump of butter, awaiting her husband's pleasure.

"How do you do?" said Denna.

Mistress Dolly Cocklebloom came to her and took her hand and smiled. "Then you will not fox-hunt with us?"

"No, but I would like to. May I have a bath tonight?"

Cocklebloom chuckled, his rolls of fat quivering. "You know, we English say you Americans take baths before you go anywhere; we take them when we get back."

Denna laughed. "I have walked twenty-five miles today." She glanced at the ancient swords and long pistols fastened to the walls, at the small tables and the semicircular bar in the corner. "It is so homelike here."

Three men entered the Partridge and Pigeon, the overhead bell at the door jangling.

Two, one older than the other, had full petulant lips. "Squire Eggleston and his son," Dolly said. "The squire will start the hunt tomorrow."

The third man, a black-thatched raffish fellow, wore a suit of unpressed tweeds. He came straight to the portrait, while the publican left to serve the squire and his well-dressed son at the bar.

"This is Bart McIntyre," Dolly said to Denna. "He owns the Tankard and Bull. Oh, if you would stay for the fox hunt!"

The tweedy young man said to Denna, "I saw you come in. I do not patronize my competitors, as Dolly will tell you, but you must have dinner with me."

At that moment the squire's son approached, having learned Denna's identity from Cocklebloom.

"I am Horace Eggleston." He bowed. "I understand you are American. You must have dinner with me." It was almost an order. His superiority surrounded him like a halo.

A twinkle of amusement leaped into Denna's eyes. "I am sorry," she said, "but I have promised Mr. McIntyre."

Before the appearance of Horace, she had no intention at all of dining with Bart McIntyre, but something about Horace's arrogance had changed her mind. She placed her hand on Bart's arm. "Where is our table?" she asked.

While the squire and Horace sulked at their own, Bart McIntyre laughed. "Our pouting pigeons," he said. "But I must tell you—I arranged the fox hunt tomorrow by doing a little midnight poaching at Granny Knowles's duck pond. The hunts are good for the old grannies, and the lads and lasses can find themselves a hedgerow."

"You are rather frank about it."

"The grannies—they all must have their stout, and then they sit on the mountain all day like old sorceresses, learning the gossip of the shire, and full of liquors."

Bart McIntyre was an amusing brigand, with tall tales of this and that. Denna found herself laughing with him spontaneously. Each time she laughed, the squire's son seemed to cringe.

"Well," Bart said at last, snapping his watch closed, "I must go

37

to my own pub." He rose and held her chair. "But I will see you tomorrow before the hunt."

As Denna started upstairs for her room, she was stopped by Horace.

He frowned. "I must say, you are very casual about your associations."

"Is that your affair?"

"Will you go on the hunt with me tomorrow?"

"I must begin my return to Keswick."

"Why do you detest me?"

"I didn't know I did."

"My father is favorably impressed by you. He would like for you to come to the hall to visit my mother."

"And why?"

"He said you were determined and independent—you might make a man of me."

"A man?"

"I have my own profession—I am a drunkard."

"I am afraid you must help yourself," Denna said.

It was daylight when Denna was roused by the blowing of hunting horns and the yelping of dogs in the cobbled common.

She went to the window in her gown and leaned out, her brown hair cascading over the sill. During the night a fog had blown in. The Ald Maen was off in the distance, she knew, but lost. The village was filled with old people, young people, and the middle-aged. All were dressed in rough clothing and brogans. There were pink-cheeked maidens from the hamlet and sturdy farm girls who had pinned or sewed the hems of their long skirts higher, and bent old grannies with protruding chins who stood shawled or capped beside their staves or crooked canes.

Where are the horses, Denna thought, and all the color of riding habits I expected? She returned to her mirror to dress, doing her hair in a heavy bun on her neck.

At breakfast she asked Dolly Cocklebloom, "Where are the horses?"

"The horses?" Dolly Cocklebloom said blankly, placing a teacup and saucer beside a plate of sausage and eggs and fried tomatoes.

"The horses for the fox hunt, the red caps and jackets, and coats with long tails."

"Oh, my darling!" Dolly laughed. "There will be no horses. We have our own time and way for a hunt. When foxes begin to come after our chickens and ducks, we walk with our dogs and hunt them down. Our hunts are all like that."

"And you mean it lasts all day?"

The eyes in their bowls of fat twinkled. "Oh, yes. But we take food and drink, yet some men take more drink than food. How I wish you could go with us!"

When she had eaten, Denna packed and went into the cobbled street. It had been almost dark when she arrived last night; she had noticed the bulk of the hill, and now she saw it was rocky and stern. The gleam of the sleekit curled at its base. The bulk of the Old Man was still lost in the fog; the small pellets beat her face.

She wore the red tam-o'-shanter, a leather jacket, and a heavy woolen gray skirt. Her shoes were flat-heeled.

There was more excitement in the street than she had seen at Wormsley when the war ended. She continued to watch the people and the shop fronts. As the fog lifted, she saw some twenty shops and three pubs—the Coach and Horses, the Ship, and the Tankard and Bull. A small intermittent stream which was retarded here and there by duck ponds ended at last in a trickle at the lower sleekit.

Two small bridges had been built across the ponds, more for ornament than necessity. The remains of the old stocks and pillory stood near the common. The houses were of stone or wattle, thatch- or slate-roofed. Each had its snug flower garden.

Mistress Cocklebloom had followed Denna into the street; Cocklebloom came to her panting. He was pulled along by six leashed mastiffs like a feather. "Can you take my rucksack?" he asked Dolly. "I can't manage until I have the dogs at the fell."

Dogs. Hundreds of dogs. They must have come from every farm and hamlet in the shire—short dogs, long dogs, tall dogs, shaggy dogs adept at hunting, others quite useless but there because of the excitement.

"Do you mean," asked Denna, "that the old women with their sticks and canes will climb that mountain, as Bart McIntyre said?"

Horace Eggleston rode toward Denna. She had already told

Bart McIntyre good-bye. Horace led a fine black mare beside his horse.

"Won't you come to the hall?" he asked pleadingly. "My mother wishes to see you."

"No," said Denna, waving a last farewell to the Cockleblooms.

She turned and walked through the crowd toward the old road by which she had entered the hamlet.

Horace Eggleston rode beside her. In the cobbled common a hunting horn sounded. Squire Eggleston had started the hunt.

Again Horace pleaded. "Then you wouldn't consider marrying me?"

"Not at all."

"Why?"

"Too much independence, I suppose."

Irritably, he swung his horse to start back to the hamlet. "Then go to hell, madam."

Denna laughed. "What an end to romance! And a merry hell to you, sir."

While the happy people clambered up the mountain, she walked on over the bleak road and turned off at the miners' path by which she had entered it.

When Denna returned to Keswick, there awaited a letter from her father:

> I am older and have grown so for many years. My rheumatism and sciatica are bad, not having improved from the war years, and my duties here have hardly left me a moment.
>
> It has been nearly ten years since I left you following the hazardous days in the Territory. I admit my error now—I should not have kept you so far away through all the long years.
>
> I have arranged passage for you. Will you return?

She knew it was over, her tour abroad and all the friends she had made in Keswick and Kendal and in the far hamlets. Of course, she would write to them, and they to her, but already they were dead.

The letters would cease, and later there would be only memories. They were all dead, as later they would be dead and sleeping in Crosthwaite Churchyard, or elsewhere among the clear lakes.

How much of her life she would leave behind her!
She replied to her father:

I will leave after winter sets in. Snow-covered Skiddaw or Helvellyn would mean nothing to you, since you have never seen them. But I will be home by summer.

To tell the truth, she had begun to tire of the constant influx of visitors to Keswick, both English and Americans, and their continual asking at her door if this was the house of the celebrated author of the sea poem.

"No," she would reply, "he lived in the great hall. Yes, the poet laureate lived there after him. Yes, Wordsworth was born at Cockermouth."

On her last day in Keswick she walked to Crosthwaite Churchyard. "If I should ever die in England," she told Amy, "I would want to be buried here. Look, there is purple heather still blooming on a flat grave. Some old Scot must be buried there."

On her last night, she awoke from a hideous dream.

She was being led along an ancient road to the sun circle, her wrists bound behind her, the long procession following. She wore a white gown of heavy material, with a green ribbon about her waist. Her toenails in their open sandals were painted green, and her cheeks were smeared with green.

Her brown hair was bound behind her neck with a green ribbon and extended downward to her waist.

She was leaned back against Old Meg and the gown stripped from her shoulders.

The robed and ocher-faced priest with his pointed knife stepped toward her, the bearers of mistletoe following, the keen blade of the knife pointed beneath her left ribcase.

She awoke in a desperate sweat.

"Amy!" she cried. "Amy!"

When she left Keswick, the meandering Greta flowed onward, gurgling and prancing as the Kent did at Kendal, onward and onward beyond the soft-colored slate roofs and into the eternal greenness with other rocky streams and rivers, rushing toward the sea.

3

Denna had written her father a last letter from Keswick:

I will arrive in Boston, then visit your old town in Connecticut for a week, if only to see a few of the friends I know you want to learn about. But, dear Father, don't expect too much. Many of them will have died, for the war took its toll there, too.

For many weeks I have had reservations on the *Mississippi Queen* out of Cincinnati. I will go there by rail, then down the Ohio and Mississippi to Napoleon, at the mouth of the Arkansas. Lest you ridicule the name of this little town, let me say that many years ago it was founded and named by Frederick Notrebe, once a French general, in honor of his old emperor, so its lineage is noble.

To tell you why I make this journey so devious, it is because I want to see again the Indian Territory we crossed when we fled from Texas, the memory of which is still with me. I will take a sternwheeler, the *Maizie Trout,* up the Arkansas into the Territory, and thence make my way down the Texas Road and to you. By then, my circle of ten years will have been complete.

I hope, too, that as I relieve you of many of your duties, the sciatica and rheumatism will improve.

She had done as planned, although in Connecticut many, or even most, of her father's old friends were dead and gone.

"Missy," Amy said, "don't you get tired of hearing day after day, 'Yes, he's dead now.' Sometimes I think nobody but dead people live in this town."

Now Denna stood on the wharf at Napoleon, watching a boxed piano being unloaded from the *Mississippi Queen* to a smaller craft, the *Maizie Trout*. She was dressed in a brown traveling suit, her bustle smart and her bust unpadded, a long feather in her hat. Amy was equally well dressed. Their round-topped trunks were beside them; the cheering crowd which had awaited the *Queen*'s arrival had disappeared.

Napoleon consisted of a post office, banks and a livery stable, a one-hundred-bed marine hospital, a theater and courthouse, and when viewed from the waterfront, half-obscured residential chimneys and church spires which rose above the trees, almost like those she had known in England.

Denna continued to watch the unloading of the piano. Oddly enough, she had felt an attachment for it ever since she had seen it loaded at Cincinnati; it had come down two rivers with her, and now faced a third. For some reason, she had adopted it as her own, as one might adopt an elephant, visiting it beneath the *Queen*'s superstructure at night to see if it was safe.

After her years abroad, she had thrilled in Cincinnati at the city's growth and industry on the Ohio, the vast artery to the Mississippi; she had marveled at the factory chimneys casting their black smoke plumes across the sky. It was like an industrial town in the English Midlands.

After their baggage had been placed aboard the *Queen,* she and Amy had left to view the waterfront, seeing the ore barges which came down from Pittsburgh, hearing the hoarse whistles as steamboats and their lines of barges put in from the South and New Orleans, their low decks seemingly made of cotton bales, while everywhere crewmen and stevedores swung huge cranes and unloaded cargo.

As they returned from their walk, a piano van had moved toward the gangplank of the *Queen*. It was pulled by two rippling Percherons; a small man in a brown derby sat in the seat with the driver. Denna could see the large wooden box in the back, lettered on all sides, "Piano, Handle With Care, Use No Hooks."

The address was in even bolder lettering.

DR. DORCH MCINTYRE
ROUND FORT, CHOCTAW NATION
INDIAN TERRITORY

Denna said to Amy, "We may have music on our trip, almost to Texas."

As the van backed toward the gangplank, a disagreement broke out among the stevedores, for an officer on the upper deck had motioned for the driver to move onward along the dock in the direction of the cranes.

The man in the derby leaped to the street; he strode quickly up the gangplank and up the steps of the superstructure to the officer. Obviously, Denna thought, the man was an official of the piano company. He wants no chance of the box being damaged by some rope slipping or cable damage or by the cranes.

The officer, followed by the piano man, came down the steps and spoke to the foreman of the dock workers; a dozen stevedores approached the van. Some climbed into it; the huge crate was slid outward and carried as tenderly as a baby up the gangplank. It was placed in a weatherproofed area beneath the superstructure, then covered by tarpaulins brought from the van by the driver.

"Thank goodness, it's over," Denna said, turning her head to watch a line of coal barges pass the docks.

Amy said, "After watching those men working, I hurt my back lifting that thing. I wonder if we'll make it."

But the *Mississippi Queen,* her appointments plush and ornate, her great stacks hurling their smoke skyward, her paddles foaming their white wake, had come down the Ohio and into the Mississippi without difficulty.

The piano box was being unloaded now at Napoleon with the same care used in its loading in Cincinnati. The quick-moving little man in the derby, Denna thought, remembering how briskly he had jumped from the van, had evidently used his influence with the *Queen's* line. Now the piano was being carried aboard the *Maizie Trout,* although her decks were deserted.

The small sternwheeler was hardly different from one of the flat insignificant floating docks moored to the banks, except for its twin smokestacks and paddlewheel. The stacks stood near the square-cut bow; behind them rose the superstructure with its surmounting pilothouse. The superstructure extended almost to the paddlewheels; now the piano was being placed in the space beneath it.

Although Denna had seen none of the *Maizie Trout*'s crew aboard, she had no difficulty in being positive of its identification. Its name was painted across the front of the pilothouse, on either side of it, and across the back. Lower down, near the stern, it was painted on the superstructure above the paddlewheel—the *Maizie Trout*. No, no difficulty in identification here. She knew it to be an old ship on the Arkansas run, commanded by a Captain Keeter.

"I am convinced," Denna said to Amy, "that we will go up the Arkansas on a vessel by the name of the *Maizie Trout,* and still with a piano."

Amy said, standing beside her brassbound trunk and gazing beyond the plying steamers on the Mississippi, "Lordy, that's a wide river. I wonder if Jordan is that wide."

Denna turned again to look at the town. The buildings stood as before, church spires and chimneys pierced the air, but she did not understand why the *Maizie Trout* was so completely deserted. So far, not even Captain Keeter had put in an appearance.

A dusty street led from the wharf, its emptiness broken by strolling cows and dogs and hogs. Toward the center of town was a slightly more active area, where men in overalls or butternuts loafed and sat on benches before the storefronts and spat tobacco juice at some unperceived object.

As the piano movers returned to the *Queen,* a big bare-shouldered Negro with a fringe of gray at his temples appeared near the gangplank of the *Maizie Trout*. Denna asked him, "Will there be any passengers or crew on this voyage, or even a captain? Is this a ghost ship?"

The Negro raised his eyebrows. "Oh, no, ma'am. All the passengers and the crew heard the *Queen* give that big whistle before she came in; they all rushed to the hotel and the taverns for a last drink or to buy a bottle. The cap'n left to round them up; they be back immediately. I stayed to sign for that piano."

"Thank you," Denna said.

The Negro asked, grinning, "That old black woman with you any good?"

"She was my wetnurse."

"I do declare! After all this time! Lady, you are my kind of people. Let me get your trunks aboard now, before that crowd gets back."

When he had pulled the trunks and luggage aboard the *Maizie Trout,* the Negro led the way up to the captain's cabin in the superstructure and riffled some cards in a file. "We got just two ladies on this trip. This card"—he ran a slow forefinger along a printed line, meanwhile moving his lips in concentration—"this card says D-E-N-N-A. And this one"—his finger moved again—"says A-M-Y. Now, who is who?"

"I am Denna."

"Then you go to Number Two stateroom—that's right beside Cap'n Keeter's cabin. He Number One. All these other steamboats name these rooms by states, but the cap'n says it's too much trouble to know if he's got a man in Alabama or a woman in Michigan or Ohio. He sticks to numbers. Well, I'll get those trunks and bags up to your rooms. We still got time 'fore those drunks come in. You go to Number Three," he told Amy.

The staterooms were hardly more than cubbyholes with a cot, a chair, a small table, and a mirror on one wall. When the luggage was deposited, Denna gave the Negro a dollar.

Once on deck again, she walked to the prow of the *Maizie Trout.* "What are those upright poles like derricks on the sides?" she asked the Negro.

"Oh, I call those the hopper-setters. We come to sand and shallow water, we grasshopper. Out in front we set pilings, then block and tackle up to them. Then we hopper them out again until we reach deep water. Or we turn around, and the paddlewheel cuts a path through the sand."

The remark convulsed Amy. "Missy, we going to have to get off and push this boat to where we're going."

"Yah, yah," laughed the Negro. "We going to push this boat right up the river. How old this old woman?" he asked Denna.

"You don't ask a woman her age."

"Anytime you don't want her, I take her."

Amy said, "You won't get me to shove no boats."

A wild honking burst from the sky. "Look!" cried Denna, pointing overhead. Three flights of geese swung upriver, shifting their patterns as they flew, making a weird yelling and cacophony in the sky.

A thrill ran up Denna's spine.

A yelping of dogs sounded up the road. Denna turned; a crowd of several dozen men, some well inebriated, including red-blanketed and top-hatted Indians, strode toward the landing, the more sober supporting the less so. At their head marched a short, brisk man in a blue uniform and officer's cap.

"That's Cap'n Keeter in front," the Negro said. "Now, you ladies go up to your cabins till he gets that mess settled down. There's gamblers and gold hunters and drunk Indians and plain outlaws in that bunch, and there's always a fight about where they sleep on deck. Some of the talk ain't pleasant, but you've got nothing to fear from the cap'n. You can see everything from the portholes or the pilothouse. What you see on the road is just the quiet before the storm."

As Captain Keeter marched down the dusty road with his following, a wag of the old Confederacy—one reason Grant won the war—who was seated in a chair tilted against a storefront began to sing in a drunken voice which mingled with the chants and shouts of the marchers, "The British are coming, tra-la, tra-la."

As if to break the town's silence, three Negro boys across the street kept time for the marchers by beating two tin pans together and playing a harmonica.

To heighten his performance, the ex-Confederate seized a broom which leaned against the storefront and stuck it under his arm for a crutch; he fell in with the procession, marching stiff-legged, as if wounded. Still another grabbed a blanket from a straight-marching Choctaw and joined the ranks, to proceed in an up-and-down shuffle. The column was marching by fours now, the remaining Choctaws joining the white man in his dance. A panic-stricken dog yelped from the road.

In sheer exuberance from the influence of too much John Barleycorn, one Choctaw gave an excruciating war whoop; he leaped into the air, clasping his legs about another's waist, who continued to carry him piggyback. Others followed suit.

Now half the Choctaws were mounted on the other half, moving with the trot of a Light Brigade to keep pace with the crew and passengers. The mounted shouted and whipped their horses. Equipped with his infantry, as well as his whooping cavalry, Keeter continued his determined march.

A liver-spotted dog with a stump tail trotted proudly before him. A whiskey bottle sailed over Keeter's head, striking the dog, which yelped and ran toward the trees. A white sow which suckled her thirteen piglets in a depression she had wallowed in the dust was struck by another bottle. She gave an impatient squeal, then she, too, fled the road, the line of interrupted piglets following. A cow flung her tail up and departed—the Negro boys' band was too close.

Captain Keeter, oblivious to the hubbub and seeing the twin stacks of the *Maizie Trout* dwarfed by the greater ones of the *Mississippi Queen,* thought, yes, here I go again, a failure at forty. Off on another voyage—to what?

Looking at the *Queen,* he remembered when he had commanded steamers on the Mississippi, some even larger and more luxurious than she; then, one night on the Memphis run had come the explosion, the tremendous loss of life, and the ruin of his career.

The cause of the explosion was never known, but the consensus of the investigating board had been conclusive; the ship was under Keeter's command, and being so, he was totally responsible.

Needless to say, no other line would place the captain in a position of responsibility again. With his savings, dating back to the days when traffic on the Arkansas was more profitable, he had bought the *Maizie Trout.*

As the years passed, he had become like a puppy in its pen, secure and confident among his surroundings on the *Maizie Trout,* but when off his own deck or among men who might know the catastrophe of his younger days, he became uncertain and silent, embarrassed and without confidence.

Keeter was short and broad-shouldered, but not heavy; his face was square and honest, and he was troubled with dandruff. He rarely thought of the ruin the war had made of his old trade on the Arkansas.

Striding down the dusty road, his eyes straight ahead, he heard the honking geese which Denna had heard. Glancing upward, he saw their shifting patterns; it was as if someone placed or replaced lines of pencils in the sky. For all his years on the rivers, he had never ceased to be haunted by the wild-geese call.

"Jessup!" he called over his shoulder.

A gangling, barefooted man with a slouch hat pulled low over his ears stepped with long strides from the throng and marched beside him. As an Arkansas boy from the Ozark Mountains, Jessup had been as lean as a split rail; he was still that, and he had become the captain's pilot many years ago at Van Buren, across the river from Fort Smith. Age had not broken his Ozark homespunness.

"There will be a piano unloaded from the *Queen*," Keeter told Jessup. "I'll have enough to do collecting fares and getting this mob settled. There'll be tarps, so see that they're tied down for a good blow."

"Now, who wants a piano in Arkansas?" Jessup said. "When I was a boy, a willow whistle and a jaw harp made good music."

Keeter grinned. "This is for Dorch McIntyre, in Indian Territory."

"Him," said Jessup. "What does a sawbones want with a piano?"

"It's none of my business," Keeter said, "but I've had instructions from him, from the *Mississippi Queen* line, and from the piano factory in Cincinnati to take special care of it. The doctor is my old friend, so if he wants a piano, I'll carry it."

"Cap'n," the stiff-legged ex-Confederate said, having eased his way forward, "can a man work his way to Fort Smith?"

"Yes," said Keeter. "The last time I put you on, you jumped ship at Little Rock. You've got your crutch with you. Just keep walking."

A bachelor, Keeter sometimes wondered if this was all he lived for—a picture such as he now saw before him, the *Queen* and the *Maizie Trout* side by side, the shining water of the wide river beyond, the distant steamers which brought back another world, and closer still the long barges of coal and cotton, the floating landings, the rowboats of fishermen. And all about, a world of smokestacks as thick as toothpicks stuck in a biscuit.

The completeness of these images came unperceived, until suddenly they leaped before him to take form and shape. He had remembered them for years, not constantly, but only when some act or occasion occurred to remind him of one, as today at Napoleon, or at some other landing with other steamers, or the *Queen* and the *Maizie Trout* side by side.

There'd be a woman on board today—two women. Complications again. Always complications with such a horde as walked or staggered behind him now.

"Keep pistols in the pilothouse," he told Jessup, "and wear one every time you are on deck."

"Women?" Jessup said.

49

"Yes."

"I remember," Jessup said, "asking an old maid up in the hills if she ever thought of getting married. She said she thought about it all the time."

Jessup, moving with his gangling stride, and two full heads taller than his captain, was surprised that no laughter followed his witticism. As they neared the *Maizie Trout,* he said, "There's the piano box, already under the superstructure. And a woman is looking down from the pilothouse."

Denna, gazing down upon the turbulence of the crowded deck, observed the casualness of Captain Keeter. As he moved among his quarrelsome passengers, settling one dispute after another as to where one man or another would sleep or stack his belongings, it seemed he had drawn some invisible shield about him which neither comment nor scathing could penetrate.

He's like a ghost, Denna thought; no one can reach him, and no one can touch him.

She noticed a band of Indian women and children moving from the river trees. Stolidly, the line moved toward the *Maizie Trout* and up the gangplank. They settled themselves at the rear of the superstructure with the Choctaw men.

Denna thought, what does Captain Keeter do in a case like this? The women are very casual; they must have been waiting in the trees while Amy and I stood on the wharf. She heard a step behind her; the gray-haired Negro stood there.

"The people who come up to the staterooms will be all right," he said, "but keep a good eye on the others."

"Who are the squaws and children?"

"They had been with the men to Little Rock from Mississippi to collect their annuities. On the way back, the men spent all their money in the taverns. The cap'n will take them to Skullyville to visit relatives."

"What is your name?" Denna said.

"Just Jim. I was old man Robson's slave, so I guess I'm Jim Robson."

"Don't tell Amy your name is Jim. Her husband was Big Jim. Many years ago he was killed in Texas and their son sold. His name was Jim, too."

"From now on, between me and you, I'm Tom Robson. But why you mention this?"

"I think Amy likes you. Maybe I'm trying to become a matchmaker."

Denna saw that Captain Keeter was faced now by a frock-coated gunman, one who wore two pistols in his crossed gun belts. Through the open window of the pilothouse she could hear the irritated voice raised at the captain.

Keeter, imperturbable, could not reason with the man. Yet he still stood in his strange aloofness, as if he existed a thousand miles away. What happened came so suddenly that Denna was hardly aware that she saw it.

A gangling man, his hat low on his ears, moved forward with the speed of a cat; seizing the gunman's right hand, he bent and threw him over his back into the river. Denna saw that he had a single pistol at his belt, but he had not used it.

Tom Robson chuckled. "Dat's Jessup, our pilot. Nobody ever know about that boy, or what he'll do. He's a mighty good pilot on this river. One thing—there's got to be law and order on these boats, and it does everybody good to see we mean business. Look how things have quieted down already. Choctaws make good passengers—see how they have already spaced out by the paddle-wheels. Back in the old days these decks were awash with Chickasaws and Choctaws—Indians the cap'n picked up from swamps and such in that Trail of Tears business. He carried them to Fort Smith or to Skullyville and didn't charge a penny."

A series of hoarse blasts came from the whistle of the *Mississippi Queen*. Her newly loaded cargo aboard, and a stack of crates and boxes left on the dock, her paddlewheels began to churn.

Captain Keeter came into the pilothouse with his pilot, followed by Amy. The little sternwheeler began its own revolutions; Jessup raised his long hand to the rope of his whistle; it gave a few quavering shrieks.

"Oh," said Amy to the captain, "why don't you get a new whistle for this thing?"

Keeter grinned. "Everyone on the rivers knows that whistle. I don't want it changed."

He gazed up at the pilothouse of the *Queen,* where her smartly uniformed captain and mate stood, glancing down at him. Once more the *Queen*'s whistle blasted and the great ship slid slowly away.

Captain Keeter raised his hand to his cap in salute and farewell; the *Queen*'s captain returned the compliment. As the *Queen* swung slowly into the current of the Mississippi, he said to Jessup in an un-nautical expression, "Let her rip!"

Let her rip!

The lowly *Maizie Trout* making her way up the Arkansas again, into the still divided and struggling Indian Territory, where even the promise of the new days had been lost to its people.

But to Keeter, at that moment everything was dead. He could see and feel the handwriting on the wall—himself a riverboat captain getting older and older, and a time, because of the oncoming railroads, when there would be no need for his ship at all.

The days when he had carried cargo to Three Forks, where the Arkansas and the Verdigris and the Neosho came together, were almost gone. No more cargo to be unloaded far north in the Cherokee country, no more pelts and salt from the Neosho works to be brought back.

Denna, too, gazed toward the luxury of the departing *Queen*. She turned in time to see Napoleon vanish beyond a wall of trees.

Perhaps it is best, she thought, that there are little places like Napoleon, as there are places like this near Coniston Water, where Cocklebloom and Dolly live. If I stayed in Napoleon for a week, I would find such people. They would be different, but their hearts would be the same.

Keeter, watching the wake of the *Mississippi Queen* as the *Maizie Trout* breasted the current of the Arkansas, said to himself, well, great ship, but for an act of God I might have been your captain.

Then he turned and introduced himself to Denna Cart.

There were twelve numbered staterooms on the superstructure.

It had occasioned some comment among their occupants that with so many elevated and refined citizens of the nation confined to sleeping quarters on the bare deck, a Negress should occupy stateroom Number 3.

The galley ran across the back of the corridor; the stateroom occupants who objected to dining in the small room, redolent of cooking smells, were served meals in their rooms. The remaining nine staterooms were occupied by four merchants, two bound for Little Rock, one for Fort Smith, and one for the Territory; there was a Department of Interior man and his marshal, and a coal-mining expert from Pennsylvania, together with a tall Arkansas politician with a frock coat and stentorious voice, Tyson Pennypacker. Jessup claimed the stateroom next to the galley.

On the first afternoon out of Napoleon, a stateroom delegation appeared before Captain Keeter, who sat at a cluttered table in the pilothouse. Denna stood behind Jessup at the wheel, listening to the fine points of piloting. A member of the delegation cleared his throat; Denna turned, and Keeter raised his head.

Denna had seen all of the delegates earlier, but three in particular interested her. Sardis Rippy, the Department of Interior man, was short, with sloping shoulders, a broad forehead, and long sideburns; Flint Murcheson, his marshal, was built like a Newfoundland dog, shaggy and wide with observant eyes; and Tyson Pennypacker, politician and orator, had silver hair which swept to his shoulders. Pennypacker's excessively long teeth were squirrelish.

Denna had gathered that the three had been sent by the government for some sort of trial at the Federal District Court in Fort Smith, although she did not know the nature of it.

Sardis Rippy, the spokesman for the delegation, told Keeter, "We object to this Negro woman you carry. Each of us has friends who will have to sleep in all kinds of weather on deck. We demand an adjustment."

Denna did not like Rippy's black eyes; there was a half-concealed cunning behind them. Murcheson moved forward to stand beside him. Little dog and big dog, Denna thought.

Keeter, not rising, fastened his eyes on Rippy. "Do I understand you represent your government?"

"I do indeed." Rippy indicated the marshal. "And here is my authority."

Keeter said, "Your marshal is not my authority. And you might tell your government to present its applications for passage on time. The party you object to was booked two months before I received your booking, or those of anyone else on deck. Good day, gentlemen."

The quietness of Keeter's voice, his impassive square face, had ended all further discussion.

Leaving with the others, the frock-coated Pennypacker showed his teeth in a grin. Whatever his personal views, he did not like government intervention in purely local matters.

Denna said, "Thank you, captain."

Keeter looked up again. "I have never liked Rippy. I don't know why I dislike him, but he is not one to trust."

Denna continued to take her instruction from Jessup, who had condescended to shove his felt hat back an inch on his forehead. "Piloting is like plowing a straight furrow—you don't watch the plowshare. See that burned pine tree up to larboard? Struck by lightning once. You pick an object like that and steer to it, then your job's half-done."

"But what if the channel changes?"

"That's what we're coming to. It shifts three times between here and that tree. Take the wheel, and I'll show you. Head straight for the tree until you come even with yon steam sawmill. Then you cut antigodlin to the mouth of the opposite creek. When you're even with it, swing back and guide by the tree again."

Denna took the wheel, half-expecting the *Maizie Trout* to leap from beneath her. When they were even with the sawmill, Jessup said, "Now, easy on the turn. See how that creek mouth opens up for you?"

"Do you mean you know the channel this way all up the river?"

"What you know today, forget tomorrow. A bank can chunk in and change the channel; then you pick new points. A thousand things can happen. But after you pilot a spell, you know about all that can happen, so you're ready for it. 'Tain't difficult at all," Jessup said, scratching his heel with his big toe.

On the second day upriver, the *Maizie Trout* pushing toward Little Rock after a stop at Pine Bluff, Denna was awakened by the sound of a shoe kicking her door. She rose from the cot, slipped on a robe, and opened it. Tom Robson stood with a laden tray in each hand, wearing a white jacket.

Tom said, "I thought you ladies would like breakfast in bed this morning. It beats that little shelf in the galley."

"You don't care whether I eat or not," Denna said, taking the tray. "You want to see Amy this morning."

"Sho', I'd like to see her."

"Leave her tray here, then tell her to come and we'll eat together. Tom, do you like her?"

"Yes, missy, I like her powerful well."

While Denna stood in the doorway, Sardis Rippy came from his stateroom, Flint Murcheson behind him. Seeing Denna in her robe, Rippy stopped. For an instant Denna felt naked. Then Rippy passed on to the galley.

Denna said, "I think Amy likes you, Tom. Did you ever ask a woman a question?"

"Yes, ma'am. I've asked a lot of questions of women."

"I mean about marriage."

Tom frowned, placing the trays on the table. "Back on Massa Robson's place, a man didn't get a chance to ask that question. It was all set for him. I liked a little high yellow once, but old Massa's boys took her."

"Go ask Amy to come in," Denna said.

"I'm a good Christian nigger, missy. I'd do anything to marry that woman."

"Perhaps I can tell you something later," said Denna.

"Precious Lord!" said Tom.

"Tell me, what is Round Fort? As we near the Territory, I become curious."

"Round Fort? That's down in the Choctaw nation, near Boggy Depot."

"I'd never known of it before."

"It wasn't really a fort. The fort was on top of a hill, all in a mess now, broken down and crumbled. The Confederates had a place built lower down the hill to store powder and ammunition. They had some German stonemasons from Texas do the work; then they went ripping off to some battle or other. When they got back, they found the Germans had built the place round, since they thought cannonballs would bounce off a round fort better than from a square one. It's still there, just as it used to be."

"Who is this Dr. McIntyre? I heard Sardis Rippy say he was being brought to trial at Fort Smith."

"Him? He was a Confederate. After the war he took over Round Fort from the Choctaws and Chickasaws. It's on the line, so he opened a hospital to treat the sick of both tribes. Of course, he takes anybody who goes there, even Seminoles and Creeks and Cherokees."

"Is he paid for his work?"

"Only for the hospital. His pappy ran a trading post back in the Choctaw country in Mississippi. The doctor is one-fourth Chickasaw. After his pappy saw most of the Indians started on their way to the Territory, he and the boy came later. But during the war the doctor ran into trouble."

"What trouble?"

"The Confederates were running a bunch of Yankee Creeks

into Kansas. One night in a battle he had his wounded to look after, and some of Opothleyahola's women—that was the Creek chief—found the wounded and began to kill them with their big hominy pestles. The doctor was alone, and to save the wounded he fired on the women."

"How horrible!"

"Yes, missy, but everything was horrible then."

"Was anything ever done to him?"

"No, not yet. The Confederacy can't do anything, because there ain't no Confederacy. The Union says he wasn't in their forces, but army men still try to get him for violating the laws of war. The Yankee Creeks want vengeance from the Chickasaws, and the federal government calls it murder. That's why the trial at Fort Smith in a few days. Some call it an inquiry."

"But why is the Department of the Interior so interested?"

"Well, the Federal District Court at Fort Smith has always been charged with enforcing the law in Indian Territory. But since the troops were moved from there and Fort Gibson some years ago, things have been turned over to the Department of the Interior. That's the reason for all the marshals now."

"I see," said Denna. "So the doctor will be at the trial, or inquiry?"

"He agreed to Fort Smith, but not to Creek country."

"How old is the doctor?"

"Maybe ten years older than you. Some say one he killed was a Creek princess. Her father is one of the chiefs who keeps the mess going. But the doctor still fights all the government men try to do. Tyson Pennypacker is one of the worst. He's been on more sides of more fences than a shoat. When he's in court, he's the spellbinder; his long teeth shine down, and his hands go up trembling. He sho' likes his own voice."

Denna said, "Breakfast will soon be cold. Send Amy in, and perhaps I can learn what she thinks of marrying you."

Since Captain Keeter would allow neither Denna nor Amy below the superstructure, Denna spent the second afternoon in the pilothouse, watching the rich soil and the cottonwoods and higher pine trees on the meandering banks of the river.

"Are we making good time?" Denna asked the captain.

"Fair," Keeter said, "in spite of a slight rise on the river. See the foam and small driftwood begin to come down? We'll be slowed, but not much. Here," he said, tormented by her nearness and taking a weatherbeaten logbook from beside the pilotwheel, "this is a record of old trips. You can see what time it takes from Napoleon to Fort Smith, and it all depends on the current."

"Oh," said Denna, thumbing through the log, "here you carried a party of railroad surveyors to Fort Smith."

"Yes," Keeter said. "The trip took ten days. There was a four-day stop at Little Rock, where the officials visited the governor to discuss rights of way, gradient, and other matters. Actually, it was six days from Napoleon to Fort Smith."

"What was it like, carrying surveyors?"

Keeter grimaced. "Like cutting my own throat."

"Do you fear the railroads?"

"They mean the end of my business."

"But why?"

"Trains can go where I cannot."

"Where will we stop tonight?"

"At Little Rock. On upriver you will see Dardenelle Rock—it's tall sandstone. Then there will be Mt. Magazine, the highest point between the Appalachians and the Rockies, and Petit Jean Mountain. You'll see steam sawmills and pine shanties and log barges at the mouth of Piney River. Then we round the bend at Van Buren, under Mount Vista, and we are in Fort Smith."

"Will you pick up more cargo?"

"Upstream from Magazine and Petit Jean are coal outcrops. I always take coal to the blacksmith shops in the towns."

After reading other logs, Denna said, "Coal, pine timber, cotton from the plantations—I didn't realize the river carried so much."

"And Indians," Keeter said. "And covered wagons and the teams of broken-down whites. My decks have been filled with Indians I carried on their Trail of Tears."

Two days out of Little Rock, while Jessup piloted the *Maizie Trout* toward the great slab of Mt. Magazine, Captain Keeter knocked at the door of Denna's stateroom and asked her to dinner.

She accepted gladly.

When Keeter left, she thought, what shall I wear on an occasion like this? Shall I be modest or bold? Somehow she pitied Captain Keeter, such a lonesome figure.

She decided upon a low-cut gown she took from her trunk. She dressed, moving now and then to the square porthole, hearing the lapping waters, the churn of the paddlewheel, the bulk of blue

Mt. Magazine a few miles distant. Then she realized the *Maizie Trout* was pulling for a bank of cottonwoods and tying up. Tom Robson had grappled to a tree; the stern of the *Maizie Trout* swung slowly to the bank. Cottonwood branches reached to within a few yards of the pilothouse.

Meanwhile, at Jessup's wheel, Captain Keeter stood in his baggy union suit, only his cap on, while Tom Robson pressed his uniform. He only hoped dandruff would not cover the collar of his coat. He always thought it as bad as a snowstorm, although it was hardly noticeable.

Within an hour the captain knocked again at Denna's door. He was immaculate and she radiant. Tom Robson stood behind him in the white jacket.

"We will dine in the pilothouse," the captain said, hardly knowing his own words with the vision before him. "It will be cooler there than in my room." He led the way to the pilothouse.

Tom whispered, "Missy, I done asked the big question. But Amy sho' put in a lot of provisions."

"What are they?"

"That she won't ever leave you. That if she die, I won't leave you."

Denna whispered, "Then you can be married at Fort Smith."

"Thank God Almighty," Tom muttered.

A small table had been set in a corner of the pilothouse; the breeze swept in, free and cool, whispering the cottonwood leaves.

"But why have we tied up here?" Denna asked as Captain Keeter held her chair.

"I thought we might dine under Mt. Magazine. It's a pretty sight when the sun goes down."

"How delightful," Denna said.

It was a pathetic dinner, in spite of the blue mountain and Tom Robson's duck and catfish, and even the old wine Keeter produced. The captain, sitting across from this vision of youth, felt the years rushing upon him. The beautiful bare shoulders, the regal neck and head, the leaves talking. Involuntarily, fearing dandruff again, Keeter raised a hand and brushed it across his shoulders, then sipped his wine.

"This is delicious," Denna said, well into her duck.

"Jim is my private cook," Keeter said.

"Jim?"

"Yes, my waiter here."

"Oh," said Denna, thinking of him as Tom.

There were drunken shouts from the deck, and the evening pressed close with the mountain.

Keeter said, his eyes on her shadowy shoulders, "Have you ever thought of just tying up with a boat, anywhere, just along a river like this in some beautiful place, and spend your life beneath a mountain like Magazine? The days keen in the sun, the nights all God could ask for?"

Once more he brushed away the imaginary dandruff.

"No," said Denna. "Such a life would be too perfect. I suppose in some way I was born to wildness. I could never live the quiet life."

She tried not to meet his eyes. Here was a defeated man, only the captain of the *Maizie Trout,* but still a man with a dream.

Dreams!

What had hers come to?

A proposal from the son of a squire, and now this.

Perhaps someday this man would find his dream.

As she sat, placing her empty coffeecup into its saucer, she heard the shriek of smaller frogs along the rim of cottonwoods and the throaty bellow of a bullfrog, then the splash of some leaping thing, a mighty fish or gar.

In the lights on deck, Denna saw the excitable Sardis Rippy and Tyson Pennypacker, his long hair brushing his shoulders, gesticulating beside the stolid marshal.

"Will you be in Fort Smith in time for the doctor's trial?"

Keeter said, "Let's call it an inquiry. That is the day the piano is to be delivered. We'll be there."

"I wonder about the doctor," Denna said.

"I imagine he wonders about himself. Miss Cart, you would not reconsider your refusal at all?"

"No," said Denna, rising as he held her chair. "I could never live the quiet life. But thank you, Captain." She rose and went to her stateroom. He held the door for her.

"Good night," he said. "It has been most enjoyable."

Within an hour Denna was awakened by the steamboat getting under way. She did not know why she worried, or what she suspected, but she slipped her long coat on over her gown and went to the pilothouse. It was deserted, save for Jessup.

"Why are we moving?" she asked.

"The captain got restless. He's that way sometimes. Said he had a deadline to get that piano to Fort Smith, but that ain't the real reason."

A row of lanterns had been lighted across the prow and hung from the derricks.

"Is it safe to cruise a winding river at night?"

"With my eyes? I know every shallow and bend. Do you see that possum hanging from its tail on Mt. Magazine?"

"It is impossible for you to see the mountain," she said, her wrapped figure rounded and beautiful in the glow of the lanterns.

"Did you ever see a gosling getting its first wing feathers wet?" Jessup pulled his hat lower over his eyes and gave a turn to the pilotwheel. "See, I've got my green and red running lights on the stacks. Well, day or night, that's old Jessup, just like a gosling. Always ready to go."

THREE

1

In Fort Smith a jaunty little hunchback walked down the cobblestones from Garrison Avenue, long ago hacked from timber to make a marching place for the soldiers of the garrison. He walked toward the lower ground and the steamboat landings and the *Maizie Trout*. Far behind him, at the opposite end of the avenue, stood the Catholic church with its spire.

He was nattily dressed, his left shoulder held higher than his right; his head was held slightly awry, and he wore a bright bow tie. His face was merry, and his eyes twinkled.

Down the cobblestones he trod toward Second and First streets, bright as the sun which shone above him, amid the shacks and stores of the waterfront, the sound of Indian and white and Negro voices on all sides. To his right, where the river circled at Van Buren, Mount Vista stood blue and bold, but without the height or bulk of Mt. Magazine, which he had seen years ago on a run up from Napoleon.

Yes, a few moments ago when he first heard the *Maizie Trout*'s shrieking whistle, she would have been perhaps halfway from the mountain to the landing.

Life had always been an old story to Timothy Baines, one into which he had been born, and one in which he lived. As a boy in New Orleans, he had owned a shoeshine stand on a corner of Canal Street, shouting his trade always.

"Shoeshine, shoeshine, sir. See your face in your toes, or you don't owe me a penny!"

A number of years before the war, a black-haired young man climbed into his chair.

"Shine," he said.

Timothy beamed. "Yes, sir. Right away, sir."

The hump on the boy's back interested the newcomer. It rose very high above his left shoulder, a monstrous mound of flesh, like some kind of waterwing filled to capacity.

The lad looked up. His face was thin, his eyes cheerful.

Dorch McIntyre, on his way home from medical school, sat listening to the snap of the shine cloth and seeing his face come out of his toes. He had always had his shoes shined by other white boys or by a few freed Negroes; he did not know why he came to this lad.

It had been many years since Dorch had dissected fishes and turtles and snakes in the leafy Tallahaga Valley with its sacred mound; he had dissected other things, too, with always drunk old Dr. Bainbridge to help him. Then, with most of the Chickasaws and Choctaws gone from Mississippi, his trader father had taken a last group overland to the river, where they had boarded a chartered sternwheeler bound for Fort Smith and Skullyville, where the annuities were paid to the Territory Choctaws.

Dorch's father had also taken a covered wagon. He was to go overland from Skullyville to Doaksville, where he had a store run by his old helper, Tom Adkins, sent there many years ago in the days of the first removals. From there he would go on to Boggy Depot, where the early Choctaw supplies had been distributed by the government, and where his second store, run by Boyce Townley, was located.

The heavy wagon was rolled aboard the sternwheeler by the Chickasaws and Choctaws, and Dorch and his father had lived in it and slept in it on the river trip through Napoleon and Fort Smith and to Skullyville. Here they bought horses and followed the old military road south to the two stores.

It had not been a Trail of Tears for Dorch or the Indians; under his father's direction, this late removal had not faced the rigors of those of the other Five Civilized Tribes when they moved, or shared the fate of Chief Chilly Black and Molly.

Trained in the Choctaw and Chickasaw academies, Dorch had left the Territory for New Orleans and medical school, and now he sat in the hunchback's shine stand.

The hunchback looked up, grinning. "Still like I say, sir. If you don't see, you don't pay."

"I'm nearsighted," Dorch said to the snapping cloth. "Maybe I can't see my face in my shoes."

While Dorch sat, he watched the passing carriages in the street, the beautifully dressed women they carried, and the late shadows of iron grillwork on high balconies which made fantastic finger patterns on the walks.

Then he turned his eyes to the hump again.

The twinkling eyes glanced up. "Are you beginning to see that face, sir?"

"Yes," Dorch said. "But you'd better stop. It looks like hell."

He did look bad; his eyes were darkly circled, and in some peculiar way an air of weariness made his features seem set and stern. He climbed down from the chair, handing the hunchback a dollar. The lad reached into an open cigar box on the stand to make change.

Dorch waved the hand away. "Keep it. When I need a new face, I'll see you again."

"Thank you, sir. Thank you."

Now, that's a real gentleman, Timothy thought, putting the dollar in his pocket rather than leaving a too big piece of silver in the box.

A real gentleman because Dorch had not asked him about his hump, or rubbed his hand over it for good luck, as almost all other customers did. But he couldn't place the odd odor which clung to Dorch's clothes.

When Dorch left the shine stand, he walked not onward to his roominghouse, as he had planned, but back to the medical school. I know, he said to himself, I'm never content to leave well enough alone. He had worked in the cadaver room for twelve hours that day, but he had become interested in the hump, and now he would work longer.

But he must get permission to use the cadaver he wanted, and the doctors would be gone now. Fortunately, tall Dr. Kinkaid in his frock coat and tall hat came down wide steps.

"Doctor," said Dorch, "I'd like to have the hunchback cadaver tonight."

Dr. Kinkaid looked at him keenly. "I should say no, because you are working too hard. But give me your report when you finish."

Dorch went down into the basement, where the cadaver vats were lined up in their perfect rows.

In the hall he hung his hat and coat on a wall peg, then hung a knee-length rubber apron about his neck, covering his chest and shoulders. Several days ago he had learned about the hunchbacked Negro girl who had been brought in; now he would find out about humps.

Pulling on his rubber gloves, he walked down the line of vats, then back on the opposite side, before he found the cadaver.

He struck a brass bell on a table which stood by the door; when Ridge, the Negro attendant, came, kept on duty for what the police might bring in during the night, he had the body removed and dried, then wheeled to a dissecting table in an adjoining room.

The girl was placed stomach-down, the hump high, and Dorch lit the overhead gas light. He had quite forgotten that he had planned to eat a good dinner and go to bed early tonight.

He began to cut into the hump to see what it was made of, probing this way and that. Then he laid the hump wide open.

He was still working when the sun rose. Through a small curtained window, open for ventilation, he heard the city come alive, voices and cries from the streets, the rumble of dray wagons over the cobblestones, the milk and beer wagons, the shrill screams of newspaper boys, "South says no compromise with slavery." "South says war inevitable." "North and South cannot exist together." "Will South secede?"

The gauzy mantle of the gas lamp above Dorch's head broke. "Damn!" he said, his face darkening. He reached up and turned off the gas, yawning. He took off his rubber gloves and rang for the attendant. "Put this cadaver back in the vat. And all the flesh in this bucket—save it."

He had literally fragmented the hump. Some flesh had been solid and sound, but there had been masses of what he could only call gristle. He had gone down every nerve; he had followed every blood line to its capillaries.

And what had he learned?

Nothing.

I've got to sleep today, he thought, yawning again. And when I wake up, I'm going to move closer to the school. Walking is my only exercise, but I don't have time for it. Later, I'll ask Dr. Kinkaid about these humps."

He washed up and disinfected himself, then started home. A fog had settled over the streets.

At the hunchback's corner he paused, then turned back toward the shine stand.

"Good morning, sir. I didn't recognize you in the fog."

"It is thick," Dorch said.

"Shine today, sir? See your face again?"

"Shine," Dorch said, already cheered by the twinkling eyes.

"You must have stayed in the bars last night, the way you look. Your shoes have been dripped on."

"Yes," Dorch said, looking down at the hump. "My shoes have been dripped on."

Several days later Dorch sat in the hunchback's chair again.

"I haven't seen you lately, sir."

"No," Dorch said. "I slept all of one day, took the next one off, then had to work overtime to catch up on what I missed."

"I know what you mean, sir. I'm always catching up."

The little fellow had begun to like Dorch. He was still the only man, even though only a medical student, who didn't always flip a tip into the air just to see him grab awkwardly to catch it, or rub his knuckles across his hump.

"It's none of my business," Dorch said, the sound of the snapping cloth in his ears, "but where do you live?"

The hunchback laughed cheerily. "Oh, I've got boxes in the alleys, and after I sweep out a saloon they let me sleep on the floor, and there are lots of porches in the courtyards with good roofs."

"How much do you earn a week?"

"Ten or fifteen dollars."

"How old are you?"

"Seventeen, sir."

"I've been thinking," Dorch said, and indeed he had been. With his withdrawn and distant nature, it was surprising how the hunchback's eager face always cheered and took him out of himself. "I'm taking a two-room apartment nearer the medical school, and I need someone to look after it. I don't want a maid—I'd drive a woman crazy, coming in all hours as I do, and never knowing what I'd do next.

"I want someone to keep the apartment clean, to cook me something to eat, no matter what hour of the day or night I want it, to press my clothes, and jump off the roof if I say so."

The lad grinned. "You mean you want a gentleman's gentleman, sir."

"I'm a hell of a gentleman," Dorch said. "I'm stubborn and broody; I don't like for people to go against my will, and when I say hop, I want someone to hop. Another thing—I play an old piano I bought. There was a piano in an old church back in Mississippi, and I studied at academies and for two years here while I prepared for medical school. You'd have that racket to endure, maybe at two o'clock in the morning, if I am in a bad mood then."

"You wouldn't want an alley boy for that job, sir."

"I told you there were two rooms—partly furnished—and one would be yours. The apartment is high up, under the attic, but it has a balcony and a courtyard beneath, all filled with stinking magnolias."

"You mean I'd stay and eat there?"

"It would be your place more than mine. I'd be there only when time would let me, and then I'd be mean as hell."

"You do look like you haven't been eating right."

"I haven't even been eating, even when I have time to eat."

"I'd almost have to work at my stand, at least part of the day, to have something for clothes and things. But living and eating at your place, it shouldn't take much."

"You'd get twenty-five dollars a week, and I'm just not throwing away money. You'd save wages for a cleaning maid, you'd save cleaning and pressing bills, and the two prices I pay in restaurants for this food I can't eat. Now, what about it?"

Dorch climbed from the stand and handed the hunchback a dollar.

"No, sir," Timothy said, almost dancing up and down in excitement. "I can't take it, sir. I'm a gentleman's gentleman now."

"I'll have Sunday off," Dorch said. "We'll move then."

"Now, let me do all the arranging, sir. I can get that piano moved for almost nothing, even up those stairs. I know people so poor they'd work all day for a dollar. I'll have a van at your house on Sunday morning, and we'll move everything at once. If you looked for a mover, they'd charge a man like you ten prices. You go on to school now and forget that dollar for the shine. I'll make this old rag pop today!"

Dorch remembered his internship days mainly because of a

cracked skull. There were those among his classmates and professors who said he should have had his head cracked earlier. He had no friends, among either the students or the doctors.

Dorch was domineering, argumentative, and aloof; he was driven by an insane urge for perfection. The climax of his academic career came in Dr. Fourche's class, in a discussion about an operation the students had witnessed the day before.

Dr. Fourche was of French descent. He had a small black mustache and always dressed in the best of fashion. He was perhaps the most adept and capable doctor in the city, and had been prevailed upon to teach one class daily on surgery. He transmitted his enthusiasms without effort.

When Dorch sat in class, he felt himself to be in a strange universe where the precise Frenchman threw whole worlds of words against each other and let them crash.

The operation had been the removal of a growth from the face of a young woman. The growth was centered in the crease line between the right cheekbone and the lip. Ruddy-faced Dr. Mayberry, who as usual operated in a half-drunken condition, had done the removal—a vertical slash from beneath the eye through the lip.

At the blackboard, Dr. Fourche made a rough sketch of the woman's face, marking the position of the growth heavily with his chalk. Then he tapped the tip of his pointer on the spot. "All of you witnessed the operation," the doctor said. "It was quite orthodox. Do I have questions or criticism?"

From his seat in the back row, Dorch growled, "It was sheer butchery. I saw the woman this morning while the wound was examined—she will have a harelip forever."

The professor said sarcastically, "Then, Doctor, suppose you come forward and show us how you would have performed the operation. I will gladly take your chair as a student."

Dorch rose, flaring. "First, I would have been sober." There was a titter among the students. Mayberry's reputation was well known; even Dr. Fourche smiled.

At the blackboard, Dorch rapidly sketched a woman's face. On the right side, where the tumor had been removed from the line above the lip, he drew the line heavily, then centered the tumor in it. When he finished, he turned to face Fourche. The straight, thin features were all seriousness; Dorch had expected to find amusement there.

"Continue," the doctor said.

Dorch used the pointer tip on the first drawing. "Here is the vertical cut, and here is the inverted V in the lip. This," he said, tapping the V, "could have been avoided."

"That is my opinion also," Fourche said. "How would you have operated?"

Dorch moved the pointer to the other picture, running the tip in the crease between the upper lip and the cheekbone. "I would have made the incision directly along this line, on both sides of the tumor. Let's forget the tumor for a moment. With the power of flesh to heal itself, the scar would gradually be absorbed or diminished and appear to be only the normal crease. Now for the tumor. If necessary, I would have made two minor incisions vertically above and below the tumor, but not cutting into the lip. In time there would be only the slight scar of the removal." Dorch tapped the harelip. "And never that hideous thing."

Dr. Fourche rose and made his way forward. "Although it involves criticizing my colleague, Mr. McIntyre, I think you are right."

"At least," said Dorch, "he could have drunk better whiskey."

Dr. Fourche always spent the hour following his lectures in his office on the second floor. One day after a lecture he stopped Dorch at the door. "Would you come to my office for a moment?"

"Of course," Dorch said suspiciously.

Once seated at his desk, the doctor said, touching a thumb to his mustache, "I have here three new surgical books from France. Perhaps you would like to take them home."

Dorch's face lighted. "Thank you, sir."

"I have what, at my wife's insistence, might be a disagreeable business to discuss. You know Amelia, my daughter?"

"Only by sight, sir."

Amelia was a brunette, eighteen, small, vivacious, with much the thin face of the doctor. Dorch had once seen her with her mother near the doctor's office, glancing at him, but she was surrounded by admiring students, and he did not approach.

"Amelia wishes to go to a ball next week, and her mother will have her go with no one but you."

"I am not well acquainted with social life, sir."

"Amelia will keep you busy. She has been all excitement for a week. Then you will take her?"

"Yes. I'd be glad to."

Strangely, Dorch felt he would be happy to go. It would break the monotony of night-to-night study.

On the night of the ball, Dorch was tall and distinctive in his black evening clothes; Amelia wore a tight black gown. Her eyes sparkled with gaiety as she touched his arm. "Oh, Dorch," she said when he and the two footmen helped her into the ornate carriage, "you make me so happy tonight." Yet he thought she struggled too desperately for gaiety.

On the way home she told him, "Father says you show more promise as a surgeon than any man he has ever known at medical school."

"You wouldn't think so, the way he rides me."

At the front door of the mansion there was the fleeting pressure of a tiptoe kiss on his cheek; then the door opened and he had a last glimpse of her running up the stairway.

Two weeks later Dr. Fourche asked Dorch to his office. Once the doctor had seated himself, his face seemed to turn gray. "Dorch," he said, "it is a malignancy."

Dorch said, surprised, "Your wife?"

"No. Amelia."

Startled, Dorch said, "It can't be."

"But it is, and I have never known one to run so rapidly. We operate tomorrow night at eight o'clock. Amelia has asked that you be there. Will you come?"

"Yes," said Dorch, sickened. That slight bit of life, so vibrant only two weeks ago!

"She said she would not be afraid if you were there. She loves you, Dorch."

"I swear, I did nothing to make her love me."

"I know, my boy, I know," said the doctor.

From the operating table, Amelia looked up at Dorch, her eyes unusually bright in spite of her preliminary injections. "Father said you would be here. Kiss me, Dorch."

He bent and his lips touched hers.

"I am not afraid anymore," she whispered. She glanced about. "So many doctors here in their white gowns!"

"The entire faculty, all but Dr. Mayberry. I gave him a bottle of whiskey. He is asleep in the basement."

"Just one thing more, Dorch. During the operation, if father asks you a question, will you answer him honestly?"

He touched her lips again. "Of course, my dear."

Her lips were paler now, and wan. "I love life, Dorch, and you."

She was soon under the anesthetic. The scalpels sliced, the nurses worked quickly. Then the surgeons looked up, searching each other's eyes. Once more they proceeded. Already they knew, or felt, the worst. All of the intestine must be removed, only a part of the stomach to remain, then a tube in her side to live with the rest of her life. God knows, not that, Dorch thought.

Dr. Fourche motioned Dorch aside. "What would you do?"

"Sew her up," Dorch said brutally. "The malignancy will continue to spread. She may last a few days or a week, but only in pain and agony."

Fortunately, Amelia died before she came to from the anesthetic.

Dorch waited in the alley of the medical school with Dr. Fourche until the hearse came. As they saw the body carried down the back steps, the doctor said dully, "She always talked of her date with you."

He moved toward his hansom cab. It was the same cab which Timothy Baines had seen at the corner so many years ago when he carried his lumber home to his alley.

"Doctor," Dorch said, as a thick fog rolled in and he helped him into the hansom, "I must tell you now what you have told so many others. You must learn to bear this."

The horses of the hearse clumped away.

"Thank you, Dorch. Good night. And Amelia would thank you."

For his internship, Dorch could have had his choice of any of the best hospitals in New Orleans.

Yet he chose a frame hospital located in the heart of the riverfront, ringed by the river and shacks and shanties and warehouses and sailors and prostitutes and brothels. At night much of the district was lighted by pine-knot flares or lanterns. Smells of tar and pitch and excrement.

On his first day, the Fourches beside him, Dorch had glanced down from an upstairs window; he saw a closer area of docks and mud and cobblestones and molasses barrels and stacked cotton bales, the distant panorama of steamboats whose whistles hooted, the oceangoing steamers and the upstream sidewheelers. Some stacks of cotton bales were roofed over and between with strips of tin to make havens for the desolate. All that and no more, but the scene ran on endlessly. This would be Dorch's home for a year.

The Fourches had tried vainly to change Dorch's mind. "No," Dorch said, pointing, "my place is down there."

The hospital was rat- and roach- and vermin-infested. Its administrator was Dr. Henderson, who also was the only physician. No doctor of repute practiced in the hospital; occasionally a doctor whose license had been revoked dropped in to help Henderson on a busy day.

Dr. Henderson was a lean and skeletal-faced man who chewed his false teeth when he talked; his two nurses were waterfront harridans who waited only for payday to indulge a weekend binge in a grog shop; then they returned to the hospital on Tuesday or Wednesday to resume their duties.

Henderson was a political appointee, but he was expecting a dismissal as another party rose to power. Consequently, he violated every rule of hospital management, and Dorch soon found that the strict rules regarding interns were also disregarded. In his first week he was performing the work of a doctor, unsupervised.

Always the cracked heads brought in; the man with the knife between his shoulderblades; a mulatto who squatted in the hall to have her baby; planters bringing their slaves for inspection, since laws on slave care were strict; a mutilated prostitute; a dead Spanish sailor; scabies, rot and fungus, gonorrhea and syphilis; in short, the life of the Big River.

Yet even on his weekly night off, when he returned to the old apartment, Dorch's tyranny over Timothy was supreme. But always after some unfortunate incident he would be stricken with remorse. One night after a particularly harsh castigation, he had gone back to the kitchen. "That was a good roast you had tonight," he said lamely.

"Yes, sir," Timothy said, inwardly chuckling, "but I wish you would let me use bay leaves."

"They sog my stomach," Dorch said.

"Then you'd better look into it," Timothy said dryly.

Dorch laughed. "There's a good performance on tonight at the Downstate. Suppose we go."

Timothy grinned. "Shall I wear my bowler, sir?"

"Wear whatever you wish," Dorch said. "I'm going in bedroom slippers. My feet are tired."

Not infrequently Dorch became a patient in his own hospital.

73

There were the stevedores, the gamblers, drunken sailors, and the solid-ilk Bully James's gang, and shills and prostitutes by the hundreds, all in their viciousness.

When Dorch's head was first cracked, it was the result of an accustomed trick practiced on the waterfront. Some seedy character would appear at the hospital, saying that his friend in some shack or shanty needed a doctor immediately. Dorch with his black bag would follow him into a maze of stacked cotton bales and mud paths, or on to some shanty. A blackjack, a stolen billy club, or a scantling or some other weapon would descend from nowhere, and on the first occasion Dorch's skull actually was cracked and his pockets rifled.

Dr. Fourche was Dorch's physician; he kept him in bed for a month.

Coincident with Henderson's anticipated departure, Dr. Mayberry, due to his constant imbibing, had lost his position at the medical school, but he had been appointed surgeon and administrative head of Dorch's hospital by rising political cronies. He spent his time with his bottle, and often might be found asleep on a cot in a room adjoining his office.

On the day when Dorch was first on his feet again, an emergency appendectomy case was brought in.

No other doctors were in the hospital—they rarely were—and Mayberry had passed out on his cot. Dorch, knowing his violation of the rules, performed the operation. With the patient safe, Dorch filled out the operation form and went to the office, then to the anteroom.

When Dorch entered, Mayberry looked up. His eyes were bleary and full of hatred. "What do you have there?" A mouse sat in a corner, gnawing a crumb fallen from some patient's bed.

"I have performed an emergency appendectomy," Dorch said. "I have filled out this report, with you as performing surgeon, and myself as intern. Will you sign it, please?"

The eyes of the two men met. They understood each other. Dorch would run the hospital; Mayberry would keep his bottle. The results of any unlikely investigation could be quashed, or the records destroyed by political means.

Meanwhile, in his convalescence, Dorch had begun to think of methods to combat the thuggery on his rounds. He would refuse to go anywhere on the riverfront unless accompanied by the same individual who made the call. A doctor could be called to a shanty, and after examination of the patient, leave a prescription. Returning alone, he could be head-knocked and rolled for money or narcotics.

But Dorch had discussed matters with the nearer druggists and had begun to say to his would-be assassins, "Your wife is a sick woman and should have this medicine at once. Some of the drugstores don't have all the ingredients for the prescription, so you'd better go back with me and we'll look them up."

So usually he had a bodyguard for protection—the very man who would have rolled him. Those who were honest became his fast friends.

As the months passed, along the sprawling waterfront the talk of war increased. It became increasingly difficult for the big Northern sidewheelers to be loaded for the return trip upriver; the waterfront brawls increased.

Dorch was tall and could hold his own with any man, except the hidden or unsuspected. But now even the boss of the front, big-eared Bully James, and his ruffians came to his aid. Dorch had treated Bully's thin wife for consumption and went to Bully's shack several nights a week.

One evening as he left the hospital, four rat-faced men in slouch hats and turtleneck sweaters came toward him from across the street.

The first stopped, grinning. "Going somewhere, Doc?"

"I was," said Dorch, "but if you want to roll me, do it here. Then I won't have to be carried back so far."

"You don't get it," a grinning ape with a cigarette in his lips said. "Bully says you saved his old lady's life. From now on you've got a bodyguard."

One day when, in spite of his new guards, he was in the hospital again—there had been a set-to between Bully's boys and a rival gang—the Fourches came to visit. As she sat by the bed, the graying Mrs. Fourche said, "Dorch, Dr. Fourche and I are opening a clinic in one of the poor districts. When you finish your internship, will you stay and help us? When you marry, you could give us another daughter and grandchildren."

"I am sincerely sorry," said Dorch, "but I can't. My people in the Territory need me more than these here do. And there is the coming war. I do not know where I might be needed more. I am sorry, but I cannot stay."

Dr. Fourche said, "I understand, my son. Yes, you have delivered babies on top of cotton bales." The doctor glanced at a clean fat Irish woman and a girl who were making a bed. "Where did you get them?"

"I fired my old nurses," Dorch said. "This woman is no nurse, but she has raised twelve children. I think she is qualified. She and the children scrub the hospital every day—perhaps you noticed the two older boys painting the hall floor. I let the family sleep in the basement storeroom."

It occurred to Dorch after the Fourches left that they, even Amelia, had made too much of his single date with her; still, if he was consolation to them, let it be.

It occurred also that in all the time he had been in New Orleans, he had never been back to Nanih Wayia. Let that also be; it was a new world now, and a falling one.

Dorch had just finished his internship when the war began. He had written his father and had seen the Confederate authorities in New Orleans. He wanted to be assigned to the Territory, among people he knew; he had been promised a captaincy, but there was a drawback, especially from the New Orleans authorities.

They would not promise him duty in the Territory, nor would the hunchback who always came to the offices with him be permitted to become his aide.

The major, mustached and goateed in the best manner of the time, had infuriated Dorch on his last visit. Seated at an oak desk, surrounded by idle captains and lieutenants who also sat at oak desks, the major had said in regard to Timothy, "That thing? Do you think we want him in the army?"

"Then to hell with you," Dorch told the major, stalking from the recruiting office. "I hope you lose the damn war."

He didn't wish it, of course, but he walked back to the apartment in fury. Timothy was out, shopping for a roast and vegetables. Dorch sat down at the piano and banged away—he fought some mad thing of Beethoven's, hitting what notes he pleased, raising a cacophonous bedlam, the grillwork on the balcony rattling.

As Timothy walked up the stairs with a grocery sack in his arms, one hand held a letter he had found in the mailbox. He had heard the violent sounds from the apartment, even from the first floor; upon reaching the door, he twisted his head and grinned. Something big had happened, or had not happened, he didn't know which. If it was about the war, Dorch could whip the whole North and South right now.

He opened the door, banging it behind him with his heel, and walked silently to the kitchen.

Abruptly the cacophony ceased; Dorch stood up from the piano bench and followed him. "Why in hell didn't you speak to me when you came in?"

Timothy turned from placing the groceries in the cabinet, saying, "I didn't know you were there, sir."

Dorch laughed. "The devil you didn't. Those stinking magnolias," he said, walking to the balcony.

"Here is a letter, sir," Timothy said, following Dorch to the overhang.

Timothy liked the scent of magnolias. He looked down into the flowering courtyard, took a few deep breaths, and carried his hump to the kitchen.

Dorch opened the letter. It was from his father:

> If you are still enduring the indifference of the military authorities in New Orleans, let me put your mind at ease. I have communicated with most of the leaders of the tribes, including Stand Watie of the Cherokees, and our own Chickasaws have promised you a captaincy immediately upon your return. A copy of your orders is enclosed.
>
> As for your friend of these past years becoming your aide, there is no problem. He will receive the rank of corporal or sergeant. I do hope I may hear from you soon, or better still, see you before the activity begins. I am worried about conditions in the Territory. The Cherokees, Creeks, and Seminoles are sharply divided on the issue, and I fear civil war among them.
>
> Do answer, please, by return mail. A great deal is at stake.

Dorch went into the kitchen. "Timothy, we are in the army."

"What, sir?" The hunchback turned from the kitchen oven.

"We're in the army, and you are my aide." Dorch glanced about the apartment. "We've been here three years, maybe we'll be three years somewhere else together."

"I hope so, sir."

"Or maybe longer," Dorch said, his eyes far away on the future.

It was not as ridiculous as it may have seemed, Timothy's becoming Dorch's aide. His mind was like a whip, as sharp as a scalpel. On one wall of Dorch's room on shoulder-high bookshelves were the long rows of a medical library. Timothy had read all the books at one time or another; he had discussed phase after phase of them with Dorch.

Not that he could operate successfully, or remove an appendix, or be an expert at diagnosis. But he did know more medicine than any other aide Dorch knew he could find in the Territory.

After Timothy left to place advertisements in all the papers for the sale of the furniture and the piano, leaving only the medical books to be stored, Dorch sat in his old chair on the balcony, smoking a panatela. A group of children played in the courtyard about the lily pond.

What would war be like? Certainly a good way to begin practice.

Dorch could see the pink and white and yellow lily blossoms in the pool rising on their tall stems above their wide leaves. He wondered how long he would remember his days here.

He thought of Timothy, of the first suit of clothes he had bought him. Timothy had always worn any old coat he could find, putting one arm through the ragged sleeve, then flinging the other shoulder of the coat over his monstrous affliction. The sleeve of this shoulder he drew downward across his chest, using a safety pin to fasten it somewhere about his waist.

The smoke from the panatela was fragrant; the shrill cries at the lily pond were distant and remote.

After Timothy had been in the apartment for a month, Dorch had said, "I've got to buy some new clothes. Let's go to my tailor and be fitted." He did not need new clothes at all, but he did not let Timothy know this.

"I don't need clothes, sir. Not with what you are paying me."

"Come on," said Dorch. "I want to spend money." And they left the apartment for the tailor's.

While Dorch was being fitted, he said to the eager man who wielded the tape measure, "Do the best you can with my friend, but make a coat he can wear over that hump."

While Dorch's fitting went on, Timothy looked into a glass showcase of ties. He came to Dorch. "There's the prettiest bow tie I ever saw over there. I'm going to buy it."

"Get two or three," Dorch said.

Within two weeks they received their two new suits apiece. They stripped and tried them on, Timothy putting on his favorite bow tie.

He looked into the mirror, grinning. "Now I do look like a gentleman's gentleman, sir."

The downward smoke of the panatela wafted across the courtyard.

Dorch heard a timid knock at the door. He rose and flipped the panatela over the grillwork. He left the balcony and opened the door. A frightened Negro boy stood there.

"What is it?" Dorch asked.

"I'se that little freed nigger boy what has that little shoeshine box down the street—that little box white folks stand up and put their feet on to get their shoes shined. Massa Timothy just come by and said I was to come up here and take that big sit-down stand he saved. He done give it to me."

"Good," said Dorch. "I'll get it out for you."

"No, suh. Please, Massa Dorch, I'll do it. I don't want to cause you no trouble."

Dorch went into Timothy's room and looked at the old stand against the wall.

A strange pang struck him.

He pulled the stand away from the wall, struggling with it across the room.

"No, suh. Please, Massa Dorch, let me do it."

"It will take both of us to get it down the stairs," Dorch said. "Catch hold."

Once at the foot of the stairs and outside the apartment-house door, Dorch said, "Where is your old box?"

"Two blocks around the corner, suh."

"Let's keep moving," said Dorch, many of his neighbors on the street smiling at his menial task.

At last they put the stand in place beside the small box.

"When you use this stand," Dorch told the boy, "always say 'You'll see your face in your toes, sir.'"

"Yes, suh. Massa Timothy done told me that."

As Dorch walked back up the street to climb the narrow stairway, he remembered a foggy morning and heard a cheery voice, "Good morning, sir. I didn't recognize you in the fog."

2

In New Orleans Dorch had spent little time on his love life. Other than the old upright piano, medicine was his passion, and after a day's work at the medical school he was exhausted. Amelia was only a child who had passed his way.

He could not work week after week on female cadavers, black, mulatto, and white, and tired as he was when he finished, trot off to some brothel nightly to see mounds of flesh he admired even less than those he had cut to pieces during the day. At least some of the cadavers had clean teeth.

Even Timothy had a girl somewhere, but Dorch had never asked how he made out with her. Dorch had known brief affairs with the daughter of Dr. Kinkaid and with the daughter of Dr. Macklenburg, the professor of epidemiology, but each had been too time-consuming for his medical ambition.

There were two possible routes to the Chickasaw and Choctaw country. One would be up the Mississippi by steamboat, transferring at Napoleon for the trip up the Arkansas. The other would be to transfer nearer at hand at the mouth of Red River, which eventually became the southern border of the two nations, separating them from Texas.

Yet each course presented an obstacle. On the upper waters of Red River, the Great Raft, as it was called—a mass of ancient and perpetual driftwood, water lilies, and hyacinths—could effectually block further progress by steamer; on the other hand, there could be the threat of Union action against any large sidewheeler venturing too far up the Mississippi, and this harassment could continue with sternwheelers through Arkansas and even in the northeastern portion of Indian Territory, where Union troops maneuvered.

Yet from the moment the sternwheeler turned into Red River, Dorch regretted his decision. It was as if the steamboat had ventured into an eternal prairie of water lilies and hyacinths, their blossoms making bright streaks across the invisible water; vines and trailers and Spanish moss hung from arching branches, like the beards of old men, and the baying and boom of alligators in their mating season made the days and nights hideous. The gray-brown snouts stuck from the lilies everywhere, like half-hidden stumps.

The male passengers presented a problem to the dainty or raw-boned females aboard; there were rough and big-fisted traders, hunters, and trappers, one- and two-pistoled, and cattle drovers from New Orleans pressing toward Texas, and trappers and hunters bound beyond Nacogdoches.

Above Alexandria laughing mulatto girls in gay blouses approached the steamer in pirogues laden with oranges, bananas, citrons, and pineapples. They took their share of ribaldry from the male passengers. Dorch was glad when the steamer's progress was slowed and could go no farther. They were in heavy bayou country when Dorch asked the captain, "You say we stop at the next town?"

Laughing, the captain spat his tobacco juice overboard. "If we make it. But I hear a new raft has formed upstream, this side of the big one. We'll make the town, but never get past the raft."

"My friend and I will get off at the town," Dorch said.

He and Timothy would need horses and equipment to complete their journey; if they left the steamer first, they would have their choice of the best livery-stable mounts before the sternwheeler returned with the other passengers.

They left the steamer at the sleepy town, with its dozen stores, and bought horses and saddles, tarpaulins, blankets, and pistols and rifles, together with bandoliers of ammunition. Timothy bought a broad-brimmed planter's hat; Dorch would continue on in his brown bowler.

They were packed and mounted in the main street, watched by laughing Creoles and Negroes. One Negro child held a squirming pet alligator in his arms. At last they heard the whistle of the returning steamer.

"Let's go," Dorch said to Timothy. "There are some in that

81

mob I wouldn't travel with. I'd be a cadaver, or make one."

"There was one pretty girl," Timothy said. "The one with the curls."

"You take her," Dorch said. "I'm going home."

"Not interested," Timothy said. "She's got a derringer in her carpetbag."

From the bayou country, glad that the sucking mud of swamp roads and green slime were behind, they made their way to the southeastern tip of the Choctaw land, then rode across the endless expanse of Wild Horse Prairie, which extended south of the Kiamichi Mountains almost to the Red River Valley.

At Doaksville, where Tom Adkins of the old Tallahaga Valley ran the store, they spent one night. Tom had been a bachelor when Dorch was a boy; now he had a grown family.

Next day they continued across the expanse of the prairie, south of the Kiamichi range, Timothy increasingly proud of his new hat. As Dorch rode across the swells and valleys and streams of the Choctaws, he began to think of Della Wano.

She was a Creek he had met at a council meeting of the Five Tribes at North Fork Town. She had white blood in her veins, but less than he. Her eyes were wide and dark, her hair black, and her face oval. She had visited his home at Boggy Depot, and he hers in North Fork Town.

Her father was a chief, but there was a complacency which was not a complacency about her. At a dance he had arranged for her in the thatched hall near the council house, and while her proud father and mother received the guests and leaders of all the tribes, she had asked, "When will you ask me to marry you?"

The tone of her voice surprised him. He glanced about at the dancers, the Creeks and soldiers and members of the other tribes, to see if any had overheard.

He answered, smiling beneath his bushy black hair, "As soon as I know you love me."

"Don't you know I love you?" she asked, feeling the increased pressure of his arm about her waist.

"You love me as the wind loves the prairies, or the mountains love the creeks. But winds slow and die, and creeks run dry."

"Why do you always try to talk like some wise old Indian in a council meeting?"

He attempted to say lightly, "Because I am a wise old Indian, and because of my dead grandmother, a Chickasaw. After all the old warfare between our tribes, she'd rise from the grave if she knew I danced with a Creek."

She pulled herself away and walked to the thatched door of the dance house. When he reached her, she said, "You are too proud, Dorch. No woman will ever marry you. But if one does, she will not be Indian."

He could hear the drums and tom-toms and guitars and a Mexican trumpet, hear the laughter and conversation of the dancers; he took her arm and walked with her past the confectionery shop and the roominghouse and the stone jail on the path to the old military cemetery with its tilted tombstones.

"Why do you say a white woman?" Dorch asked. "You didn't say it, but that's what you meant."

She turned toward him in the yellow moonlight. "Look at me," she said, her eyes clear. "I wore a white woman's dress for you tonight. Look at my bare shoulders, my high bodice and tight waist. See how long my gown is." She raised her head proudly. "I went to Fort Smith to buy this gown, and I did my hair for you."

He was seized with a passion he could not control. He clasped her close, kissing her again and again.

They drew apart. She sighed. "Then you will marry me—now—tomorrow?"

He backed away, aghast. He knew now what she had thought, and what everyone had thought, that the dance was an engagement dance. "No. Next week I leave for New Orleans and medical school. That is why I gave the dance."

"Then I will wait for you."

It all came back to Dorch as he rode with Timothy through the thick grass of the prairie, with mottled thunderheads muttering above.

Where was Della Wano now? He had gone down the Arkansas on the *Maizie Trout,* and that had been the end of things. Neither had ever written the other. Perhaps pride had prevented her. Or why had he never written? But had she waited, although he had given her no reason to wait, or had she married?

"This is damned wide country," Timothy said. He rode his horse slouched on one side, which made his humped shoulder

83

seem lower. He rode that way because, never having ridden a horse before, he had accumulated saddle sores.

After one night's camp they crossed Clear Boggy Creek, and an hour later Dorch said, "Look, there is Boggy Depot."

Timothy saw a smattering of houses, a large store with smaller ones scattered about, and a few white mansions and church steeples. "Let's turn to town," he said.

"No," Dorch said. "We'll turn off at the next road. My father's home is there, and I haven't seen him for years. We'll visit him tonight and join the army tomorrow."

At the same time, Abel Cart's little family of Denna and Amy fled northward from Texas through the troubled Territory.

In the first year of the war, Colonel Cooper of the Fourth Texas Cavalry led a wedge of Texans into the Creek country.

At first Dorch had been assigned to irregular Chickasaw and Choctaw units; they had captured the southern line of forts which had been built to defend the Civilized Indians from the wilder Plains Tribes, and to protect the covered wagons which used the California Trail and other trails leading westward.

But already, even before he was sent to join the Fourth, Dorch knew what obstacles he faced. In the new and ragtag army of the Territory, he had no supplies, no drugs, no medicines. And he knew it would continue that way—always shortages—perhaps to the war's end. Even for the established Union Army things would be bad enough in this theater of war.

Military activity among the more northern tribes had not yet become full-blown; the divided Cherokees and Creeks and Seminoles received emissaries and promises from both sides.

Yet by November it became evident that the Creek chief, Opothleyahola, who had buried his nation's treasury in a barrel, had made preparations to escape with some five thousand of his partisans to Kansas.

A Confederate force from Fort Gibson was sent to contain the threatened movement or to defeat the chief. The advance guard of the expedition was the Fourth.

At Fort Gibson Dorch sat his horse on the hill overlooking the small landing on the Neosho. The buildings of the fort were behind him; he had scowled as the expedition moved out. Captain Keeter and his sternwheeler had not arrived with supplies. Although his saddle pockets and Timothy's were packed with drugs and medicines, almost nothing was carried in the short ambulance wagons. For bandages, Dorch knew he must tear shirts from the backs of wounded men.

"It's a hell of a war," Dorch said to Sergeant Timothy, "even if it is only seven months old."

Four days later Cooper's advance guard caught the Creeks of Opothleyahola.

Dorch would never forget the evening; it was cool, and in the distance, near two round mounds, he could see the Creek campfires blinking among the trees like fireflies.

The scouts of the Fourth had reported back to the advancing cavalrymen; the charge began. In an open space near the edge of the timber, having had the ambulance wagons drawn close, Dorch set up his field hospital. Meanwhile, he had sent Timothy to advise those in command of his location. His hospital was bare ground and no more, and now the appalling gunfire and screaming filled the timber.

Soon the wounded began to straggle in, stuck full of arrows, or with bullet wounds—arm wounds, leg wounds, chest and belly wounds. Dorch worked first with the worst cases, then had them sent to the rear in the ambulances. On all sides the gunfire increased; Dorch wondered what was wrong. The Fourth had anticipated an easy victory.

He was working steadily with Timothy, but now other wounded were seeking him, staggering in under their own power, or carried or helped by other wounded. Already he had more than enough moaning and shrieking men on the ground to fill the remaining ambulances. He had expected the battle to be over quickly, and not give him all these injured.

He had sawed a shattered leg off; then the soldier died.

The last ambulance left for the rear.

He cut an arrow from another soldier. "More arrows?" he asked.

"Hundreds of them. That's what we ran into when we charged the trees. Then we got their gunfire. We are whipped—we are already retreating. Even the Creek women are fighting."

Against his better judgment, Dorch began to work by lantern light. There was no other way in the increasing darkness. Timothy went again and again to the front, returning always with more wounded.

It was grim business now. The scattered Texans fought as they retreated, their horses' throats cut, or hamstrung. Lost, surrounded, they fought hand to hand.

Then the lantern flickered out.

In spite of danger, Dorch had Timothy build a fire to work by.

More Texans rushed through the clearing, throwing their weapons aside, stepping on the faces of the dead or dying. A white-jacketed orderly was felled by a stray bullet. Dorch's scalpel was slashing into a man screaming with pain. He was held down by two soldiers.

Timothy was stopping the runaways, getting what men he could to assist the wounded who could walk or even crawl to the rear.

Dorch called to the hunchback, "We must clear these grounds quickly. Go to the rear and find if there is an assembly point somewhere; ask for volunteers; I want these wounded moved."

A scalped soldier ran through the fire and into the farther trees, terrified, his face in the firelight a mass of pouring red.

Dorch never knew how much later it was when the attack on the hospital came. He was alone, but miraculously he had almost cleared it of its wounded; able-bodied men had come from the rear to help. Only some twenty wounded lay on the ground. Distantly, he could hear the screaming of dying horses.

Turning from one patient to another, Dorch saw a sudden shadow move behind the bushes. It disappeared beyond the circle of light. He thought it was a woman—a squaw.

Then the screams rushed upon him.

He saw squaw after squaw and young girls rushing upon the wounded; the women carried their big wooden hominy pestles; they were pounding the heads of the unmoving injured into pulp.

"Stop!" he called. "In the name of God, stop!"

He acted instinctively; he seized a pistol, then a rifle from the ground, firing upon the murdering women. Some fell; the rest ran back into the trees, screaming their hatred.

He took a fagot from the fire and walked the circle of his dead, looking at the battered skulls and faces, faces that were not faces, but only bloody pulp left from the heavy pestles.

Stooping, he rolled one squaw over to see if life remained, then another. He moved to a younger figure, which lay face down.

He rolled it over also; the glazed and dead eyes of Della Wano gazed upward into his own.

As the weeks passed, Dorch was to wonder what he had thought at that moment. The answer was—nothing. He had simply knelt there.

When he emerged slowly into life again, he remembered how proudly Della had stood before him in her new gown at North Fork Town. He remembered their kisses at the old soldiers' cemetery, not knowing then that he would become a soldier or that he would be at the Battle of the Mounds. He had learned from a captured Creek that Della was still unmarried. Had she waited for him, after all?

It was not in consolation, but only in bitterness, that he had ridden in the campaign a month later when Opothleyahola was defeated at Shoal Creek. A pincers movement was begun between the Verdigris and the Arkansas, but now other cavalry had dismounted, charging on foot among rocks and trees, their rifles sure. Repulsed, they returned to the charge; the battle was over before Stand Watie and his Cherokees arrived.

The defeated Creeks of the Union fled northward into Kansas, through bitter cold and snow, provisionless and miserable, all their belongings lost or left behind, their cattle slaughtered, with some women trampling their babies to death in the frozen muck rather than have them living fall into the hands of the rebel Indians.

Dorch had told the colonel of his murders in the clearing.

The weatherbeaten face was serious. "Hell, man, what could you have done? In another moment, it would have been your own hide. Anyway, you and your sergeant are in for a medal for getting most of the wounded out."

"I'd never touch it," Dorch said.

The colonel nodded.

It was perhaps well that Della Wano had died early in the war; she did not live to share the penury of the lean and wasted tribes which wandered northward or southward across the Territory as the fortunes of war changed again and again, or fall into a fate perhaps worse than that which had overtaken her.

And when the conflict was over, a haunted man on a black

horse rode with a tattered hunchback down the Texas Road to his father's home near Boggy Depot.

That evening, as he sat with his black-bearded father before a flickering fireplace, an oil lamp with a green shade on a table behind them, Dorch asked, "What has happened to the old Round Fort?"

"It is still on its hill, intact."

"What will happen to it?"

"Since there is no longer a Confederacy, the land will revert to the Chickasaws and Choctaws. It's on the boundary, you know."

"I want it," said Dorch. He rose and paced the floor, his dark face frowning. "I have lived in hatred for myself for four years. I thought I would live there and build a hospital, you might say a memorial to Della Wano."

"Lad," his father said, "ye must put out of mind what has happened. It could have come to anyone."

As Dorch stopped at the table to take a panatela from his father's box, his shaggy hair seemed even blacker.

"It is not healthy to live as I do. I must make restitution, or lose my mind. The war—doing something for others—has kept me going, but now I must find something new."

"But why Round Fort?"

"Because I would be among our own people, near enough to help both Chickasaws and Choctaws. The Texas Road will open up again, and thousands of immigrants from the North will follow it to new lands. Boggy Depot will grow, and it will be a good place to receive my supplies."

"Lad, did you love Della Wano?"

Dorch sat again, inhaling the panatela softly. "I've asked myself that question in a thousand bivouacs. You know how it was—I had known her so long. She had lived in Doaksville, and here, and I saw her whenever I went to North Fork Town. I may have loved her—I don't know."

"You want solitude. Why?"

"I don't want to see people, except the sick and impoverished Indians who come to my hospital, or would die otherwise. I may as well tell you now—since the Union has won, influential Creeks who have returned from Kansas plan to try me for murder."

"Aye, I have heard that."

"So it's talked even here," Dorch said.

"But what you did was an act of war."

"Do you think tribal revenge will end because of Appomattox? No, it will last for years. Already I've met old friends—Cherokees, Creeks, Seminoles, and some Choctaws—and they have turned from me. That's why I want solitude, some memorial to Della, and a chance to work."

"I have heard," the black-bearded old man said cautiously, "that there could be a federal charge against you—from either Washington or the Union Army."

"I hadn't wanted to tell you that."

"Damn the mad world! Well, there's no official among the Choctaws or the Chickasaws at Tishomingo I don't know, and my stores at Doaksville and Boggy Depot helped keep their armies in the field. I even freighted from Mexico. In a few days we will see about Round Fort, but tomorrow I want you to rest."

Dorch laughed harshly. "Rest? That is the last thing I want. Since the tribes own their own land in common, suppose you ride to Doaksville or Tushkahoma, and I will go to Tishomingo. I hear the Chickasaw council is meeting. Perhaps in a week we can settle things."

Dorch and Timothy rode up the steep slope of the hill to the old fort.

It was on the boundary line of the two nations, a brief ride from Boggy Depot. The crumbling mass loomed like a broken-winged monster on the summit. As they dismounted beside the ruins, a green snake slithered away in the sunlight.

"Let's go inside," Dorch said.

There were two buildings—the headquarters, or officers' rooms, and the soldiers' barracks, far larger and taller. They tramped about the stone floors, the open sky above, gazing up at the ragged walls.

When they came out, Dorch led the way to the round powder-house, which overlooked the valley of Clear Boggy Creek and which gave the fort its name. As they approached, Dorch saw that the heavy oak door had been carried away, as had stones from the other buildings, for building purposes elsewhere.

"The door can easily be remedied," Dorch said, taking a panatela from his vest pocket.

Once within the powderhouse, they looked about. The round room had a smooth stone floor; it was over forty feet in diameter, a perfect circle.

"A few windows and a fireplace," Dorch said, "and it would be livable."

He came outside and stared down at Clear Boggy Creek and the green valley. Yes, that was his too; he had leased the valley from the Chickasaws.

The council had been excited by the plans for a hospital; he had faced no difficulty in obtaining the grant; perhaps the council members, as had the Choctaws, felt the need to do something worthwhile for their beaten people.

He turned, and for the first time in years Timothy saw a genuine smile on his face.

"Old friend," Dorch said, "we've got our work cut out for us."

It was numbing and progressive work on the hill. First, Dorch had it cleared of scattered brush and undergrowth, using Chickasaw and Choctaw laborers. Even the women helped, while others stayed to cook for their men.

Dorch and Timothy headquartered in Round Fort, the somber outlines of the old barracks above them. For days Dorch paced the hill, circling Round Fort a hundred times, evolving this plan, now that, for the hospital.

At last the hospital came clear, something he could visualize. They would use limestone building stones from the old ruins to run a rectangular extension from one side of Round Fort; it would have a long hall down its center, with hospital rooms on either side and with nurses' apartments, small, but still apartments, at the far end. Where the rectangle joined the fort, he would curve out two small rooms at the angles—rooms for visitors, if ever he had any.

A door must be opened through the walls of Round Fort into the hospital, and windows cut into the walls of their living quarters, and Dorch looked forward to the building of the fireplace. There would be fireplaces in the hospital, too, especially in the nurses' quarters.

But where to begin?

At the end of a week Dorch rode across the Texas Road to see his father. Over the old gentleman's whiskey in the living room they discussed the proposition.

"Ye'll want it well made," the old trader said. "Come to think of it, I'd cross the river into Texas. There are good stonemasons in Denison, old Germans, some of them are, and they could tell you more in an hour than I could in a week."

Without returning to Round Fort, Dorch and Timothy loaded their saddle pockets and forded Red River, heading to Denison. After a night in a hotel, they rode about town until they saw construction work on a busy corner—a stone store building going up.

Dorch and Timothy climbed off their horses, and Dorch walked straight to a young stonemason who tied his guide string to a stake. "How many of you masons could join me for dinner tonight at my hotel? I have a big job in mind."

"Why tonight?" The young mason grinned. "This is Saturday—we quit at noon. Is that soon enough? Only one thing, though. We've got some old Germans with us, and they like their beer. After lunch they'll spend the afternoon in a tavern."

Dorch grinned. "That is something I can do equally well."

The old bald-headed German in charge of the job was one who had helped build Round Fort.

"Yah," he said at the table in the saloon. "I helped build the fort from the ground up." He held his hand up, his fingers splayed. "I know it like I know my hand."

"I'll tell you what I want," Dorch said, taking a notebook from his pocket and sketching the plan he had evolved. "Now, can you do it?"

The old German raised his mug of beer. His name was Kirsten, and his ears stuck out from his bald head like a pair of red biscuits, the color matching his nose. "Yah, we can do it, but there is much to talk about."

"Then talk," said Dorch, raising his own mug.

"The cement, what about that?"

"That's what I came to find out about."

"We can build a kiln, grind the limestone, and make cement. But you want this hospital quick. It would be best to ship the cement from here."

"Agreed," said Dorch.

"Where you want windows and a door in Round Fort, those stones must come out."

"I can get Indians for that."

"No. They would not do it properly. It would take a stonemason. I will send a man ahead of time."

"When will that be?"

"There are more masons in town who will finish a job next week. I can get them to help finish my building, then we will all be at Round Fort three weeks from today."

"Then I can count on you." Dorch placed a stack of gold pieces on the table.

"You can count on me," the German said, ignoring the money, "but for one thing. We masons work hard, but when we finish a day we like our beer."

"We've got good Choc beer," Dorch said, "with rattlesnake heads brewed in, but if you want Texas beer, ship it across the Red. I'll pay the bill."

The deal closed, the German raised his mug, then pocketed the gold.

The mason old Kirsten sent back to Round Fort with Dorch was the young man Dorch had first talked with at the construction site. His name was Hedges. He had a long nose and a prominent chin.

After the first day's work and a supper served on the bare floor of Round Fort, Dorch pulled out a gallon fruit jar from a stack of straw. "This is the beer you'll drink until Kirsten gets here."

"No." Hedges laughed, stretching back on the stone floor beside the open door. "I'm a teetotaler. In spite of what Kirsten says, why don't you get some Indians up here? In a week I can train them to take the stones from the old barracks and clean them properly. We can have them all stacked on the hospital grounds before Kirsten gets here."

"A good idea," Dorch said. "The poor devils need money anyway."

So when Kirsten arrived with his masons and the barrels of beer and cement he had floated across Red River, the grounds of the hill were as clean as a pickled onion, the stones for the hospital were neatly stacked, the window holes and the door to the hospital were opened, and stacks of firewood were available for colder weather.

Day by day the work went on, the walls of the hospital rising upon the hill, their outlines as straight as the strings which marked them. The barrels of beer and the cement continued to come from Denison in laden wagons whose horses struggled up the hill.

Dorch had written a medical-supply house in New Orleans; one day a shipment of twenty-four cots came to the hill, with bale after bale of sheets and blankets.

The masons cheered; they had been sleeping on the cold stone floor of Round Fort while the fireplace and chimney went up, shivering in their blankets in spite of the Denison beer or the Choctaw beer, both legally prohibited. Dorch had stretched a point here, but so had the lighthorse of two nations.

Now well wrapped in blankets, the older Germans would sit with their beer before the fireplace, then pull out slender old pipes, fill them with tobacco, and sip them as old women might sip tea.

On yet another day, when the roofing was being placed on the hospital peaks, a shipment of lamps arrived, and a wagonload of drugs, bandages, medicines, and two operating tables. Then another load of drugs came from Boggy Depot.

Dorch's first care was to finish his operating room.

One day his father came to see him. He was stooped and as yellow as a pumpkin. The old man got off his horse. "How are ye, lad?"

"Fine," Dorch said. He wanted to ask, why are you so yellow all over? But already he knew the reason. Cancer.

"I should have seen you before now," Dorch said, "but I've been busy here."

His father said, "Show me around the place."

Dorch wanted to say, are you sure you can make it? They walked up the hill together to the old barracks.

"I tried to leave the old outlines as they were," Dorch said, slowing his pace to his father's. "In spite of the stone we took out for the hospital, it looks almost the same."

"Yes," the old man said. "It's just as I remember it." He turned. "And Boggy Creek and the valley are still the same."

"I run a few cows in the valley," Dorch said. "Food for the hospital."

"I want to see the hospital," his father said.

Dorch led the way back down the hill. They walked through

93

the long corridor, the small rooms on each side of them. Dorch turned toward his operating room, its table and the shelves of drugs. "Look at my lamps," he said, pointing overhead. "How bright they will be!" He struck a match and lighted one. "See, with two on, it will be brighter than sunlight. The painters will finish in a week, and it will all be over."

In the round room they sat in new chairs before the fireplace.

"There's a bottle of Scotch in my saddle pockets," the old man said. "Will you get it? There's also a box of panatelas."

While they sat before the new fireplace, their drinks and the cigars beside them, Dorch said, "I should have seen you before now."

His father said, "No, you have been too busy, and I am happy for you. You were a good boy, Dorch, and you are a good man. Some part of you is dead, but something will never die."

He opened his lips to speak again, but Dorch said, "No, don't say it. I already know. Tomorrow I'll make an examination," he added, looking his father straight in the eyes.

For several days he pondered. The diagnosis baffled him. He had learned that for years—all during the war—there had been stomach upsets, that his father could not hold certain vegetables on his stomach.

There was consultation about this organ and that.

Dorch made a wild guess—he decided on the pancreas.

Should he go in from the front or back? Night after night while his drugged father lay on a cot beside the fireplace, he pondered.

At last he reached a decision.

One morning he said, almost with enthusiasm, "We'll operate tomorrow. Timothy will trim your black Scotch beard down; he's better at that than I."

The glazed eyes looked up from the cot. "One thing, lad. It's not a question of right or wrong now, but there are forces in the Territory and in the Fort Smith courts who are determined to convict you because of Della Wano. Never give up. Fight through every court."

Dorch sent Timothy to Boggy Depot for Boyce Townley's daughter. She had taken nurse's training during the war; once they had worked together at the same field hospital for two weeks.

Yes, with Timothy administering the anesthetic in the operating room, the overhead lamps glaring, it was the pancreas. Dorch removed it, and a section of the intestine. With Elfreda Townley's assistance he removed other cancer particles with a suction pump and put a new father together.

He was afraid of the third day.

On the fourth morning, exhausted from watching his father and sleeping in an adjoining room, he felt Elfreda Townley's hand on his shoulder. "Doctor, it is a stroke."

The old trader mumbled and talked of the days in Mississippi.

"Doc Bainbridge, what is wrong with that boy of mine?"

"No, I won't give you another drink. You've had one over the eight now."

"Dorch is always cutting something up. Snakes, frogs, turtles. What will I do with him?"

That afternoon the old man died. Dorch embalmed his father, although he hardly knew him in his short-cropped beard. But he did know that hundreds or perhaps thousands of Chickasaws and Choctaws would come from miles to view the body, bringing their meat or hominy, walking or on horseback or in family-laden wagons, among them the friends and chiefs of the old Tallahaga Valley.

His father had never forsaken his two tribes, the people who had made him rich. His body would rest in state outside the almost completed hospital in a thatched arbor.

On the day of the burial, Dorch and Timothy dug the grave near the high barracks. Every Indian on the hill watched and would have done it, but each knew it was a task the doctor had set for himself.

When the Indian sun flung a thousand swirling colors across the sky, Dorch McIntyre buried his father.

3

Timothy Baines continued his walk down the cobblestones of Fort Smith toward the *Maizie Trout,* the bulk of Mount Vista rising to his right.

Yes, sir, he thought, that old mountain is just where it ought to be. It really gives something to this town, standing over there like it owned it, solid and high and good.

He was nearing the thick of the waterfront now, its noise and hubbub, the *Maizie Trout* before him; on the lower ground, the church would have been out of sight.

Behind him and to the left rose the high buildings of the old fort on the Point—Belle Pointe, named by the French explorers. Everything bustled with activity; First Street, or sometimes called Commerce Street, or because of its fancy ladies, the Row, was filled with traders, Indians, travelers to the West, and the girls from the Row's shanties and roominghouses who promenaded in long skirts on the cobblestones, twirling their parasols.

Steamboats were moored to the riverbanks, and bales of cotton bound downstream were being loaded. Black stevedores with red bandannas wrapped about their heads sang at their work, watched by Indians in leggings and jackets or in white man's clothes.

Timothy began to whistle merrily. Now and then he tipped his hat to the town ladies strolling up from the landing or to some pretty prostitute, who also bowed and smiled.

The only thing Timothy was ashamed of in his natty attire was his old bow tie. It was the one he had found and liked many years ago in New Orleans; now it was only a thin rag.

He didn't know why he had wanted to wear the tie today; he had many new ones, but perhaps he had been overcome by some sentimental attachment he felt for this one.

Yes, over the years things had gone well at Round Fort. Dorch had moved some of his father's furniture into the round room—the massive dining table and its chairs and the huge secretary.

His father had always done the book- and paper-work of his business at home; as a boy, Dorch had watched him at night for more years than he could remember, sitting before the hinged panel which opened downward as a writing shelf, a lamp beside him, with the glasswork and shelves of the secretary above.

It, with the dining table, had been brought from Mississippi to the new Territory.

There were the mastiffs, too, three huge spotted brutes which had guarded the master's home, since always he had money stored in the house.

Dorch had allowed the mastiffs the run of the room, except at meals. Then they knew they were to remain at the hearth, their tongues in and out; they would sit patiently while Dorch and Timothy laughed and talked, each knowing that soon he would have a bone or biscuit or some other delicacy tossed his way.

Traffic on the Texas Road had increased, and on its prong through Boggy Depot, bound for the fertile and cow-raising lands of Texas. Colbert's Ferry across Red River was always busy, the store at Doaksville and at the depot prospered, and in the spring the drivers of Texas cattle and sheep went north, passing through the green valley below the hill.

Suddenly Timothy laughed. There had been the training of Chickasaw and Choctaw girls to become nurses or assistants at the hospital. At first Dorch had despaired. Although intelligent, some of the girls showed no aptitude for the work. Some did not like to scrub floors; others had a superstitious fear of working with the sick.

One ludicrous mistake Timothy would always remember. Dorch had sent a trainee to give an enema to a person soon to be operated on; there was a scream, and an Indian boy who had just been brought in to have a broken arm set rushed out the rear door. The Chickasaw girl had gone to the wrong room.

It was perhaps the trainees, those who had aptitude and grew older and remained, who gave rise in some quarters to talk that the doctor maintained kept women in his home. Some nurses, after assisting at a long or tedious operation, did eat with Dorch and Timothy in the round room, but that was as far as matters went. He and Dorch slept on collapsible cots near the fireplace; these were removed during the day.

Dorch devoted his days and nights to sick Indians who came from the hills and valleys, even Seminoles and occasional Creeks, or he rode almost impassable trails to reach those who could not be brought. From the poor he accepted no pay. If a year or so later an Indian brought a rabbit, a blanket, a bucket of wild honey, or a quarter of beef to the hospital, it was enough. This was his memorial to Della Wano.

But he still brooded, and he was always restless. It was bad enough that he should always hear from the Union Creeks that he should still be punished for a wartime crime, but the subject had become more and more discussed in the Chickasaw and Choctaw lands. Not in the manner or with the intent of the Union Creeks, but merely in conversation, as casually as one would discuss the weather.

Yet he did not know how near lay his first reckoning.

He had promised to visit a cancer-stricken squaw who lived up Muddy Boggy Creek. The ride would take the better part of a day, and this was the first time he would have even half a day free.

He told Timothy before noon, "I think I'll ride up Muddy Boggy to visit my cancer patient."

"But it looks rainy, and you wouldn't be back till after dark, maybe even midnight."

"That's true, but the hospital is quiet today, and it's not likely that anything would happen tonight. Anyway, you'd have two of the best nurses with you."

With misgiving, Timothy watched Dorch ride down the hill, a slicker tied behind his saddle. The weather of spring had been intermittently rainy, with sudden clouds doubling their size almost in minutes, and violent thunderstorms raking the sky. Dorch could ride into such a storm this afternoon, or even at night upon his return.

Timothy turned and glanced upward toward the gaunt walls of the barracks. A thin scud raced overhead, pressing the outline lower. As lightning flashed from heavier clouds, the walls seemed to shimmer. When Timothy turned and looked for Dorch again, he had disappeared into the brush of the creek.

In the late afternoon Timothy visited all the hospital rooms with Elfreda Townley, his favorite among all the nurses, and with a young trainee.

They had come from the room of a frightened Negro boy whose appendix had been removed. "Do you think he will live?" Elfreda asked, almost laughing. She had blue eyes which were placed rather far apart above a sensitive nose.

"Live?" Timothy chuckled, raising his hump. "Of course he will. He's just scared to death—he doesn't see how he can live with a part of his innards missing, even if it was only an appendix."

"When you have time," Elfreda said to the trainee, "go back and sit with him for a few moments. Tell him you had your appendix removed."

The rain began shortly after the inspection. Water ran from the hilltop in sheets, then spread among the trees into Clear Boggy. Apprehension seized Timothy; if the rain continued, Dorch would not get home tonight. But within an hour the cloudburst ceased; the sun shone from a clear sky.

Timothy had just finished supper when another storm struck. He went to the door, looking into the boiling clouds revealed by the lightning flashes. He should never have let Dorch make the trip.

The rain settled into a steady drumming. Midnight came, but no doctor. It was two o'clock now; the mastiffs whined, until Timothy forced them to settle beside the fireplace.

Timothy went to the door again and opened it. As he stuck his head outside, he heard two shots fired in rapid succession.

Heedless of the rain, he took a revolver and raced toward the location of the sounds, slipping and sliding.

He saw a slickered figure stretched in the mud, a hat beside it. The horse had spooked into the trees.

Dorch sat up.

"What is the matter, sir? Are you hurt?"

"Just stunned a little—one shot missed me."

"Where are you hit? Under your slicker?"

"No. Creased across my forehead. Blood is in my eye."

"Let me take you up the hill."

When they reached the rear door of the hospital, Dorch saw a trainee on her knees scrubbing the stone floor. "Take my boots off," he told Timothy, "then yours. The poor girl has almost finished her work. No use to make her do it over again."

99

As they walked down the spotless corridor, Dorch held a folded handkerchief across his forehead.

The two night nurses met him at the door of the operating room. "Oh, Doctor," one cried.

"Get on the table," Timothy said. "Let Doc Baines work on you."

It was a good crease, no doubt about it. Part of the bone of the skull was grooved.

"I'm going to give you a shot," Timothy said. "You'll be hurting in a minute. I've got to shave part of your head to get the chips of bone out, and you've got to sleep. How was your patient?"

"Hopeless," Dorch said, staring vacantly at the overhead lamps. One nurse was washing blood from his face and eye. A second trainee stood in the doorway, waiting.

Timothy was already cleaning the wound. The sharp sting of the antiseptic roused Dorch.

"Because of the flood, my horse had to swim Muddy Boggy five times. You know how the trail winds over it. No wonder these Texans call it the graveyard of cowman's hopes. I hope I never again see Muddy Boggy that high, especially at night."

Then he slept.

When he awoke at noon, Dorch found that he had been moved to one of the hospital rooms. Timothy and Elfreda Townley stood beside the cot.

"What did you do to me?" Dorch asked.

Timothy laughed. "I nailed a horseshoe to your head, sir."

"It feels like it."

"You'll have quite a scar."

"To hell with it. Do you know what I think?"

"Maybe I do," Timothy said, handing Dorch a cup of coffee as he sat up, gingerly placing his bare feet on the stone floor.

"What do you think?" Dorch asked.

"Someone saw you leave here, or saw you on the trail. Anyway, he knew you'd come back in spite of the rain, if just for the hospital. So he waited—it could have been all afternoon—at the edge of the trees until you came in."

"To have waited that long," Dorch said, "would show patience and purpose."

Elfreda refilled the coffeecup. "Tenting on the old camp

ground," Dorch said to her, thinking of their war days. "Many are dead and gone. You never mind being a beautiful young nurse, do you?"

"No, Doctor."

"It's purpose that worries me," Timothy said to Dorch. "You haven't been riding with a pistol. Maybe you'd better begin."

"I will," said Dorch. He placed the cup on the cot and felt his wrapped head. "A good bandage, Doctor."

When Timothy investigated the site of the shooting, there had been no tracks at the edge of the trees. Dorch's horse had not returned.

Dorch recuperated rapidly, pacing the hospital and the round room restlessly. But how could what he thought about the shooting possibly be true? Were old grievances among the tribes to be started all over again?

When the rains diminished, Elfreda Townley asked Dorch if she might have a day off. Before the rains, her mother had been ill, and she was worried.

"Of course you may go," Dorch said. "You work too hard anyway."

"I love it, Doctor."

"Timothy tells me the hospital at Fort Smith wants you for special training. Unless you just happen to like Fort Smith, I'll raise your salary one-third."

"You don't have to, Doctor, I feel I am helping here."

When Miss Townley returned from Boggy Depot, she reported that her mother had improved and that there was a box of narcotics and other supplies which the stage had left at the store.

"I'll send Timothy for them tomorrow," Dorch said, "and have him call on your mother. If he thinks it necessary, I'll visit her. By the way," he said, his black hair more askew than usual, his dark face flushing, "on your next day off, I wonder if I could dine with you at the hotel? Or if not that, go to the store and eat cheese and crackers from the barrel?"

Elfreda laughed. "You place me in such a predicament. When I was a child, I always liked the barrels. But the answer is yes."

"Thank you," said the doctor.

God alone knew how much he needed some other form of companionship besides Timothy's faithfulness, some woman to sit with before the fireplace in the round room at night, someone to talk with of untouched things, instead of his endless pacing of the floor, his mind prodded by a thousand torments.

Timothy went to Boggy Depot for the narcotics, but when he returned he was beaten, bloody, and bedraggled.

He told the story to Dorch. He had ridden into Boggy, trotting his horse past the churches and their steeples and the several white mansions, and had tied his horse at the hitchrack between the wheelwright's and the blacksmith shop.

A few Texas cowhands had come from a roominghouse as well loaded as their pistols, but all in good fellowship; he watched them for a moment, then entered the McIntyre store.

One corner of the front was used by the stage line. It had a counter, a few chairs, and to separate it from the rest of the store, it was fenced in by chicken wire; in the opposite corner of the store was the United States post office, similarly fenced. Timothy considered this good business on Townley's part; the two offices brought more people into the store.

Townley, as soon as he finished selling a horse collar to a Chickasaw, turned to him. "After your supplies, Timothy?"

Boyce Townley was more than a six-footer, heavy but not fat, with direct eyes and a clean-shaven face, the muscles of the jawbones rather bunched.

"Yes, sir," said Timothy.

"Elfreda was home the other day," Townley said, taking a key ring from his pocket and moving toward the chicken-wire cage.

"Yes, sir, that's another reason I'm here. The doctor wants me to go by and see your wife. If he's needed, he'll be here this afternoon."

"She's much better," Townley said, unlocking the door to the express stand. "I think it was only biliousness."

"I'll go by and see her," Timothy said, with the persistence some little men have. "Those are my orders."

"All right." Townley laughed. "She's your patient."

He shoved a waybill beneath the grill of the window of the cage. "Sign for the supplies, then there'll be three copies to sign for the narcotics—it's a new law. The government is getting strict on drugs."

"Did you ever think," Timothy said, "that if a man signs his name three times, he's three different men? He's a different man to everyone every place these papers go. Everywhere his name is read, people have their own idea of him."

Townley laughed. "You are too deep for me today," he said, shoving the packages through the window. "Do you want something to carry these in?"

"I've got my saddle pockets for the narcotics."

"Let me give you a bag for the rest. It will make it easier."

Once in the street again, Timothy gazed about. The cowhands were gone; only at the far end of the street did he see anyone besides a Choctaw and his wife, and four men who sat their horses before the livery stable.

He sighed. Someday he would like to ride in to Old Boggy, put his foot on a forbidden saloon rail, and enjoy a few beers. Not that he had tired of Dorch. That man was his life; he had made him what he was, given him opportunity.

But what was he? He didn't know, but anyway he was damned happy about it. He wondered if Dorch ever became tired of him—not really tired—but only wanting something a little different. After all, the years had been long—the New Orleans days, the war years, the time at Round Fort.

After he made his call on his patient, he concluded that Townley was right—it was only biliousness. That was what Elfreda had thought too.

As he left the house with the package of narcotics in his hand, he noticed that four horsemen waited in the street a couple of hundred yards away. He put the narcotics in his saddle pockets and mounted up.

Funny, he thought, beginning to jog his horse out of town, those riders look like the bunch I saw before the livery stables. One rider had a black horse; when Timothy looked behind again, the riders had disappeared.

He was about two miles out on the leafy trail beyond the old graveyard when a tomahawk flew through the air; then four horsemen burst from the trees, one on a black horse Timothy would have sworn was Dorch's, the one which had spooked on the rainy night when Dorch was shot.

The tomahawk struck his head; as he fell from the horse, he felt himself beaten and pommeled.

When he regained consciousness, he found himself curled up in the road, his hat ten feet away. His horse, with the narcotics in the saddle pockets, was gone. The bag of other supplies lay in the road, untouched.

"My God," Timothy groaned, rising and rubbing his head and his hump, "now I've done it. I'll put the master out of business with this stunt. Maybe they left me for dead, but someone knew about the narcotics."

Aching all over, Timothy bent and picked up his hat. He walked unsteadily up the road with the supply bag to the first farmhouse and borrowed a horse.

"And you think the black horse was mine?" Dorch asked, working over Timothy in the operating room.

"There's no doubt," Timothy said, wincing from the pressure of Dorch's fingers on his battered hump.

"I'll have to ride in and report this," Dorch said, "especially since it involves narcotics." He turned to Elfreda. "Would you like to go? We'll have to be back tonight."

She laughed. "Cracker barrel?"

He smiled. "No, the hotel. But I'll have business with the Choctaws, so I won't see much of you until dinner. Meanwhile, you can visit your mother."

When he left Elfreda at her mother's, he rode to the store and told Townley, "The narcotics were stolen from Timothy on his way back. Have you see any Creeks in town lately?"

Townley's jaw muscles knotted. "It's odd you ask that. Yes, four Creeks have been around for ten days or so, since about the time you were shot. They were in the store. I sold one of them a bridle."

"I hear there will be a Choctaw council in town, instead of at Tushkahoma. Are any of the chiefs here yet?"

"The principal chief, Albert McIntosh. He is staying with the Shadwells."

"I won't ask you now," Dorch said, "but remember what the Creeks looked like. And send some lighthorse to the Shadwell home."

"I see," said Townley. He noticed that Dorch wore a pistol belt under his long coat. He noticed also the bulge of a shoulder holster. I'll remember your Creeks," he said.

Dorch turned to leave the store. "By the way," he called back from the front door, "I brought Elfreda in. We'll have dinner at the hotel."

Townley watched him go.

Elfreda!

Townley thought, perhaps someone could enter that troubled soul after all.

Dorch found Albert McIntosh with the Shadwells in their rose garden. The late rains had brought full blossom again; they stood with the Shadwells in a riot of color.

In spite of Albert McIntosh's mixed blood, he looked more Chinese than American or Indian; he was of small to medium stature, with a face more likely to be inscrutable than not.

The doctor greeted the chief and the Shadwells, then said, "I come on a matter of urgency. If the Shadwells will excuse us, could we talk for an hour?"

"Suppose," the chief said, "that we sit on yonder settle. The day is too pretty to be inside. What brings you, Dorch?"

"Della Wano."

"I have told you not to think of that; in fact, those were my words to you at your father's funeral."

"Something moves to a showdown," Dorch said. "The word was out among the Union Creeks even before I returned from the war, and it has spread to all other tribes—Dorch McIntyre killed Della Wano."

McIntosh was silent.

"I built my hospital to atone for my sin; today I wear two pistols. Now I will tell you why."

Dorch told it all, stressing the long wait of someone who had lurked among the trees of Round Fort in the rain, of Timothy's injuries and the theft of the narcotics, Townley's statement about the four Creeks, and the stolen black horse.

Albert McIntosh rose from the settle and walked to a rosebush. He picked a white rose, placing it in his lapel. As he sat again, he turned his Oriental eyes to Dorch.

"Very little of what you told has not been known to me before."

"But how? And why?"

"You have chosen to regard these things as personal matters, since you have not wished to trouble our two nations with them. But they involve our nations, more than you think."

"But how have you learned what happened?"

"You know my niece, of course, a trainee."

"I see," said Dorch.

"I instructed her to have me or the lighthorse informed of anything which would indicate that outside action was being brought against you. As I say, this is a matter of two nations."

"But why should my trouble extend to that?"

"Because the Creeks are still in political upheaval. Remember, their numbers were almost equally divided during the war. A struggle for power exists among their leaders. Dorch McIntyre is a pawn between two political parties."

"It is still not clear," Dorch said.

"For months I have received letters from influential leaders on both sides, some indicating their desire for restraint, while others advocate violence. Also, I have had a letter from the Creek council at Okmulgee, asking in very diplomatic words, of course, that you appear before a board of inquiry at North Fork Town. There was, of course, more than pleasant and innocent words behind the letter. They could demand by our own laws that you be extradited, although the letter was not couched in those terms. You ask my advice—I believe, for the sake of tribal peace, you should go to North Fork Town. I am looking into the future, my son."

"I could not promise to go so suddenly, after what has happened here."

"What has happened proves my point. The Creek dissidents are determined upon vengeance."

"Then I could be the cause of war?"

"You must think of the Choctaws and Chickasaws, of which you are a member."

"Was anything else mentioned?"

"Yes. The federal army, the government itself, and even the Department of the Interior, are interested in the case. In fact, I have heard that some of them will demand that you appear before the Federal District Court at Fort Smith."

"My God," said Dorch. "Is there no statute of limitations?"

"Under Reconstruction? No. The army feels that until a criminal is brought to trial, there is no statute of limitations."

"But what of the others?"

"You must consider the corrupt situation in Washington. Men in each department wish to advance themselves. To those who know you as we do, you are a doctor; to those elsewhere, a criminal. Dorch, I have known you and your father well; believe me, I had told neither of you these things before, because I have tried to handle them myself. Your father suspected, but he did not know everything. But with what you have told me today, I have spoken. I have no faith in the Fort Smith District Court, where a case, if it is a case, would be tried."

"Then it's between a hard place and a rock."

The Chinese eyes twinkled. "The Choctaws are old in diplomacy—the centuries of contact with France, Spain, England, and the colonies made them so. It will do no harm for us to procrastinate, to explore the intent of certain Creeks further, and so secure vital information for ourselves. And remember, too, that the Chickasaws also have their way of doing things, or there would not be Chickasaw lighthorse with the Choctaws at the gate now. Your principal chief has three men stationed here."

"But you do want me to go to North Fork Town?"

"Let us say to consider it."

"I could not consider it. It is not neutral ground, but I might go to Fort Smith."

"Should you go, the lighthorse of our two nations would accompany you. You would go to prevent tribal dissension and perhaps guerrilla warfare; your willingness to appear would pacify the mass of the Creeks. It would not be a trial, only an inquiry."

"I am concerned about the narcotics," Dorch said. "If I am suspected by the government of illicit use of them, I could no longer practice at Round Fort. That is why I came to you first, to tell you everything."

"Continue your work. It is necessary. And you will bear no ill will toward my niece?"

"No. In fact, I had already selected her and a Chickasaw to go to New Orleans for special training." Dorch laughed. "But perhaps now I should keep her."

From the Shadwell's white mansion Dorch rode to the Townley home, before and behind him the lighthorse. He did not like what he considered ostentation; still, for a day or so, at least, it was necessary.

When he entered the large living room, he saw Elfreda dressed in an evening gown. He placed his hat on a sofa and walked to Mrs. Townley, who sat in her chair.

He felt her pulse. "Stick out your tongue." When she did, he said, "Ugh! The case is hopeless. In a week you will beat your husband, and your toenails will fall out."

"Dorch, you could always be so ridiculous." The gray-haired woman flung her shawl from her shoulders, laughing.

"Too much meat, madam. Eat more vegetables."

"I don't like vegetables."

"And meat doesn't like you." He turned to Elfreda. "And what are you? A vision?"

She smiled. "I hope so." Her gown was cut low, but not too low; the bodice swelled, and the waist was small.

Townley came in from the store. "Hello, Doctor. I see your lighthorse arrived in time."

"Yes, and thanks," Dorch said. "It's between me and the Creeks now." He glanced at the thinning sunlight through the curtained windows. "How shall we go to town?" he asked Elfreda. "Walk, ride, or send for a carriage?"

"Suppose we walk. We are both shut up too much." She took a light wrap for her shoulders.

As they walked down the wide street, the late sunlight still lingered. The lighthorse rode casually, bluejays shrieked in the trees, and robins hopped on the grass. Somewhere a church bell tolled.

Dorch asked, "What do you think of a doctor who forces a nurse to have dinner with him?"

Elfreda laughed. "It will depend upon what I have to eat."

"It's a beautiful evening," Dorch said. "Look, you can almost see the stars, and there's no doubt about smelling the stinking magnolias."

"Don't you like magnolias?"

"When I was in medical school, I had two smells always—magnolias and cadavers. I'll never like either."

"You've done a good job here, Doctor."

"Call me Dorch. You used to."

"I'm a nurse now."

"A beautiful and hungry nurse."

When they finished their dinner at the crowded hotel, alone at a separate small table covered with a red-and-white-checkered tablecloth, Dorch said, "I've enjoyed tonight."

"You should have more enjoyable nights, not with me, necessarily, but with some other nurse or person."

"Time," said Dorch, "what time would I ever have for that?"

When they left the dining room, he saw the lighthorse again, some sauntering about the street, while others had remained mounted. In spite of their presence, he tucked the right tail of his coat behind the pistol butt. At least, he thought, I have this right.

At the Townley home, Elfreda changed to a riding habit, and they set out on the leafy trail to Round Fort. Three lighthorse rode before them, and three behind. Dorch rode silently.

Elfreda said, "Why don't you tell me, Dorch? You have not been yourself tonight."

"Of course, you know the story of Della Wano."

"Yes."

"Honestly, I don't know whether I loved her or not. I know only that in one hideous night I killed her. Now the matter has other implications, perhaps even tribal warfare."

She hesitated, then said, "If there was a reason for you to kill me, I should not blame you." She drew her horse closer. "Dorch, did you hear something in the brush?"

"Yes, but only a fox or coyote. It moved too fast to be anything else."

"What did Chief McIntosh tell you?"

"We will wait the Creeks out, although I may go to Fort Smith as a gesture of conciliation."

"Never, Dorch. Don't do it."

"Why?"

She turned her face to his. "Because you could never trust anyone."

He wished only that there was light enough to see the large eyes which had gazed at him across the checkered tablecloth.

At the rear door of the hospital they stopped the horses. A Chickasaw groom came to take the beasts to the stable.

"Give them plenty of oats," Dorch said, "and rub them down."

Elfreda looked up at him. He said as awkwardly as a backward boy, "You look radiant tonight."

He felt it would be almost improper to enter the rear door with her, then walk down the corridor to the door of her room, then go out to his own door of the round room.

"Promise, Dorch, you won't worry about the past, or the present."

Once more he wished he could see her eyes, the alive eyes looking up at him, and not think of the dead ones.

Again he said, "It was a beautiful evening."

She rose on tiptoe and lightly kissed him, then opened the door and went inside.

He turned and walked around the hospital to the door of the round room. He could see the lighthorse stationing themselves about the hill.

Timothy was still awake. "How are your wounds?" Dorch asked.

"Fine," Timothy said. "Did you have a good evening, sir?"

"Yes," Dorch said. "A very good evening."

4

The winter had passed, cruel and keening, disturbing the old soldiers' ghosts which kept their vigil on the hill. The valley of the Boggy was white with snow or filled with piercing winds.

During these days, after his mornings were finished, or until his afternoon inspections began, Dorch paced the hill restlessly, or if the weather was too inclement, he paced the round room.

There had been a stage holdup on the Texas Road—only narcotics for the hospital had been taken. This had not helped his black moods.

"What you need," Timothy said one night, "is a piano like you had in New Orleans. Then when you get into these moods, you could pound hell out of it the way you did that old upright."

Dorch clapped a heavy hand on the table. "Why didn't you think of that before?"

Timothy grinned. "Because I am a gentleman's gentleman, sir. I don't intrude on your thoughts."

After a lengthy correspondence with a piano manufacturer in Cincinnati, Dorch decided upon the piano he wanted, a large walnut square. He wrote:

> I must caution you about the care to be taken with this instrument. I am acquainted with a steamboat captain on the Arkansas who can make the transfer from the Mississippi. It will be your responsibility to deliver the piano intact to Captain Keeter. I will be called to Fort Smith in the spring on other

matters, and I shall assume responsibility there. Include two tuning hammers and all items incidental for tuning. The dates of shipment and transfer we can agree upon later.

The other matters involved, Dorch thought, standing in the center of the room, his hand on the table, concerned the Creeks and Della Wano. Odd how it always concerned Della, and not the other women he had killed. Perhaps it had been her youth; perhaps other things.

His agreement to go to a federal conference at Fort Smith had resulted from a visit by Albert McIntosh to the hospital. Dorch had been at the old barracks when he rode in; he walked down the hill to greet him.

The chief said, after they had shaken hands, "I continue to hear good things about your hospital. I came again to see for myself." He asked curiously, "What are the wooden buildings in the distance?"

"Isolation wards," Dorch said. "There has been an outbreak of smallpox up Clear Boggy and on Blue River. I want it stopped before it reaches Boggy Depot. Also, I've asked all people to remain at home until they can be vaccinated."

"Thank God, you didn't bring the matter before the council—it would still be argued."

"Let me show you the round room first," Dorch said. "I'm rather proud of it now."

He held the heavy iron-banded door open.

Within the room the chief said, "Ah, your father's secretary, and the old table and chairs. How many times have I sat at each with him, dining or working on the accounts of the nation. A warm fireplace you have, too."

Dorch opened the door to the hospital corridor. On the left he indicated the door of the first room. "Go in," he said. "My operating room."

The chief looked at the overhead lamps, the operating table, and glanced toward the shelves where drugs and medicines were kept.

"Suppose we look in on some patients," Dorch said. "A visit from their chief would be good therapy."

Albert McIntosh's Oriental features smiled. "It would be therapy to me if they approve the way I handle the affairs of the nation."

They went from room to room, the nurses at attention, a little trainee struggling from her knees from a wet floor, a scrub brush in her hand, to stand shaking against the wall, awed by the presence of the small but great chief.

In one room a pregnant woman said from her cot, "I will name my baby Albert McIntosh."

The chief smiled. "Then I must visit you again."

At the doors of the last rooms, Dorch stopped. "These are the nurses' quarters. I would show you in, but some may be sleeping."

"Here is where you have your kept women."

"You have heard that too?"

"Dorch, let us go to the old barracks. I always think better when I see the lands of our nations about me."

They sat at a low point of the wall, facing the valley and Boggy Creek.

McIntosh asked, "Where do you keep your narcotics?"

"You ask that because of what happened to Timothy and the stage holdup?"

"Yes."

"In each case, only my narcotics were taken. I have thought of that circumstance many times. But you ask where I keep them."

Dorch reached into the pocket of his long coat and drew out an old pipe and tobacco pouch. He drew the pouch string and took out a dozen small vials.

"Here are my narcotics," he said, "any one of which I may use on a given day. The vials are with me always. No nurse or trainee in the hospital knows where I keep the rest."

"Where do you keep them?"

"After all the Creek talk, and after Timothy was waylaid, we removed a hearthstone and replaced it with one not so thick. A locked metal box is buried beneath it. When I need more for daily use, we take the stone up; then a thin layer of cement is used to hold it in place again. The area is blackened with ashes."

"I suppose your opinion is mine."

"Yes, to involve me in violation of the law. It could be said that I robbed the stage to get narcotics for illegal purposes, since I alone would know what stage they would come on. Yet, on the other hand, every stage-stand operator from Kansas to Boggy Depot would know what the shipment contained because of the waybills. The information could be spread easily, especially among the Creeks in North Fork Town. Even a stage driver could arrange a holdup."

"What is your theory about your black horse, which returned after the stage holdup?"

Dorch said, surprised, "You know of that too?"

"The lighthorse reported the incident within an hour, also my niece."

"The horse was wounded," Dorch said. "Its shoulder was full of buckshot. It's probable that the shotgun rider on the stage was not a party to the plan. He did his duty and fired, killing the outlaw and wounding my stolen horse before he himself was killed. I worked half a day with the horse, taking out buckshot."

The chief said, gazing into the valley, "The dead outlaw was a Creek."

"It would have been the same gang which shot me and waylaid Timothy."

"Have you taken more precautions here?"

Dorch laughed. "By law, I am limited in my precautions. I can't hire a regiment. But I no longer allow the nurses to ride to Boggy on their days off, unless several Indians of our tribes ride with them. Some men beg for the privilege, because they cannot pay the small bills they owe the hospital."

"I am assigning six lighthorse permanently to Round Fort, and I will request an equal number from the Chickasaws. They will be under your orders. Now, there is something else."

Dorch was amused at the chief's deviousness.

"You will recall that at the Shadwells' I mentioned my communications with the Creeks, as well as with certain elements of the federal government. Since then I have tried to conciliate everyone—you, the Creeks, and the government. You raised the point that a meeting in North Fork Town would not be on neutral ground. I impressed this upon the Creeks—that even their own council, as strongly as our two peoples are aroused by the case, would hesitate to appear in our council houses for such a purpose, although we would do our best to provide adequate protection.

"Consequently, the adamant faction has agreed to a meeting at Fort Smith and to our guard of lighthorse. This will not be a trial, but merely an official gathering of information. I must say, too, that the government is sending an agent of the Department of the Interior, Sardis Rippy, and a federal marshal, Flint Murcheson, to investigate the first theft of narcotics."

Dorch said, "Now they will have another."

"Even if there is unfavorable evidence at Fort Smith, you will still be allowed to return. A trial, if any, would come later. Go, Dorch, to prevent the dissension and the guerrilla warfare we spoke of. We can still have genuine peace among our peoples. You alone can give it."

"I will go," Dorch said.

Dorch wrote Captain Keeter of the *Maizie Trout* and the officials of the piano-manufacturing company of the date of his arrival at Fort Smith; the captain always plied the Arkansas, especially between Fort Smith and the Mississippi, so he would have no difficulty in meeting the *Mississippi Queen* at Napoleon.

"Even if I lose my neck," Dorch told Timothy, "I'll get a piano out of the trip."

He told Elfreda over the red-and-white-checkered tablecloth at the hotel one night, "When I leave, you will be in charge of the hospital. You know my rules and regulations. See that they are followed."

"Oh, Dorch!" Her eyes looked into his pleadingly. "I could never do it properly."

He replied, "But who else could? Once you ran a field hospital under artillery fire. This is a time when you will have to take charge. On operative cases, you know how I try to build the patient up first. Do everything you've seen me do; keep them alive until I get back." He lowered his voice. "About narcotics—there may be times when you must give them. But watch carefully, and give only half of what I give, and let no nurse or trainee see you do it. I can't let some poor Indian or cancerous woman die in pain. That last hour can be a big thing. But with those who simply desire morphine—like my amputee, old Willie Turtle—use a placebo solution. I'll leave written instructions that Willie is to have one morphine injection; after that, it's placebo."

She said, "But I don't know where the narcotics are."

"Tomorrow we will talk of what you'll need and before I leave arrange a hiding place."

"Dorch, I am glad you once told me something."

"What?"

"About Della Wano. She has become a spirit to me. I think, in spite of all the war and terror which claimed her, she knows what you do here."

"I am at my limit. I've been in touch with several young doctors—one, Dr. Dennis, may come."

She put her hand on his. "Then you can rest."

"No, I can never rest."

As they rode home on the Round Fort trail, the lighthorse some distance before and behind them, she said among the trees of the creek, "What a moon!"

"A good night for possums," Dorch said. "Do you see the shadows of the next big trees?"

"Yes, I see them."

"When we get there, bend toward me. I want to kiss you."

Two days before he left for Fort Smith, Dorch found two off-duty trainees, a Chickasaw and a Choctaw, curled in the big chairs of the round room, each reading a medical book.

He pulled a footstool before the chairs and sat facing the girls, who put down their books. "Are you ready for a surprise?" he asked.

"What, Doctor?" the Chickasaw asked.

"First," Dorch said, "I have talked with your parents about this, and they have agreed, although they leave the decision to you. When I go to Fort Smith, I will take you with me. We will have an escort of lighthorse, and you will have a tent for privacy. Then you will go to New Orleans for two years of special training at my old medical hospital."

"But, Doctor," Albert McIntosh's niece said, "we do not have money for that, and neither of us has ever seen any town but Tushkahoma and Tishomingo and Doaksville. Even my uncle, the chief, is almost poor. He gives everything to the nation."

"The expenses will be paid by the hospital. You will receive full salary, plus your expenses. You will go to New Orleans to work, and not to play. You will have no vacations; in the summer you will attend special courses at my old medical school."

The Chickasaw began to sob. "Doctor, you have never said anything nice to us before—you even fuss at the way we scrub floors."

Dorch said gruffly, "It's just my way. Forget it."

"But why do you choose us?"

"Because you are my two best trainees. Someday you will run this hospital. Now, here is the rest of the plan. Captain Keeter, an old friend of mine, will take you by steamboat to the mouth of the Arkansas, where you will transfer to the *Mississippi Queen*.

The *Queen*'s captain will look after your comforts. An old professor of mine and his wife will meet you in New Orleans, and you will live with them. That will be good; he will talk medicine all night if he has a listener, and you can discuss all you have learned during the day."

"But, Doctor," the Chickasaw said, "we don't have clothes for a trip. We dress all right here, but New Orleans would be different."

"The eternal feminine," Dorch said. "At Fort Smith you will get the most fashionable clothes money can buy. The hospital will pay for them."

The Choctaw said, "But why don't you train white girls?"

Their dark eyes were intent on his.

Dorch said, "Very few white nurses understand our Indians. Now, what is your decision?"

The trainees glanced at each other, then nodded.

"Fine," Dorch said. "Now ride home and tell your parents. A lighthorse will go with each of you. Be back tomorrow night with what you need to take, since we leave early next morning."

He saw the old balcony at the apartment house.

"And tell my other old professors hello, if they are living."

Next day Dorch and Timothy removed the firestone above the narcotics box. Dorch called Elfreda into the room, being certain that the hospital door was locked.

"You have several pairs of shoes in your closet?" he asked.

"Yes," she said.

He extended the tobacco pouch. "Here are the narcotics. Stick the pouch in a shoe, and let the shoe look as if it had been tossed carelessly upon the floor. Anyone looking for narcotics would first search the operating room. Keep the door of your room locked, and remember, there will always be lighthorse near. I have told them to watch you always."

Timothy coughed and left the room.

Dorch seized Elfreda closely.

"I'm terribly afraid," she said, her arms about his shoulders. "Can I do what you want done?"

"You'll have to," he said, kissing her. "There's no one else."

Dorch and Timothy trotted their horses up the Texas Road, accompanied by the Chickasaw and Choctaw lighthorse. The air was brisk; there were the flights of geese soaring north, shifting their flight lines across the sky; whooping cranes moved in wide-winged clouds.

Dorch glanced before and behind at the twenty-four lighthorse the chiefs of two nations had sent him. They were all above average height, reserved, and quietly confident.

There was no predominant uniform among them. They carried rifles, pistols, and knives; ropes were at their pommels, yet beneath the wide-brimmed hat of each might have been detected one thing in common.

This was the color of green each man wore, perhaps a green bandanna, a green shirt, or green trousers or leggings, or a green armband. Captain Tiger Panton, the leader of the Chickasaws, had cut up his wife's dress to make a sash; he had passed other green sashes to four of his fellows.

Dorch looked with admiration at his bodyguard. "Why does each man wear green?" he asked Tiger Panton.

Panton said pessimistically, "So if there is an ambush, we won't kill each other." Panton was supposed to have second sight, because when he was a boy, a crazy old Choctaw woman had placed her hands on him. But because of this gift, he was often laughed at. He was broody, but one of the best lighthorse.

Dorch had been given a pair of silver spurs by the Chickasaw nation, and a new Colt pistol with silver inlays on the butt by the Choctaws; the gifts, while not impressive, conveyed a message to other tribes. Dorch spurred now to the forward position, which Captain Dade Rothney, the high-cheekboned Choctaw leader occupied.

"Tiger Panton looks for catastrophe," Dorch told him.

Rothney laughed. "He'd be unhappy if he had an egg as big as the sun for breakfast."

As the sun rose higher, more and more covered wagons came from the trees, where immigrants had slept overnight; soon the road teemed with its usual traffic, the wagons and men on horseback moving everlastingly south.

At the junction of a creek, a dozen riders, to all appearances seedy but well armed, came from the brush. Captains Tiger Panton and Dade Rothney rode forward to confer with them.

After a few moments the lighthorse started again, the strangers straggling with them, before and behind and even on the sides.

"Are these men with us?" Dorch asked Panton.

"They're lighthorse, all right. Had you thought that any man we meet on horseback, or anyone hidden in a passing wagon, could end you with one good bullet? These men can work in and out of the wagons and spot anything that looks suspicious."

Having been confined to Round Fort for so long, Dorch had not realized how little he had known of the Texas Road since the war days. Then it had been a pathway where warring armies had advanced or retreated. He had been present before Perryville was destroyed.

He was not prepared to see now the great herds of Texas cattle and sheep driving north to the Kansas railheads, although from the Round Fort hill he had seen many pass through his valley. And the wagons were filled with all types of humanity, but not all the faces he saw in the wagon seats or peering from beneath the tailgate bows were happy faces; some, those of wives and children, were old and tired and worn from travel.

Yet behind them would always be the new generation, itself born of the old urge, moving restlessly forward, the sons of the men he had fought with, or against.

At Perryville, where he had helped poison the wells before the Union capture, the lighthorse stopped for consultation. They had made the usual good time for unpushed horses, forty miles a day in a good trot, camping by night. Thus far, no untoward incident had marred the journey.

"I'll be freighting a piano back with us," Dorch told Panton and Rothney as they began another day. "I'll want the easiest road from Fort Smith."

Dade Rothney shoved his hat back on his forehead, the sun striking his prominent cheekbones. His candid eyes squinted. "Then we'll turn off on the old California Trail. You don't want to cross the South Canadian into Creek country, and with the light rain we've had, the *Maizie Trout* couldn't get over the rock ridge at Webber's Falls with a full cargo. We'll turn northeast and take the trail to Fort Smith. The road is still used by freighters, and by staying south of the Canadian, we'd be among Choctaws and not near the Creeks."

Tiger Panton grunted. "Yes, and we could be charged from four directions at the intersection."

On their last night out, they camped near the old Choctaw town of Skullyville on its gravel hill. It's odd, Dorch thought, trying to sleep and watching a sky of stars; I don't think of the trial at all, only the hospital and Elfreda.

His concern was for another doctor. He knew he could not continue indefinitely the pace he had set for himself. Of all the young graduates with whom he had corresponded, only one, Anthony Dennis, had shown the slightest interest in Round Fort. Money, position, prestige—that's all the others want, he thought.

But he'd make out somehow.

They had been in Fort Smith for a day now, spending the night uptown at the new Le Flore, instead of at the old Rogers Hotel on Washington, or Second, Street.

Timothy continued to whistle merrily as he walked toward the landing. This old tie, he thought again, why in hell did I wear it today? And to a trial?

But he didn't care, really. The sun warmed his back, and he felt good. The tie was something like an old corn, or an itch, a part of his life, just as Mount Vista was part of the town. The tie was Timothy Baines as much as his hump.

If it hadn't been for Dorch back there on the Point at the morning meeting of the board of inquiry in the Federal District courtroom in one of the old fort's buildings, he wouldn't have had a care in the world.

There had been bearded and mustached government officials seated at the heavy table, Creek dignitaries anxious to be circumspect, and the Chickasaw and Choctaw lighthorse. Only half their number had been allowed in the room; these had been disarmed, but they surrounded Dorch solidly, sitting beside him or standing close as witness after witness was presented. Informality was the rule. Actually, Timothy had seen no reason for the hearing; it presented only a rehash of what had been known in the Territory since the first year of the war.

Yet it might serve the purpose Albert McIntosh had hoped for.

Suddenly Timothy stopped whistling and began to laugh. In the midst of a long and tedious harangue by some black-coated government official, a quavering blast from the waterfront had entered the open courtroom. One who had heard that sound before could never forget it. Sitting beside Dorch, Timothy nudged his foot and grinned. "The *Maizie Trout* is in," he whispered.

The official had stopped speaking to regain his composure. Now he began again, only to be interrupted a second time. There was laughter even among the Creeks.

"Thank God for Keeter," Dorch whispered to Timothy. "He's turned this thing into the farce it is. Go down and tell him we are here and I'll be there when the session ends."

A little prostitute with a red feather in her hat pushed her way before Timothy on the cobblestones, stopping him. Timothy tipped his bowler.

"I've got a nice room on Second Street," she said. "It's much nicer than on the Row."

"The trouble is," Timothy said, "I'm going down beyond First Street, down to the river. The *Maizie Trout* just came in."

Three men, carrying their luggage, rushed past them at breakneck speed. One, a tall man with squirrelish teeth, tripped and fell headlong to the cobblestones. His companions paused and helped pick him up; the three raced on toward the avenue.

"Who is that bunch?" Timothy asked.

The little prostitute laughed. "Everybody knows them. They are Department of Interior men who were supposed to be at the inquiry today. What was that tune you were whistling?" she asked.

"That? Oh, that was the 'Stephanie Gavotte.' My gentleman used to play it when he was in a good humor, or sentimental."

"Your gentleman?"

Timothy tipped his bowler again. "I am a gentleman's gentleman."

"When I was a girl, I used to play the 'Gavotte.'"

Timothy looked at the red lips in surprise.

"My folks had an old organ in the farmhouse. We had a little sheet music, but not much. I used to make up pieces to play. I made up some pretty ones—'When April Rains Fall in Autumn' and 'When Bullfrogs Sing Beside the Sparkling Spavinaw.' Did you ever see the Spavinaw?"

"Not that I recollect," said Timothy.

"Green as leaves in the spring, fields and meadows stretched all about. Huddled little hills. I used to rake hay in the meadows. If we could go to a piano, I could play you 'When Bullfrogs Sing Beside the Sparkling Spavinaw.'

The Spavinaw!

Some other stream in this harsh but beautiful land; a child

sitting before a tallow candle in a half-lighted cabin, her small fingers stretched on ivory keys.

Timothy said, "Maybe I'll see you again. Where are you going?"

"Just walking. Maybe up to the fort to hear the Della Wano trial."

"I've just come from there. A lot of windjamming—statutes of limitation, the rights of the federal army, the rights of the Indian Commission, the rights of the whole human race except those of my gentleman."

"Oh." The brown eyes began to comprehend. "The three men who just passed—they are Sardis Rippy and Tyson Pennypacker and Flint Murcheson, a marshal. They won't help your gentleman any." She looked at Timothy wistfully. "Could I see you tonight? We can find a piano and I can play the 'Sparkling Spavinaw.'"

"You'd better forget it," Timothy said. "I come up to meet the *Maizie Trout* for supplies sometimes. Maybe I'll see you again."

But he thought as he left her, that girl has possibilities. I really believe she wanted to play the piano.

When Timothy walked up the gangplank of the *Maizie Trout*, he found Captain Keeter talking with Jessup and Denna Cart at the prow. The roistering passengers had left for the grog shops; the Choctaws from the stern had joined other Indians they met at the landing to go with them to Skullyville, a few miles upriver.

Jessup was speaking. "Do you know why Indians hang meat high in the trees?" he asked Denna. She and Amy had at last been allowed on deck.

Denna laughed. "No, I don't know."

"Because flies don't fly high," Jessup said.

"Captain, sir," Timothy said.

Keeter turned. "Timothy Baines!" He took Timothy's hand. "So we all made it."

"It's been a long time," said Timothy. "Do you have the piano?"

Keeter nodded. "It's under the superstructure."

Denna said, "You are Timothy Baines, Dr. McIntyre's gentleman. I am Denna Cart."

"Pleased, ma'am," the little hunchback said, lifting his bowler.

"How goes the trial, or whatever it is?" Keeter asked.

"Around and around, with more wind than a tornado."

FOUR

1

Dorch walked out of the District Court building. In the dungeons beneath the courtroom, the Territory outlaws were confined. He could see the other structures of the fort, the old stone commissary rising high.

Something else he saw, too.

The gallows of the court, stark and dismal, equipped for twelve hangings at once, although only six men had been its greatest load. On the days of execution of Territory outlaws who had taken their toll of human life, many of the whites of the town came to the gallows as if on holiday, and Indians from up the Arkansas and its tributaries came in their best regalia.

Holiday—holiday for everyone, red, white, and freed blacks alike.

Food—fried chicken, biscuits, boiled yams, venison, and barbecued beef. Yah, yah! Guffaws. Smoked ham. Eating on the grounds around the gallows. Special invitations to illustrious or important men. "You are welcomed to the hanging of so-and-so," with the condemned outlaw's picture printed on the invitation.

Light bread, cornbread—sour hominy, plain hominy, and hominy with meat. A gala holiday, a short shrift and a long rope.

Dorch walked a block toward Garrison Avenue, his silver spurs glinting, then down the cobblestones toward the river, following Timothy's path to the *Maizie Trout*. The combined lighthorse walked unobtrusively before and behind him and on his sides. He had noticed a preponderance of Choctaws near the court building;

he had heard their muttered approval as he left; he wondered if Albert McIntosh had conveyed to Choctaw officials at Skullyville that a show of numbers might be desirable.

Once aboard the steamboat, Dorch talked with Captain Keeter, Timothy, and the lighthorse captains.

Keeter said, "The river is low, and at Webber's Falls we'd face grasshoppering or being pulled by horses across the stone ridge. I'll load cargo here for another day, so suppose on the next we cast off for Skullyville, and we'll arrange for a wagon and horses and transfer the piano."

"A good plan," said Dorch. "The trainees can stay at the Le Flore, and you can pick them up on the way back."

Timothy said to Dorch, "Why don't I ride back to Skullyville tomorrow; then I can hire a team and drivers and have them ready by the time you put in." Timothy had already been questioned at the inquiry; his part in the trial was over.

"A good idea," Dorch said.

He turned and moved to stand at the prow of the *Maizie Trout* beneath the starboard derrick, gazing upstream at the flowering river, his features stern and brooding.

Denna came to the pilothouse to talk with Jessup; it was then she saw Dorch for the first time. In that instant, she knew she loved him.

He had taken his hat off, letting the wind blow through his bushy hair; never had she seen a face so dark and distant.

"That is Dr. McIntyre beside the derrick?" she asked Jessup.

"Sure. Like a black crow that don't know which way to fly, one the whole roost has turned on. Do you know how crows do that? One of them violates a crow law, then he's chased all over the sky, or lands on a limb to wait his end when the flock comes down. The doc is an outcast."

The Negro Tom came to the pilothouse. "Missy, could I see you outside?"

"Of course," Denna said.

"Just tell me something, missy, when a man asks a woman the big question and she busts out crying and says yes, what's a man to do? Why do women cry that way?" he asked, wiping his own eyes.

Denna laughed. "I don't know, Tom. But it's still early—why can't Captain Keeter marry you and Amy now? Jessup says we won't leave for two days. You could go ashore and have a honeymoon."

"But there's the license and that business."

"Captain Keeter can handle it. He'd be glad to. Tell Amy to be ready in an hour."

"You've done got a man, missy. Amy says she won't ever let me leave you."

"You can help on the ranch, Tom."

When Tom turned away, Denna went back to the pilothouse and looked down on Dorch again. He had not moved.

Once she had heard the slope-shouldered Sardis Rippy say to his marshal, "He keeps women at Round Fort. He sells narcotics on the side. That's why we are here—to nail his hide to the wall. And he killed women during the war."

On the deck before the superstructure, Captain Keeter married Amy and Tom. He asked, "Who gives this woman in lawful matrimony?"

Denna was disturbed. Some man should give Amy away, not herself, not a woman. The deck was empty, save for the bushy-haired man who still stood at the prow. "Couldn't a man give Amy away?" Denna asked the captain, who had paused with his finger in the closed Bible.

At the derrick, the dark man turned. He bowed and said to Denna, "At your service, miss."

He moved to stand beside Amy. "I, Dorch McIntyre, give this woman."

Tom and Amy walked down the gangplank, carrying their carpetbags.

"I have not had the honor, miss," Dorch said.

"I am Denna Cart, from Texas."

Dorch bowed again. "As you know, Dorch McIntyre."

"Yes. I think you owe me a dinner tonight, Doctor. I have watched and cared for your property for weeks."

"What do you mean?"

"Your piano. I saw it loaded at Cincinnati, transferred at Napoleon, and every night on the Arkansas I have had Tom check to see if the tarpaulins were tied properly."

"I do owe you a dinner," Dorch said, a sudden smile breaking his somberness. "In an hour?"

"Yes."

"I will call at your stateroom."

When they left the *Maizie Trout* and walked up the cobblestones toward the avenue, the lighthorse, which had scattered themselves along the waterfront, moved into place.

"You have an excellent bodyguard," Denna said, Dorch marveling at her height and the proportions of her body.

"Unfortunately, it is necessary."

"Yes, I know. Mainly from a conversation I overheard from three of your enemies."

"The marshal and Pennypacker and the Interior man? They were in the courtroom when I left."

Denna said, "But to tell you something else—I am returning to Texas from England. I was in the Lake District for two years. I knew a McIntyre near Coniston Water—his name was Bart; he owned the Tankard and Bull."

Dorch grinned. "After being chased out of Scotland, my ancestors settled at Coniston or came to this country. Bart must be some left-handed cousin."

"He was very nice. We had dinner together."

On the wide avenue, they walked on for several blocks, the spire of the church fading in the dimmer light. They returned to the new Le Flore and entered the dining room.

"The best cuisine west of the Mississippi is served here," Dorch said.

When they were seated at a table with silver threads woven into the tablecloth, the mirrored walls about them, he removed the light wrap she wore; under the subdued lights her shoulders gleamed. While they ordered, Dorch thought of Elfreda at their table in the hotel at Boggy Depot.

Denna said brightly, "Are you moody?"

"I have had a hard day. Tell me about Bart and Coniston."

"There was a fox hunt, but instead of having horses, everyone walked. The night before, a squire's son fell in love with me, but later I had dinner with Bart."

"Did the squire's son propose?"

"Yes, but when I refused him, he told me to go to hell. I returned the compliment."

One of the new independent breed, Dorch thought, putting a knife to his steak. Still, she was a regal wench, and damn good-looking.

"I've been thinking," he said. "You will want to reach the Texas Road as quickly as possible, and Captain Keeter is worried about the rock shelf at Webber's Falls. Why don't you leave the *Maizie Trout* at Skullyville when we transfer the piano, and we'll take the California Trail to the Texas Road. Then you could stay over for a few days at Boggy Depot or Round Fort. Anyway, you'd have the best lighthorse escort in the Territory."

Over her wine, her eyes were brilliant. "I'll do it. It would be like roughing it in the Lake District again."

"I have a favor to ask. I have brought two hospital trainees with me. They will go to New Orleans for two years' work, but are visiting friends in Skullyville tonight. They will return in the morning, and I wonder if you would see that they are properly outfitted. Money is no object."

She smiled. "It never is for kept women, Doctor."

Dorch laughed. "And I hope I can keep them forever."

Since leaving Fort Smith on the eight-mile run to Skullyville, the *Maizie Trout* had clunked beyond the bluffs of the Poteau and old Fort Coffee; the inquiry had been inconclusive, and on its last day neither Sardis Rippy nor Flint Murcheson had appeared, but now Dorch, leaning against the side of the superstructure, had his attention drawn to a frock-coated and two-holstered gambler who wore a flamboyant vest along with other trappings of his trade, the obstreperous man Jessup had flung over the side at Napoleon.

The gambler's name, Dorch had learned, was Capshaw, and he was on his first trip into the Territory.

As the sternwheeler approached the mouth of a creek, a naked Choctaw lad sat on the bank, his fishing pole extended. The boy glanced toward the *Maizie Trout,* waving, and Jessup responded with a whistle blast.

"Damn!" said Capshaw, moving to the side, "I've always wanted to get me a redskin!"

Drawing his pistol, he raised it and fired. For a moment the boy sat rigidly, then slowly bent forward and followed the pole into the water. Tom dived over the side to recover the body.

Dorch was outraged. "Capshaw!" His voice rang. "You will do me the honor!"

The gambler, still holding his pistol, saw the silver inlay on the butt of the pistol in Dorch's holster; one side of his thin face twitched. Dorch had worn a short leather jacket on the trip to Skullyville; the butt showed cleanly.

Capshaw raised his pistol; Dorch drew and fired. The gambler slumped to the deck but remained in a sitting position; he stared in puzzlement at Dorch, then curled over and lay still.

"A nice-looking lad," Dorch said, going to kneel beside the dead youth, Tom still dripping and standing over him.

They would meet most of the other lighthorse at Skullyville, but Captains Tiger Panton and Dade Rothney stood close. Dorch rose from the boy, shaking his head.

"The lad will belong to someone in Skullyville," Captain Keeter said. "We'll take him on." He added with unexpected sternness, "Doctor, I don't think you have helped your other case a bit; still, if you hadn't shot, I might have."

A Skullyville merchant in a brown bowler said to Dorch, "Enough of us saw the Indian boy killed and saw the gambler raise his pistol toward you. We will go to the council house the moment we dock. You have your witnesses, sir, and will not be detained. You may be recalled for trial, but that will be a formality."

Denna, in the pilothouse, looked down on the two bodies and at Dorch, still standing beside the Indian boy and holstering his pistol. She had been strangely thrilled by the incident; a tingling was in her spine.

Skullyville lay three miles from the river, and there were wagons and carriages to meet the sternwheeler as it edged to the landing. Timothy Baines had come also, together with the lighthorse who had left early with him. As the two bodies were placed in wagons, Dorch explained to him.

"Well," said Timothy, "that's tough, but we'll get this second inquiry over tonight and pull out with the piano first thing in the morning. The freighter's wagon will be here by sunup."

Awaiting Dorch's return from Skullyville, Denna was restless. She paced the deck until she was tired, then went to her stateroom. From the porthole, she sat staring up the dusty road to Skullyville. At last the porthole was blotted out by darkness. She did not understand the strange desires which overwhelmed her.

She rose from her cot and went on deck again, just as the men from the *Maizie Trout* returned. She saw Dorch come up the gangplank and immediately went to him.

"What happened?" she asked breathlessly.

"Nothing. It was only a matter of taking statements from witnesses."

"You are free?"

"Until a trial, if there is one. But there would be no doubt of the verdict, in spite of my challenge."

The strange thrill persisted in Denna.

"Unless you are tired, would you want to walk?" she asked.

"Of course," Dorch said. "There's not much to see but the woodlot for the steamboats, or we could walk along the creek."

"I would like to see the creek in darkness," Denna said, half-leading him down the gangplank. As they walked, she had taken his hand, and held it tightly. They reached the creek. "Could we sit somewhere?" she asked.

"If you wish."

"Then here," she said. "This is a pretty spot."

They sat. Dorch seemed to hesitate, then leaned forward and kissed her. He was stunned with surprise; he was being kissed more passionately than ever he had known in his life.

He was fumbling with her; she with him.

He was gazing down into dim eyes, living and demanding eyes, not the dead eyes of other woods and other times.

"Dorch!" she cried. "Love me, love me!"

Capshaw was sitting on the deck, and he rolled over stupidly and lay still.

The fact that Sardis Rippy and Flint Murcheson had not appeared on the final day of the inquiry at Fort Smith had preyed on Dorch's mind; now, as he left Skullyville, his suspicions became a certainty. They had taken advantage of his being in Fort Smith to leave to investigate the hospital in his absence. What could Elfreda do?

On the second night on the trail, he awoke by two in the morning by the stars, the night chill. He was convinced of his suspicions; nothing could change him. He sought out Tiger Panton, who was in charge of the night guard.

"Get your men up and wake Dade Rothney. I'm afraid for the hospital—we'll start riding tonight."

"But your piano?"

"I planned to go with it only to the intersection with the Texas Road, then burn daylight to Boggy Depot. Timothy can see it through."

Tiger Panton walked a few yards to where Rothney slept and kicked his back end, under his blanket.

"Get up, Choctaw. We're riding."

Rothney said, his pistol pointed, "Chickasaw, look at this little eye I've got on you, then tell me to get up."

"Forget it," Panton said. "Get your men ready."

Timothy had joined them, and now Denna Cart came from her tent wrapped in a night robe. "Amy can ride," she said. "There's no reason why we can't all go together."

"It will be hard riding," Dorch said.

"You forget I was born on a Texas ranch." Was there some mockery in her smile in the thick moonlight? She had conquered a man she had not expected to conquer, and conquered him easily.

Tiger Panton said, "I am still afraid of the intersection. After Fort Smith, the other faction of the Creeks could look for us to be in a let-down, and there would be no better place for an ambush than the four corners. I've said that before. As we turn into the Texas Road, they could come at us from four sides, and we'd be caught in a crossfire."

Rothney grinned. "Chickasaw, what do you suggest?"

"We'll cut off from the California Trail, say ten miles from the intersection. We'll take the brush and creeks and hit the Texas Road later. The piano can go on as planned."

Still laughing, Rothney said, "You guarantee this?"

Tiger Panton said, "I wouldn't guarantee your soul a roost in hell."

On the next day Dorch's party cut off the trail and began the brush and creek riding. It was slow going, but perhaps best. Once more Denna was strangely excited. What part did violence play in her nature?

Once on the Texas Road, they would stop only to rest the horses.

Tiger Panton said, "Once I rode ninety miles in a day, but my horse was trotting cross-legged when I got there."

Dade Rothney still needled. "Why did you ride so far?"

"To get away from Choctaws."

As soon as Dorch reached Round Fort, he showed his guests to the round room, while the lighthorse led their weary horses to the creek.

As Dorch entered the hospital corridor, a hawk-faced, slightly stooped young man in a white gown and rubber gloves emerged from the operating room.

"Dr. McIntyre?" he asked, taking off a glove and moving quickly to shake hands. "I am Anthony Dennis. You may remember our correspondence. I came to seek employment, but it seems that in your absence I have employed myself."

Dorch liked the young doctor immediately.

"What have you had here?" he asked.

"A hysterectomy—cancerous."

"Any spreading?"

"No. A few particles, but I removed them with a suction pump."

"Anything else?"

"Two—an appendectomy and a lung removal."

"How are the patients?"

Dr. Dennis grinned. "Still surviving."

A nurse came to the door. When she saw Dorch, she returned to the operating room. Elfreda came out.

"I must tell you about the narcotics," Dr. Dennis was saying. "Some were needed immediately. Miss Townley cooperated nicely. She gave me morphine for a terminal case. And may I say your secret is safe with me. I understand the situation perfectly."

"Dorch!" Elfreda cried, running to him. "So much has happened!"

"Everything looks very well," Dorch said.

Elfreda began to laugh almost hysterically. "Yes, but look at the clock above the round room door."

Dorch turned; a bullet or a pistol shot had taken the hands out at the center. "What caused it?" he asked.

Elfreda said. "On the day Dr. Dennis arrived, two men from the government, a Sardis Rippy and a marshal, came to inspect the hospital for narcotics. Because of their authority, the lighthorse had admitted them. They were shoving me into the operating room, just as the doctor came in."

Hawk-faced Dr. Dennis laughed. "I'd bought a pistol, just to look like everyone else who came down the Texas Road. I thought I had walked in on a holdup, but I had never fired a shot in my life. When I tried to draw the gun, it went off and put the hole in the clock. The government men made a record run going out the round room. If I am employed, I'll buy a new clock."

"I know your men," Dorch said. "They were witnesses at Fort Smith."

"But what happened at the inquiry?" Elfreda asked.

Dorch laughed shortly. "Nothing. Status quo."

Elfreda opened the door to the round room, as if they would go and sit there and talk for a few moments. She came back, saying, "Who are those people, Dorch?"

"Denna Cart and her servants. They came up on Captain Keeter's boat. She has been in England. Her father owns a ranch in Texas, but due to her interest in the hospital, I asked her to stay for a few days."

"Oh," said Elfreda.

Denna would never forget her first visit of Round Fort, of the old walls on the crest of the hill.

The barracks loomed like the remains of old castles she had known in England; the valley of Clear Boggy Creek was like English valleys she had known. She was quartered in one of the rooms between the hospital angle and the round room; Tom and Amy had the other.

She felt again that she was home. She did pretend an interest in the hospital, but it was only pretense. Her interest was in the shaggy-haired doctor who at table tossed bones to his mastiffs like an English lord, then sat nightly beating out his strange and maddening cacophonies on the piano.

The large fingers which operated so successfully were equally adept upon the ivory keys. Driven to exasperation one night, Denna said, "In God's name, Dorch, is there nothing in you but madness?"

He lifted his hands from the keys, flexing his tired fingers, which were unaccustomed to playing for so many years. Even the muscles in his wrists and forearms hurt.

He turned, scowling. "Yes, I suppose I am mad."

"Do you want to come to my room tonight?"

"I expected to."

"Then I hope you will be more cheerful tomorrow."

"And I hope a good tussle in bed will make you less irritable tomorrow night."

She slid her arm about his neck, then bent, kissing his forehead. "Dorch, why are we like this? I love you, and you were my first. Why are we so quarrelsome?"

"Our damned natures," Dorch said. "Both too proud, too free, too independent. We are too much alike. Someday we will hate each other."

"No," she said. "We could never hate. We are alike, but we will see what time brings. Since first seeing you, I have loved you."

"You have loved me for your own vanity. You are troubled, Denna, within yourself."

She sat beside him on the long piano bench. Impatiently, his fingers struck the keys discordantly.

He continued, "You never took the simpering college boys or the squire's son. Why did you take me?"

"Must we always analyze the most beautiful moment I will ever remember? I am beginning to think you never knew what happened."

"I know very well what happened. Let's don't talk about it. Later, tonight might change things."

"No, our meetings at night will never change things. What is wrong between us is too deep for that, Dorch. We are only sparks at night to kindle an explosion—a nice explosion, I admit—but the next day we are always the same, the same pride, the same independence."

Dorch kicked roughly at a mastiff which came too near. The animal yelped, then settled itself on the hearthstones again.

A timid knock sounded from the hospital door. Dorch rose and opened it. Elfreda stood there. "Doctor, a woman needs you."

Dorch grinned satanically. "Why don't you say that several women need me?"

Within a month, Denna Cart left for Texas with Tom and Amy.

In the round room, she kissed Dorch lightly before going outside to the horses. "I'll see you again sometime," she said casually.

"Yes," he said. "When your father makes a cow drive, come along and stay over. You like the rough life."

"What an idea!" she said. "Perhaps I will."

On the next evening Dorch took Elfreda to dinner at the Boggy Depot hotel.

She said, seated beyond a red-and-white-checkered tablecloth, "Are you glad she is gone, Dorch?"

"I don't know," he said frankly. "It could never have lasted. But there is something inside which still hurts. I suppose it will always hurt."

"You have had three women in your life, Dorch. Della Wano, myself, and Denna Cart. Somehow, each of us has failed you. Della, because you made too much of her and lived in her shadow; myself, because I dared not press for what I wanted; and Denna, because she would have taken all that there is of you. You will always be alone."

When they rode back to Round Fort, the lighthorse showing clean and clear in the moonlight, they came to a dark gloom on the trail—the wide shadow of heavy trees.

Here, once before, he had asked to kiss her. Tonight he rode on, saying nothing.

A year later, in the round room one night, Dorch heard a knock at the door. He opened it, expecting to see some late patient from the hills.

Instead, a small cry came from a bundle at his feet.

Another baby.

Not unusual, because some poor Indian or white in the hills and valleys always left a baby at the hospital, or some impoverished parent might bring one up from the Texas Road. Dorch saw the babies safely along; then the nations claimed them.

He bent in the open light and picked up the bundle. He crossed the round room, then kicked the hospital door with the toe of his shoe.

Elfreda appeared.

"Here's another one," Dorch said.

"Goodness," Elfreda said, "people never cease to be people, do they?"

They took the baby into the operating room and placed it on the table, lighting the overhead lamps. Elfreda unbundled the child. It was a black-haired boy, dressed in warm flannel.

"This is odd," Dorch said. "Clear skin, no chafe, no rash. Why would anyone leave a baby this well kept?" He took the pulse, blood pressure, and temperature.

"Where shall I put him?" Elfreda asked, dressing the baby.

Dorch laughed. "In what we call the baby ward."

"He has such black hair," Elfreda said, gathering the bundle in her arms.

Two days later Timothy Baines brought a letter in a blue envelope addressed to Dorch from Boggy Depot:

Dearest Dorch,

I know you have our baby by now, because I with Tom brought him to you. I waited in the trees until I saw you carry him inside. I loved bearing your child, and he will always be mine as well as yours.

The gods have crossed us, Dorch, and we both know that because of our temperaments we could never live together. It is exactly as you said one night. Keep our child, Dorch, and do for him what I could never do.

Whatever I am, I will love you always. I can see our child when he grows up; he will be like you.

Denna

Dorch placed the letter in the secretary and walked down the hospital corridor to look at his son.

Next day he told Elfreda, "This is my son. I am placing him in your charge."

When Denna Cart had first reached the Texas ranch upon her return from England, she found Abel Cart plagued with more troubles than Job. He was white-haired and stooped now.

It had been a dry spring and early summer; he was plagued by the rise of the freebooters.

It had become an almost accepted practice on the arid range that if a rancher found a cow which had famished for lack of water, he could skin it and keep the hide. Things broke about even, since each rancher gained about as many hides as he lost.

But abuse of this practice rose among wandering outlaws, freed Negroes, starving whites, and Mexicans with their two-wheeled carretas. Riding upon a cow too famished to move, a freebooter waited until it fell to its knees or turned on its side to die. This provided quick temptation.

It was only a moment's effort to knife a standing or kneeling animal, skin it for the dollar the hide would bring, take a quarter of meat if wanted, and move on to the next cow. The bolder of the freebooters hid the hides in brush piles, awaiting nightfall to send wagons or carretas for them; at last any cow, famished or not, was killed.

The rope trick developed; the freebooters would stretch one through the brush, then drive the cows into it. The tripped cattle fell; off their horses in an instant, the riders stuck their knives in the point of the backbone and skull, thereby avoiding gunfire which some searcher might detect. Then the unfortunate animals were skinned.

The ranchers formed vigilante committees, but to no avail, and with the breakdown of range law, rustling increased.

So Abel Cart's cowhands rode the mesquite and cactus, ready to use a hangman's noose on an offender as quickly as a pistol. Sometimes on learning of a freebooter camp, Denna rode with her father and his men; this was excitement, flushing outlaws from the brush, until at last the old colonel forced her to remain at the hacienda.

"Too risky," he told her. "They're fighting back now. You could be shot."

By now, Denna knew well of her pregnancy. "Father," she said, "Anthracite, a girl I knew at Lady Burroughs', has moved to Dallas with her husband, Brian Doyle, an attorney. She expects another baby and fears a difficult birth. She wants me with her."

This was true; the two friends had corresponded throughout the years; Anthracite's births had all been difficult; there was no reason to suppose this one would be otherwise.

"Go ahead, child," the colonel said. "I'd as soon you stayed away until the freebooter question is settled. It's too dangerous here."

Anthracite had her baby first; then Denna had hers. She had taken Tom and Amy with her; they lived in servants' quarters behind the Doyle home. Amy kept the baby.

"Brian Doyle," Denna said one night in the living room, "you were a good attorney in the East. Why did you come to Dallas and Texas?"

"It's a land of promise," Brian said, sitting in an easy chair and puffing his pipe. "It has a few rough edges, but they'll rub off."

She told him the story of Dorch McIntyre.

"Obviously," Brian said, "it's a fight among governmental bureaus and agencies, each trying to get ahead of the other in Washington politics. It would be the same at Fort Smith and in the Territory."

"If you had the case, what would you do?"

"Honestly or otherwise?"

"Which would be best?"

Brian grinned. "With what we are dealing with, otherwise. Your man should have maintained that someone else killed the women, that he had remained instead of retreating to serve the

Union—not the Confederacy—by revealing the Confederate plan of battle. Such a yarn would easily hold water, since the Texans were whipped so suddenly and completely. Other Confederates returning to help the wounded could have killed the women. The possibilities of raising doubt are unlimited, especially with a battle."

"But Dorch has already admitted it."

"Coercion because of fear for his hospital." Brian grinned. "But this would be one way through all the corruption."

"Could you go see Dorch?"

"It would be at least a month before I could go," Brian said. "But after the thousand-dollar check you gave me and Anthracite when you were at Lady Burroughs', I'd seek out hell if you asked me."

On the night Denna and Tom rode up the dark trail to Round Fort, Denna with a bundle in her arms, she feared some interruption from the lighthorse.

And one did come—he plunged his horse suddenly from the trees and asked, "Who are you?"

"Captain Panton," Denna said, "don't you remember? Tom and I returned from the *Maizie Trout* with you and stayed at Round Fort for a month."

"Miss Cart! Of course, I remember. Well, make your way up the hill. I have men on the far side I must see."

He noticed the bundle she carried.

Clothes, he thought, or luggage. She hadn't brought as much this time.

As the months passed, hawkish Dr. Dennis repeatedly told Elfreda, "I don't see how Dr. McIntyre operates. He has such large fingers, but even at medical school I never saw a man work with such delicacy. No wonder they love him here. By the way," he said, "would you have dinner with me at Boggy Depot on your next day off?"

Elfreda hesitated. "Yes," she said. It had been months since Dorch had asked her to dinner.

Dr. Dennis liked his work; he also liked Elfreda.

When young Dorch was in the toddling stage, the doctor and Elfreda sat among the old barracks stones on the hill, watching the child play and run about.

"Dorch, I must ask you something."

"Yes?"

"It is evident you will never ask me to marry you."

"I can marry no one."

"I asked because Dr. Dennis wants to marry me. But I don't want to give you up, not if I have even the most remote chance."

"Dennis is a good man. You will deserve every happiness."

"There is one thing more," Elfreda said, watching the black-haired boy toddle on a stick horse among the ruins. "If something should ever happen to you, could Dr. Dennis and I adopt young Dorch? I have reared him for you; he is like a child of my own."

"For my part," Dorch said, "yes."

"I hoped you would agree."

"There is only this—Denna, as his mother, could still claim him. I suppose she could even take Round Fort, because she lived here as what could be called a common-law wife. But since she returned the child to me, I do not know what she would want with him, now or later."

"But you will arrange everything, so it will be legal?"

"Yes, and I will even arrange for your wedding, my dear. Would you and the doctor like two weeks at the Le Flore in Fort Smith, with the compliments of the hospital?"

"That is nice of you, Dorch."

He watched a herd of longhorns with its riders and chuckwagon pass through the valley toward Clear Boggy Creek and looked at his watch. "I must be at the hospital at three. Do you want to go back now?"

"No, I will sit here a little while."

Since Denna had told Brian Doyle of Dorch's case, he had visited Dorch many times; he often practiced at the Fort Smith court and stopped over at Boggy Depot.

One night while they visited in the round room, Dorch said, "I have been told a new rumor about myself."

The lawyer puffed his pipe. "What?"

"That the reason I stayed behind at the Battle of the Mounds was to inform the Union of the Confederate plans and those of future campaigns. I helped the Union cause by betraying the Confederates, but the Creek women did not know this and attacked."

"I can't imagine who would start such a tale," said Brian. His eyes twinkled. "Have you thought how much new sympathy such a rumor could bring you, and make those who damned you first begin to doubt? For all they know, the rumor could be true. Your real friends, of course, would never believe it."

"But its purpose?"

"More element of doubt, which could prevent the matter from ever coming to a head."

Dorch said bitterly, "So now I am a traitor."

"And I your lawyer," Brian said, laughing. Then he sobered. "About the matter of the youngster and Miss Townley. Denna is strong-willed, but I think even now she does not know her full mind about the child. She could be quite unpredictable. Nothing has happened to raise her instinct—a mother's instinct—for her child.

"Now, even though the child is not with her, she still has some memory to cling to, and she is what we will call a common-law mother. With court reversals so common, I think this matter should rest quietly for a few more years. When Miss Townley bears children by Dr. Dennis, the boy's loss—if it should become that—would not be so hard for her to bear. We must be certain Denna knows her own mind. You would want her full consent, and not a court case, for you could not stand the publicity. By the way, I stopped over at Skullyville. The matter of the dead gambler is settled."

"You have been a good friend," Dorch said, "to both me and Denna."

"My only regret," Brian said, rising to leave for his horse, "is that the fates did not arrange for you and Denna to stay together."

2

After Elfreda's baby was delivered, Dr. Dennis stood in the doorway of the hospital room.

Dorch laughed. "Go to the highboy in the round room and take a drink. Take two drinks. I'll stay until the nurses are back."

He closed the door and stepped to the bed.

She smiled up wanly. "Was I awfully bad, Dorch?"

He bent and kissed her forehead. "You were wonderful."

"What is it, Dorch? A boy or a girl?"

"A seven-pound girl," Dorch said.

She tried to smile again. "Then little Dorch will have a playmate." She looked at him fully, her eyes brimming. "Do you think they might marry someday—your Dorch, my daughter?"

Dorch was strangely moved. "That is what we'll count on."

Dr. Dennis came back to the room. "How are you, darling?"

Trying to be gay, she whispered, "I am fine, Doctor."

"Doctor, hell," Dennis said. "I'm your husband!"

Dorch left the room.

At first Timothy was greatly disappointed. Elfreda was his favorite nurse; had the baby been a boy, she had promised to name it for him. Now his hope for a namesake had vanished.

On the third day after the birth, Timothy tapped lightly at Elfreda's window. She opened her eyes and saw his eyebrows raised questioningly. He motioned toward the back of the hospital, then crooked a finger around, meaning could he come to her room.

She smiled and nodded.

When he entered the room, he led little Dorch by the hand. The child carried a package.

Timothy said, "The lad and I rode to Boggy Depot yesterday to get a present—for a girl baby," he added accusingly.

"I couldn't help it, Timothy."

"Sure, I'd not be blaming you," Timothy said. "It's the way of the world. Anyway, my lad wants to give the baby a present. Take it to the bed, Dorch."

The boy, long-legged for his four years, placed the package beside Elfreda. She opened it; she saw two night dresses and a tiny day dress.

"Oh, Dorch, how Lucy will love them!"

"We'd have got shoes too," Timothy said, "but they were all too big."

"This is for you," the boy said to Elfreda. "It was by the horse collars."

"A little box of rouge! Whatever made you think of it?"

"You used to put it on when you saw Daddy coming." Dorch looked about the room. "Where is Lucy?"

"Come to the other side of the bed."

Dorch looked in amazement at the puckered face; he stuck a finger in the baby's mouth. Somehow, the baby managed to grasp the finger; Dorch stood there, holding the chubby fist.

"She's real," he said, grinning.

"Will you look after her, Dorch, the way I have looked after you?"

"It will be my baby girl."

Timothy was terribly tired. "We'd better go now," he told Dorch.

Yes, Timothy was terribly tired. Tired of living alone.

Every man ought to have a woman. It got very lonely without one. He ought to have a woman, if only to help place something like that puckered little baby beside a woman like Elfreda.

He went into the round room and sat. The doctor dozed on his cot.

Out of a clear sky came a vision of the little prostitute he had met walking up the cobblestones at Fort Smith, the one with the red feather in her hat, the one who as a child had made up a song

143

on an old foot-pedal organ, "When Bullfrogs Sing Beside the Sparkling Spavinaw."

What was the other song? Oh, yes, the other was "When April Rains Fall in Autumn."

But it was neither the red feather nor the songs she had composed which made Timothy think of her.

She was one of the few women who had looked into his eyes first, without looking at his hump.

A man going through life like a damned camel, with a hump riding his back. He had always felt guilty for not trying to find a piano for the girl. If he ever saw the red feather again, he would.

"Oh, well," Timothy said aloud, "I've been pretty lucky after all."

"Lucky about what?" the doctor asked, yawning and rising.

"Why?" said Timothy. "I've been thinking that when life is over, you might find you've known some good people after all. Some you wish you could meet again in the next world."

"There'd be a lot of them," the doctor said.

Sardis Rippy and his marshal had returned to Boggy Depot after a prolonged stay in Fort Smith.

"Oh," said Dorch when Timothy told him, "it's just the beginning of another harassment."

But the incident did plunge him into one of his moods. He was banging at the piano that night when three Chickasaws from the adjoining valley rode to Round Fort. They were poor, but hard workers; they seated themselves uncomfortably on the large sofa and made their statement.

They wanted to build a school on the hill; there was a one-room cabin in the valley which was used, but other children had to travel great distances from other places to reach it. The Chickasaws could get money from the nation to help build a new school, provided the location was suitable to all, and they did the work themselves.

A school, Dorch thought. He had seen Choctaw and Chickasaw children riding three or four on a horse or mule through northers and blizzards to reach the cabin, or had seen some frozen and lonely child, blue-faced with cold in cutting winds, trudging some snowy hill or valley, two or three textbooks held beneath his ice-coated jacket.

He thought of young Dorch and Lucy, inseparable, except when the boy rode to his school in Boggy Depot, how young he had been when he started; he, too, had ridden in snow and ice. But Dorch would graduate this spring, and Lucy would begin next autumn.

A building at Round Fort would give Lucy a place to attend classes without the long ride to the Boggy Depot school when Dorch graduated. "Where would you want the building?" he asked the Chickasaws.

The mastiffs sat at the Indians' feet, sniffing the unaccustomed leggings.

"We must have your permission first, but anywhere on the hill, so all the children could reach it easier."

"Look," said Dorch, "why couldn't it be built inside the old soldiers' barracks? The walls would break the cold winds, and the stone floor is still solid. We'd need only to build up walls and add a roof. There would be good play places on the stone, good in any weather. In fact, our work is half-done. We could have at least three rooms and a hall."

So here he was off again on an errand of mercy, if it could be called that. But on sleepless nights, while he pitched and tossed in his cot, other words came back, Elfreda's words: "You have had three women in your life, Dorch. Della Wano, myself, and Denna Cart. Somehow, each of us has failed you. Della, because you made too much of her and lived in her shadow; myself, because I dared not press for what I wanted; and Denna, because she would have taken all that there is of you. You will always be alone."

And he would rise, put on a worn robe, and walk the hospital corridor.

The two trainees he had sent to New Orleans had long since returned; they were poised and confident and had relieved Elfreda of much of the administrative duties. But for himself, the hospital meant too much to Elfreda to leave its management entirely in the hands of others.

Tonight, after the Chickasaws left, he met Elfreda in the corridor.

He was strangely proud that the Chickasaws had come to him about their school; he told Elfreda what had happened. "Someday it could amount to something," he said. "It's taken a long time to build up the hospital."

"I don't see how you've done it, Doctor."

"Good friends, faithful nurses and trainees. You have four children now."

"Yes."

"I begin to wonder about Dorch and Lucy. They are inseparable."

Elfreda laughed. "Do you know, she still keeps the baby clothes he bought her?"

"Do you think they are together too much?"

"It seems to be a healthy relationship. He has taught her to ride. They even ride at night, many times. They are safe with the lighthorse about."

"Where do they ride?"

"You would be surprised. In the trail-driving season, they ride to the camps of the drovers in the valley."

"I'll talk with Dorch. They shouldn't do that. It could be risky."

"No, Dorch," she said, forgetting her hospital manner. "You would be surprised how many Texas drovers know them. They eat at the chuckwagons, and can tell every brand between here and the Pecos."

"Why has Dorch never told me this?"

"He said you always had too much to do, but as long as I knew, it would be all right. The coosies always have a special meal when they ride down, and the children take them things they can't get on the trail—fruit, tomatoes, and canned goods."

"I still must talk with Dorch. You don't worry about Lucy's being with him so much?"

"Not a bit." Her eyes misted. "I love him as I love my own sons."

The doctor went back to his own room but he was tired. Tired ever since he had started his hospital, tired of a past that would never leave, tired of Creek talk, of marshals and Department of Interior men, of the courtroom at Fort Smith, where he had been called again with Brian Doyle.

Names in his mind—Della, Elfreda, Denna. Not one had ever left him.

On his cot he tossed again as usual; then he slept.

Next day the doctor talked with young Dorch in the round room.

For the first time he seemed to see how lean and tall his son had grown. Fourteen now, and Lucy ten.

"Why do you go to the valley so much with Lucy?"
"Why, we like it there." The dark boy stood before the table in a pair of heavy boots, a sombrero in his hand.
"Why do you like it?"
"I just do, and Lucy does."
"What do you intend to do in life? What do you intend to make of yourself?"
"Be a cowhand, or maybe have a ranch of my own."
"And not be a doctor?"
"I wouldn't like that. I want a ranch."
Dorch felt a pang of regret. It was more than a pang; it clamped his heart as if a vise squeezed it. "You don't want to be a doctor?"
"I'm not made for it. I want the outside."
"This year you graduate at Boggy or at the new school here; then you could go to the academy."
"I don't know yet."
"Why?"
"I want to learn cowhand business. I'd better start young."
Start young!
Dorch remembered a faraway day on a creek, when he had dissected a turtle. His father had wanted him to become a trader but had helped him become a doctor. He could do no less for his own son.
"Have you talked this over with anyone?"
"With Elfreda—I mean Nurse Dennis—like I always do."
"What did she say?"
"That I'll have to strike out for myself someday."
"Do you have a place in mind where you would want to go?"
"There's good grazing in the Chickasaw country, but some of these cowhands say Wild Horse Prairie down in the Choctaw Nation is good."
"Yes," said the doctor, "I know Wild Horse. You'd be near Doaksville and Tom Adkins, too."
"The cowhands say get a place with good water. I guess water would decide what I did."
"I tell you what," Dorch said. He stood up, moved to the piano, and struck a few chords. "We'll have a new doctor on the staff next week, and that should help Dr. Dennis. You and I will ride to Wild Horse Prairie and lease or buy a ranch. How does that suit you?"
"I wasn't asking for that, Daddy."

"I know you weren't. But you can start now and know what you're building for."

"Gee," the boy said, overcome and turning his face away. "I never thought it would be like this. I thought you'd be mad because I didn't want to become a doctor."

Dorch reached and placed a heavy hand on his son's shoulder. "Mad? No, son, not a bit. I'm glad you know what you want."

"Could I ask one thing?"

"Of course."

"Lucy and I have always been like brother and sister, but I know someday we'll get married. From watching those cows go through the valley, we have always thought of having a ranch ever since she learned to talk. Could she go with us?"

"You'll have to ask her mother," Dorch said.

When his son left the round room, Dorch thought of a new world which had been born beneath his very eyes, one he had hardly seen or known.

The trip to Wild Horse Prairie was a wild and wonderful thing to Lucy and young Dorch. Brown-eyed and brown-haired Lucy wore fringed doeskins, and he woolen trousers and chaps and a new sombrero. Timothy had stayed behind to work on the new school.

Whenever they came upon a herd of longhorns which headed northward to strike the Texas Road, it was young Dorch who always swung his horse to move back to the head of the plodding and dusty line to join the point riders.

There he talked trails and cows and water.

Once the doctor had followed him back to listen to a conversation.

"Traveling?" the tan, long-jointed point rider said. "Got any makings?"

"Makings? Sure," said the boy. From his jacket pocket he pulled out a Bull Durham bag and papers. "I've a few more," he said, reaching into another pocket. "Pass 'em back to the swings and the drags."

"Thanks," the point rider said.

"What's your handle?" the boy asked.

"Jack Leavitt. And yours?"

The happy boy grinned. "Dorch McIntyre. But don't get me mixed up with the sawbones there. He's Dr. Dorch."

At this the doctor chuckled. His son did know how to get along with cowhands; the time he and Lucy had spent in the valley had not been wasted.

"Everything going okeh?" the boy asked. He used the old Choctaw word.

"Well," said Leavitt, shoving his hat back, "we got chased across ten counties by a tornado, had two stampedes, lost our makings and one man in a flash flood on the Red, but you might say it's been tolerably quiet. We've still got a few hurt boys, and Lame Duck's in the wagon."

"When do you throw off? Maybe my dad can fix the boys up."

"We'll stop at the next creek for water, and I'm tempted to stay close for the night."

The doctor looked back down the line of longhorns; it lumbered along like a long snake as it wound its way through dips and over higher ground. The doctor knew his son did not smoke; he began to appreciate his forethought. This was made more evident a moment later.

The boy asked Leavitt, "Got any drags you want left?"

"Ten or fifteen calves we'll have to kill when we stop. They can't keep up."

"A buck a throw," the boy said.

"Sold," Leavitt said. "When we stop, pick 'em out."

"Mind if we bed down tonight?"

"Company's welcome," the point rider said, exhaling again, then turning to motion to a swing rider. He tossed the extra sacks of Bull to the ground.

Clockwork, the doctor thought, clockwork. Gazing behind, he saw the swing rider reach to the ground and come up with a tobacco bag. The swing rider signed back to the other swings and the drags. The doctor knew that in turn they also would reach for the grass. Things like this had gone on in his own valley under his very eyes, and he had known nothing of it.

Young Dorch said, "Reckon I'll cut through the herd and give the other boys some Bull."

Jack Leavitt looked worried. "Maybe you'd better not. I don't want this herd headed. Cutting through this line of longhorns, you might upset them."

The boy laughed. "An old cowhand like me? Take a look—I've been practiced with."

He dropped farther behind the point rider; halfway back toward the swing rider, he turned his horse again and rode slowly beside the strung-out herd. Then he edged his horse close to a longhorn and cut easily behind it.

Now he was among the dust of the herd itself, moving forward with the cows, only slightly faster, cutting behind one cow and then another, never breaking the line, but always pressing forward and to the opposite side.

"How in hell did he learn that?" Leavitt asked the doctor.

"I don't know, but he would have made a damned good doctor."

Lucy, who had come forward and rode beside the doctor, said, "It's the way cowhands showed us down in the valley when we used to ride herd and camp out with them."

Leavitt said, "If he had made the wrong move, these longhorns would be in Kansas by now. And the way this outfit is wrecked, I don't want to get there that quick. But the boy is a natural cowhand."

Dorch was on the far side of the herd now, moving up to the opposite point rider. He passed out the tobacco sacks.

"I didn't hear your name," Lucy said to Leavitt, her brown hair blowing, "but my friend and I are going to buy a ranch. Maybe you could be foreman."

"Leavitt's the handle," the point rider said, laughing and choking on his cigarette. "If you furnish the makings, I might do anything."

It was a good night, the fire and chuckwagon some distance from the creek, cowhands moving out under the stars for their two-hour watch on the bedded herd, the singing sounds and lullabies, the Big Dipper high, the North Star blinking in a film of gauze, and the old coffee bucket plunged into again and again. And yarns at the fire plausible and implausible enough to keep the boy and Lucy dreaming for a lifetime.

"Do you like this?" he asked Lucy.

"It's like I've been here all my life," the girl said.

At the fire, the doctor fixed up a few mesquite cuts, a ringworm case, two broken fingers, Lame Duck's fractured leg, and one ingrown toenail. The coosie hung a lighted lantern from the propped-up wagon tongue to guide the night riders in from the herd.

"Do you want this for a ranch?" the boy whispered to Lucy.

She nodded.

"Then we'll tell mama when we get home."

The doctor had formed his opinion of Jack Leavitt around the fire that night. Next morning he asked, "What would you think of cow business for my son?"

"He's a natural cowhand, and he understands animals. But times are changing, or they will change more within a few years. When the future comes, he'll never see much more of what he saw here last night. The old ways won't get the job done. The open range will be gone, there will be selective breeding for a better meat animal, and the trail towns will die. He'll ship direct to the big markets, and he'll have to know them."

"You don't sound cheerful."

"No, I feel exactly the opposite. A boy in your son's place could be ready for the change; he should study breeding and marketing and management, and when the change comes, he'll be two jumps ahead of the pack. The day of the old longhorn is about over. The kid has a great future if he tackles it right."

When the longhorns tailed out for the Texas Road, the doctor told Leavitt, "If you'd be interested in bossing a ranch here, see me at Round Fort when you come back."

Leavitt nodded.

The three prospectors left and rode deeper into Wild Horse Prairie, with twenty-two calves and as many she cows. "Hell," Leavitt had said to the doctor, "keep the she stuff. It will even it up for your work on the boys last night."

By nightfall, after moving the herd all day at an amble, they came to miles and miles of prairie, broken only by a few groves of low trees valuable for shade in the hot summers. A low ridge ran across the northern extremity of the prairie, something to break the winter northers. Beneath it lay a single swell; from its crest the view of the distance was wide and long and endless. A leaping freshwater stream from the blue mountains beyond the ridge promised indefinite water.

"How do you like this spot for a ranch house?" the doctor asked Dorch.

"It looks good. Unless we find something better, this is what we want."

They made night camp near a clump of persimmon trees beneath the swell. They sat on the ground, cooking their supper. Lucy, a blue apron tied over her doeskins, burnt her biscuits; the doctor ate them and laughed. In this brief absence from the hospital, the days of youth returned.

"I'm sorry about the biscuits," Lucy said, her eyes full of tears.

The doctor patted her shoulder. "There's nothing as good as burned biscuits and a strip of bacon with the ashes of the fire on it."

Youth and promise. Two glowing faces beside a fire, riding their big adventure, into what? A boy of fourteen and a girl of ten.

Lucy brought him a cup of coffee. "I hope it's better than my biscuits," she said, her hair a wreck in the wind.

Young Dorch and Lucy would not consider letting the doctor ride night herd; they decided instead five hours for the boy, then three for Lucy. The doctor slept fitfully; he was awake when Dorch came in to wake Lucy. As soon as Lucy left for the herd, the boy was asleep.

But the Territory was still a land of outlawry, from the Cherokee country in the far north, the Creek country and the Belle Starr hangout at Younger's Bend on the Canadian. Other gangs from the grog shops across in Arkansas infested the Chickasaw and Choctaw lands.

After Lucy left, the doctor took his rifle, wrapped a blanket about his shoulders, and walked to the persimmon grove. He sat among the thin trees, hearing Lucy sing some soft lullaby as she made her rounds of the herd.

The doctor could see the shadow of the moving horse, but the sounds of Lucy's singing grew fainter and fainter. He threw the blanket from his shoulders, took the rifle, and walked cautiously forward.

Lucy was riding around the herd, her head on her chest, sound asleep. As good a way to sleep as any, the doctor thought. Maybe the horse knew its business and made its rounds as usual, regardless of its rider.

The doctor walked back to the grove and sat again with his rifle.

Lucy woke with the sun, the longhorn shes and calves rising from the bedding ground. In the red sunrise she saw the doctor walking toward her, a blanket over his shoulders, the rifle in hand.

"Thought I'd try to get a deer for breakfast," he called, "but perhaps we scared them off."

"I feel like I've been riding all night," Lucy said.

"What you need is a good breakfast. Let's go wake Dorch."

After they ate, they rode out and admired the scrawny herd. "It's a good start, isn't it?" Dorch asked.

"A good start," the doctor said. "But what will you do with them? We can't drive the calves home."

The boy's face fell. "I hadn't thought of that. But I sure hate to go back to Round Fort and leave these cows behind."

"We'll want to look for other locations, in case this one is leased. We might find someone to keep the herd; anyway, I don't think it will wander today—the grass and water are too good."

They did find someone to keep the stock—an old gray-haired Chickasaw and his shrunken wife. The Indian wore an open shirt and a loincloth; his bare legs were as thin as broomsticks. He and his wife had lost their two sons in the war and lived in a one-room log cabin several miles down the ridge.

"I am too old to ride to look after cows," the old man said, standing beside his wife at an ash hopper while she prepared to make hominy, "but I can look after the calves like my father used to in Mississippi. He would build a calf pen, then let the cows wander. But they always came back in the evening to let the young suckle. Then next morning he would drive the cows out of the pen. I can do this for a few months, until the calves are too large. But you must build the pen."

"Good," said the doctor. "Within a few months we should have cowhands here."

Two Choctaws with sharp axes lived over the ridge; the doctor hired them to split rails, but it took three days to finish the pen. It was a heavy stake-and-rider fence with a smaller pen at the gate. An old she could be guided to the poled gate, the bars closed, then admitted from the smaller pen into the larger. Coming out was similar; the poles of the small pen were slid, the cow admitted, and her calf pulled back into the larger pen. Then the cow was driven through the outer gate.

The Chickasaw's wife had complained of stomach pains; the doctor had examined her and given her a supply of pills. He had learned from the Indian that the prairie land was not leased; on the day they left he said, "Within two months, have someone write me a letter to Round Fort and say how your wife is. I have a man, Jack Leavitt, who may come here. Anyway, I'll see that you get more medicine for your wife."

When the doctor saw Elfreda after his return from Wild Horse Prairie, he said, "I've got two cowhands fixed up, provided they don't want to turn sheepherders within a week."

"It's wonderful. I've never seen such happy children." She eyed him closely. "You look years younger."

"I feel better."

"You've had too much on your mind, and now I must tell you something else. While you were gone, there was a visit from the Department of Interior man and his marshal."

"Did you let them in?"

"Yes. This time they had a warrant. They went to every patient's room, then to the operating room. Both Dr. Dennis and Dr. Warwick were out on calls; this time the men were orderly, and as long as they did no harm, I thought it best to leave them alone."

"You did right, but there's got to be an end to it."

"In some way they had learned of Willie Turtle, the crazy old Indian whose leg you amputated before you went to Fort Smith for the piano. He likes to be under the influence of morphine, and when I refused it, he became angry. He told Sardis Rippy we sold it to rich Indians."

"I imagine Sardis Rippy trapped the old man with leading questions. I understand Rippy rides from cabin to cabin in the hills, gathering what he hopes will be evidence. Well, in Willie Turtle's case, you gave the last injection I prescribed; then the others were placebo. Both of us are safe there. What did Dr. Dennis say about the visit?"

"I never saw a man so angry. He rode to Boggy Depot and found Rippy and the marshal at the hotel. He called the search a raid and said that such a thing without proper supervision and preparation could endanger the lives and health of patients."

"Your husband has character."

She smiled slightly. "Yes, I think he does."

"He knows of the last injection to Willie Turtle?"

"Yes."

"Good. And tell him of the placebo solutions."

She nodded. "Dorch, since you have been to Wild Horse Prairie, I feel strangely at peace. Boys, if they have what they want, can always look after themselves. And Dorch will look after Lucy."

"You seem quite certain they will marry."

"Like Tiger Panton, I have the gift of prophecy."

Within two months Jack Leavitt, the rangy trail boss Dorch had met on Wild Horse Prairie, stopped at Round Fort. Dorch had been called from the hospital by Timothy; he found Leavitt seated casually in one of the big chairs before the empty fireplace.

Leavitt stood up when Dorch entered the room, extending his hand. "My boots are clean, doctor, so I took the liberty of sitting."

"Damn your boots," Dorch said. "Here," he added, taking the box of panatelas from the piano, "have one."

"Thanks, no. This time I've got the makings."

"A drink?"

"Not in daytime or on the job."

"Then sit down."

Instead, Leavitt moved to the piano. "You've got a real one here," he said, standing before the ivory keyboard. Timothy sat down.

"All the way from Cincinnati," Dorch said, lighting a panatela. "But that was a long time ago."

Leavitt laughed. "When I was a kid, my mama always wanted me to play the piano. She came with my dad from Tennessee— it was a little more cultured than Texas in those days. Anyway, we had this old organ they brought, and she'd stand over me day and night and make me play it. She thought I'd be a great musician."

Leavitt sat at the bench and began to finger the keys, his hands stiff and awkward. "Hell," he said. "I don't remember anything." Then he struck a few clear chords. "Yes, I do," he said. "I was thinking about this tune on the way back. I always think about it on the way back."

He began to play, this time surely, a folksy, gay little tune. It was simple, but with an appeal that startled Dorch.

"What is the name of that?" he asked, lowering the panatela.

"'When Bullfrogs Sing Beside the Sparkling Spavinaw.' I've always been a loner and like to come back on the trails by myself. One time I ran into a rainy season up in the Cherokee country. The creeks were booming, and I asked some white folks who had leased the land if I could stay at their cabin. They were poor as church mice, but when I stepped inside, there was this little girl pumping and playing an organ, just as I used to do.

"She made up her own tunes, and I was shut up there for four days. The child would get so tired of staying inside with the rain pouring down that she'd pretend to dress up fancy and walk around the room like going someplace. She always wore something with a little bit of red on it. The name of this tune she wrote," Leavitt repeated, following the exaggerated complicity of cowhand talk, and beginning the tune all over again, "is 'When Bullfrogs Sing Beside the Sparkling Spavinaw.'"

Timothy sat mutely.

Always wore a little bit of red. He could see the hat with the red feather bobbing toward him up the cobblestones.

"Play that again," Timothy said when Leavitt finished.

"Yes," Dorch said. "Play it. I want to learn it."

"Agreed," Leavitt said, "but I don't want to monopolize the conversation."

Dorch sat beside him at the piano bench.

Leavitt slid over. "No, you're too high there. It's a C you want. After that, give it a do-re-me sound."

At last Dorch rose, having mastered the little tune. "Now let's talk about Wild Horse Prairie."

He told Leavitt, who rolled and continued to smoke and roll his makings, "The kids will marry someday, even though now they don't know what marriage is. When they do marry, I want a good ranch set up for them."

"Sure," said Leavitt, his eyes squinting through the smoke.

"I'd like for you to go down to Wild Horse as foreman. You've got twenty-two shes and twenty-two calves in a calf pen to start with."

Leavitt grinned.

"The calves are being looked after by an old Chickasaw couple, and they'll show you the land I've leased. Build yourself a house or cabin, get a few good hands, and start buying cows, good stuff, a grade or so above the average. Enlarge your house or bunkhouse as you need to. Make your drafts on the Doaksville store or here at Boggy."

"A tolerable proposition," said Leavitt.

"The kids will take summer vacation there. I want you to watch them and teach them. If it's a deal, name your own salary."

Leavitt rose from his chair. "It's a deal. We'll thresh the salary out later. Right now, I'm more interested in the deal."

"The old Chickasaw woman is sick," Dorch said. "I've had a letter from a Quaker preacher in the hills, so I'll send her some medicine by you."

Leavitt nodded. "Could I see my new boss? The boys really appreciated those makings after the rampaging Red."

"Yes," Dorch said. "He's in class in the new school at the soldiers' barracks. But don't tell him yet what we've agreed on, or he wouldn't look at his books for a month. Neither would Lucy."

"A nice pair," said Leavitt. "Well, if you'll get the medicine, I'll be vamoosing."

"Can you use a thermometer?"

Leavitt nodded.

"If the old woman's temperature gets above a hundred, send a rider to me. Let's go up and see the kids."

When Dorch and Leavitt left for the school, Timothy continued to sit before the fireplace.

So that was how it had started!

Wide, innocent eyes in an isolated cabin, and an old organ.

A girl walking about beneath a rainy roof, a bit of red in her dress.

Once more he saw the hat and the red feather bobbing up the cobblestones.

" 'The Sparkling Spavinaw.' If you can find a piano, I'll play it for you."

She had talked with him, a slight thing, looking straight into his eyes and not at his hump. If I'm ever at Fort Smith again, Timothy thought, I'll look her up.

He rose and walked about the round room. What a fool I was, he thought, what a fool I was!

At the beginning of summer, Jack Leavitt and two of his cowhands rode into Round Fort. He had left a wagon and driver at the store in Boggy to pick up supplies.

Young Dorch and Lucy were ready, their four pack horses laden for the summer. Leavitt had built a bunkhouse for his cowhands and a two-room cabin for himself; he and the boy would bunk in one room, Lucy in the other.

When the horses disappeared under the creek trees, Elfreda said, "We've done all we can do, Doctor."

"Yes. I hope it works."

"Dorch wanted me to tell you that he has decided to go to the academy and take the courses you wanted him to."

"Why didn't he tell me?"

157

"He worships you for all you have done for him. He is very manly, but still only a boy. I think he feared he would break down had he told you what he thought."

"Two new lives," Dorch said. "Two new lives from two old ones."

3

With the future of his son assured, and with two new doctors to assist Dr. Dennis at the hospital, Dorch began more and more to ride the outlying districts of the Chickasaw land with Timothy, going to the cabins on the upper Clear Boggy and Muddy Boggy and Blue River, and even to the fertile valley of the Washita and to Tishomingo.

He rode between endless, low parallel upthrusts of limestone, some barely a few feet above the earth, the deep grasses between them brushing his horse's belly.

He rode without weapons, as if inviting disaster. The silver spurs showed from his heels, and the black bag from the pommel. A pack horse carried blankets, bandages, and medicines.

Often he would find impoverished bands of Seminoles never recovered from the war; he would stay with them for weeks, tending their sick and dying.

Or he would ride into far Choctaw lands among the Kiamichis, or the Jack Fork range, or even northward almost to the Sans Bois Mountains.

Then after weeks on barely passable trails, finding isolated people where no people should live except by tradition and love of freedom, he would return worn and tired to the hospital and resume his place in the routine of doctors. Another thing he did, too. Each year after the return of the first two trainees from New Orleans he had sent others there, those chosen after consultation with the doctors and nurses. Now he sent nurses for specialized training to Eastern schools.

There would be room for all of them in the far and sordid places he had visited, where husbands struggled at being midwives, and disease swept among the young, who were without vaccination.

One morning after breakfast he walked to the top of the hill.

He thought of the changes which had come with the years, the railroads which had pushed southward, but bypassing Boggy Depot to the east, the new bridges over Red River, and how his hospital could rank with the best anywhere.

But he felt old, very old, although he was not old.

Only the past and a name bore down upon him.

His hospital—a complete record on each patient he had ever admitted. He had been strict with his records; each new patient had always been asked, "Is there any epidemic or disease in your valley? Smallpox, scarlet fever, roseola?"

If the answer had been yes, he had gone himself or sent one of his doctors into the region, stopping an epidemic before it started.

But he was tired already today.

He walked toward the old barracks to indulge the only luxury he had ever allowed himself.

A lily pond, with a solitary high-podded cattail rising in its center.

A rectangular cool lily pond cut in the stone flooring behind the school building and the barracks walls. He had thought much lately of the New Orleans days, and of Timothy. Timothy, too, was becoming gray.

He reached the hilltop where his father's body lay and climbed the remaining stone walls of the barracks. Here he sat and looked down on yellow and pink and white tall-stemmed lilies, a panatela in his teeth.

In this lost spot it was almost like sitting on the old balcony at the apartment in New Orleans, even then with a fragrant panatela, gazing into a courtyard filled with lilies. While he sat on the barracks walls, he could almost hear the shouts and cries of laughing children in the old courtyard, as sometimes he heard the laughing Indian children here.

Today as he sat in this seclusion, he thought, what else is left? There was a hospital on the hill, and a school, a school and hospital where once soldiers had marched and trained for murder. If he were gone, others could carry on as well as he.

He thought continuously of the past, of Della, and Elfreda, and Denna.

What had it all come to?

There was no longer reason for life. He had done all he could do for others. If he were gone, there would still be teachers in the school, nurses and doctors in the hospital.

Names, words, and faces.

A turtle's head beside a creek, the hunchbacked cadaver of a Negro girl, the founding of the hospital, Denna's face in their only happy hour.

While the railroad engines whistled north and south, almost on the old Texas Road, he thought more and more about the Creeks and Della Wano.

Could he expiate his sin?

A gust swept over the wall, and the lilies trembled. The balcony of the attic apartment had been high, so high.

There were other winds, too—political winds among the Creeks. They had a new council now, and while it had been chosen on grounds other than the Della Wano matter, it did consist of a majority of those who had urged vengeance. Over the years he had taken the Creek newspapers; he had followed each political event closely.

He would not yet admit to himself what he had decided.

He walked slowly back down the hill.

As he passed through the hospital corridor, Elfreda in her white cap said, "Doctor, you look worried."

"Just a problem," he said, looking at her wide-apart eyes and sensitive nose. "I always have problems."

He walked on. The years—how they pressed even here in the corridor.

In the round room he wanted something light to play, not his usual thunder; he fingered the 'Sparkling Spavinaw.'

"Would you play that again, sir,?" Timothy asked, rising from dusting the shelves of medical books.

"Gladly," said Dorch.

Why did the piece haunt him so? Something that closed about his heart and brought peace.

Even as he played, Dorch came to decision. He stood up, saying to Timothy, "The lad and Lucy may be getting homesick. Why don't you ride down to Wild Horse Prairie and stay for a week?"

The little hunchback grinned. "It would be a pleasure, sir."

Next morning Dorch dressed in his best black suit. He put on his silver spurs, but left the revolver given him by the Choctaw nation in the secretary. He had his packed and saddled horse brought to the front door, then opened the door to the hospital; he motioned Elfreda to come in.

"I am going on a little journey," he said. "As usual, Dr. Dennis will be in charge of the hospital."

"Dorch, you look at me so strangely."

He put his hand on her shoulder, then kissed her lips tenderly.

"Good-bye, my dearest."

He left Boggy Depot on the black horse without seeing Boyce Townley at the store, or the principal chief, Albert McIntosh. He rode up the old Texas Road, when he could have taken the railroad or stage.

It was almost the first flush of autumn, although days as hot as summer would still come. Along the roadside the leaves already changed color.

At night he camped leisurely, enjoying the flickering campfires, thinking of the Texas Road and Boggy Depot. With the old town not on the railroad, soon it would begin to pass away, and later with progress the road itself would be gone. Brush and trees would grow back, hiding its path forever.

He reached North Fork Town on the fifth night, as he had planned. He rode past the council house and other places he remembered. A few lighted lanterns hung along the walks; he avoided them and rode to the livery stable.

He could see chinks of yellow light through the cracks of the weatherbeaten office.

"Haloa!" he called, stopping the horse.

A stooped old man opened the door and came outside; he stood framed in a slanting rectangle of light, white-haired. Dorch was conscious of the pungent odor of the livery barn.

"Speak, Tom Mikish," he called.

The old man blinked, still not seeing the black horse in the shadows. He reached for his pistol, gazing into the darkness.

When Dorch was certain the shack was empty, he rode into the light. "Dorch McIntyre, Tom."

Tom Mikish had once kept a livery barn at Boggy Depot; at sight of Dorch, he seemed to shudder. "Dr. Dorch, out of town with you! Go now, before you are seen."

Dorch climbed down from the horse. He handed Tom Mikish

several gold pieces. "This should look after my horse until I settle some business. Who is in charge at the jail tonight?"

"The lighthorse are out spilling liquor. The jail is empty; only Captain Duane Vann is there."

"I know Vann."

"If you are caught, you will be killed."

"No, I will be executed. I will walk a little, then surrender to Captain Vann for the murder of Della Wano."

Dorch walked slowly about the old town, avoiding the lanterns which hung from the remaining storefronts. The affluence of North Fork Town had vanished with the decline of commerce from the California Trail and the Texas Road. The council house and the dance hall still stood, but the confectioner's shop near the corner was gone. Small store buildings were closed or dilapidated.

Dorch left the council building and walked toward the old soldiers' cemetery. At last he stood before the tombstones, tilted more than ever now. He looked about, as if expecting to see a girl in a beautiful gown come toward him, her hand extended.

"Della, I have come back," he said.

He turned and walked toward the jail.

As he approached the small stone building, he saw Captain Duane Vann standing beneath the overhead lantern of the doorway. He wore a broad sombrero and a red jacket.

When Dorch was close, Vann motioned him aside and into the shadows. The two men stood, studying each other curiously. "Doctor, you are a fool to come to North Fork Town. Tom Mikish was here. I repeat what he told you—get out of town."

On the occasions when Dorch and Duane Vann had met at the inquiries in Fort Smith, their relationship had been pleasant; here, in the Creek stronghold, there was no apparent change.

"I am sorry, Captain. But I am here for a purpose."

"You know of the political campaign?"

"That is why I came. As they say in Fort Smith, a short shrift and a long rope."

"I know how too many Creeks feel," Vann said. "The last election was not based on the Wano matter, but on other things. By a coincidence, most of the elected council do have strong feelings against you, but they do not represent Creek thought. I will not admit you to the jail."

163

"If I emptied a pistol into the air, you would have to."

"Doctor, I was a Unionist in the war. I may have killed Confederate women—I don't know. In the Territory, many of us are still divided, in spite of our struggles to forget. I can blame you no more for your act than I could blame myself."

"Shall we go inside?" said Dorch.

"There was an old drunk in jail yesterday," Vann said. "His eyes hurt, so we hung blankets about his cell to keep out the light. You may go there, Doctor, and if you want out later, beat on the bars. Tomorrow morning, when my lighthorse come in, it will be too late."

In the cell, Dorch sat on the cot, Vann opposite him on a three-legged stool. Dorch gave Vann a panatela.

Dorch spoke monotonously, his head bowed in his hands. "You say you may have done the same thing I did. But do you know you did? Did you see a woman die before your eyes, a woman you might have loved? I was put here and trained to save life, not to take it. That is what has borne on me for so many years. I can no longer face it. When I was younger I fought it; but now I am tired and wish it over. Continue to be my friend when you leave, Captain, and take these blankets from the cell."

"Your pistol then, Doctor."

"I have no pistol."

"You still may leave if you wish."

"No," Dorch said. "I will stay."

Denna Cart had sold her ranch in Texas.

Her ranch because old Abel Cart, who had helped string up many men in his Texas days, had been caught by an outlaw band and was himself strung up.

Denna had moved to Dallas to live with the Doyles. Tom and Amy had long since died.

"Darling," said Anthracite, hugging her, "how many years has it been?" She appeared more fragile than ever in the large puffed sleeves she wore. She looked at Denna's still Junoesque figure. "You are as beautiful as ever, or at Lady Burroughs'."

At dinner that evening, Anthracite said, "What will you do now, darling? A trip abroad, perhaps? To the Lake District?"

"After all my years spent among freebooters, the Lakes would be rather tame. I don't know what I want." Denna said, an evasiveness in her eyes.

Brian said bluntly, "As an old friend and one indebted to you for many years, I think you are miserable and alone. With all your early promise and abilities, you have never tried to make anything of yourself, and you have never been useful to others. You have become an emptiness behind the glittering shell of Denna Cart."

"You cut nicely, don't you?" said Denna.

"I am worried for you. You are a strong woman, but someday your strength can break. That is when I shall fear for you."

Denna said harshly, "Yes, sometimes I, too, am afraid."

"Brian," Anthracite said softly, "enough, now, or I'll make you eat with the children."

Brian grinned. "Not with that crew."

A week later Anthracite handed Denna a letter. It was from Timothy Baines. Denna opened and read it.

She turned suddenly, agony in her face. "Dorch is to be executed in the Creek nation for the murder of Della Wano. I must go there."

The trial, or the events of the sentencing of Dorch McIntyre, had been extremely decorous. The council had not been elected on the basis of the Della Wano matter; this, then, was something which had been pressed upon it by the sudden appearance of the defendant himself.

The trial would be held at North Fork Town, and not in the stone council house at the capital in Okmulgee. Yet this fact did not prevent others who had been implicated in the old Fort Smith hearings from presenting themselves before the council to express their own opinions; among these were the silver-haired orator Tyson Pennypacker, sent from Washington, who happened to have been in Fort Smith when the news broke, and Sardis Rippy and his marshal from Boggy Depot.

The hearing was held in the old thatched council house. The council itself was composed of extremely serious men who sat at an extremely large table, each showing more or less white blood; they wore the best suits of the period, mustaches or sideburns, and had been educated in mission or white schools; several were experts on tribal and American law.

Dorch sat in a heavy chair a short distance from the table, surrounded by Captain Duane Vann and a dozen Creek lighthorse.

After several preliminary matters were discussed, the council turned to the case of the Creek nation against Dorch McIntyre. Immediately, Tyson Pennypacker was on his feet, bowing and moving forward. Here was his opportunity, too long delayed.

The council chief struck his gavel on the table.

"You, sir, will return to your place. Yet I am glad we have been interrupted, for it introduces a point the council should discuss."

From the discussion emerged the fact that the defendant had presented himself to the council as guilty, and of his own volition, having come to North Fork Town for that purpose. There would be no need for a trial in the usual sense of the word. The council would question the prisoner, since the matter now was between it and the prisoner alone. Upon the prisoner's answers would depend the council's decision. Furthermore, there would be no interference, questioning, or oratory from outsiders. The lighthorse were instructed to remove any such person from the crowded council house.

The proceedings began, the doctor standing.

The principal chief asked, "Your name, sir?"

"Dr. Dorch McIntyre."

"Your place of residence?"

"Round Fort, Indian Territory."

There were more short questions; then the chief reviewed the facts of the death of Della Wano. "These are our facts, sir. Do you wish to present others?"

"No."

"Then you admit the truth of the allegations as specified?"

"Yes."

"That on the night of the Battle of the Mounds, you deliberately killed Della Wano."

"Yes."

"How did you kill her?"

"By pistol."

"You have stated to members of the council prior to this meeting that you want no mercy shown?"

"That is correct."

"And even here, you still will not ask for mercy?"

"No, but I demand my right of execution under the laws of the tribes, execution by my own hand, and with my choice of weapons."

166

Cyrus Wano, a slightly built Creek, had not sat at the council table; his work was done; having disqualified himself, he watched the proceedings from the background. At Dorch's request, the members of the council leaned forward across the table and conferred. Then some drew back, almost in humiliation.

The principal chief said, "Sir, your plea of execution is granted. Do you have last wishes?"

"To write my last letters."

"Granted. Two weeks from today you will stand beneath the execution tree."

Money had never meant anything to Dorch; he would have slaved for his medical training, with or without it.

But back in his cell he began his will, and wrote his last letters while word of the pending execution swept the Territory like a prairie fire.

The first letter was to Albert McIntosh:

> It is my wish that no political element of our nations make any effort to render void the death sentence imposed upon me by the Creeks. My act was voluntary; it was not made a political issue by these peoples.
>
> While it is true that I did not take you into my confidence at the time of my departure from Boggy Depot, it was not due to lack of love for you, my father's old friend, nor did I intend to render the Choctaw or Chickasaw nations capitulate to any other in the Territory.
>
> Rather, because the virus of this case—the death of Della Wano—has entered into the fiber of all our nations and has led to hatreds and suspicions, the cause itself should be removed. By this act I do, I can perhaps give some aid to a new promise.
>
> My will, of which you will later be advised, is quite implicit, yet in regard to the hospital at Round Fort, may I recommend to you personally that it remain under the direct charge of Dr. Anthony Dennis, until such time as he desires to retire, and that the nurse in charge remain Elfreda Townley Dennis, his wife.
>
> There is no more to say, sir. If I have had any purpose on this earth, I feel that by this act I do now I have fulfilled it.
>
> > With the full affection of years,
> > Dorch McIntyre, M.D.

He sent a similar letter to the principal chief of the Chickasaws. Albert McIntosh placed his letter on his desk, his face inscrutable. With Timothy Baines, it was another matter:

> Friend Timothy, for I am certain you know I have always regarded you so, I must tell you that the time for parting has come. I reached conclusion after my son agreed to attend the academy, the better to learn those subjects for the life he intends to follow. All my usefulness has been accomplished; the investigations at the hospital will cease, our nations can rest, and life will be better for everyone.
>
> I make one final request of you—that you intercede with my friends and those who may have loved me and whom I might have loved, and state to them my appeal that they do not attend my execution. I would not want that final sorrow brought upon them.
>
> I trust, dear Timothy, that you choose to remain in the service of young Dorch and Lucy when they marry. I shall imagine it so, and this will lift a last burden from my shoulders.
>
> You are amply provided for in my will, for never was there a more perfect gentleman's gentleman.
>
> With all my affection,
Dorch McIntyre

Weeping, the little hunchback placed the letter on the dining table of the round room and walked about, one hand rubbing his face.

I failed him, thought Timothy. All the time when he brooded so, I ignored him. But I thought he wanted to be left alone. My God, my God!

He had stopped his tears; then he thought of the New Orleans days. He began to weep again.

"My God, my God!" he cried aloud.

"What shall we do, Anthony?" Elfreda asked Dr. Dennis, her voice sounding strange to herself and even stranger to the doctor.

"I don't know," he said. "But we will do what you wish."

It was not much now for Elfreda to look back upon and have left to remind her of a man she had loved—the old checkered tablecloth she had shared with Dorch at the hotel on their first dinner engagement, hidden away, and which she had asked her mother that night to buy for her the morning after.

She said, "We have known him so long, and for him to die alone like that."

The doctor hesitated, then spoke. "I think, dear, that he has built up such a strength for this deed that he fears he could break, if at that last moment he saw those he loved most. He has always been proud; it would humiliate him, even that close to death, to lose his strength before his friends."

Dry-eyed, Elfreda said. "Then you think he should die alone?"

"Yes, dear. It should be as he wishes."

A buzzer sounded. Elfreda rose. "I have a patient." She bent and kissed his forehead. "Thank you, dear."

Execution day was hot, with bright sun. The dust of horses and wagons hung heavy near the council house.

As the door of the stone jail swung open, Dorch stepped into the sunlight, a panatela in his hand. He was without his coat, wearing a white shirt with ruffles at the cuffs, the collar open. He was thinner, and squinted into the unaccustomed light.

The crowd which had gathered between the jail and the tree near the council house was sullen. The majority of the nation had not favored the execution. It was a faction of the Creeks, and not the nation, which had convicted Dorch McIntyre.

Captain Duane Vann in his red jacket walked beside him, followed by other lighthorse. The doctor had asked that they be kept from his sides. He walked slowly, his step sure.

At the halfway point to the execution tree, a little hunchback who wore a wide hat stepped from the crowd, then walked with him, a small box in his hands.

"Do not blame me, sir," said Timothy Baines, "but I received permission from the council to carry your weapons. It will be my last act as a gentleman's gentleman."

"I forgive you, Timothy."

The tree was nearer now. How much better this death, Dorch thought, than dying like a hanged dog on the Fort Smith gallows where criminals and outlaws had strangled among feasting and laughter.

The sun was hot on his back.

Sun, he thought, yes, once I felt sun. He began to think of the places where he had felt sun. One, when he had run naked in the Tallahaga Valley. Then all thoughts of sun left him, and he thought of nothing, only the steady walk toward the tree, the crowd still opening.

Now the walk was over. He stood, his back to the tree, the bright light in his eyes, he squinted.

He saw the plank coffin on the ground; it had been carried behind him by the lighthorse.

Captain Duane Vann was reading from a scroll: ". . . for the crime of murdering Della Wano, a Creek, death by your own hand, by pistol."

Then Vann said, "You may select your weapon, sir."

Timothy Baines stood beside the doctor. Dorch inhaled the panatela, then dropped it at his feet. Timothy extended the plush-lined box.

"Thank you, Timothy."

The doctor raised the pistol to his head.

But suddenly his eyes were swimming. Was it the sun, or something else? The sun. No.

In the glare stood Denna Cart, her face agonized, his lean and rigid son standing beside her. There was only that instant; then he pulled the trigger.

But he had been distracted and aimed poorly; the bullet had grazed the frontal lobe, but it did not kill. It would kill in a few moments, but not now.

He was on the ground squealing and screaming, his body bouncing, only human flesh in agony, his shirt bloody.

Drawing his pistol, Captain Duane Vann stepped forward to render the coup de grace.

"No," said Timothy Baines, taking the other pistol from the box and dropping the case to the ground. "I am his gentleman, sir."

He bent and fired a shot into Dorch's head.

The long body flinched and lay still.

Only the smoke of the panatela was alive, rising straight and clean like the smoke of a campfire.

Dorch's head had been bound in white wrapping, his neck and shoulders washed free of blood. He had been placed in the coffin and carried to the council house, although blood still trickled from beneath the bandage.

The coffin had been placed on a waist-high platform.

Already the muttering crowd which had witnessed the execution passed by the coffin in tribute. Here lay a man who had helped any poor of their kind who had ever gone to him at his hospital; young people, Creek and Seminole babies then, stopped at the coffin to view the man who had delivered them.

The line entered through the far door of the council house, passed the coffin, and left by the opposite door.

Denna Cart and young Dorch were in it. By now the doctor's body was almost covered by gifts, small turquoise talismans or bits of magic, personal trinkets and glass beads, elks' teeth, bits of Indian craft, bright feathers, and tiny images made of the sacred clay of Nanih Wayia, for many of the older Creeks had often visited in the Tallahaga Valley and taken back mementos.

The boy stopped at the coffin, gazing at the placid face. Father, he thought, for the first time thinking of him as Father, and not Daddy, I would not have come against your wishes, but she made me. Then Timothy came. But I will do as I promised. I will go to the academy and graduate. Then Lucy and I will marry and go to Wild Horse. Do you remember how we laughed over the burnt biscuits? No, you can't know, not now.

He saw the silver spurs Timothy had placed at Dorch's feet; he took them from the coffin. You don't mind if I keep these, do you?

The boy moved on, and Denna Cart stopped at the coffin. She bent and kissed the dead lips. Thank you, Dorch, for giving me the only hour which ever took me out of myself. No, we could never have lived together, although I will love you for always. A part of me rests in the coffin, but what I must do now is so clear.

What shall I do with the rest of my life? Dorch, I will devote it to vengeance to all who have done this thing. My love, I shall spend my life at vengeance, and always remember our hour.

Denna kissed the dead lips again, and with her son moving slowly before her, followed him in the line into the open.

She now had a purpose in life, and the upbringing of her son, who also would avenge his father.

The Texas Road took Dorch McIntyre home for the last time. Denna had hired a wagon and driver and four horses from Tom Mikish. She and Timothy rode in a *carriage*; young Dorch stayed by choice in the wagon bed, his father's horse following. He rode at the foot of the coffin, the wagon tailgate down, his feet dangling, holding the silver spurs. He scarcely ever looked at the carriage.

The leaves had turned color with the first touches of autumn. The boy thought, yes, Father, you rode up the Texas Road in the changing colors; we take you back the same way. Next week the academy will open. I will begin to fulfill my promise.

But he feared what this strange determined woman might do to him. She might take him from Elfreda, who had always been his mother. And what would she think of Lucy, and the life they planned on Wild Horse Prairie?

When Denna had come from Dallas, he had been summoned from the prairie, but he had refused to go with her to North Fork Town because of his father's wishes. He had known the old story, but he had never known his mother.

"You will go," Denna had said. "You are my common-law son."

The boy remembered Elfreda's pale face in the round room.

He would have to be careful until he learned what this new woman intended to do. She could destroy all he wanted, and ruin his life with Lucy.

On the afternoon of the third day on the road, it was hot, as hot as midsummer. The carriage stopped at a thatched roadside arbor with a sign before it, "Watermelons—Last Water for Fifteen Miles." Denna sat on a bench under the arbor and ate the pink heart of a watermelon, meanwhile talking and laughing with the watermelon man and his wife about the sign. It would not be fair to say that she had forgotten or meant disrespect for Dorch; it was hot, and they had had no water since leaving McAlester.

"Out with you, lad," Timothy said, walking to the back of the wagon.

"No, I'll just sit," the boy said.

"Aren't you thirsty?"

"Not enough to sit with that woman. Give a watermelon rind to my father's horse, will you?"

"When we have a chance, we'll talk things over."

At Round Fort, Denna buried Dorch beside his father. At the service, two black-eyed Indian children approached Denna, their arms full of late flowers. One child asked, "Do you want flowers, lady?"

"Yes," Denna said.

Within a week she had the father's cross taken down, and set up two duplicate markers of stone taken from the old barracks.

When young Dorch entered the academy—a two-hour ride from the hill—Timothy accompanied him with a pack horse for his luggage.

The boy spoke little until they were well on their way and wound their trail through shaggy hills and valleys. At last he asked, "Timothy, what kind of woman is she?"

"Your new mother?"

"She could never become my real mother."

Timothy said cautiously, "She came of good Eastern stock, but she was born in a hard part of Texas. Maybe she knows a little of the rough and seedy side of life, too, since I know for a fact that she rode with her father against the freebooters."

"Is there any law we can go to?"

Timothy said, "Until your father's will is read, we'll play it close to the vest. I wonder if what Denna plans to do isn't atonement for the way she has neglected you, just as your daddy sought atonement for something else."

"She already wants me to go somewhere else to school."

"If anyone says anything about your father, hold your head up."

"Don't worry—I'll hold it up."

They came from a wide valley and up slightly rising ground to a great limestone building several stories high. It was so solid that it appeared to have been cut from a single block of limestone. About it were scattered the academy buildings.

The boy saw that the steps were broad and high.

He was ready to go to work.

4

Timothy Baines had not liked the way in which Denna, once she settled herself at Round Fort, began to put her fingers into so many things. She had bought an expensive bed and vanity in Dallas and installed them in the round room. Under her instruction, Timothy had dismantled and moved the large dining table to storage and had moved his cot into a schoolroom.

Denna had begun to question Elfreda and Dr. Dennis about the inner workings of the hospital, the payments which came in, the drugs, and if strange men visited the nurses' rooms. She added that Sardis Rippy had told her in Boggy Depot that the doctor had once maintained kept women in the round room.

"Rot," said Elfreda, surprised at her boldness. "I have known him longer than anyone. You were the only woman who ever stayed there."

Elfreda's defiance created a twinkle of amusement in Denna's eyes. She thought, very well, my dear, if you want war you'll get it.

But when the will was read by Brian Doyle in the Boggy Depot hotel, with a great many of the curious standing about, Denna found that she did not own the hospital; Dorch had given his interest in it to his two nations; out of its income would come salaries and the expense of upkeep and improvement.

Of the two stores—those at Doaksville and Boggy Depot—young Dorch was to receive one-half interest in each, the remainder being willed to the respective managers, Tom Adkins and Boyce Townley, trusted men who had been with the McIntyres for years.

Young Dorch and Lucy were to receive the Wild Horse Prairie ranch jointly; the doctor's personal fortune would go to his son. Denna had been left nothing, except what she might after due litigation secure under common law. This she had half-expected, hence her claim to the round room, which she meant to maintain against all odds.

More by pique than necessity, since she had ample funds of her own, she returned to Dallas with Brian. One afternoon in his office she became very definite.

"Why," she asked, "did you draw such a will for my husband?"

"First," Brian said, eyeing her keenly and taking his tobacco pouch from his coat pocket, "I did not draw the will; the doctor did, and mailed it to me. Secondly, he was never your husband. I doubt that any court, Indian or white, or even the Supreme Court, would grant that you were ever even a common-law wife. Thirdly, assuming you were such a wife, you abandoned him, and when your child came, you left it at his doorstep. You neither saw nor made any effort to see your child or the doctor again, not until the time of execution."

"How you twist facts," she said.

"I can twist them even more," Brian said. "In view of what I have mentioned, do you think any jury would conclude anything but that you returned to Round Fort only for what money you could get, and the estate?" Brian smiled. "I see you are angry, my dear. You are my client also—now, what do you really want?"

"This," said Denna. She had money; it was power she desired. "I want and expect the right to remain in the round room." She rose haughtily. "Now drag that out through the courts. But I intend to live at Round Fort."

"Things are happy there. Why don't you let them remain so?"

Denna did not reply. "I also want the right to use the valley along the creek. Though I have a claim to it, I will lease it from the estate. I may run cows there."

The best way out, Brian thought. Pacify her until the whole affair is cleared in the courts. He said, "The lease can be drawn tomorrow. You can take the papers with you, but have them filed subject to the approval of the tribes."

"I think," said Denna, "I will have no trouble there." What she intended to do was work slowly for control of all the property, since young Dorch was not yet of age.

"My cab will be here at five," Brian said. "Suppose we try one of Anthracite's dinners tonight."

As the cab drove through the busy streets, Denna thought, I was secure and safe with my one night, as long as Dorch still lived. Was it vanity that made me leave a man I had won, to hurt him, and return my child to his door? Did I think I could humble him by this, a man who could not be humbled? Do I seek power and vengeance now to use against myself, a self I am beginning to hate, or has it all proved I was the insignificant, I, who thought myself the proud one?

"We're here," Brian said cheerfully, and helped her from the cab.

When Denna returned to Round Fort, Brian had an almost immediate appointment at the Fort Smith court; he wrote Timothy, asking that he meet him at the Boggy Depot hotel.

"I am worried about Denna," he said in the dining room. "I have known her for many years, but a strangeness has come over her. If she appears to become ill, or in any way unsettled, will you write me?"

Across the table, Timothy nodded. Even at the reading of the will, when he had heard the sum left to him by Dorch, he had hardly listened.

His mind was far, far ahead, down another road.

When young Dorch returned to the academy after the Christmas vacation, Denna Cart took the train to Texas. She had spent the autumn riding the near and distant hills and valleys; she had covered the land by horse, much as she had covered the Lake District in other years on foot. By now she knew every ridge and slope and each possible hideout, and was ready to act. Her features had hardened, and her skin was rougher.

Yet in her riding across Muddy Boggy Creek she had returned to one spot again and again, drawn to it irresistibly. It was no more than a few acres in circumference, with shriveled and dwarfed brush at its edges, yet its desolation reminded her of the savagery which, though different, had surrounded Gaits Water in her rambles around Hawkshead and Coniston.

Within these acres there was no vegetation at all, only a salty whiteness surrounded by the dwarfed bushes. The spot was dominated on the south by a shaly hill, where once a landslide had occurred, spreading its debris fanlike upon the crusted whiteness. Near the foot of the debris a gnarled and twisted oak stood, one which for perhaps a century had reached its roots beneath the hill, gaining its sustenance there.

She knew sulfur springs were to the west, and northward lay the Great Salt Plains; she had knelt to taste a pinch of the white crust; it was bitter and salty, but she could not account for this single spot of death among the colorful hills. In bright moonlight it looked like a shimmering lake, and she thought of it as Gaits Water, although it went by the Indian name of the Licks, and wild animals rarely went there.

As she left the train in San Antonio, Denna thought of this isolated spot, for she had visited it only the day before she left Round Fort, half-expecting to see the bulk of the Ald Maen rearing in the distance, and not the huddled hills.

From San Antonio Denna took the stage line to Victory. But as the bouncing wheels spun over the endless miles, raising a plumed feather of blowing dust, from station to station the quality of each stage became progressively worse, until after the last change she wondered if the rickety thing she sat in would reach Victory at all.

Her nights on the road had been spent in plank hotels or roominghouses set among desolate cactus and chaparral, with constant dust and blowing sand.

When she reached Victory, she found it had become almost a ghost town; its blank-faced buildings stared into the almost deserted streets. She stayed at the frame hotel for a day, resting, the wind howling, and on the next bought a horse and saddle at a livery stable.

She rode out to the old ranch to visit the Willacys. In town, she had gone neither to the grave of her father nor to those of Tom and Amy, for other things were on her mind.

David Willacy was a stocky John Bull from Lytham, in Lancashire, England, and a cousin to Dolly Cocklebloom who had run the Partridge and Pigeon in Coniston with her husband. When Dolly learned that David planned to enter the cattle business in Texas, she had put him in touch with Denna.

It was shortly after the death of Abel Cart when David and Kate

Willacy arrived in Victory. Denna had just sold her father's bank and other properties; she sold the ranch to the Willacys at an exorbitant price, honestly believing, as she told them, that the town would flourish and the property become more valuable.

David Willacy could have bought a very good ranch elsewhere in Texas for half the price, but he paid Denna considerably over half down on the purchase, the remainder due in yearly installments.

But years of drought and freebooters had taken their toll; David was hard-pressed to make his payments, in some years paying only the interest on the installment.

The stocky little Englishman had become a favorite in Victory; he was stuffy to a degree when offended, but he was generally agreeable and never one easily to ride false horses.

As Denna rode the familiar old trail to the hacienda, she knew where she could find men she could trust, killers all, if they were ordered to kill, and if their old loyalty remained the same.

At the hacienda, now strangely desolate, Denna found a big-waisted woman whose hair stuck out in the wind like broomstraws and who battled to hang a line of clothes in the wind.

"Kate Willacy!" Denna cried, stopping the horse beside her. "Let me help you."

"Denna Cart! Oh, this forbidden land!" Kate Willacy moaned.

Denna slid off the horse and proceeded with the clothes hanging. It took one of them to hold a wind-whipped sheet on the galvanized wire, while the other fought to clip the clothespins in place.

"I should never have left England," Kate Willacy said through a clothespin she held in her determined teeth. "But my husband! All he talked about was Texas, and he had to come here. God rue the day!"

Denna laughed. "It's not all that bad," she said through her own clothespin. "My father had the same ambition."

"David is humiliated that we still owe you, but it could not be helped."

"Don't worry," Denna said.

"Oh, that awful interest! But David will make a cow drive in a year or two, and we will be on our feet."

Kate dragged a basket of still-to-be-hung sandy clothes farther along the ground. "How glad I will be to have it over."

"The squire's son," Denna said. "Have you ever heard of him?"

"Yes. He hanged himself in a garret." Kate added with her usual English practicality, "I suppose it was too cold to go outside."

David Willacy rode in with his cowhands at sundown after spending a day in the brush. He was broad-shouldered and bow-legged, but his legs were from a natural formation at Lytham, and not brought on by Texas horses.

Denna achieved her purpose with the Willacys; she was invited to stay all night. They dined on a flat-topped trunk and talked of the Cockleblooms and the Partridge and Pigeon and the Lake District until midnight.

"Oh," sighed Kate, battling a dozen millers which fluttered around the lamp. "Oh, for Lytham on the Ribble, and the white fog rolling in from the Irish Sea." Her cowlike eyes glanced at David accusingly.

Denna was given a single candle and placed in her old room, which Amy had kept so immaculate. It was now a storage place, cluttered with old churns, broken furniture, and a single cot. She saw her father's books strangely stacked and torn in the corners; undoubtedly they had been ripped apart to start fires in cold weather.

But everything showed how badly the ranch had gone, and what the Willacys had sold of the old furniture to keep it on its feet.

Next morning at the scanty breakfast for Willacy would not eat his own beef, Denna asked him, "Is Devil's Den still here?"

That was where she had often ridden with her father to raid the freebooters' camps.

"Aye," said Willacy, "and full of outlaws still, worse than it used to be." He added stuffily, "Miss Cart, if I have one regret about our business arrangement, it is that I was not told of the constant freebooting and outlawry here."

"In turn," Denna said stiffly, "you had your own attorney witness the count on the cattle; you were aware of the freebooters and outlaws as much as I."

Willacy, fearing he had gone too far for one who still owed a debt, said, "If you ride today, don't go toward Devil's Den. Those men are beyond the pale."

"I know," said Denna. She knew the hidden dens in the red canyon as well as she knew her hand. And from Willacy she had learned what she had wanted to know without arousing the suspicion she might have aroused in town.

When Willacy and his heavily armed cowhands left the hacienda, Denna rode toward the canyon. Two hours later, moving into its gaping mouth, she saw all its old features—the heaped rocks and ledges, the struggling mesquite and cactus holding to the walls, and the rattlesnakes. She rode without haste, surely, knowing what she would find.

At last she approached a campfire, two dozen men hunkered about it, at its edge a gallon can of coffee boiling. As she stopped the horse, there was only silence; no man seated had raised his head to look at her or the horse. She knew that the stolid pace of the horse had not alarmed them; also, that a signal of acceptance had perhaps been given from some higher point.

"Good morning, gentlemen. Don't any of you remember me?"

One raised his head and glanced at her steadily.

"Hello, Kent," she said.

"Sure," Kent said, rising. "Denna Cart."

He was sharp-eyed, of medium build, with a trim black mustache.

"Light and rest your saddle," Kent said. "Coffee? Pinto, give her a cup."

Denna slid from the saddle. She took the proffered cup and sat on the ground; Kent took the makings from the pocket of his brush jacket and hunkered beside her. He had been her father's foreman in the war against the freebooters.

"What can I do for you?" Kent asked. "People don't come to me for nothing."

"Are you a freebooter now, or a plain rustler?"

Kent shoved his sombrero back and grinned. "I've got a new religion, Denna. If you can't beat 'em, join 'em."

Denna was conscious that all eyes were fixed on her now.

"I want twelve men and you to come to the Territory. I'd say more than twelve, but it wouldn't be wise right now. Others can come later—cowhand wages, plus a half."

"And for me?" Kent said.

Denna laughed. "That depends on you. You've still no notches on your gun?"

Kent said, his teeth shining, "No reason to advertise my trade. Somebody might take those notches for evidence."

"You are in charge here?"

"Call it that."

"Let's go off and talk," Denna said.

When she had transacted her business with Kent, he asked one question. "You want four or five hundred cows driven up there to put in the Round Fort valley. Where do I get them?"

Denna laughed. "Kent, I'm surprised. A little Englishman lives up the way. He has thousands of cattle and still uses the old brand."

She rode back and spent the night with the Willacys.

When she left for Victory the next morning, her only regret was that she had not visited the narrow creek where as a child she had watched a horned toad until Amy had come for her.

Denna had completely claimed the round room for her own, and having returned from the Texas ranch, she rode again and again to the desolate acres of the Licks. Perhaps a salt lake had once been there, or a pocket of an ancient ocean bed of the Ordovician not yet eroded and washed away.

Timothy Baines had from the beginning moved his cot into the school building; since the doctor's death his life was completely disorganized. He built the early-morning fires in the school, so the rooms would always be warm when the Indian children arrived, and during the day he helped in the hospital. But the old manner of his life had ended, and he was lonesome.

Before going to bed in a schoolroom, Timothy added a few pieces of wood or coal to a potbellied stove and slept with the foot of the cot toward the heat, always warm under some of the hospital blankets. When he woke, he folded the cot and blankets and placed them out of the way in the back of the classroom.

On some nights, he might fry bacon or make coffee on one of the stoves. On these nights he missed young Dorch and Lucy. Since the doctor's death, he had taken them under his wing completely, but Dorch did not get away from the academy often, and with Denna occupying the round room, Elfreda had limited Lucy's freedom.

As a consequence of his loneliness, Timothy took up teaching.

Not that the teaching was real; it was imaginary. On some nights, after he had drunk his coffee, he would get up from his seat beside the stove and sit at the teacher's empty desk.

"One and one make what?" he would ask, his eyes steely on a miserable little Choctaw seated on his splintery bench, only a long plank before him to hold his tablet and pencil.

Before the child could answer, a black-eyed Chickasaw maverick from the back row would yell, "Two!"

"Shut up," said Timothy. "I asked this boy."

"Two," the first child replied. At least, thanks to the interruption, he was over the mountain. He hadn't known what one and one made—at least, not in English.

On other nights Timothy would take a pupil's place on the seats and face the lank teacher at the desk. There would be questions and answers. But tonight was different because of what he had seen in the valley this morning.

It was not unusual for Texas drovers to use the valley on their trail drives to Kansas—that was how young Dorch and Lucy had learned their love of ranching—but it was unusual so early in the year, when grass was barely green, to see a strange herd of some six hundred longhorns rise from its bedding grounds.

This would have meant that the herd had come to the valley late last evening, or even during the night. But more unusual, as the day advanced, was that the dozen or so riders with the cows made no effort to continue the drive, but seemed quite content to remain in the valley.

It was such a strange herd that even Lucy had not ridden down to greet its cowhands.

But next day Timothy investigated.

He rode down the hill and set a straight track across the valley, as if going directly to a certain point on the creek; he hoped, without arousing suspicion from the men loafing about the chuckwagon, to pass through a portion of the herd and identify its brand. He was rewarded.

The lank longhorns bore the old Abel Cart C Bar brand which he had often heard Denna mention, but there was one odd thing which struck him. Not only did each cow bear the Cart brand, but each had been dewlapped; that is, the brisket had been slashed and left to heal in a hanging position. One way to change ownership, Timothy thought. On some cows he passed, the flesh had not yet healed.

He waved casually toward a rider with a black mustache who trotted his way, then continued on into the opposite trees. Well, it works two ways, Timothy thought; he wanted to know who I am.

He knew the cows were not Denna's; she was out of the cattle business, but how had the cows of the old Cart brand found their way into the valley? And whose were they? How long were they to be kept here?

When Timothy returned to the hill, he made a point of seeing Denna. "Have you noticed the strange herd in the valley? It's got the old Cart brand. I thought you might be interested."

"No, I haven't noticed the herd," Denna said, "but because it bears the old brand, I might ride down tomorrow. Perhaps they are old cows my father sold."

Timothy started to say that a cow sold that many years back would really be getting pretty old by now. However, he let the matter drop.

But as he paced the schoolroom that night, he felt that the fat was in the fire. He forgot all about the patient black-eyed pupils who sat in their places waiting for their questions.

Timothy Baines was greatly relieved when Jack Leavitt and three of his cowhands rode to Boggy Depot with the account book of the Wild Horse Prairie ranch. He happened to be in town at the same time, having come for the hospital mail.

When Leavitt finished his conversation with Boyce Townley, Timothy said, "I want to talk with you, not for a few minutes, but for an hour."

Leavitt shoved his hat back, grinning. "Getting married?"

"Yes, to hell and high water."

Leavitt said, "Let's go outside to a bench."

They sat watching the street, and each reached for the makings. Timothy began the story of the strange herd, how it had been in the valley for two weeks, making no effort to move, and how Denna Cart had begun to ride to the chuckwagon almost daily. Was it a cow camp or an outlaw hangout?

"Well," said Leavitt, "I reckon three of my hands will equal twelve of their skillet-lickers and saddle tramps. No better time than now. Let's ride and take a gander."

"Young Dorch is home for the weekend. While you are here, we'll talk over a few things."

They circled the base of the hospital hill along the creek,

183

rather than climb the hill and then descend, and entered the valley from below. The gaunt longhorns grazed in the distance. As they neared the camp, riding through the cows, Leavitt squinted. "It looks like a cow camp, provided that wreck in the middle is a chuckwagon."

Dorch and Lucy rode down the hill to join them. It was their first ride into the valley since the arrival of the herd. They all neared the chuckwagon with the fire beside it. At last they could make out the faces of the strange cowhands, who watched them come.

"Know any of them?" Timothy asked Leavitt.

"I'm sure of one. I've been up the trail with him."

They reached the chuckwagon and pulled up. A dark man who hunkered beside the fire, one with a black mustache, squinted up at Leavitt.

"Hello, Kent," Leavitt said. "Mighty big herd you're wintering here. And that same clean gun butt—never killed a man yet, have you?"

Kent grinned. "Never this boy."

"What's that?" Leavitt said, indicating the ancient chuckwagon. "Looks like you found it among the bones of the first longhorn. And dewlaps on an old brand I know."

"Now, don't criticize us or our hospitality. Look at this good coffee coming up."

"Fine," said Leavitt. "We'll light and take a few cups."

Timothy sat and studied the close faces of the cowhands. He might trust one of them from here to Round Fort, but not beyond it.

Young Dorch said nothing. Too many strange things had happened at Round Fort lately—this herd, and Denna's long rides and absences. Some of the boys had seen her riding even far beyond the academy. Lucy sat closer, not liking the way the strange cowhands observed her.

"Back to the dewlap on a C Bar brand," Leavitt said to Kent.

"Brand comes from near Victory," Kent said, holding his tin cup. "Some Englishman owns the spread now."

Leavitt lied with a straight face. "Didn't know that."

Kent said, "A few years ago I bought some cows from old Cart; then we had a run-in. My cows having his brand, you see, he accused me of a little poaching. So I dewlapped for my brand."

"Then judging from the time old Cart died, these three-year-old

184

shes you have here must be the great-great-grandmothers of every mossy-horned steer left in Texas. Aren't there more regular and legal means of showing ownership?"

Kent flushed. "I subleased this valley from Denna Cart, and my own way of changing a brand is all right with her."

"But you bought the cows from her father."

"To hell with you."

"You've got a bill of sale, of course," Jack Leavitt said, "just so I can quash some suspicions I heard in Boggy."

Kent pretended to be surprised; he reached into his jacket pocket. The paper he handed Leavitt was brown and ragged, one side burned. "Look it over," he said.

"Looks right to me." Leavitt returned the paper to Kent. "Well, old son," he said, rising, "I'll see you. But one little tip—keep your saddle tramps away from Wild Horse Prairie. Thanks for the coffee."

Leavitt's party mounted their horses and rode up the hill.

"Denna Cart," Leavitt told Timothy, "is getting into something deep. It's my bet she had Kent steal that herd from the Englishman, so Kent and his outlaws could set up here by pretending to be in the cow business. You noticed how Kent took my insults; he didn't draw on me, because he's here for bigger game. On the bill of sale, Denna had faked Abel Cart's signature, then roughed up and dirtied the paper to make it look old. The date was a year before her father died, yet here come these young dewlaps."

Timothy said, feeling the pull of his horse on the upgrade, "How sure are you about that signature?"

"As sure as Judgment. I've seen old Cart sign his name dozens of times in cowtowns and saloons, and I've been getting letters from Denna over her signature."

"What has she wanted?"

"She's trying to edge me off Wild Horse—claims she wants to look after the ranch herself—for the boy, of course."

"So she's lining these men up for mischief."

"From what I've learned in Texas about Denna, she'll lead them herself. A Belle Starr number two, if you get what I mean."

Timothy knew only too well what the foreman meant—the villainy of this slouch-hatted, horse-faced female. Living up at Younger's Bend on the Canadian, beneath Hi-Early's rocky heights, Belle Starr provided a mecca for Texas and Kansas and Missouri and Territory outlaws alike. Is that what I'll see happen

As she slid from the saddle, Denna said, "Come inside, Timothy. I would like to talk today."

Within the round room, she took off her dusty hat and tossed it on her bed. Timothy seated himself before the fireplace, watching her almost eager movements as she tidied herself at the vanity.

"Wine, Timothy? There is some in the highboy. Get us wine."

Timothy placed one glass on the vanity, the other on the piano. Seated on the piano bench, he began to one-finger the notes of the "Sparkling Spavinaw."

"What is that tune?" Denna asked, brushing her hair before the mirror.

"'The Sparkling Spavinaw.'"

"Where did you learn it?"

"First from the foreman at Wild Horse; then later my gentleman played it."

"I can't imagine the doctor playing that piece. By the way, what do you think of Jack Leavitt?"

Timothy measured his words slowly. "In a tough spot, or in any kind of a mess, I'd want Leavitt on my side. I wouldn't want him against me." He was emboldened to add, "If I were you, I'd be careful."

She turned from the mirror, flaring. "What do you mean?"

"Just what I said," Timothy said. "I'd watch my step."

"You hunchback!" she cried. "You are a fool!"

"Yes, I am a hunchback. I've been one all my life. It doesn't hurt me to be called a hunchback any more than if someone said I had a hand or a foot. I'm used to it, but I'm not throwing myself to the dogs. I'll tell you once more, I'd rather have Leavitt on my side than against me."

"But why should Leavitt be against me?"

"I think you know the answer, and the reasons."

"And what are those?" She moved from the vanity, her cheeks rouged, and placed the wineglass on the piano.

Timothy thought, God, she's beautiful. But she's taking every wrong in the world out on someone else.

"Tell me," Denna said, raising the glass.

"Since you know the reasons as well as I do, I won't take time to tell you. You have few friends now; the time may come when you won't have any."

"Have more wine, Timothy. I want to sing."

"No." He had seen her this way once before—the day after she had ridden away with half the outlaw band when Dorch was there. On the next day, a murdered Indian and his burned cabin had been located in the hills. The Indian was part-Creek.

Timothy rose, not touching his wine. "I've got to go to the school and start the fires for some meeting tonight. But I'll tell you another thing—I hear old Albert McIntosh is looking pretty close at you. Maybe he thinks you are buying off someone on the council."

He opened the door and left, closing it behind him.

The murder of a second Creek came within a week.

In Boggy Depot and in Boyce Townley's store, the subject became an immediate subject of conversation. The store was crowded with those avid for information.

Who had done this murder?

And why?

In this last case, an old Creek couple from North Fork Town had decided to take a holiday on horseback, as they had done many times in their younger days when the Territory was new. They had decided to follow the Texas Road to old Colbert's Ferry —now a bridge—on Red River, then return to spend a night to fish on Blue River before proceeding back to North Fork Town.

But as Captain Dade Rothney of the lighthorse began his investigation, a singular fact emerged. The murdered Creek, Jonas Whitecotton, had been a member of the council which had convicted Dr. Dorch McIntyre.

The act had occurred only a few miles from Boggy Depot; Rothney, stationed there at the time, was at the scene immediately. The dead Creek lay crosswise in the ruts of the Texas Road, and beside him knelt his weeping wife.

When the woman became coherent, the lighthorse asked, "How did it happen, Mrs. Whitecotton?"

"Four men and a woman rode from the trees. The woman was tall and masked. She pointed to my husband and said, 'There is your man.'"

"Did your husband appear to know them?"

"No."

"What were his last words?"

"'Forgive me for what I did to Dr. Dorch McIntyre.'"

"But what could the connection be?"

"My husband was on the council which convicted the doctor; he always regretted it."

"You saw none of the men closely?"

"No, only the woman."

Rothney's continuing investigation brought no results; at times he thought that fear prevented the country people and poorer Indians from telling all they might have known, as they had in the earlier case, of people they may have seen near the spot on the day of murder.

While some people passed away both murders as mere outlawry, a newspaper in the Territory, one mailed regularly to the hospital, had a different story and indicated another viewpoint:

WAR AMONG NATIONS?

The slaying of the Creek councilman Jonas Whitecotton on the Texas Road near the boundary of the Choctaw and Chickasaw nations brings alive again the sordid story of Della Wano and Dorch McIntyre, the Chickasaw doctor who murdered her during the past hostilities.

The incident is too well remembered to repeat here.

Suffice it to say that our interviewer asked Mrs. Whitecotton, in seclusion at her home in North Fork Town, if she had seen or heard anything from the outlaw band to indicate that this sad affair could be related to the Wano case.

Mrs. Whitecotton replied to the contrary, but stated that her husband's last words were, "Forgive me for what I did to Dr. Dorch McIntyre."

In spite of the sporadic murders committed by both sides since the doctor's death, in the opinion of this column there will be no war between the Creek nation and its sister nations to the south. There are calmer heads in these days, and it should be the obligation of the remaining nations to prevent a war.

Could it be that the mysterious woman in the case is none other than the secretive Belle Starr, who though aligned by a previous marriage of sorts with the Cherokees, for reasons of her own took part in this matter with her own tested outlaws?

Readers of this column are invited to return their opinions for publication.

When Elfreda and Dr. Dennis read the column, she asked, "Anthony, do you think the woman could have been Denna?"

The hawk-faced doctor said, "Damned if I know. But more than ever, from now on we'll watch everything that goes on in the valley."

FIVE

1

With the doctor's death, Timothy Baines had adopted Lucy and Dorch as his own, as much as ever he had adopted the boy's father. With Dorch, it was the weekly visits to the academy; with Lucy, his constant safeguarding on the hill and his watchfulness on the valley. Each morning he was mounted and armed; the hill was inspected and safe before Lucy came from the hospital apartment to make the short walk to her classroom.

Lucy and Dorch filled the vacuum which had come to Timothy's life; in them he found his only happiness.

Young Dorch was serious; his mind was always on his studies; Lucy was equally determined, but in a different way—she wanted the life she and Dorch had set for themselves.

"We don't let Father and Mother know," the brown-eyed girl told Timothy one day, "but Dorch and I are worried."

Timothy had become the melting pot of their thoughts and the discussions of their future, and because of it he was also happy. "Cheer up," he told the worried girl, a little hard core in his heart warming, "just leave everything to Old Timothy; things will come out all right."

She put her hand on his arm. "Oh, Timothy, what would we do without you?"

But Timothy had never mentioned to Dorch that the doctor in his last letter had wished him to become his son's gentleman; this Timothy would tell when the time came or when the boy was older.

After a ride through driving snow one Friday afternoon, Timothy sat in Dorch's cold room in the academy. The boy was coming to the hill for the weekend, but he could not leave until noon on Saturday; Timothy was worried for his safety because of Denna's riders, as he was always worried about Lucy's; he did not want Dorch to return to the hill alone.

Timothy sat on a cot across from Dorch's, oblivious to the cold stone walls of the room, watching the tall boy who sat opposite him.

"I had your cot moved in," Dorch said. "I thought you might want to stay here instead of in a separate room, and we can talk more. How is Lucy?"

Timothy, his ears still frozen from the ride, grinned. "Headstrong as ever for her ranch."

Dorch rose and stood at the window, watching the whipping snow. Each time Timothy had seen him since his father's death, he seemed to have grown taller.

"I've got bad news for you," Timothy said, "so keep standing and face the music. Dr. Dennis had a letter from Jack Leavitt this morning."

Dorch turned. "What did he say?"

"Someone tried to burn the grass and the bunkhouse."

"Do they know who?" Dorch asked, his dark eyes snapping.

"Jack said that after the shooting was over, one man who had his face shot off might have looked like one of those we saw in the valley that time we rode down to the chuckwagon. It was a case where he couldn't be certain."

Dorch sat again on his cot. "Timothy, I'm not afraid of anything. But some things are just not in the cards, are they?"

"It's like unraveling an old sock," Timothy said. "It will take longer than you think. From now on when you come down to the hill to visit, don't leave the academy by way of the big valley."

Surprised, Dorch stood up again.

Timothy said, "Tomorrow we'll head north first, before turning back. We'll lose ourselves in timber, then strike back for the Boggy. Old Timothy is watching you, just as he watches Lucy, snow or no snow. But from now on, never start your trail in the direction you want to go. Make it like a sidewinder's, for that's what you're dealing with."

Two roughly dressed and holstered women sat in a thatched lean-to beneath the ruggedness of Hi-Early Mountain, the Canadian River before them. On the opposite side of the river stood another mountain.

So this, Denna thought, is Younger's Bend, named after one of Belle's old sweethearts.

"You know the newspapers," Belle Starr said. "They say I did it."

"Good," said Denna, "for you can prove you didn't, because at the time Jonas Whitecotton was killed, you were in the Fort Smith court."

The harsh face with the agate eyes looked at Denna contemptuously. "And you?"

"Supposedly, I was at Round Fort, but who would suspect me?"

"Why have you not been here to see me earlier?"

"Because I thought you would come to see me."

Belle Starr said, surprised, "Why should I have come to see you?"

"Because I have great plans for both of us. And because in the valley of Round Fort there would always be shelter for your friends who pass back and forth through the Territory."

Denna saw a flicker of interest in the uncompromising eyes. She had heard that this woman was in love with her own son and that she had known many lovers among her outlaws, that when her illegitimate children appeared in court with Belle they used the names of their supposed fathers; she knew Belle's uncouthness.

Belle watched the mustached Kent, who sat outside the lean-to. "What you really want," she said, "is another hideout for your own band, as well as a chance to strike the Creeks easier."

"It would all fit, wouldn't it?" Denna said, smiling. "And I would give you the same right at Round Fort."

"Who is this man with you?" Belle said, watching Kent as he put his face into the wind and cupped his hands to light a cigarette.

"Kent, a Texan."

"A man is like a goat," said Belle. "He can be led by a smell." She wore a blue off-colored blouse, boots, and a dirty skirt. She may have had some attractiveness in past years, but this was not now. Her black hat was tossed on the ground near a blanket roll.

"You have a beautiful view here," Denna said.

Belle snapped shortly, "I never think of views, unless my boarders are coming up the rise."

Denna felt that Belle was dismissing her as an upstart. Still, she persisted. "Isn't buried treasure supposed to be on Hi-Early?"

"Do you think I'd climb a damn mountain to look for treasure?" Denna was thoroughly irritated. "Hell, no," she said, leaving the lean-to to mount her horse. "Not you."

"Stay," Belle said, rising to follow, now completely interested because of Denna's abruptness. "We'll make some candy. I have a nice recipe for sugar candy."

"Sorry, but I've got business," Denna said, waving her hat toward the opposite mountain. "When my men cross the river, don't be alarmed. They are not looking for you."

"I have only to raise my arm, and I will have twelve men here."

"I have already raised my arm, and I have twenty-four."

On her way back to Round Fort after burning a Creek valley, Denna made love with Kent under the curlicued leaves of a gigantic sycamore tree.

At his desk, Dr. Dennis looked up from a crushed and battered letter written by Jack Leavitt. "I'll have to go to the old Chickasaw woman on Wild Horse," he told Elfreda. "She is worse again."

"Couldn't Dr. Ballinger go?"

"No. She is peculiar—it has taken almost a year for her to accept me."

"When will you leave?"

"At noon. Even then, I'll ride most of the night to get there, but I know the trail, and the moon will be out. I'll take an extra horse."

"Anthony, could we go to the barracks? I have something to tell you."

"Of course. It's a little cool—slip your jacket on."

When they sat on the lower walls of the barracks, Elfreda said, "It's about Denna."

"What about her?"

"All that Dorch gave his life for, to keep peace in the Territory, she will destroy. On days when there is a stage holdup, or some murder, she is always away somewhere. An Indian woman who was a patient here told me that even Belle Starr has been to see her. Once there had been some disagreement between them, but Denna won her over. Denna wants only to antagonize the Creeks."

"Are you positive she rides with the men, especially Kent?"

"Yes. Timothy bought a brass telescope at the store—one of the old pull-out kind. He hides in the cedars on the opposite side of the hill; he has seen her meet them all in the creek trees."

"I don't like it. Perhaps Belle and Denna have divided the country—Denna lets Belle hold up a stage here, and she gains a base for raiding the Creeks."

Elfreda said, "The woman told me that when Denna's men from the valley leave on long raids, they leave singly, then meet with Denna and each other in other valleys; she has seen them meet from her mountain. She also said that Denna sometimes spends an entire day alone at some gnarled and savage spot north of Muddy Boggy. She broods there as if fascinated. What could be wrong with her?"

"A released savagery."

Elfreda turned to face the doctor squarely. "Anthony, Jack Leavitt also wrote another letter. It was to Denna, and I read it."

"How did you get it?"

"Once when she had been gone most of the day, and I knew she would not be back before dark, I went into the round room. I searched everywhere for something, anything, to throw light on matters and to know what she intended to do with Dorch. I found the letter beneath the piano fallboard."

"What was in it?"

"Denna is starting a court action with some Fort Smith lawyer to gain control of young Dorch's estate and Wild Horse ranch, claiming she should manage everything until Dorch is of age. She also wants to send Dorch East. She evidently wanted Leavitt to—what is the word?—throw in with her. Leavitt brought this out in his reply, I think deliberately, to have it on record that he condemned her."

"What else did he say?"

"That he had agreed with the doctor to manage the ranch until Dorch is of age, and still intends to. Also, that no loose—he had underlined it—that no loose Texas cattle would be allowed on Wild Horse. I wish that were all," Elfreda continued, "but since the Department of the Interior man and his marshal have come back to Boggy Depot, Denna has been seeing him at night at the hotel."

"Romance?"

"I don't know, but something is back of it."

"I'll go on and see Leavitt at the ranch."

Elfreda said, rising, "I'll pack your clothes and bag."

As they walked down the hill, the doctor's hawkish face brightened. "By George, I've got it. Somehow, Brian Doyle has had his eyes opened. He wouldn't handle Denna's case; she had to take a Fort Smith shyster. That means Brian is free. When I go through Boggy, I'll write him, and have him file a cross-petition for our own guardianship of Dorch. If things do end up in court, we can cause our own confusion."

"Anthony, you are an old conniver."

"I am a conniver, but am I really old?"

"Not too old."

"You know, in spite of all the hell popping, I've had an idea about the hospital. We have Dr. Warwick and Dr. Ballinger now, and Dr. Michaels is coming. With four doctors, why can't we set up a circuit riding organization—not exactly that—but build three strategically located cabins within less than a day's ride from the fort? One west of here in the Chickasaw land, another to the north, and one perhaps toward Wild Horse Prairie and the Kiamichis.

"These places could serve as epidemic or vaccination centers, and sick Indians could come on certain days a week, and the doctor could go out to see those too ill to come in. It would not only relieve the load on the hospital, but give service to those too far away to get it. I have been in touch with the government, and the plan meets with its approval."

"The old doctor would be glad to know what you have done here."

"I hope so. We might even place the first two trainees he sent to New Orleans in charge of these base hospitals. They could alternate their rounds, and we have many ambitious trainees to help them."

"Denna Cart," said Elfreda. "If she would let us live in peace!"

Dr. Dennis found the old Chickasaw woman dead, her body placed on a high platform beneath an oak tree. Some Choctaw blood there, he thought, glancing up in the thin moonlight, the old man beside him.

"Choctaw blood?" the doctor asked.

"Some. She wanted me to find bonepickers, but few are left."

"There are two very old men from the Tallahaga Valley who

live near Boggy Depot. In three months' time, I will send them here." In the weak light, he studied the Indian's drawn face keenly. "You do not look well. Let us go to your cabin; I will examine you."

"When the end came," the Chickasaw said dully, "I knew the signs you told me to watch, and gave her the little pills. I do not think she felt death."

In the lamplight of the cabin, the Indian removed his shirt. The doctor examined him thoroughly. It was advanced tuberculosis—what laymen called galloping consumption.

"You must go back with me and stay in the hospital."

The old man nodded; then he seemed to think. "If I go, what will happen to the spring garden? We have always worked it together, but this year she cannot work it."

"Nor you," the doctor said, slipping the shirt over the skeletal shoulders.

"You will stay here tonight?"

"No, I must go on to the ranch. You must come with me to Round Fort, so gather what you need. Since you have no horse, take my extra one."

It was daybreak before the doctor saw a cabin off to the left, which he took to be Jack Leavitt's, and saw the friendly smoke rising from the bunkhouse chimney; after the long night ride, he would sell his soul for a cup of coffee.

"Where do I find Leavitt?" the doctor asked.

"In the little all-alone cabin," the Chickasaw said.

"He doesn't live in the new bunkhouse?"

"He says men who work all day don't like to stay with boss at night."

Dr. Dennis guided his horse to the cabin. "Haloa," he shouted. "Jack Leavitt! Awake in there?"

Leavitt appeared in the doorway, grinning and pulling his brush jacket on. "So you got my letter, but a day late. Sure, I'm awake. Let's go for the bunkhouse grub."

The bunkhouse, although new, was a typical cowhand hideout —bunks along the walls, each unkempt, a splattered deck of playing cards on a table in the center of the room, a buxom *Police Gazette* pinup in tights plastered beside a window, an overturned spittoon on the floor, a thousand cigarette butts, and rising and belly-scratching cowhands yawning and pulling their boots on.

Behind a partitioned section at the back reared a cook stove, a slender, clean-cut Mexican tending it.

"You look beat," Leavitt said. "There's my private table back here. Come sit and eat."

"Eighteen hours in the saddle," said the doctor.

Leavitt grinned. "It makes a man of you. Since you are a doctor, we don't have anything for you here but eighteen hydrophobia cowhands, one that stutters, one that's still hungover, so just shoot the pack and have it over."

When Leavitt reached the spittoon, he kicked it across the floor and stopped to face the cowhands. "I told you to keep this bunkhouse clean, and I mean it. I don't want you down with scabies or rot; the doctor won't give this free treatment forever. And wash your stinking socks and blankets." As he and the doctor sat with the Chickasaw, Leavitt called, "Aduna."

The Mexican cook came from behind the partition.

"Three big orders," Leavitt said, glancing at the thin bones of the Chickasaw. "Pancakes, maple syrup, bacon, and steaming coffee. A pot of coffee. A few cans of peaches."

When the cowhands had gone from their own table and they finished eating, the doctor said to Leavitt, "I think you're an honest man."

Leavitt leaned back in his chair and began on the makings. "Now what do you mean?"

"I read a letter of yours to Denna Cart. That is, I didn't read it, but my wife did, and told me about it."

Leavitt's lips were stern. "Denna Cart has had her fling—a few killings and holdups—and now she feels power. Remember what she is, born in tough Texas country, and wandering all alone in England. She's a loner now, for some pretended or imagined reason, and a mad one. She's buying influence in the councils. Two Creeks have been killed on Wild Horse within two months, and I'd swear they were killed by her gang—solitary, that is."

"Here's more," the doctor said, and told Leavitt all that Elfreda had told him of Denna's other activities. "How many cattle do you have?"

"We're running a thousand head, good stuff. They're safe. Aduna!" Leavitt called.

The Mexican came from the kitchen. "Sí, señor."

For the first time Dr. Dennis studied the cook. Along with Aduna's easy slimness, he was intelligent.

Leavitt was saying, "You used to work for old Abel Cart, C Bar, down Texas way, and you cooked for the Mason House in Abilene. And Denna Cart always had a fancy for you."

Aduna grinned. "Many women have had a fancy for me."

"Do you want to get your long throat cut?"

"It is a good throat, señor."

"Here's my proposition. I'll write the Mason House and say you want a job again. You will get a letter of acceptance; then you'll ride up by Round Fort. When you see the C Bar camp, pretend not to notice it. But they'll stop you for makings, or something else, to check you over."

"They could check me too well."

"Show the letter from the Mason House, and say you were going for the job. That will make you up and up. Because you are old C Bar, and with Denna's say-so, they'll keep you. I'll pay double salary."

"Above or below the grass?"

"Before your letter gets here, I'll give you the rundown, and what you will watch and listen for. Until we figure a better way of contact, tell Boyce Townley of the Boggy Depot store what you run into. Got it?"

"Sí."

Still without sleep, the hawk-faced doctor rode back to Round Fort with the old Chickasaw on fresh horses. Before leaving Wild Horse, he did take time to inspect the ranch and the corrals, so he could tell Dorch and Lucy about the progress made.

In the months which followed the Creek murders, Denna, through no wish of her own, had entered into a long period of introspection.

It was as if a thousand small voices beat at her ears, inquiring about the sudden surge of power she desired. Their persistence was such that she had begun to wonder.

Was it only revenge and vengeance for the doctor's death, or had this been only the means of opening a new world for her? Had there always been this latent sense within her, awaiting only the right moment to burst into being? Nor did she understand the sudden surges of passion which swept her.

Was she no longer her old self, but another, shoved and pushed along to some destiny, as if she were a different person? The small claws which raked her brain impelled her only to more violence, and why was it that she, who had scorned all men, held dear only a single hour beside a creek bank many years ago near Skullyville?

Only one man had broken her from her shell—Dorch McIntyre.

Yet in her new self she had turned to Kent, as she would in time turn to others, perhaps to Sardis Rippy.

Why did she do this?

Did the second self revel in power and debasement, more than the first had, even though the seeds had been there always?

In the valley one day, she had seen a strange Mexican working at the chuckwagon. Then she had called, "Aduna."

Slowly he turned toward her. "Miss Cart," he said.

"Why are you here?" she said. There was a strange beating in her heart.

"I was passing through to cook for the Mason House, but Señor Kent gave me a job."

"You haven't forgotten the old days at the C Bar?"

"Never, señorita. Sometimes I thought it was not wise for your father to put us so much together, even though I was your bodyguard." Aduna was emboldened by the warm look in Denna's eyes. "We had many good times then."

"Yes, but you stayed too much away from me. That is . . ." she began.

"It was my place to stay away," Aduna said. "We were both young then. You know very well what could have happened."

A flurry of girlhood thoughts came back. "Yes, but why did we get along so well?"

"That will be for you to decide."

"The night my father was delayed at the bank meeting, he had you take me home. You put my leg over the curved horn of the sidesaddle. Then you rode close, but were very silent."

"I was a Mexican, señorita, and still am."

"Yet if you had done only one little thing, the way I felt then, you might have changed my life. After that, it seemed nobody wanted me."

"But by morning I might have been hanged from a tree."

"Don't say that. But while you are here, come to the hill to visit me. You are always welcome in the round room. And while you are on the hill, see if you can learn anything, what the people there think of me."

"Gladly, señorita."

She had an insane desire to press close to him, but with the outlaws and Kent hunkered about the fire, she couldn't, but an old hunger gnawed at her heart.

Something, she thought—if it had only happened then.

Denna was agreeably surprised one afternoon to have a visit from David Willacy, the stocky little Englishman from Victory. She had, in fact, been reading one of her Lakeland books, and was thinking of the Cockleblooms, when a determined knock came on the door of the round room.

The spring weather was still cool, and there was a light fire beneath the huge chimney. She rose from the deep chair and went to the door. Opening it, she saw Willacy, dusty and heavily holstered.

"David Willacy!" she cried. "Come in. But why are you in this country? Sit down, and we will have tea."

Willacy said stiffly, "No, I do not have time for tea. Miss Cart, I am driving two herds to Kansas. I would like permission to cross your valley. What is your fee?"

"Fee?" said Denna, seating herself. "Why, no fee at all. You are welcome to cross."

Willacy still refused to seat himself. "While reconnoitering the valley, I found many of my cows and their increase there, dewlapped. Six hundred of my cows disappeared soon after you visited my home, and today they roam your valley with no riders to watch them. I am convinced, Miss Cart, that the purpose of your last visit two years ago was to gather cattle and outlaws."

Denna said haughtily, "If you accuse me of stealing your cows..."

"Let us say they are missing."

"Mr. Willacy, my father sold many cows to many people before you bought the ranch. A complete record of each sale is available in the courthouse. May I suggest that you check these records before making such accusations."

Even as she spoke, Denna realized her mistake. This determined and stuffy little man, immediately upon his return from Kansas, would go to the courthouse and search every available record.

One of Willacy's cowhands appeared in the doorway. The stocky rancher took this opportunity to ask again, "And you say, Miss Cart, that there will be no fee to take my cattle across your valley?"

He wants everything quite legal, Denna thought; he wants a witness to my statement. "There will be no fee. How could I ever charge an old friend for something so trivial?"

"Thank you, Miss Cart. And I hope to pay you in full for my ranch when I return."

Willacy and his cowhand mounted their horses and left. The visit had not been so agreeable after all.

Restlessly Denna paced the round room. Yes, she had made a slip, and it was not like her to do that. There would be no record in Victory of the sale of the valley cows to anyone. It would mean one thing—rustled stock. In her new position, she could never afford that accusation and its proof.

That night she rode to the valley and called Aduna from the fire.

"You have always liked me, Aduna. I have a favor to ask, but you shall have your reward."

Aduna's eyes were tightly masked, only the firelight revealing their glints. "Sí?"

"I want the courthouse at Victory burned—every plank, every paper, every document. I do not want one stick of the place left. And let the whole town burn," she had added, thinking of the desolate buildings which bordered the lip of the canyon.

"I have never burned," Aduna said. "But you promise me this reward?"

"Yes, on the night you return. And bring a dozen new men with you."

When Aduna had saddled and gone, Kent said, "What did you do to him?"

"I sent him to Texas for more men," Denna said lightly.

While young Dorch continued his studies at the academy, Denna Cart had become strangely exhilarated. Her court proceedings against the McIntyre estate were moving nicely, she was influential in the councils of two nations and in the judgments of the Fort Smith court, and she had recently had the pleasure of four dinner engagements at the Boggy Depot hotel with Sardis Rippy, the Department of the Interior man.

Her only worry was the action of Brian Doyle. With his eyes opened to the past, he was a worthy opponent; sometimes she wondered if she would ever beat him. His decision to take no more of her cases had held to one thing—sincerity or insincerity.

He could only contrast the sincerity of the dead doctor and Anthony Dennis with the insincere opportunism of Denna.

"I hate to throw her over," he told Anthracite one night before the fireplace. "At one time she meant a great deal to us."

"Darling," fragile Anthracite said, cuddling in his lap, "long ago we repaid the money she lent us. You made the only possible choice."

Brian chuckled. "Seven kids for a thousand dollars. That figures a little over one hundred forty-two dollars and eighty-five cents per child—provided you are through. Are you?"

Anthracite kissed his cheek. "That depends on my husband. But I've thought lately that even at Lady Burroughs' Denna lent us the money only to show her superiority."

Denna's methods with the council members of two nations had been equally devious; her money and figure had brought power.

Yet, in spite of her continuing engagements with Sardis Rippy, it could honestly be said that she hated him for himself alone. She had hated him instinctively from the moment he had stepped aboard the *Maizie Trout* at Napoleon, he and his broad forehead and excessively long sideburns and sloping shoulders. He was built like a wedge, if one could call a man that small a wedge.

In the years when she had met him in and out of the courts and the hospital, she had never trusted his narrow black eyes; they were direct, but with a half-concealed cunning behind them. She would never forget the quickness with which he and his marshal and Tyson Pennypacker had run to the court proceedings at Fort Smith when the *Maizie Trout* pulled up to the landing.

She had once respected the marshal, Flint Murcheson, marveling at his quietly observant eyes. Yet throughout the long years she had rarely heard him speak. As she came to know him, his eyes conveyed only stupidity, looking as a child's might upon some incomprehensible object, something without meaning, and only as an object. His silence, too, had become obvious—he simply had nothing to say. Behind his badge, he was only a protective backdrop for Rippy.

For her dinner engagement tonight she had dressed carefully, her shoulders bare, as usual, something which always caused comment at the hotel.

Rippy and Mucheson had been riding the eastern hills today; the appointment had been for seven. She had ridden into town, a loose wrap about her shoulders, and had reserved a room at the hotel.

A curly-haired Mexican lad took her horse at the hitchrack. "Señorita, may I guard your horse?" She slid from the saddle and stood beside him.

"Chico, you always guard my horse." She handed the boy a coin. "There will be more later."

"Then I will bring the horse oats and rub him down. But I will not give him oats too soon, or much water at first."

Denna always paid Chico and other urchins well; she never knew when they might be of greater service, although they themselves might not suspect the nature of it.

Seated now in the dining room with Sardis Rippy, glancing distastefully at the cheap tablecloth on their table, she thought of the ornateness she had once shared with Dorch at the Le Flore in Fort Smith. She also thought, watching Rippy's narrow and excited eyes, if this is a game, my little friend, it is being played two ways.

She hated him for the part he had played in the execution of Dorch McIntyre, hounding him to self-destruction, and still annoying the hospital after all the years, his always secretive investigations in the hills and valleys and his court appearances.

"This subject of narcotics," Rippy said over his duck, "it interests me."

"Why?" asked Denna, cutting a canned pear with her fork.

"Three things are on my mind," Rippy said. "On my first investigation, there was the amputee Dr. Dennis' wife injected. When we questioned her, she drank the drug in the vial, claiming it was only a saline solution. Then there were the times when Dr. McIntyre's narcotics were stolen. Now I have learned through investigation near Wild Horse Prairie that Dr. Dennis himself left drugs with an old Chickasaw to give to his wife. As a result, she died from them. Unfortunately, the old man died of tuberculosis, so he cannot be questioned."

"Yes, he died last week in the hospital."

"I know," said Rippy, almost distracted by Denna's shoulders. "Such things hinder investigations."

Denna leaned across the table. "You do try hard, don't you?"

"Yes. Are we finished?" he said, rising to hold her chair. "My marshal is not at home tonight. Shall we go by for a nightcap? Then I will see you to Round Fort."

He thought, she might at least let me kiss her on the way along Clear Boggy.

Denna laughed softly. She pressed his arm. "Why go to Round Fort at all? Suppose we go to your house?"

It would be like going to bed with a frantic little monkey, but it didn't matter.

Over many months Aduna had made constant appearances at Round Fort. This had been a plan on the part of Kent and Denna to have Aduna gather what information he could, and to know if the activity in the valley was suspect.

Today he rode up the hill to borrow a can of coffee.

When the almost languid Mexican was seated in Dr. Dennis' office, the physician asked, "Well, what is up now?" He sometimes wondered at the attachment which seemed to exist between Denna and Aduna, but nothing had happened to make him suspect Aduna of disloyalty.

The Mexican said, "I have given Señor Townley much information, and it has begun to interfere with their plans. Within a month, two raids have gone wrong. They think someone must be watching from the hill; I am to find out."

"Only Timothy watches, but the credit goes to you. You still have not been on any of their raids?"

"No. A cook is always needed to feed those who are left behind, and the others when they come back."

"And by now you know they did kill the old Creek councilman?"

"Sí. Kent fired the shot."

"Two Choctaws who worked at the ranch were killed."

"Yes. They were hauling logs from the hills. Now, here is what I must tell you. Next week there will be a shipment of gold from the Creeks to settle a loan from the Chickasaws. They have agreed to meet in Boggy Depot. The Creeks think they are very smart. Since there have been many train robberies lately, they will send the gold down the Texas Road by ordinary stage."

"Will the stage even arrive at Boggy Depot?"

Aduna laughed. "That stage? It will never arrive."

"Where did the gang get this information?"

"From the woman of the north."

"Belle Starr?"

"Yes, and she obtained it from one high in the Creek nation."

"If you learn more, let Townley or me know."

"Until the robbery is over, I cannot see you again. It would be too risky."

"I agree," said the doctor. "But for what good it will do, I will get this information to the council and the lighthorse, yet action with some comes very slow now. Well, pick up your coffee at the commissary, and talk with the schoolchildren and the men at the stables. Stay as long as you wish—they may have a glass on you. I suppose they think you are safe because of Denna."

"Sí. Kent said she would release me." There was a flicker of something unreadable in Aduna's eyes.

When the Mexican left the office, the doctor walked to the window. He looked down at the camp in the valley. Unmitigated gall, he thought, and Denna here in the round room, using this means to learn if she was suspect.

But the stage robbery.

The doctor turned from the window and walked to the far side of the office, where even a glass trained upon him from the valley could not probe his thoughts. He had determined upon his course of action, or inaction. In some way, this thing of constant warfare must end.

In his business, death was death; let it happen. Let the stage be robbed, let the driver and shotgun riders and even passengers be killed. He knew that in time these would be hailed as honored dead, as Dorch McIntyre was honored, that this robbery must occur to provoke wrath against a greater evil.

And thinking of the doctor again made him think of Elfreda. He had always known that Dorch had loved her, and she him, although nothing had passed between them.

He could still remember Elfreda's doubting eyes, troubled eyes, when he proposed to her, yet no woman could have been a better wife. But in the last months Elfreda had almost broken, although still doing her work in the hospital and caring for Lucy and the three boys.

But the fear she felt for the future of young Dorch would not leave her, or the threat of harm to Lucy. "Anthony," she would say in their rooms in their cramped apartment at night, "we must keep Dorch. He is like my own, like one of ours, and he must have Lucy. Since Timothy gave him his father's pistol, he is like an old man and needs her. What will he do with the pistol? He is old enough to use it. Would it be against Cyrus Wano?"

"We don't know, dear," the doctor said, patting her hand. Then he would go down the corridor to check the hospital.

No, he thought, as he paced his office, let the stage be robbed. Let the Creek gold be taken. The robbery will do more good than I can by informing. A strange lethargy has crept among certain members of the councils, and among the lighthorse; if I spoke, these outlaws would be informed, and desist. Let the stage be robbed. It will create action, anything on earth to stop this menace. If to accomplish this, people have to die, as we all do, they must die.

Denna sat at the table in the Boggy Depot dining room.

"Did you know," she asked Sardis Rippy, "that the North Fork Town stage has been robbed? Somebody took the Creek gold payment being sent to the Chickasaws."

"I heard of it," said Rippy, thinking already of another night with Denna, provided he could get the marshal out of the house. If not, he wondered if there could be a good throw in the grass when he took Denna back to Round Fort.

"I have heard that Belle Starr did it," Denna said, wearing a new evening dress tonight.

"It would not be surprising," Rippy said. "Belle Starr is a wicked woman."

"Wicked?" Denna laughed. "Shall we go?"

When they reached the house, the bulky marshal was curled in his chair, snoring.

They had barely had a drink in the kitchen before Rippy said, "I suppose I must take you home now."

Denna's eyes twinkled. "Really? But it is so soon."

On their way back to the fort, he shoved their horses into the trees.

"Do you mind?" he asked timidly.

Denna laughed. "No," she said.

Old Belle had been right.

The old Choctaw bonepickers of the Tallahaga Valley, Dead Man Joiner and Chimney Katchee, were in consultation in their cabin on Clear Boggy Creek.

"There is not much left for us now," said Dead Man one night, sitting on the floor before the empty fireplace and looking at his taloned nails. "Most of the Choctaws have taken to the white man's way and wish to be buried."

Dead Man held his fingers before his eyes to see how long his thick nails had grown. If he and Chimney Katchee went to Wild Horse Prairie to strip the old dead woman on her platform, his nails would have to be longer and sharper.

Chimney Katchee said, sitting beside Dead Man, his lank rib bones showing, "It will never be like stripping Chief Chilly Black. Even though he had been rotten for months, he had the toughest meat I ever worked on. We could tear it out only in thin shreds, and even then it was almost impossible to get it off the bones. Molly, his wife, was easy."

Dead Man Joiner rose and waddled in his shirt and breechclout toward a lantern which hung by a wire from the ceiling. He held his fingers up to the light. "It is a pity the old man died. He would be pleased we make our trip."

Chimney Katchee rose and followed Dead Man, also holding his fingers high. "Everything has changed now," he said, "even at the schools we have. Once, if a boy misbehaved, he was lashed. If he misbehaved a second time, he was given a hundred lashes. On the third offense, he was lashed to death."

"Yes, there has been change," Dead Man said. "The Tallahaga Valley is no more."

"When will you sharpen your nails?" said Chimney Katchee.

"On the day before we leave for Wild Horse," said Dead Man.

2

Anthony Dennis was correct in believing that the stage robbery would produce action.

A delegation of Creeks appeared before Albert McIntosh, making it clear, however, that neither the Chickasaw nor Choctaw nation was suspect, but wanting most of all assurance that those implicated would be found and punished. The monetary loan must also be extended for a year; the gold coin sent on the stage could not be immediately replaced.

To these things the Chickasaw and Choctaw councils agreed, even adding that a detachment of Creek lighthorse would be welcome to assist in the investigation.

When she heard of these agreements, Denna Cart laughed. No one but she knew the real purpose of the theft, or where the gold rested, except Aduna and Kent. Almost the final step in one plan of vengeance was complete.

As she rode down the trail from Round Fort to Boggy Depot, Denna thought of the doctor as she had known him so many years ago. What had it been, what sudden fancy had come to make her love him so? How had she taken him so completely for her own? Today the promise she made at his coffin in North Fork Town would be kept again.

Yet there had been one other thing, even before her meeting with the doctor, and that had been the persistence which Sardis Rippy and his marshal had shown in their constant struggle for advancement; Rippy would use any means to achieve his ambition. Now, in her, he had met his match.

As Denna gave the horse its head down the leafy trail, at last passing the old graveyard just out of town, the image of the doctor faded, and all her past life vanished, the life she had wanted then, and in its place stood the life she lived now.

Excitement, her own will!

Once within town, Denna turned into the street which ran from the livery stable to the Townley store. Now she must be doubly vigilant; the success or failure of an entire plan must come with the first opportunity which presented itself. She did not know what the opportunity would be—it could be one thing, or another.

Before she neared the green house of Sardis Rippy and the marshal, she noticed a number of young girls playing skiprope farther down the road. Also, a group of mixed-breed boys had drawn a ring in the dust and had set up their taws for a marble game.

Denna swung her horse to Sardis Rippy's side of the street; she slowed, and seeing curly-haired Chico moving in her direction, his head down, his eyes on his bare feet, her right hand moved quickly, and her thumbnail and forefinger flipped what appeared to be a gold coin into Rippy's yard, where it fell near a lilac bush.

She flipped several more coins, then swung to the middle of the road again, continuing to drop gold pieces. She was glad Chico came nearer; she knew him better than she did the other children.

When he was almost at the horse, she cried, "Chico, look almost before your feet. It is a gold coin in the road!"

The curly-haired boy looked up. He had been playing what he called his heel game, moving at a shuffling gait, dragging one heel behind the other in the dusty road, leaving a trail of two heels, like the paths of large snakes. Surprise on his face, Chico's eyes followed Denna's pointed finger.

"Sí," he shrieked, leaping forward. "It is a gold piece, señorita." He reached and picked it up. Then he cried again, "And another one!"

Denna turned the horse, following him back down the road. "You have found two gold pieces, Chico?"

"Three now," Chico shouted, following the golden trail like a spaniel, "and four!"

Now Chico held six gold pieces in his hand; he followed the glinting trail across Rippy's yard to the lilac bush.

Then he ran back to Denna. "Señorita, I think much gold is hidden under the lilac bush. A hole was there, but covered up, with a gold piece on top of it."

"Do you think," Denna asked, "that it could be the gold stolen from the Creek stage?"

Chico's black eyes looked up at Denna fearfully, then with confidence. "Sí, that must be it. It is the Creek gold. But I am innocent."

"Is the Creek delegation still meeting with the Choctaws and Chickasaws?"

"Sí, and Madre de Dios, I could not keep stolen money, señorita."

"Then run to the hotel and tell the councils what you have found. Perhaps they will reward you. If they doubt your word, I will be at Townley's store."

Chico ran toward the hotel, calling to the other children as he ran, "The Creek gold—I have found the Creek gold!"

Denna was selecting a pattern for a new dress when two lighthorse captains, Dade Rothney and Duane Vann, in his red jacket, entered the store.

Denna turned from the counter. "Captain Vann," she said, "and Captain Rothney."

The Creek bowed slightly. "Miss Cart," he said.

Denna turned over a bolt of print material on the counter.

"A Mexican boy . . ." Dade Rothney began.

"Yes, I know him. Chico—he always looks after my horse. Is it about the gold he found? I told him I would bear out his story."

"Then you did see what happened?"

"Yes. But please, not now. You know how it is when a woman picks out a dress."

"Of course. We will wait."

From the direction of the hotel, Denna heard a sudden shouting; she turned and saw other lighthorse and citizens moving toward Rippy's house. The council members followed with shovels, along with more whites and Indians.

When the bulk of the stolen gold had been removed from beneath the lilac bush, the councils reconvened. Denna had been seated in the lobby of the hotel, the bolt of cloth beside her. The council sat at a very large table in the dining room. Tiger Panton came to her and asked, "Will you testify before the combined councils?"

"Of course, Captain. Yes," she told the members. "Chico's story is true. As I rode into town I saw the children playing, and then I saw the first gold coin in the dust. I called Chico's attention to it, and he followed the trail back and told me about the lilac bush."

That afternoon when Sardis Rippy and Flint Murcheson returned from their sleuthing in the valleys, they were arrested by the three lighthorse captains for the holdup of the Creek stagecoach.

Within two days Sardis Rippy sent to Round Fort for Denna. She was shown to his cell in the stone jail, and stared at him through the bars. He was a miserable little wedge of masculinity now, his cocksureness gone.

He said pleadingly, "Why did you do this to me?"

"Because while you have pretended to check on the hospital, you have also checked on me. When you asked me to dinner at the hotel, you thought me quite blind, didn't you? I have always hated you, but never so much as now."

He said, almost rising on his toes, "I don't think you can get away with it."

"What do I have to prove? It is your defense."

"You, with Belle Starr, robbed the stage before I had dinner with you that night. I know Belle was in the country, because people saw her. You had someone bury the treasure in my yard while I was taking you home."

Denna asked, her eyes merry, "Would you say that to a court of justice, when at the time we were both together in the bushes? Remember, you shoved me off the road. What would that testimony do to a government servant?"

"I have underestimated you."

Denna said, "Where were you the afternoon of the robbery? Three people were killed, and you were seen with your marshal and three other men and a woman within a mile of the attack."

"It was an old woman and her grown sons from Texas. They were going back north on a visit and wanted to know where the old water stand used to be. I tried to show them."

"Belle said that you have had her before the Indian commissioner several times. That, too, was political, for your own advancement."

Rippy placed his hands about the cold bars, his face peering between them.

He spat in her face. "Why I never saw through you!"

Denna laughed, touching her face with a handkerchief. "Little monkey, you have given me great amusement. Now you can hang, or go to a federal penitentiary."

Still laughing, she turned and walked down the corridor.

But the complications of the great stage robbery were not yet over. Things were exactly as Dr. Dennis had thought they would be.

This morning Aduna had ridden up the hill again. "Have you learned when the Creeks will go back from the council meeting?" he asked the doctor.

"I think," the doctor said, hawking about his office, "that it is tomorrow, but it is not known yet."

"They will go back tomorrow night, and by stage again."

"Why do they fear the railroad?"

"They think if gunmen are in the cars, they would have no safety."

"What safety have they on a stage? They have just had the experience with one."

"This time there will be an escort of the lighthorse of three nations."

"How do you know this?"

"Kent has learned it, and Denna too, from certain council members, and others in high places. We talk these things over in camp, when we make our plans."

"When will Rippy and the marshal be taken away?"

"When the next prison wagon from Fort Smith comes through."

"Denna's trick on Rippy was a masterpiece. I have noticed many more outlaws in the valley today."

"They are for the plans of tomorrow night."

"You don't know the plans?"

"The women decide tonight."

"What women?"

"Denna and Belle Starr. Belle camps in the trees."

"My God," said Anthony. He paused, then said, "So the worst of this trouble should soon be over. You've already had too much luck at your job. Why don't you leave now for Wild Horse Prairie?"

Aduna shook his head. "No. If they missed me for only an hour, they would pursue me. The same orders go for everyone. If I leave, it would be better to go tomorrow night, when many of us will scatter. Kent has already told us to disappear then."

When Aduna left, the doctor stepped to the window and gazed into the valley. He stood pondering, then returned to his old decision. No, he would still do nothing. To reveal this new knowledge would, for the long pull, solve nothing.

If the lighthorse of three nations were to accompany the stage, enough was already known, and his few words would not matter, only for the timing. With Dorch McIntyre buried on the hill, he would wait and see this tragic comedy played out to its bitter end.

With all the new riders appearing in the valley, and with Belle Starr camping in the trees, the doctor could see only that this was the final showdown resulting from the execution of Dorch McIntyre.

On the morning when Aduna had appeared on the hill, Timothy had worried at the sight of the new riders who had come to the valley.

Hidden in his clump of cedars on the opposite side of the hill, his elbows raw from holding the brass telescope before him, he continued to spy out the outlaw camp. He glanced up at the sun. It was still early.

The bulk of the riders had come in after sunup, singly or in pairs. After reporting to the chuckwagon, they had dispersed to the trees, leaving a watcher at the edge of the timber to report any signal from the wagon. Even now Timothy could see them, some hunkering about small fires, others still sitting their horses.

Something is going to happen, Timothy thought. There's that woman again. While he watched, he began to whistle his thin little tune. I guess my hump has been sticking up like one of the Alps, he said to himself. I hope they haven't spotted it.

He had been worried this morning, and he had worried all night. But last night he had worried about the telescope, and not what he saw now. Sometimes Lucy watched with him in the cedars, or at other times alone. But if some sharp-eyed little Indian saw them, there would be a yell, and every boy in the school would want to look through the telescope.

Timothy didn't trust his girl students, either. They wouldn't be as loud as the boys, but they might talk even more. Last night, drinking his coffee beside his stove, he had said to his imaginary pupils, "Don't tell anyone about my telescope. If you mention it at home or to some stranger on the road, it could put me in trouble with the outlaws in the valley. You wouldn't want Old Timothy strung up, would you?"

Now, with his elbows aching still more from holding his weight and the outstretched glass for so long, his mind took on a third worry—young Dorch.

The gathering of the outlaws in the valley had brought all his other worries about the boy to a head. If Denna was successful in what she planned—and it would be something big—she would then be free to devote all her time to Dorch. Timothy had wondered why she had even let the boy spend two years at the academy and then return this term. Perhaps Denna had too many irons in the fire to decide Dorch's future immediately, other than the action she had started to control his property as guardian. With her time devoted to her son, her power over him would be complete.

Through the telescope, Timothy saw Aduna ride up the hill and go to the hospital. He came to decision; it was still early; if he left for the academy now, he should be there by noon. No need even to tell Dr. Dennis about the gathering in the valley; he may have seen it himself, but certainly he would learn of it from Aduna.

Timothy collapsed his scope, stuck it in his inside coat pocket, then walked to the corral. If he made good time through the hills, he might even eat lunch with the academy boys and get Dorch off for a talk to warn him of what appeared to be shaping up.

When he was mounted, he guided the horse around the hill to the road which came down from Round Fort, rather than be seen on the side of the hill next to the valley, although that way would have been shorter.

With all that's in the woods today, he thought, no use to show my hand all at once. I won't meet one of those gentlemen or ladies until I have to.

Timothy fixed his rifle in a pommel sling for quick readiness, the way Texas cowhands had showed him, and kept the right tail of his long coat clear of his holstered pistol butt.

He grinned as he crossed the creek. Ready for bear—provided they don't see my hump first.

At his first sight of the stone academy building, he looked at his gold watch. "Twelve o'clock on the dot, and came at a good trot all the way."

That afternoon he and Dorch sat on the stone wall which surrounded the building. "You must be a good student," Timothy said. "You look bleary-eyed today."

"It's that animal-husbandry teacher," Dorch said. "He's an amateur astronomer, and if you get caught with him about sundown, you don't get away before sunup. I can't complain, though. I know the name of every star in the sky. It will help my business."

Timothy said brutally, "What business?"

Dorch said surprised, "Why, my cow business, and Wild Horse ranch."

Timothy said, "In a few days, the biggest bolt of lightning since the flood is going to hit this country. That's what I'm here to tell you. And when it's over, judging by the number of outlaws in the valley, Denna Cart will have enough power to put Belle Starr to shame. She'll get her way in the courts, in spite of all Brian Doyle does, and when she does that, you won't have a ranch, you won't have property, and you won't have Lucy."

"But it's not right."

"As your guardian, Denna will control everything your father left you. You're about grown, but not of age; when a lick comes, you've got to take it."

"I don't know what to do. But you'd back me, wouldn't you?"

"Yes, I'll back you. That's what I'm doing now, telling you what the next few days could bring. Don't get out of this building. With as many men as Denna has in the valley, you—or even Lucy—could be kidnapped and hidden in Texas until you agree to what Denna wants. That would mean going East to school and giving up Lucy."

"I'll never give up Lucy."

"When pressure is put on her and Elfreda, you might change your mind."

"Never. This trouble you look for—when will it come?"

"Any day or night from now on, and I'll bet a bale of shinplasters it's against the Creeks—still from that old feud about your father."

Dorch said, "Why can't that die?"

"Because people aren't meant to let it die." Timothy glanced down at the ground. "Why don't you do something with these fornicating horned toads? Hasn't that amateur astronomer figured out a more productive use for them?"

Dorch laughed shortly. "Maybe he's trying."

"Elfreda told me the government has asked Dr. Dennis to open a small hospital up on the Sioux reservation. It would be a log house to begin with, but the doctor's not sure of going yet."

"It looks like everything is going," Dorch said. "Elfreda is my real mother. I've never been away from her, except here. There may be peace for my father, but it may be best that Lucy and I go somewhere else and that the doctor and Elfreda go to the Sioux. There will be no peace here, not with Denna."

Timothy drew a battered letter from his coat. "This is your father's last letter to me, a gentleman's gentleman." He handed it to Dorch to read. "I did not want to trouble you so soon, but if ever there was a time to become your gentleman and serve you, it is now. Could you let it be that way?"

Dorch read the letter and said, "I will do what you say. From now on, you are my gentleman."

"Then, thank you, sir. I am very happy." The hunchback hopped as nimbly as a cricket from the wall and said, hearing an old shoeshine rag on Canal Street go slappity-slap, "My first duty is to remind you again that you are not to leave the academy, even on short hunting trips with the boys. You will not come to Round Fort unless I have arranged an escort for you. And from now on, avoid Denna as you would a rattlesnake."

Timothy went to his horse.

"Are you leaving now?" Dorch asked, following him.

"Yes." Timothy grinned. "I want to be back by four o'clock. When school is out, I always watch your Lucy for you."

Timothy climbed back into the saddle and rode toward Round Fort.

When Denna left Round Fort next morning to make a surprise visit to Dorch at the academy, she was well satisfied with herself.

So far, everything had gone perfectly. She had done it all so cleverly, and now Belle, hidden in the creek trees, would repay her trapping of Sardis Rippy by aiding in an ambush of the Creek delegation. Not the entire delegation, necessarily, but one man especially among it.

She wore a brown slouch hat and a dark-tan riding habit—one which could not be easily seen at night. To all appearances she was a woman off on a holiday.

Her pistols were carried in her saddle pockets, with the exception of the little derringer concealed on her person.

But it was odd how stupid the Creeks and Chickasaws and Choctaws were—they could have hired an entire passenger car on the Katy line, one to hold all the lighthorse needed, and have been reasonably sure of reaching their destination, rather than attempt the ludicrous plan they had evolved.

As Denna rode through the widening valley, the rectangular academy bulking in the distance, the low hills reminded her of the Lake District and the moors she had known so well. She thought of Gaits Water, both here and in England.

She thought of another thing—this foolishness between Lucy and Dorch. She should have stopped it long before now. Well, she would stop it, and today.

Before the night was over, her son would have an entirely new opinion of her. That would be good, for Dorch would know that she could be strong and that her strength meant his acquiescence.

When Dorch was called from the academy by a student she saw in the yard, she was surprised to notice the somber change which had come over him since her last visit.

"Come," she said. "Get a horse. We'll go for a ride."

It was early; he had just finished breakfast. She must have been up long before daybreak to have arrived at this hour. Standing lean and straight on the broad stone steps, he stared steadily down at her. His expression was one of mingled curiosity and wariness. "But I was out with Timothy yesterday. I can't take too many days off."

"Your mother has rights too. I told the boy to say that we had business to discuss. Now, get your rifle and the pistol the Choctaw nation gave your father. As we ride, we may get game for the academy."

It was the first time she had ever mentioned the pistol, although she had felt that only Timothy could have taken it from the secretary.

Dorch returned from his room holstered, with his rifle and crushed hat and jacket under his arm. Yesterday he had been with Timothy—was something like this what the hunchback had warned him about? He still did not trust his mother; he felt that her overture of finding game for the school had been made simply to disarm him.

He pulled his hat over his bushy hair and went to the stables. He thought it was wrong to leave the grounds after his promise to Timothy, but he would be doubly careful. When he returned riding a horse from the stables, he bent from it to pick up the rifle and jacket he had left on the steps.

"Are you ready?" she asked. Denna had suddenly become austere and distant. She said, as if shifting her mind from one thing to another, "We'll go toward Muddy Boggy today." The horses began their steady jog.

"But deer are better to the west," he said as they rode into the trees.

Denna was already incensed with Dorch, but without knowing why. Then suddenly she knew the cause of her irritation. She rode a good horse, the best in stamina, but Dorch's horse was over a hand taller than hers. When she spoke to Dorch, she was in the position of having to look up at the tall stripling on even a taller horse. No longer did she have her feeling of superiority. It was lost in humiliation of being physically lower than he.

How she hated that dark face that never looked at her!

Dorch did not know that Denna meant to lead him carefully over a trail she had selected with Belle Starr and her outlaws. Trotting their horses, they crossed Clear Boggy, the water low.

Denna asked, "What did Timothy talk about yesterday? He was building his fires in the school when I left, so we didn't speak."

Dorch was relieved. He had feared some of the outlaws might have seen Timothy, or even shot him. If she tells the truth, he thought, Timothy is still alive. He glanced toward Denna. There was no veiling in her eyes; she returned his glance steadily.

Since she knows Timothy was here, Dorch thought, I'll have to talk about something. He tried to pass the matter off lightly, laughing and saying, "Timothy talked about becoming my gentleman."

Her voice was harsh. "No, that hunchback will never become your gentleman. And I must tell you that Lucy will never become your wife. I have greater plans for you."

"Lucy is what I want. We have been together for so long."

"That is exactly why you should not marry her. Forget Lucy." She snapped her fingers impatiently, as if the separation could be accomplished that quickly.

"You know I couldn't forget Lucy—leave her the way you want me to. Aren't we riding pretty far?"

"I want to ride far, and let's not argue about Lucy." She added tightly, "I have told you my decision." Still the horses trotted on. She watched Dorch's dark face harden.

"And I have told you mine."

Infuriated, she cut her quirt across his chest.

A voice said, "He is too nice a one to hurt."

Too late Dorch realized he should not have disobeyed Timothy, that he should have remained at the academy.

Belle Starr, dusty and dirty, one side of her jaw hanging heavier than the other from a hornet sting, and followed by a dozen outlaws, rode from a copse.

Dorch stared at his mother in disbelief, not because of the blow she had struck, but how she had lured him.

He was to be some part of a raid, what part he didn't know, but there was no doubt in his mind, especially when he saw the mustached Kent and his band of outlaws ride toward them from the opposite side of the trail. By Kent's satisfied expression Dorch knew that he had helped plan the scheme with Denna and Belle.

He was, as the two women put their heads together and rode slowly onward toward the Texas Road, no more than a prisoner of the dust-streaked men of each side who surrounded him.

In the early afternoon of the day when the Creeks were to leave for North Fork Town, the delegates, together with those of the two tribes, rode for privacy and instruction with their respective lighthorse to an open prairie a mile from town. Its only growth was a stand of vertical persimmon trees in its center.

Ringed by the delegates and lighthorse, Albert McIntosh spoke. Even as he began, an old and small Creek, Cyrus Wano, had trouble holding his horse steady, but finally got it under control. He backed it into his place in the circle.

Albert McIntosh said, "Gentlemen, we have met in privacy to discuss our last difficulty, that of seeing the Creek delegation safely home. But one or more of you, gentlemen, have been bribed. Be it a curse to the nations which bear these men, for all our discussions have gone to ears elsewhere.

"But this we have planned for the Creek departure. Since you wish to go by stage, it shall be a special one, driven by our own lighthorse. We will also supply a mounted escort, and you have yours."

Captain Duane Vann rode his horse into the circle. "I do not like it," he said. "We Creeks are still in a trap. We will not get out alive."

Albert McIntosh said coldly, "How do you know this?"

"It is something I feel."

"But since your own delegates wish it, we must accommodate them."

The principal chief then outlined his plan. Later in the afternoon, a portion of the Chickasaw and Choctaw lighthorse would go outside of town singly for the purpose of watching the Texas Road from the brush.

Others, including the Creeks, would be the escort for the stage, which would be made up behind Townley's store, but with only two or three Creeks stepping aboard. As the stage progressed through the town to the Texas Road, other delegates would come from certain houses; the last, Cyrus Wano, would come from the last house at the edge of town.

Meanwhile, as the stage rolled on up the Texas Road, the unobtrusive lighthorse hidden in the timber would appear and form before and behind it. The only possible early ambush would be at the new bridge on Muddy Boggy, but other lighthorse had already sent word to Clear Boggy that the region appeared safe.

From the bridge onward, all lighthorse would converge upon the stage as escort. This veritable company of men would accompany it to North Fork Town.

At the conclusion of Albert McIntosh's remarks, Captain Duane Vann of the Creek lighthorse turned his horse toward his men. A very good plan, if he could believe it.

But if . . . But if . . .

3

When the Creek stage left the last house in Boggy Depot, Captain Tiger Panton of the Chickasaws fell in with his Creek counterpart. They preceded the stage, riding side by side.

The red-jacketed Creek captain said, "The sun will sink red today."

Tiger Panton looked at Duane Vann in surprise. "You feel it too?" He had not taken Vann's riding his horse into the circle about the persimmon trees seriously, thinking it was only the matter of procedure he had objected to.

Vann said, "I see no way out."

Panton grunted. "It will not happen today. It will come after dark."

Vann said, "As long as you agree it will happen, we will not argue when."

Panton had a long upper lip; it seemed to add another dimension to his face. He glanced back over his shoulder; two Chickasaws rode shotgun in the seat beside the stage driver. He and the other captains had gone over their plan completely. They had arranged for changes of horses along the way, and tomorrow as the stage neared the Creek lands, Creek lighthorse would be in the driver's seat, men familiar with that portion of the Texas Road, knowing the sites of possible ambush as the Chickasaws and Choctaws knew those at this end.

Again fixing his dark eyes on the wide and rutted road, Panton brooded.

How he hated the gift of prophecy and the old Choctaw woman

who had cursed him with it. His lighthorse always laughed and said that when Panton was under its spell, he was as crazy as the old woman. He was laughed at good-humoredly, of course, but still laughed at.

Sometimes he was feared by the purebloods in the hills and valleys, those who believed him to be in league with some woodland witch, all because of the touching.

The old woman was one who had accepted Christianity from a mission preacher. In her fits, writhing and twisting on the floor, she had shrieked weird incantations or put curses on unbelievers. The mission preacher had not intended her to go this far.

He did not know that she had been demented long before she had embraced his creed, and in her native religion had employed the same incantations and curses she now used.

Once she had predicted a flood; next day it came. The village and its church had been swept away; she had been executed by strangulation and left unburied.

Panton could feel the old woman's cold hand on his forehead.

"You will know all that will happen," she said, "and you will predict your own death."

"Will the stage be lighted as usual?" Panton asked Vann.

"Yes, they want it to appear to be a normal affair."

Panton had achieved the gift of prophecy. He attributed this to two things. He was always certain to think each new matter out completely, and being by nature one who brooded, he worried at his conclusions, things other people would never consider. Often, a few days after he said a certain thing would happen, it did. But he always thought, all the signs were there—anyone should have known it.

"I was surprised that Cyrus Wano would accept the stage," Vann said, drawing a package of Turkish cigarettes from his red jacket. "Smoke?"

"Thanks. Wano—you mean the old man who couldn't hold his horse steady this afternoon? At the council near the persimmon trees, I mean."

"He is hated even by many Creeks," Duane Vann said.

"Della Wano. It happened a long time ago, didn't it?"

"It's not dead yet," Vann said. "It's living now and tonight, on this very road. Wano was a strong chief, but he lived only for hatred."

They reached a swath of prairie which spread on either side of the road. Vann looked westward and said, "Sun's down. Only the red rim left on top."

He and Tiger Panton had ridden farther ahead of the stage, allowing for the formation of the other lighthorse who had come from the trees. Panton turned his horse back down the long line to talk with Dade Rothney, the Choctaw captain who brought up the rear. It was a fine group of men—the pick of three nations.

Some wore sashes; from the gear of others, fox tails or other ornaments dangled; they were armed with knives and pistols and rifles. As Panton returned to the head of the line, the stage stopped and the shotgun lighthorse lighted the lamps.

Now Panton's worried eyes took in the length of the road again.

Riding beside the red-jacketed Duane Vann, he inhaled deeply on the cigarette once, then twice.

He knew it was the last good smoke he would have on this earth. They could laugh at him later.

As twilight fell, Belle Starr rose from the ground and beat invisible dust from her skirt.

Beside her, Denna rose.

Dorch stood against a tree, his thumbs in his gunbelt. His rifle had been taken from him.

At the same moment, several miles away, the stage had stopped on the road for its lamps to be lighted.

Belle said, her face gaunt and her eyes shadowy, "Our other men are already across the road, so we will take our places on this side. I will cross the road and join the others, who wait at the bridge. You," she said to Kent, who stood smirking, "will have the place of honor with Denna, opposite me at the bridge. Those who have already been placed to attack will strike, then scatter for a few months east or west to Arkansas or to the Arbuckles."

A lewdness crept into her voice. "Take care of him," she said to Denna, looking at Dorch.

Belle mounted her horse to cross the road, some twenty riders following. "In a month, come up to the Bend," she told Denna.

Kent put his arm about Denna, then helped her to her saddle.

Cyrus Wano jolted along in a lonely corner of the stage. He was an old man, tired, with nothing to live for. Everything had left him; even his wife was dead.

He sat next to a window; while he thought of the past, he could see the shadows of bordering trees along the road, or sometimes the lantern of a covered wagon headed south. Perhaps, he thought, in some small way I have helped avert a war among our three nations because of the gold robbery.

It had taken Cyrus Wano many years to reach this inward peace. Once vengeance had gnawed into him, eating him like a cancer, but the old life he had known was dead now.

"Cyrus Wano," a voice said beside him, "do you have tobacco?"

"Yes," Wano said, reaching into his pocket and passing the pouch to his side.

Wano's single word evoked laughter within the coach.

"Wano is thinking of angels tonight," a Creek said from the opposite side of the coach. "He has not spoken a word since leaving Boggy Depot."

Yes, I am thinking of angels tonight, Wano thought. He had seen the two lighthorse captains smoking their cigarettes. Then the stage had been lighted.

Yes, thought Wano, I am thinking of angels, angels of mercy.

After his wife's death, he had embraced one of the white man's faiths, one in which he could unburden himself to a black-gowned priest who was hidden in a little cubicle or behind a curtain. As he revealed what troubled him, it was like talking with God.

"Then why did you do it, my son?"

Wano had seen the priest on the streets of North Fork Town or riding his donkey or bicycle about the countryside; he himself was an old man, but now a young man, one young enough to be his son, had called him "my son."

"Because I could not forget. Because I sought vengeance."

Yet when he went home to a very desolate, a very alone home, he saw the tall bushy-haired man walking unbound from the entrance of the stone jail.

"God forgive me," Cyrus muttered in the stage.

"Here is your pouch," the Creek jolting beside him said.

"God forgive me," Cyrus said, his words indistinct.

The stage jolted again. "I said I thank you," the Creek said.

Wano, thought, it was a very red sun this evening, all bolstered upon the earth, then sinking until only the top rim showed like the top of a moon tip on the other side of the world. He huddled beneath his blanket, for the night had come cool, and a stiff north wind whipped old leaves against the slight glare of the stage windows.

The sun had reminded him of the sunsets and pine trees back in Georgia many years ago, when as a boy he had run naked through the trees, as later Dorch McIntyre might have run in Mississippi.

They had shared one thing in common—youth.

Youth, and for him marriage, and Della's birth.

He had understood that there was a young Dorch.

Cyrus Wano heard a sudden crackle of gunfire from his side of the road, and then from the other; now it was heavy on both sides.

He heard the shouts of the surprised lighthorse; then the six horses began to plunge, dragging the stage behind them.

Captain Duane Vann, riding with Tiger Panton, felt the fusillade; it seemed that both sides of the road had burst into flame.

But now he was slowly slipping from his saddle; Tiger Panton had already fallen from his. The stage driver and the shotgun riders lay slumped in the seat.

Another crash of fire came from the trees, and then, above the outcries of the demoralized lighthorse, Vann heard the firing cease and the cracking of brush begin as many horses galloped away from the road, from either side of it.

Bracing himself in the saddle, Vann tried to call out, to give orders, but somehow his throat wouldn't work. In the darkness, trying to move his horse toward the stage, he held both hands tightly to the saddle horn.

The screaming and wounded mounts of the fallen lighthorse bolted, scattering up and down the road, and now the stage swung wildly toward the bridge on Muddy Boggy.

Duane had feared the narrowing road at the bridge; there, anything could happen. Not that the road really narrowed, for it was as wide as ever on the sides of the bridge; it was only that at the bridge the ruts converged from their wide swath as if to seek the narrow end of a funnel.

The remaining lighthorse had dashed in two directions from the road, pursuing their assailants, and above the shrieks of wounded men and horses, Duane heard their own thunder as they crashed through the brush in pursuit, the sound drowning out the more distant sound of those who rode scattering before them.

It will still be the bridge, Duane thought, or they would not have run so. This attack is only a diversion. It has served its purpose; the stage goes on alone.

A Choctaw underofficer, Felix Duchon, staggered toward Duane's horse. "Captain," he gasped. He held himself upright by grasping Duane's leg.

"The men," Duane croaked the words at last. It had taken them years to come from his throat, which seemed bubbly inside. "And where is Dade Rothney?"

"The men are scattered, and Rothney dead."

Two lighthorse, leading horses, came to Duchon. Duchon pulled himself into a saddle.

"The men . . ." Duane tried to say again.

Duchon, gaining strength rapidly, turned back from his two lighthorse to shout, "We'll get them, Captain."

No, Duane wanted to scream. No, you fool! Not the men who ambushed us, but get our own men back. The bridge is the place!

Once more he tried to shout but felt himself strangling from the blood in his throat.

His hands would no longer hold the horn; he felt himself leaning; then he continued to tilt from the saddle until he fell. His red-jacketed shoulder struck the ground first; his sombrero fell off, and his face turned slowly downward and rested in a rut.

"Here comes the stage," Denna whispered to Kent.

As the coach approached the bridge, there was an outburst of rifle fire from the roadsides, but it was tentative, designed to probe rather than annihilate. A lamp was shot out.

"Stop!" A woman's voice rang from the opposite side of the bridge. "Stop!"

A Creek who had managed to open a door of the stage had climbed over the dead shotgun riders into the driver's seat; he sawed frantically at the lines.

The horses stopped. The off-lead horse, wounded in the first ambush and shot again here, attempted to rear; instead, it gave only a scream and dropped dead in its tracks.

The Creek looked down into the face he saw in the light of the remaining lamp. By now all of two dozen riders had come from the trees, surrounding the stage. The face was dark, but the Creek could see the white eyeballs and the black mustache.

Kent said, "How many in the coach are wounded?"

"Two."

"Any killed?"

"No."

"We want Cyrus Wano. The rest keep their seats. Which side of the stage is he on?"

"The other."

Kent rode his mount behind the coach and around it to the other side. He called into the shot-blasted window, "Wano, step down!"

As yet, no sound had come from the stage; none came now.

But the door opened slowly, and Cyrus Wano moved out. He stood in the road, the blanket still about his shoulders, looking at the horsemen and the bridge. A woman's voice—Denna's voice—rang from across the creek. "Bring him here!"

Kent caught Wano's arm; a rider bent and grasped him, and he was swung upward to sit behind Kent's saddle. As Kent rode past the stage horses, he could see glistening smears of blood on all of them.

"Shoot these horses," he said, and rode across the bridge.

The outlaws followed, leaving the remaining Creeks on the stage. Once across the bridge, the horses strung out through the timber in a long line, led by two slouch-hatted women, the shadow of a lean boy riding between them.

Wano thought, could that be the son of the man I killed? Could the woman who called out at the bridge be his mother? Yes, I remember. I saw her at the execution. She was a tall woman.

The other woman—he had seen her often—was Belle Starr.

But the women did not concern Cyrus Wano—it was the boy, who rode looking neither left nor right. Yes, thought Wano, his eyes searching beyond Kent's shoulder, the boy could only be the son.

There was something definite in the trail the women took, but it became still cooler. Wano glanced upward; the pointed stars flickered in their black kettle. Dorch did not know that they rode to the Licks.

This trail, Wano thought, they must have ridden it dozens of times; they know exactly where they are going.

It was a long ride between hills and through valleys; after an hour they rode around a low hill; as they came closer, Wano saw that it was sliced more sharply on the north side than on the others. Before it lay an area of shrub-bound desolate whiteness.

Riding beside her silent son, Denna Cart was seized by a sudden chill. It was only momentary, but it seemed that another self walked beside her in a white robe, her toenails painted green, moving up a long road with a procession of ancients following.

There was a crusty sound as the horses' hooves sank into the salty brackishness. Denna and Belle pulled up at the oak tree, the men dismounting behind them.

"Aduna," called Kent, hampered by Wano behind him as he dismounted, "light the lantern, then get wood from the hill. Build a fire."

"Dorch," Denna called, "get off your horse!"

Dorch sat motionless, looking across the burning lantern and the whipping fire at the face of the slight figure still mounted on Kent's horse.

Wano did not take his eyes from the boy.

"Kent," Denna called, "get Wano down. Damn you, Dorch, get down, I say."

Dorch climbed off the horse.

"Lead Wano to the tree," Denna told Kent, the wind snapping her long skirt.

Kent pulled Wano toward the twisted oak, then spun him to face the fire. "Stand here," he said.

Denna pulled Dorch forward, facing Wano. She pointed. "Do you know who that man is?"

Dorch spoke slowly. "I think I do, or you would not have brought me here."

"Then you know what I want."

"Yes."

Dorch could see the gaunt face of the other woman within the outlaw ring.

Denna told Dorch, "Then wait until I speak." She took a step nearer Wano. "You murdered the father of this boy."

Wano drew his blanket closer. "Yes."

"Why did you do it?"

"For vengeance."

"That is why my son is here now. He will kill you, as you killed his father."

"Stop," Dorch said, stepping forward. "I will kill no one." His

233

eyes sought those of the blanketed Creek. "So it was you who had my father killed?"

"Yes, and I beg your forgiveness."

"I forgive you. It is what my father would have me do."

Wano said, "Will someone hand me a pistol?"

"You will not be allowed that privilege," Denna said. "Shoot him," she screamed to Dorch. "You wear the pistol the Choctaw nation gave your father. Shoot this man!"

Dorch drew his pistol, but flung it to the ground. "I will not kill him."

Belle Starr laughed harshly.

Wano's lips moved silently, the firelight graving his small face; he had crossed himself. The wind had swept the blanket from his shoulders; it blew his long hair back.

The outlaws laughed.

"You!" Denna screamed at Dorch. "You saw your father killed. Now I must kill for you!"

She drew her pistol and fired at Cyrus Wano. The Creek fell.

Denna screamed again at Dorch, "I gave my life to you for this moment. Why didn't you kill him?"

Dorch raked his hand so hard across her face, her teeth shook. "You have given your life for yourself, never for me or my father."

He picked up the pistol and without looking at Denna or Cyrus Wano's body rode from the Licks.

Denna ran to Belle Starr and sobbed on her shoulder.

SIX

six

In the weeks which followed, a strange numbness fell upon Round Fort. The outlaws were gone from the valley, and the herd had wandered away.

Aduna had been slain by Kent in a quarrel which broke out over the possession of Cyrus Wano's blanket at the execution site at the Licks. Denna had brought the body back and buried it on the hill beside the McIntyres. She had built a circular veranda about the round room; now she sat almost listlessly, gazing into the valley or moving to the farther side of the veranda to sit facing the barracks.

"Can it be the end?" Elfreda asked the doctor hopefully.

"If it is the end, it is the end of only one thing, and the beginning of trouble for Dorch. She is free now to devote all her time to him."

Oddly, while seated on the veranda, the spread of hills and valleys and the creek before her, Denna's thoughts reverted to the Lake District, and she was rarely without some book or volume of poems on the region. She was thinking one day of Greta Hall and the writer of the sea poem and the ancient graybeard loon and wondering if anyone lived in the hall now. She laughed aloud, wondering if the same questions so often asked her were asked now of others.

One morning while she sat on the veranda gazing at the creek, David Willacy and two of his cowhands rode up the hill. Willacy dismounted; she noticed how heavily armed his men were. The stocky Englishman had learned one hard lesson of the West.

Willacy stepped to the veranda and said, "Miss Cart, the time for amenities is past." From his inside coat pocket he took a very large wallet. "Here is a certified check for the balance due on my ranch. And you may recall that when I drove two herds north last spring, I did receive permission to cross your valley—that is, your leased valley."

"Of course," Denna said.

"I spoke to you then of the dewlapped cows in the valley. You said your father had sold them before I bought your property and that there was a record of the sale filed at the courthouse. Yet why, Miss Cart, was the courthouse with all records destroyed, all within a month from the time I was here?"

"I am sure I don't know," Denna said. But her thoughts were on Aduna, killed with a knife because of a stupid quarrel over a blanket, and Kent was still gone.

"Now I am completely free of you, Miss Cart," the stuffy little Englishman was saying, "but I intend to remain in Boggy Depot and to continue my own investigation, then seek my recourse. Good day. Even an Englishman knows the age of a cow."

Yes, thought Denna, watching Willacy mount his horse, he is the last one of the past off my mind. From now on I am truly free. She sat again and picked up her book, placing the check within its pages.

Although she spent much time on the veranda, she made a determined effort to break her lethargy. She began to take long and solitary rides, exploring the Chickasaw country as Timothy and Dorch had once done on their medical rounds, riding between the endless and low parallel rows of limestone upthrusts, grassy between, mile on mile, like stone fences bounding a road in England.

Or she rode among the Arbuckle Mountains, seeing ancient fossils imprinted on the shale of shady creeks, or sometimes she rode to the Licks again.

Yet steadily, as time passed, she was seen more and more in the shade of the veranda. The harsher lines in her face had vanished; her complexion, free of constant sun, regained some of its old creaminess.

"I wonder if Aduna had loved her, too?" the doctor said one day in his office.

"It would be quite possible," said Elfreda. "Have you heard more about the Sioux hospital?"

He grinned. "Yes, but I've waited until you asked before talking about it."

"Why?"

"To know if you think about it also."

Elfreda laughed. "Anthony, I married you. I will go where you go. It's a beautiful day. I would like to walk to the barracks."

Dr. Dennis slouched to the window. "If you go, you'll see nothing but that old buzzard roosting over her graves."

"I want to see her anyway," Elfreda said, taking a brush jacket from the clothes stand.

"For the last month, whenever you go outside, you wear that jacket," the doctor said. "Why not your cloak?"

"Because I like this better," Elfreda said.

As she walked up the hill, she saw Denna's brooding figure sitting at the officers' barracks. She thought, Dorch has been to visit Lucy only twice since the murder—is it fear, or to avoid Denna?

Denna had found Dorch and Lucy sitting against the wall of the hospital, facing the valley. The windows had been up, and Elfreda, with a postmaternity case, had heard Denna's sharp voice, "Dorch, leave this girl alone. Come to the round room with me at once."

Rising angrily, Dorch said to Lucy, "I'll see you in an hour." Lucy remained seated against the wall, her hair windblown.

Elfreda had gone to the door of the round room; she dared not open it, even ever so slightly, but she could hear the rising voices, at first only a word or two, and then complete sentences. "Lucy . . ." "Wild Horse Prairie . . ." "Who would know what I did that night? I have a dozen witnesses who would say I was with them."

She heard a strange and older boy's voice, one tempered by bitter experience. "Yes, they are the poor Indians you have intimidated, people who grub for every turnip or melon they get from their little land. If they did not say what you wished, they would be shot or have their cabins burned. You should be proud of yourself."

"Have you forgotten the power I have in the councils, what I could do for you?"

"From you, I will take nothing."

A voice had risen to a scream. "Ungrateful! As stubborn as your father!"

239

Then Lucy's name again. "I will not leave Lucy."

"I have ways of making you leave her," a colder, calmer voice had said.

Elfreda passed the three gravestones set before the barracks. She had wondered how Aduna, in his divided mind, had remained so faithful to two such different things. As she neared Denna, Elfreda was quite confident; despite the heart which beat so strongly beneath her jacket, she was quite sure of herself.

Denna asked, the flesh beneath her eyes dark, "Why are you here?"

"I wanted to walk," Elfreda said, "and I want to ask you some questions." She determined to throw everything to the wind at once. "You look very nice there, seated above your lovers. Do you want young Dorch added to them someday, as Belle Starr might do her son?"

Elfreda had seen rattlesnakes coil; it was nothing to what she saw now. Denna seemed to writhe within herself, sparks almost flying from her eyes.

Elfreda was elated; she had succeeded beyond her hopes. Never had she seen Denna brought so low. "You," she said. "And you loved Dorch's father."

Denna muttered, her face stark, "As you loved him."

"Yes, I loved him. No one will ever know how much I loved him, and still do. But it is not the father I came to talk of, it is the son."

"He will never marry Lucy," Denna said, with a return of her old fire.

Elfreda drew a derringer from the jacket pocket. She said, "I want to show you this."

"I have wondered why you wear that jacket, instead of a cloak," Denna said, comprehending everything.

"My husband also wondered," Elfreda said. "Now I will tell you something. You should not talk to Dorch in such loud tones in the round room. I will tell you more—if ever you do one thing to mar the happiness of Lucy and Dorch, I will kill you. I will kill you as I would a snake. You will never know where or when, but I will kill you. And I will watch you carefully, so you and your band will not kill me. Do we understand each other?"

"It will not change one thing I plan."

"Remember my warning," Elfreda said. She turned and walked

down the hill, trembling. Good Lord, how had she ever had the nerve? She was still agitated when she entered the doctor's office and hung the jacket up.

"You didn't stay long," the doctor said, looking up from his microscope.

"No. I told Denna that if she interfered with the happiness of our children I would kill her, and I mean it."

"Come here," the doctor said. He unbuttoned his white jacket, and she saw in his belt the butt of the pistol he had bought when he first came to the Territory. "I saw it all, my dear. And once I investigated the bulge of your jacket pocket. I think we understand each other."

"Oh, Anthony!"

He took her blood pressure. "Um-huh," he grunted, "Not fit for a pretty nurse. You've never learned to tell me the truth, have you?"

"I tell you the truth, Anthony."

He rose and took a glass from the cabinet. He measured a teaspoon of a white powder and stirred it rapidly in water. "Drink this."

But there were to be two miserable nights for Elfreda. A voice too near the round room had shrieked, ". . . threatened to kill me, threatened to kill me!"

"Why?" said Dorch, who perhaps had followed Denna across the room.

"She doesn't want me here. She hates me!"

Dorch's reply was lost as they moved from the door.

Elfreda had not known Dorch was on the hill that night; perhaps he had seen Lucy secretly. She walked to their apartment; Lucy lay on her bed in her undergarments, one arm drawn over her eyes. Her riding habit, tossed over a chair, had a slightly horsey smell; perhaps she had ridden to meet Dorch as he came from the academy.

Asleep, Elfreda thought, or pretending to be. Still, any girl her age should pretend and deceive; I still do. "Lucy," she said aloud.

Lucy removed her arm from her eyes. "Yes, Mother."

"Could I have a talk with you?"

"You mean a mother-to-daughter talk?"

Elfreda laughed. "No, it will probably be a daughter-to-mother talk."

"What is it, then?"

"You and Dorch must be patient, just a little longer. We have a very good attorney, and we hope to delay everything until Dorch is of age. Then you can be married as you should be."

"Nothing is certain, Mother—not with Denna."

"Try to remember what I have told you."

Lucy turned her face to Elfreda. "Kiss me good night like you used to."

"I have always kissed you good night."

"But this is so special," Lucy said. "Good night, Mother."

Next morning at breakfast Elfreda did not see Lucy. She thought nothing of it, nor did the doctor, since Lucy often grabbed a bit of toast or fruit and ran to the school before the pupils came to help Timothy with the fires; often she even ate lunch with him over some bacon-and-egg or steak fire near Timothy's old spy place in the cedars.

But Elfreda did worry when Lucy did not appear for supper. She walked to the school and found Timothy sweeping the floors. "Have you seen Lucy today?"

"No," Timothy said, surprised. "Isn't she at the hospital?"

"I haven't seen her all day. Where could she be?"

"Come to think of it," Timothy said, "I'm afraid of something. Dorch left the hill about midnight. He stuck his long hand down my good shoulder and looked me in the eye and said something like 'Timothy, old hoss, if I don't see you again, keep your powder dry.' I thought, with the handshake and all, he was just kidding. Now I know he wasn't. He was telling me good-bye forever."

Elfreda went to the round room and found the iron-banded front door open. Denna, in a red dress, sat before the empty fireplace. Without asking for entrance, Elfreda walked to her. "Have you seen Lucy today?"

The harsh face looked up in surprise. "Lucy? No, I haven't seen her since last night. I was walking on the hill and found her talking with Dorch."

"And then what?"

"I sent Lucy to her room and brought Dorch to mine."

"And what right do you have to order Lucy about?"

"To get her away from my son."

"I see," Elfreda said. She knew Denna had told the truth, for there had been the voices through the door, and she had found Lucy in bed.

She left the round room and found the doctor leaving the operating room. She tried to say lightly, "Tired?"

He hawked toward her, taking her arm roughly. "What is wrong?"

"No one has seen Lucy today. Come, I'll fix you a cup of coffee."

When they were in their apartment, she told him what Timothy had said. "What do you think, Anthony?"

"She and Dorch have probably left together."

"I see it now," said Elfreda. "They had made their plans before Denna separated them. After I left Lucy's room I heard her go outside, but I thought she was hanging out her riding habit. Yes, she wanted me to kiss her good night—she said it was something special. Now I know what it was."

While the doctor drank his coffee, she sat beside him on the couch, her hands tightly clenched. "What will we do?" she asked. "We must know positively if Denna had part in it."

"I don't think she did—it's too soon after the other matter, and too close to home. I'll send a Chickasaw to the academy now to learn if Dorch returned." He placed a hand on her knee. "I'm like Tiger Panton and you used to be—I may have the gift of prophecy. I don't want Denna to know until she has to, but I've got a hunch. I'll have Timothy at the Boggy Depot post office in the morning the moment it's open. But we'll know positively about Dorch as soon as the Chickasaw gets back."

"Where are our boys?" she asked, taking his cup.

"Off like a bunch of hoodlums hunting a coon with the Chickasaw and Choctaw boys. That means we will have dinner alone tonight."

She smiled. "Yes, we'll have dinner alone."

"Come back here," he said. "I want to tell you something."

He kissed her lips, the coffeecup rattling in its saucer.

"Yes?" he asked.

"Yes," she said.

Before daybreak, the Chickasaw rider returned from the academy. Dorch had not been seen for two days. His blankets and all his possessions were gone. He had not said good-bye to his instructors.

243

"Thank you," the doctor said in his bathrobe at the back door of the hospital.

Timothy stopped his horse beside the Chickasaw's. "I can't sleep," he said. "I'm going to Boggy now. Townley will open the store before the post office opens, but I'll be first in line for the letters."

The doctor returned to his quarters. Elfreda was sitting up in bed. "Was Dorch at the academy?"

"Not for two days."

"Are our boys in from their hunt?"

"No. They'll drag in about sunup, and we'll have coon and maybe possum and taters for a week. A week, because it will take that long to eat the stinking mess."

They were in the doctor's office when Timothy returned with the mail.

There was a letter in Dorch's handwriting, addressed to them, postmarked yesterday. The doctor rose from his desk chair; Elfreda sat, fumbling with the envelope. Timothy stood against the wall.

"Here," the doctor said roughly to Elfreda, "let me open the envelope."

Two letters were enclosed. The first was from Dorch:

Dearest Mother,

You know how much I have always thought of Lucy, and while I ask your forgiveness for our leaving, I believe it is best, not only for us, but for you and the doctor, who has always been a second father to me.

Last night in the round room Denna told me to give up Lucy, that she had only to sign certain papers, then I must beg for everything. I do not mind the loss of money or property, or having to give up Wild Horse ranch, which meant so much to us, but no one will ever take Lucy from me. If I remained at Round Fort, Denna would only make life miserable for all of us.

I know we are young, but Lucy and I were married today at daybreak in old Preacher Parsons' cabin—you remember how often we used to laugh at his name. That woman may have all my father willed me, the money and everything.

But Lucy and I will have each other, and tonight we will be

244

in Texas and go on to New Mexico or Arizona and try to find a place to start a ranch. I can work, and Lucy can work, and no one will ever find us.

Always your son,
Dorch

Elfreda then read Lucy's letter:

Dearest Mother and Father,

I hope you will forgive us for what we have done. Dorch and I have talked so many times of having both of you stand beside us when we were married.

But last night before Denna found us on the hill, we had agreed it was best to leave home now. Do not blame Dorch; I, too, think he is right. We will find our own lives, free somewhere, and Dorch at the wedding ceremony did seem so much older. And I felt older too.

Farewell, dear parents, and someday, somewhere, we will meet again.

With all my love,
Lucy

"What are you crying about?" the doctor asked gruffly.

Elfreda rose and flung her arms about him. "Because I am the happiest woman on earth. They are free, Anthony, free at last!"

He thrust her from him and turned to gaze into the valley. "I'm glad it worked out."

He stood there so long, she flung herself toward him. "Anthony," she cried, "what is it?"

"Herds of longhorns," he said, holding her closely. "Herds of longhorns, always driving north. Well, old wench, it's all over."

"No," she cried, "it's just beginning, for them, for us. We'll go to the Sioux camps. It won't be heaven in a log cabin, but it will be home, and we'll go with our three coon-hunting hoodlums."

The old dry-cell-battery-operated buzzer on the doctor's desk began to whirr.

"Emergency," said Elfreda.

"Yes," the doctor said, slipping into his white gown.

Together they walked into the spotless corridor. A little Choctaw trainee stood stiffly at the doorway of Room 14.

"Emergency, Doctor. Room fourteen. The nurse is inside."

Left alone in the office, Timothy Baines decided to go outside and look at the weather. Leading his tired horse, he walked like an old man back up to the stables.

Dorch's departure brought a complete change in the life of Denna Cart. She was alone now, completely alone. Even Kent was forever gone, killed while attempting to hold up a train on the Katy line. Even the days of her father's life fell farther away, and she lived in an agony of introspection.

Occasionally she thought of Anthracite and Brian, of Tom and Amy, and the long-dead doctor who rested on the hill. But there was always the inward gnawing as she paced the floor of the round room at night, passing the piano only to strike some discordant sound from the keys.

The nights with the doctor came back, and they hurt.

They hurt deeply.

She remembered his words. "You have loved me for your own vanity. You are troubled, Denna, within yourself."

They had sat on the piano bench that night. She crossed the floor and sat there now.

What hardness was in her?

Why had the places she loved most on earth been harsh—the old Texas ranch, the mountainous Lake District, and these hills and limestone rows? Did things which repelled other people serve only to attract her?

Was some latent hatred, a love of harshness, the power to break or hurt, necessary to her existence?

Sometimes she slept in a confusion of dreams, of the long road she walked in a white robe, or the endless path between parallel rows of white limestone she rode with grass to her horse's belly, or some lonely trail she sought at night, a trail to nowhere.

She would awake sweating, throw her gown aside, and toss and turn.

But whatever she was, she could not tolerate this act of defiance by her son.

She rode to Boggy Depot and gave orders for the lighthorse to send notices of detention to the officials of Texas, New Mexico, and Arizona, to apprehend and to hold Dorch and Lucy McIntyre for their return to Boggy Depot.

She must return within a week to sign the necessary papers,

which must clear through Tishomingo and the Choctaw capital at Tushkahoma.

No one ever knew who killed Denna Cart.

The day had been sunny, and in appreciation of the work of the hospital personnel, together with the rumor that Dr. Dennis might leave, there was to be a dance that night honoring the doctors and nurses at the Boggy Depot hotel.

Denna had taken a nap after lunch; then she had bathed and dressed. She was agreeably surprised at what the long days of rest at Round Fort had done for her figure and complexion; free of wind and sun, her face had begun to blossom again.

As she gazed at herself in the mirror, she was all radiance. It was almost as if the Denna of old smiled back at her.

Timothy was going to the dance, and Elfreda and Dr. Dennis, but Denna had preferred to ride in early and alone. She found the outside of the hotel festooned and decorated, and new planking placed over the old walk for those who might wish to promenade or dance outside.

As usual, the curly-haired Chico stood by the hitchrack. "May I keep your horse, señorita? There will be many people for the dance tonight, but I have rented the vacant lot around the corner."

"Which corner?" Denna asked, getting off the horse.

The urchin pointed. "That one. I will have lanterns up, and I will take special care of your horse."

"Good, but will you take my bag inside?"

Denna took her usual room upstairs. Here she could rest and freshen up, have her gown pressed, and make her entrance down the stairway to the cleared dining room, resplendent in her low-cut gown after the dance had begun. This would let her slight Elfreda and the doctor, who were to lead the grand march.

She was irked by only one thing—she would have no escort. There would be dozens of men on the dance floor all eager to dance or walk with her under the lanterns of the new promenade. But her pride suffered; when the dance was over, there would be no one to see her to Round Fort.

For various reasons current in the town and the two nations, most men would not care to be seen alone with her, although they might under pretense of courtesy dance or talk with her as long as others were present. No one wanted his association with her to be misinterpreted.

At nine o'clock Denna came down the stairway. She had tinged her nails with light green. The orchestra had been splendid, and it was between dances. As she moved one hand lightly along the banister, she was conscious of many eyes raised to her from the floor, eyes of many expressions, curiosity, admiration, hatred, and suspicion. It was as if people thought, what alibi will her presence here serve tonight?

Surprisingly, she met Timothy at the foot of the stairway. "How nice to see you," she said mockingly. "Will you have the first of my dances?"

Timothy was dressed in his black suit and black bow tie. He said stiffly, "My dances are taken. But you should know that Sardis Rippy has hanged himself in the Fort Smith dungeon. Word just came of it."

There was no change in Denna's brilliant expression. "It is too bad," she said indifferently. Someone drew Denna away, and the string instruments and the trumpet and drums began their music.

Timothy watched Denna go. If she signs papers to get Dorch and Lucy back, he thought, she might end up as dead as Sardis Rippy.

Between dances Denna walked the lighted promenade with her partners, from one corner of the street to the other. Many poorer-class Indians stood along the rail; they watched her closely, silently.

She saw Jack Leavitt standing against a storefront, dressed in cowhand clothes, rolling a cigarette, and merely watching.

As she entered the hotel for another dance, she met Elfreda.

"How charming you look," Denna said. "What a beautiful gown!"

The gown was a beautiful dark satin with a few sequins, but Elfreda, standing beside her father, flushed. It was as if Denna hinted, now, Elfreda, look at my gown.

Denna turned to the arm of a new partner; it was then that she saw the stocky figure of David Willacy standing against the wall. The little Englishman watched her without expression; obviously he had watched her all night. But he doesn't stand there, Denna thought, with nothing on his mind. I wonder what it is; why does he watch me so intently?

Elfreda and the doctor left with Dr. Ballinger at eleven; they would relieve Dr. Michaels and new Dr. Tomlinson and if they and the remaining nurses rode at a good trot, they also could enjoy several hours of the festivities before the evening, or morning, ended.

But Denna was being left alone. Perhaps the talk of Sardis Rippy was spreading.

Within two and a half hours the other doctors and nurses from the hospital came in. Denna had been neglected for three consecutive dances; she walked to Boyce Townley and pretended to discuss business matters.

"May I have the next?" Dr. Michaels asked.

"Of course." Denna laughed, once more her radiant self. "Excuse me, Mr. Townley."

Dr. Michaels danced with her; his obligation ended, he left her alone. She missed the next two dances, her eyes smarting with rage. Dr. Tomlinson ignored her.

During an intermission she was also left alone; she moved toward a group of councilmen. The austere principal chief of the Chickasaws, tall and rail-thin and with his hair curled on his neck, stared straight through and beyond her. "Miss Cart, your son's father was my friend. You have driven the boy from us, and I do not approve your further persecution in forcing his return. Although your legal papers will come through for signature, I demand that you let the boy and his young wife have peace."

He turned and left her without even a bow; the silent councilmen avoided her and dispersed. She was left alone in the center of the floor, her face flaming. In the deathly silence which followed, every eye in the room was upon her. She walked to the doorway, the pouty little Englishman watching.

Standing just inside the dorway, waiting for his horse to be brought around, Timothy had overheard the chief's remark.

Denna said, "Timothy, I feel faint. Will you walk me to the corner—the corner to the left?"

Timothy took her arm; she noticed that now he was leaving, he wore his pistol; men with pistols had checked them at the hotel desk before the dance began.

"What the chief said hurt, didn't it?" Timothy said.

"I don't care to discuss it." When they reached the corner, through the crowd of merrymakers, she said, her head high, "Go back to your dance now. I'll stand here for a few moments."

"I'll stay," said Timothy. "I was just waiting for my horse."

"Then go to it."

As Timothy disappeared back toward the hotel, Denna slipped around the corner to Chico's lot. Thank God, Timothy had saved her the final humiliation of having to walk for her horse alone, in plain view of all who strolled and laughed on the promenade.

Chico sat on a packing box beside a lantern; horses were tied to a long hitchrack he had built. "Señorita," he asked, jumping from the box, "would you like to have your horse? Look, I have kept him nearest my box."

"Yes, I will take him now. Here are two dollars."

"Gracias, señorita. May I help with the stirrup?"

"No. I have been getting on these things all my life."

"Buenas noches, señorita."

She rubbed her hand in his curly hair. "Dear Chico," she said.

Still hearing the distant music, she turned the horse toward the leafy Round Fort road.

It was a familiar trail to her now, once she had entered the trees. She had used it so many times, for so many purposes. Now the branches and the night could hide the rage which still lingered on her face.

Dark riders came and went on the trail; she trotted the horse past an open wagon, an Indian and his wife in the seat, a lantern resting in the space between them, the wagon bed full of children, their faces looking up when she passed.

Ah, if only she had Kent and Aduna again. Then she would have power she never dreamed of.

She was a mile beyond the wagon when the shotgun blast came which ended all thought.

It was three-fifteen in the morning.

In the operating room, Dr. Dennis looked down upon the once-beautiful head and face, now torn away. Even so, the shotgun blast had been poorly aimed; only an edge of the buckshot pattern had struck the side and back of the head; the perfect profile remained intact.

Dr. Dennis, assisted by Elfreda and a nurse, had given Denna injections for shock and pain. Now, under the shaved and cut hair to stop what bleeding he could, and remove buckshot and bone chips and splinters. "Another blanket on her legs," the doctor snapped.

"Amy," Denna whispered. "Help me!"

Her head tilted to one side; she was dead.

The doctor went into the corridor. An Indian stood with his short wife, surrounded by five children, two boys and three girls. The children were sniffly and ringwormed. The doctor asked the Indian, "You said she passed your wagon only a few minutes before she was shot?"

"Yes." The Indian was tall and long-haired and ragged, with a cracked cold sore on his lip. "She was trotting her horse; then we heard the shot and found her in the road. We laid her in the back of the wagon."

"Why were you in Boggy Depot?"

"Our children had never seen a white man's dance."

Dr. Dennis saw Denna's blood on the clothes of the parents and all the children. He said, "When the other doctors and nurses come in, we will have to report this to the lighthorse. You must go to Boggy Depot with me." The doctor motioned to a trainee. "Take this family to the tubroom. Give them medical soap, and have them all bathe for a checkup. Get another trainee to wash their clothes and put the family in hospital robes."

The trainee motioned to the tall Indian, who led his family down the hall.

Elfreda came from the operating room, closing the door behind her. "Did you kill her?" she asked.

Surprise on his face, he said, "No, I thought you did."

"Thank God!" she said.

Yet each would always wonder.

She hesitated. "But she cannot be buried on the hill. Too much good has been done here for that."

"When I go to town, I will make other arrangements."

So who had killed Denna Cart?

Timothy Baines, because he would prevent her from signing papers which would put in motion the search for Dorch and Lucy?

Or was it Dr. Dennis, or Elfreda, and for the same reason?

Or Jack Leavitt, the lounging-point rider turned foreman, who in integrity to a promise fought on against the dissolution of a ranch?

Or vengeance from Belle Starr, because Denna had never kept her promise to visit Younger's Bend after the Wano execution, and because she resented being used by another woman?

Or an act by a friend of Sardis Rippy?

Or David Willacy, who had learned the truth of the C Bar cattle?

Or was it an act of a member of the combined councils of the Choctaw and Chickasaw nations for the good of all their peoples?

Or any one of a hundred poor hounded Indians she had persecuted?

Or had Denna Cart simply killed herself little by little since the day she bathed in a Texas creek, these things making the sum of life?

She was buried in Boggy Depot graveyard.

SEVEN

1

Timothy Baines had moved from his schoolroom back to the round room. Here he rearranged things until they stood as they had back in the old days when the mastiffs guarded the hearth and his gentleman played the piano. He removed Denna's bed and vanity and reassembled the large table, and asked only that he have some out-of-the-way corner—if a round room has a corner—to place his cot at night.

He kept the room spotless, cheerful as usual, using it as a lounge for tired nurses and doctors when they were off duty, serving them hurried snacks or coffee in his white jacket, or going down the hall to serve the busy ones.

He did like the veranda, now that he could enjoy it more, and its couches and chairs; it broke the stern lines of the fort, giving the hill a certain softness; in the hot summer it shielded from the sun, with always ventilation, a haven for the convalescent.

Sometimes, after putting the round room in order, he would sit at the piano and pick out the "Spavinaw" tune, then hunch his way down the hospital corridor to see if Elfreda or one of the nurses wanted coffee. He was happy, knowing that his years here were nearly over and that in time he could seek his own future.

Future, he thought one day, feeling his thin face, knowing he had flecks of gray at the temples, and reaching up to pat his hump significantly, yes, it's a hell of a future I've got. My life is like the old Chickasaw's broken-down farm wagon that would go forty miles an hour—five miles forward and thirty-five sideways, shaking itself to pieces. That Indian would start for Boggy Depot with a load of corn, and because of the cracks in the wagon bed grinding the ears down get there trailing cornmeal behind him. Then, after a good chuckle, Timothy would sit at the piano again.

Elfreda, too, was happy, and Dr. Dennis. She moved on light feet, thinking, too, of the future, and the future of others. Only the recent death of her mother marred her thoughts. But she knew that always people walked over the bodies of the dead, always to somewhere.

One day in the office Elfreda handed the doctor a stack of mail which Timothy had brought. "One letter, I think, is from Washington."

He looked up from his desk, an odd grin on his lips. "I have a hunch," he said. "Open it."

She read the letter quickly, then, still clutching it, bent to throw her arms about his neck. "It has come through," she cried. "You are a Sioux man."

"Do you still have that thing called courage?"

"Yes," she said. "I will be sorry to leave for father's sake, now that mother is gone. But father will understand—he always has."

"Could we celebrate with dinner in the round room tonight? After all, this is a family matter, and we should discuss it with the hoodlums. It will take a big table; it might awe them to silence—I hope."

Elfreda placed the letter on the desk. "I'm afraid they already know."

"But how could they? We've never discussed it with them."

Elfreda sighed. "No, but Anthony was skinning a coon outside the office once and heard us talk of it."

"Privacy," the doctor grunted. "What a word! Still, we will eat in the round room."

"I'll tell Timothy."

"Do you think he would go with us?"

"Something makes me doubt it."

When they entered the round room at seven, young Anthony, the quietest of the boys, sat at the old secretary reading a ledger bound in brown parchment.

Timothy had lighted the slim candles on the table; the two other boys, Carl and Langley, sat on the bench banging the piano, first with their hands, then elbows, then with entire forearms.

"Here, here," the doctor said, taking each by the ear. "We have important matters to discuss tonight. How can we, in this uproar?"

Elfreda had gone to young Anthony. "What are you reading?"

Anthony glanced up from the ledger. "It's got old figures in it, from way back in Mississippi."

"Yes," Elfreda said. "It is the account book kept by the father of the first doctor here, together with your grandfather, who runs the Boggy store now."

"All the big Chickasaw names are here, and Choctaw names." Anthony's blue eyes twinkled. "You aren't this old, are you?"

"No, young man, but I will be before I raise three boys I know."

Carl and Langley had got back to the piano, banging and yelling, "Hoodlums, hoodlums!"

"Quiet," said Elfreda, "all of you. Now go to the table for your father to say grace."

Langley sat first. He opened his fingers wide to put them over his eyes. "Who's Grace?"

The doctor said, "You know where it hurts to sit down sometimes. Now shut up."

Meanwhile Timothy had set steaming platters on the table. After the dinner Langley asked, as Timothy placed coffeecups and saucers for Elfreda and the doctor, "Can we have coffee tonight?"

"What?" said the doctor.

"May we have coffee tonight?"

"Since we have something important to talk about, yes. Half-and-half," he told Timothy.

When coffee was finished, the doctor said, "I understand you young gentlemen know that we may go north to the Sioux country."

An outbreak of war whoops from three hand-patted mouths.

"Silence," the doctor called. He glanced the length of the long table to Elfreda. "A fine bunch you put on earth."

"Doctor," Elfreda snapped, "don't sit there so sanctimoniously."

"Old Sanctimonious!"

"Old Sanctimonious!"

"Old Sanctimonious!"

"Oh, my God," the doctor groaned. "Your mother and I wanted to give you a voice in how we travel. Shall it be stagecoach, or railroad as far as we can make it?"

"Covered wagon!"
"Yoke of oxen!"
"Yoke of oxen!"

"Ah!" said the doctor, a gleam of malicious satisfaction in his eye. "Yes, you give me an idea. Your mother and I wanted your opinion because the Old West we have known is fast going. We wanted you to know how it was in the old days—that's why I said stagecoach. But you go me one better. Yoke of oxen it is."

By George, he thought, by the time they walk a thousand miles and goad oxen at every step, they'll know what the West was, and they will be so tired they can't open their heads for a month. By the time we reach the Sioux country, they'll really know the West.

He laughed to Elfreda. "Weeks and weeks of silence."

She asked wonderingly, "What do you mean?"

"All right," the doctor said, "stagecoach, railroad, or covered wagon. Anthony, Carl, Langley, now vote."

Unanimous covered wagon.

"But, covered wagon," said Elfreda. "Why, those were used . . . Those were used . . ."

"Oh," the doctor said carelessly, "you still see a few on the Texas Road, even now. You know," he said, putting his elbow on the table and cupping his chin, meanwhile giving her that odd look she knew so well, "you know, I have always wanted to be an adventurer, to strike out somewhere, something I could never do, being a doctor. That old pistol I brought into the Territory—it's been fired once, the day I got here. This will be the only chance of my life. Afterward, work, work, work. Take yourself, Elfreda. Haven't you ever wanted to strike out for the new, and leave a thousand things behind? I vote oxen."

"Well," Elfreda said slowly.

The doctor laughed. "Motion carried, unanimously. Tomorrow Timothy can go to Boggy Depot and try to find a wagon and oxen. Meanwhile, we'll begin to pack."

While he was on duty that night, Dr. Dennis talked with Timothy Baines. "Would you go with us?" he said.

They were standing outside the back door of the corridor, and Timothy, looking into the bright night, was touched. He had always liked Elfreda, and his opinion of the doctor was good enough. And there were Lucy and young Dorch he might hear of again.

"I . . . I . . ." Timothy started to speak, then couldn't.

"I understand," the doctor said.

Timothy said, "I've just got to strike out on my own, like everybody else. For most of us old ones, Round Fort is over. We've all got to fly the coop. Too many thoughts are here that haunt. But if it wasn't that I've got to find my own place, I'd go with you to the Sioux."

"I understand," the doctor repeated, taking his arm.

Violently the little hunchback tore himself away and raced toward the barracks, as if to a haven. In the schoolroom he paced the floor until midnight, all doubts resolved.

The eight oxen and the covered wagon stood before the livery stable in Boggy Depot.

Old Pip Waddleston was grizzled and gray-bearded; the wagon was a sway-backed old Conestoga with hind wheels which seemed twice as large as the front two.

"Yes," the old man said to the doctor, "I'm selling out, and there's no place I haven't been with this team or another. Old Spot there will make a good lead for you. I came back from the Sioux country with him two years ago. Soon as you get up the road, and he can smell a Sioux, he'll lead you straight as a star.

"I wouldn't sell Spot or the outfit for a million, except for my rheumatiz. I'm finished for the roads and trails. All I want is a warm room in the winter, a drink by the fire, and a warm bed. Well, you take Old Spot and the gol-durned outfit, and God bless you, if you can get through the wire fences."

"It's a deal. If you don't mind, I'll take the bullwhip back with me."

The doctor, not used to driving oxen, did not want to learn on the narrow road from Round Fort, so the family possessions were packed, including Elfreda's long-hidden-away red-and-white-checkered tablecloth in the bottom of her trunk, and carried in a mule-drawn wagon to Boggy Depot.

"It is utterly ridiculous," the doctor said as he watched Timothy drive the wagon down the hill, "to think that after all these years a family could accumulate no more than what is in that wagon."

"No," Elfreda said. "It is not at all ridiculous. We have lived in hospital quarters, with our needs furnished. When we have our own cabin, we can begin to accumulate."

He said in alarm, "You're not pregnant? Not more hoodlums?"

"Doctor, by the time you drive eight oxen to the Sioux country, that would be impossible for the next ten years."

Laughing, they went back to the hospital.

Next morning they left Round Fort.

Their horses were outside, with a mounted Chickasaw to drive them back. The doctor and Elfreda had said good-bye to the other doctors and nurses and trainees; in parting, they had been given a silver coffee service.

Now they were in the yard, ready to mount, the hoodlums squabbling over which horse each would take.

"Are you ready?" the doctor asked Elfreda, snapping the bullwhip.

"Yes, but I want to go up the hill for a moment."

She walked upward into the wind, remembering the day she had first come to Round Fort after the war to see the stern and tall doctor with his shock of black hair, the day before his father's operation.

The old barracks loomed higher, and at last she stood beside the grave.

"Good-bye, Dorch," she whispered. "I have always loved you. And may our lost children stand someday where I stand now. God rest you."

Turning, she walked back down the hill.

In old Boggy Depot a number of the curious and various friends had gathered to see them off, some in ridicule, some in sincerity; the team of oxen and the Conestoga stood before the old store.

But the town itself was turning to decay, its streets half-empty, the old cisterns cracked and drying.

"Good-bye, Father," Elfreda said, holding him close. He was thin, and his eyebrows brushy white. "I would not leave you after mother's death, but we must go on."

"Go, lass, go," he said.

"Hey, Grampappy," young Anthony yelled from the tailgate of the wagon, "I'm taking this old Mississippi ledger with me."

"Gladly, son. Keep it. It has good names in it."

"Well," said the doctor, "off to the kangaroos and cantaloupes."

"You didn't say there were cantaloupes," Carl yelled.

"Or kangaroos," cried Langley.

"I must have forgotten," the doctor said.

He may indeed have forgotten. He had wanted to leave Boggy Depot in good form with the oxen and Conestoga; he had practiced for hours at Round Fort learning to pop the long bullwhip in an explosive manner.

With Elfreda beside him in the seat, the doctor threw the whip forward and snapped it and shouted; there was an explosion indeed over the head of Old Spot, accidental or not.

The Conestoga creaked and moved out behind the oxen, heading north.

"Ain't you going the wrong way?" someone yelled.

"No," the doctor yelled back. "We're headed for the kangaroos."

The hoodlums were having a wrestling match in the back of the wagon.

"A covered wagon going north," a wiseacre yelled. "I never thought I'd see the day."

Before they knew it, they were out of town and on the Texas Road.

Timothy Baines rode beside the oxen. He would be with the voyagers until they reached the junction of the old California Trail; then he would leave them and turn east for Fort Smith.

He had taught the doctor all he knew about oxen, gee, and haw, but he didn't know which word started them or which stopped them. He was not quite right in his assumptions but he was just thankful that the doctor had got the Conestoga out of town without making fools of everyone. He began to whistle his "Spavinaw" tune.

In the seat of the great cocoon, the doctor and Elfreda sat in their rough jackets. Dr. Dennis glanced toward her. Poor child, he thought, she did go back to the grave; she had to. She looked very stark against the sky. I hope she can forget.

Elfreda placed a hand on his arm. "We're on our way," she said.

He smiled toward her. "Yes, dear." He thought of the past, of all the people he had known, the good and bad, the laws and outlaws, the clean and unclean, the poor and the rich, the black-haired doctor who had brought him here on a fool's errand he had learned to love, or why would he go north now? He left behind a new Territory, perhaps someday a new state.

"There is only one thing," he said.

"Yes?"

"I am taking the best part of the years with me—you." There was an uproar in the back of the wagon. He added, "And your three hoodlums. Two others got away—our eagles in the sky."

She leaned toward him. "Thank you, Anthony." She kissed him.

So the ghost of Della Wano had gone from the hill, and Denna, and now Elfreda.

Yet still on its eminence and among its old ruins young people moved about, forgetting the old people who had once been there. Yet still older people came into the hospital to talk of the other old people who had left.

Dorch McIntyre slept on, knowing none of this.

At the junction of the old roads, Timothy parted from the Dennises.

It had been a wonderful, ridiculous experience, Elfreda laughing over the campfire each night, listening to all the sorrows, the doctor entangled in his oxen's gear and arm-weary from popping his bullwhip, the boys silent and tired from constantly walking beside the oxen and plunging their sharp goads at the impenetrable flesh.

Yet one day at noon the time for parting came.

The covered wagon and its oxen moved on northward amid shouts and hand waving, into a strange land where distant snow-covered mountains would loom, and Timothy turned off the road to Fort Smith, the road on which the old piano had gone to Round Fort.

As he rode among prairies or through blackjacks or among deep hills, he whistled his tuneless tune, his hump high.

But often a twinge tore his heart, his mind, and his whole being, when he thought that he, a hunchback, had done the deed he had.

When the little caravan had been well out on the Texas Road from Boggy, riding beside the oxen, hoping they would keep moving, he had overheard a few words—"eagles in the sky."

Yes, Timothy thought, as he trotted his horse onward, I did right. Eagles in the sky. They may have been young and foolish, but that's what they were, eagles in the sky, the past not mattering. I did only my last act as a gentleman's gentleman, as I did once before. I killed my gentleman, and I killed her.

Yet there was no guilt in his mind or in his heart. I did right, he thought, I gave him the coup de grace, and I killed her. I was indeed a gentleman's gentleman, a gentleman for two gentlemen.

When he camped at night and ate his food, he wished that Elfreda was there, laughing across the campfire.

Once more a pang tore him. No, I was right. Yes, they should go on alone, as I am doing.

It was the morning after as he approached Fort Smith and neared Skullyville on its gravel hill that a weird sound swept from the Arkansas River. He straightened and turned in the saddle; no one, even after a thousand years, and certainly not in this brief span, could ever forget it.

The sound rose shrieking and wavering, as if the very soul of the old *Maizie Trout* wailed in despair and screamed in agony; Old Jessup was yanking the rope of the pilothouse whistle.

Good Lord, thought Timothy, is that old sternwheeler still living? It couldn't be anything else; that's Captain Keeter's old steamboat. The old duck, I'll ride over and see him. He'll be at the Skullyville landing.

The sun midway of the sky, Timothy cut off the road and trotted his horse across the open fields, or let it leap the crisscross rail fences; about him the scattered clumps of papaw trees were beginning to bear their bananalike fruit. A denim-clad Choctaw boy chased a spotted calf across a field. Once more the disembodied wail drifted from the river.

Timothy Baines rode past the old town and made his way through other sprouting fields to the landing on the Arkansas.

Captain Keeter sat despondently in a canvas chair on the empty deck of the *Maizie Trout*.

Over the years there had been no ups and downs in his fortunes; they had all declined steadily. There had been the invasion of his beloved watershed by the network of hated railroads; his once lucrative trade on the Arkansas had turned to sand and silt.

From the mouth of the river upward, at all the old stops and landings, there were only dilapidated docks and wharves and lonely pilings standing knee-deep in water. Sometimes only ankle-deep.

Some people said that all the farming of whites and Indians had helped make the river shallow—with the old native grasses turned under, the land left bare by the corn and cotton crops began to wash away in heavy rains, filling and choking first the creeks with silt, and then the river.

With vegetation not left to hold the rain, and with the excessive runoff, in the flash flooding the banks of the river were undercut and dropped in half-acre chunks with splashes heard hundreds of yards away.

Along the river as it changed course farms could be lost overnight, and steamboat stops had vanished. Vanished like old Napoleon at the mouth of the river, washed away in the flood of '73—no, '74, it was. After the first flood, most of the people moved away, but the next ended everything. The banks chunked in— nothing left now but part of a shanty and one gaunt chimney rising.

Keeter could remember the prosperous and boisterous town with its floating landings as it was the day the *Mississippi Queen* slid away into its big river, the day he had met Denna Cart to bring her to Fort Smith. God, what a woman! He remembered their dinner in the pilothouse; now she was dead and a corpse in the Boggy Depot graveyard.

Keeter sighed, crossing his legs and looking up the dusty road toward Skullyville. He was neatly dressed in an open-throated brown shirt and brown trousers, clean-shaven; his captain's cap sat steadily above his square face, although his temples were gray.

He still had money, enough to let him subsist for the rest of his life, but what could he do with the *Maizie Trout?* The old flat-bottomed sternwheeler was like a part of him, even though today the last member of the crew had deserted. He was a gangling Negro and had left with steps twelve feet long up the dusty road to Skullyville.

Jessup wouldn't have left me, he thought, thinking of the homespun faithful pilot who had died five years ago. Jessup had been telling some first-run passengers his usual tall tales about his boyhood in the Ozarks, how, standing upright, he could fire a rifle at a catamount on a limb with his bare big toe. "The way I used to hunt for a living," he said, "before I got the river blood."

But as he fired the rifle in a show-off gesture, Jessup's other foot had slipped on the deck; the bullet had gone beneath his heart. No, Jessup wouldn't have left, not willingly, Keeter thought, but everyone else has.

Keeter laughed aloud at a trick Jessup had pulled during the war. The *Maizie Trout* had been beset by an armed Union sternwheeler just in on the Arkansas near Napoleon. Jessup had swung the craft into a deep creek.

He ordered the crew ashore to cut brush and cover the boat, but there still remained the tall smokestacks—a dead giveaway. Jessup solved that problem too. He ordered two thin pines cut and their lower branches stripped; he had positioned them in the open stacks, using the starboard derrick and pulleys and ropes and a branch of a large tree on the bank. He had used a rope with a hook on it to climb the stacks and had himself done the positioning; then more brush was piled high.

The Union sternwheeler searched the river and creeks but never found the *Maizie Trout*. After a few days, it left.

But because of the delay, Keeter and the hospital supplies bound for Fort Gibson on the Neosho had not reached the fort in time for what was to become the Battle of the Mounds.

Keeter gazed about at the battered and rundown wharf. Twenty years ago it would have been as neat as a pin, with Indians come to Skullyville for their annuities and turbaned Negroes clustered about, and whites standing or conducting business beneath stovepipe or bowler hats, and his own bare-chested crew loading and unloading cargo.

Now, when you put your foot on the dock, even the pilings trembled. The town had dwindled; almost nothing but a few tribal buildings and cabins remained.

In sheer irritation, Keeter rose from his chair and walked briskly up to the pilothouse. Why he wanted to do this, he didn't know. The view from the pilothouse would only show the desolation more.

A small head of steam was still up; glancing between the twin stacks and the outside derricks, Keeter reached for the hanging rope of the whistle, yanking it and sending a frustrated blast shimmering beyond the distance, meanwhile gazing defiantly ahead. This was the shriek Timothy Baines first heard.

By God, I'll whip it yet, Keeter thought. I'll whip it yet. Somehow I'll whip it.

He was ordinarily an even-tempered man, and now he began to smile.

Yes, he could whip it. Take the old steamboat anywhere on the river he loved, along woodlands, or near a town, tie up, and live the rest of his days there.

If he went to a town to live, he'd tie up thousands for a house, and lose money to boot. The old *Trout* wouldn't bring a dollar on a hundred, or a thousand, and it held for him all he could ever want, more than he could find elsewhere.

The streak of defiance still remained, and once more he raised his hand to the rope and sent the despairing wail trembling across the countryside.

I feel a lot better, he thought. I got that out of my system!

He wished Jessup still stood here beside him, talking things over as they used to.

Even as he stood, he saw an odd little rider trotting his horse toward the dock.

Now what, he thought, his mind going back into the years, what can that be? Then he knew.

The devil! Keeter grinned, seeing the little man better as the horse trotted closer, the wide-brimmed hat, the boots, and the rising hump.

"Timothy Baines!" Keeter shouted.

He gave a welcoming blast with the whistle, then tumbled down the stairs to the deck.

Timothy Baines, his horse scattering a dozen hogs which rooted hopelessly for kernels of corn on the planks of the dock, rode to the prow and looked down.

"Captain, sir!" He grinned.

"You old rapscallion!" Keeter shouted, waving his cap in the air. "You cheer me up. Get down and come aboard. By God, you're as gray as I am."

"Only at the temples, sir, only at the temples."

Timothy left his horse on the dock, and Keeter walked briskly to the deck below the superstructure, bringing out another chair. "Sit down," he said.

Timothy sat, dropping his hat at his feet; he looked about at the utter desolation of the *Maizie Trout*.

"Well," said Keeter proudly, "how does she look?"

Timothy lied like a deep-sea sailor, and he knew it. "Quite the same, sir."

"At least, you are a gentleman," Keeter said. "You might have told me she needed paint."

Timothy said, "Maybe a drop or two wouldn't hurt her." He added, "Skullyville is not as large as before."

"No, but many new towns spring up along the railroads. I read in the Fort Smith newspapers about the trouble you had at Round Fort and at Boggy Depot. Do they know who killed Denna Cart?"

"They're still looking," said Timothy.

"And where do you intend to go?"

"To Fort Smith, maybe. What have you been up to?"

"Reading the writing on the wall. But there's no use for you to ride down. Bring your horse aboard, and we'll leave early tomorrow. It will be a job without a crew, but we can make it."

"Where is Jessup?" Timothy asked.

Keeter told him. "And a damn good pilot he was."

That night under a moon as big as a washtub, the two men sat in their chairs and began to talk.

Along the creek the bullfrogs roared, a few lights shone distantly on the Skullyville road, a cow lowed near the deserted dock, and beside the old woodlot a slice of bank chunked into the river, the splash swaying the sternwheeler. They swatted mosquitoes over the cool beer bottles Keeter had pulled up from beneath the paddlewheels.

"I don't know if I'm a fool or not," Timothy said, watching a string of whirlpools racing in the moonlight, "but I want to find a girl I saw a long time ago. She won't be the same, and I won't be, but I want to find her. She's something I've dreamed about."

Keeter said, swatting at a mosquito and lighting his pipe and taking his cap off, all in the same motion, "I've told you what my plans are. If you don't find the girl—she'd be a woman now—why don't you throw in with me? I've enough money to last us. We'll float and drift and tie up somewhere, and we'd still have the *Maizie Trout* underfoot."

"Money would be no object, sir. My gentleman did quite honorably by me."

"Then you'll consider it?"

"If I don't find the girl, yes. But I'd be pretty restless."

"No, you wouldn't, and neither would I. We wouldn't have time to be restless. We'll get the old tub shipshape, paint her from stem to stern, and sit and fish with our feet in the water. Jessup had a lot of common sense. He said he liked to sit with his feet in the water—it eased his mind. Well, let's get your horse aboard before the moon goes down."

Timothy grinned in the yellow moonlight, although so much had happened at this deserted landing so many years ago—the murder of the Indian boy, the shooting of the gambler, Dorch and Denna, and the transfer of the piano. Now all was gone. "If we bring the horse aboard," Timothy said, "do you have a shovel, sir?"

At Fort Smith Captain Keeter hired two riverfront boys to begin the scraping on the *Maizie Trout* and prepare her for painting. He didn't want to monopolize space at the landing, so he moored the sternwheeler to a cottonwood several hundred yards upstream near the junction of the Poteau.

This was fine for Timothy's horse; he could stake it out in green grass during the day and bring it back for oats before dark, provided some thief hadn't taken it.

While Captain Keeter scraped and sanded with the sweating waterfront boys, Timothy began his search for a red feather.

He left the *Maizie Trout* each morning, walking past the first shanty on First Street, which may have housed some sort of restaurant, since smoke always poured from its round tin chimney pipe. As he walked, the bulk of the slablike mountain in the distance, he looked closely at each woman he met, stopping some to question them. At the end of First, he turned right and walked a block over before hunching into Second Street.

Along his way, he passed the hotels and stores and rooming-houses of frontier glory where Forty-niners and bustling traders had stopped on their way to the California Trail, buildings now running down or in decay.

Having worked the river trade and prostitute areas, Timothy would turn up the cobblestones to the slightly higher ground of Garrison Avenue. He did this day after day, eating in one dive or restaurant or another, if he ate at all.

But it was a different world on the avenue—the taller buildings, the glass storefronts, saloons ornate or common, the hotels, the wide street with the planks across it at the end of each block for better crossing when it was muddy, the spire of the church still at the farther end on gently rising ground on what was now Thirteenth Street, the cross streets being numbered consecutively up from the river.

And there was another difference from the old days. The soldiers were long since gone from the garrison, there was no longer military drilling to harsh cadences as during the war days and later, and a new and overworked federal judge who abhorred capital punishment sentenced Territory and Arkansas outlaws to be hanged on the efficiency gallows, but losing in the process almost as many of his marshals as he succeeded in hanging outlaws. The town was spreading in all directions from the avenue; the stone and brick buildings of the old fort were still used by the town, the courts, or the government.

Once a crowd of Indians and Negroes straggled past Timothy on the cobblestones, going to the gallows to witness the hanging of an Indian outlaw. But even as Timothy walked and searched, the locomotive whistles shrieked their triumph, the sound causing him to wince.

Late one afternoon Timothy stood on the avenue looking into a display window which held a perky brown hat with a slanting red feather; the hat had a round turned-up brim, a close-cupped crown, and an elastic band to fit under the chin. And the perky feather! The hat was set quite alone in a ring of a dozen black bustles and other female finery.

The nearest I've come to her yet, Timothy thought, his heart sinking.

He turned from the display window and walked slowly up the street toward the church. He and his hump were familiar sights on the avenue now; people he met smiled and nodded, for his face was always cheerful, no matter how he felt inside.

But could he ask forever the soiled doves of the river trade or the ladies of the roominghouses if they had known a prostitute who wore a red-feathered hat? It had been foolish, after all these years, to come back at all, even to begin a search.

Common sense and reason had overtaken the enthusiasm which had guided him since he left Round Fort.

Another thing—these fancy ladies moved around too much; any one of those he had spoken to when his search began could be in Little Rock or Memphis or even New Orleans by now. These girls might never have known his girl, even if she were still here, and she, too, could have drifted away.

The prostitutes could solicit by day but must remain in their quarters at night. Timothy saw one now and stopped her.

"Well, what was her name?" a smartly dressed young woman with a parasol said, tapping her foot impatiently on the plank walk.

"I never knew her name, but she always wore something red."

"Sooner or later, everyone wears something red. Anyway, I wasn't even born then."

Timothy walked on up the street toward the church. As he reached Texas Corner, or the Plaza, where the old wagon trains had made up for their travels, his stomach began to ache. He thought, it's from this poor and greasy food I've been eating in all the dives and shanties while I questioned everyone.

The only thing for him to eat in these places now would be hard-boiled eggs. At least they would be cooked right—there was only one way to cook them. He was hurting so much, he groaned; he would have to return to the *Maizie Trout*.

Although bent almost double by the pain of cramps, on his way back down the street he stopped again to look at the hat in the bustles. Then he humped on down the cobblestones to the *Mazie Trout*.

Somewhere a locomotive whistled, and a steamboat wailed.

"Timothy," Keeter said that night while they sat in their chairs, the smell of fresh paint clinging to everything. "Why don't you give it up? We'll be finished with the painting in a week and can cast off. You're beginning to worry."

"I know," said Timothy. "There's not a prostitute's shanty or roominghouse I haven't been in, and even asking at all the hotels uptown. I've tramped this town over. People all think I'm crazy. But if I could only see her, I'd know in a minute."

"As long as you won't eat on board, pick one good place uptown and stop this upset-stomach business. You're making yourself sick."

Timothy said dismally, "I can't help it."

During the night thunder and lightning rumbled and cracked. The *Maizie Trout* strained at her moorings.

Timothy rose in his stateroom and went to the pilothouse.

Keeter was already there, looking out into blinding sheets of rain. The branches of the cottonwood tossed and swayed.

"Do you think she'll hold?" Timothy asked.

"She'll hold," Keeter said. "I've tied up here for years. How is your stomach?"

Timothy belched. "That soda you gave me helped."

He woke at daybreak, the smell of new paint close in the stateroom. Stretched on his side, he blinked his eyes at the porthole but didn't move.

Now that he had convinced himself that his search would prove useless, he felt better, and almost his normal self again. Or it could have been the soda.

He closed his eyes and slept again.

2

When Timothy Baines woke in the morning, it was to the sound of Keeter's hammering and sawing.

He was refreshed and glad that he had come to his decision to give up his search for a wife. He got off his cot, dressed, and went to the pilothouse. Keeter was nailing a bracketed bookshelf to the wall.

"What's that for?" Timothy asked.

"Reading," Keeter said. "It's how I'll spend the rest of my life."

"I'm going to walk a little," Timothy said.

"If it's breakfast you want, I'll fix it."

"No, I'll just go over to that shanty for a cup of coffee."

Keeter grinned. "No hard-boiled eggs?"

"No."

Timothy left the *Maizie Trout* with his slicker pulled loosely over his hump and walked through the mud. No use to look for anything anyway, he thought, this is all there would be, mud, mud, mud. No one would be out in it.

When he entered the shanty, he found only a wispy girl in blue gingham who was washing dishes at the counter.

"Hello," he called cheerfully. "Any coffee today?"

The child looked up from the pan. "Yes, sir," she said, sliding an unwashed plate back into the water. "Where will you sit, sir?"

Timothy glanced about the shanty. It was hardly even that—only planks nailed upright with cracks between them. I hope the roof is good, he thought, if it rains again.

Four rickety tables with oilcloth covers stood in scattered locations; for seats, there was only one chair, and it had a rung out of its back; the others were wooden boxes turned on end.

"I'll take the table with the chair," said Timothy.

He picked up a broken string guitar with a warped neck from the table, placed it across one of the boxes, and sat in the chair. The girl busied herself at the wood-burning cook stove; soon Timothy was taunted by the smell of boiling coffee.

"That smells good," he said, by way of making conversation as the frail figure placed a cup and saucer and spoon on his table.

"It is good coffee, sir." Her brown eyes sparkled. "Big Agnes always buys the best. Will you have cream and sugar? But our cream is just milk."

The remark touched Timothy. My old soft heart, he thought. He liked his coffee black, but now that the child had said the cream was only milk, it could hurt her feelings if he declined.

"Yes, cream and sugar," he said.

Timothy noticed how carefully she placed the cream pitcher and sugar bowl on his table, then returned to the counter for the coffeepot, pouring and filling his cup.

She curtsied. "Would there be anything else, sir?"

"No," Timothy said, still strangely touched. "I didn't feel well last night."

A gleam of merriment came to the large eyes. "You weren't drinking, sir?"

"No." Timothy laughed. "Only baking soda."

"Let me see your tongue."

He stuck it out.

"Ooh!" She shuddered. "I think you are sick."

"I've been looking for . . ." Timothy began. He changed his mind. "Who is Big Agnes?" She must be a battleax to work a child this way.

"Big Agnes is my mother."

"Where is she?"

"She's gone to the avenue for groceries."

"Then that is why you are here alone." The child couldn't have been more than twelve or thirteen. "Do you do well here?"

She lifted her head proudly. "Yes, sir. We do very well."

Hurt by the inference that perhaps they didn't do well, she half-ran behind the counter and dipped her hands into the suds again.

273

Timothy apologized. "I just meant," he said, "that you might do better up the street where more people are."

A tear rolled from a large eye and dropped into the dishpan. What an old fool, he thought; everything I say is wrong.

She said with spirit, "Mother does well enough to send me to school on the Point, and there are people on the street she doesn't want to be around."

She ran around the counter and came to him, her hands dripping. "Please, I know what you need for breakfast. Some fresh tomatoes and bacon and toast, and two poached eggs. I know you can't pay for it, so just pay for the coffee, but let me fix a breakfast."

"Very well," Timothy said, watching her eyes moisten. He wondered if she would accept the tip he would leave. "Do you work here often?"

"Except when I am in school. But we live here. And today is Saturday." She ran behind the counter to begin his breakfast.

"Live here?" Timothy glanced about the shanty again, and he hadn't known it was Saturday.

"Yes, sir. We live here. Our cots are in the back."

"Don't you get tired of so much work?"

"Oh, no, sir. It's a play game with us. I tell Big Agnes to do something, and she tells Little Agnes to do something. Then we laugh about it."

"It's beginning to rain again," said Timothy, hearing the wind come up. He started to rise and go to the door to look outside, but another rung had become loose in the back of the chair, and he turned to shove it back into place.

"Everything comes apart here." The girl spoke impulsively.

"All but you," Timothy said, straightening and sliding his slicker off, "and you are about the sweetest thing I ever saw in a gingham dress. That bacon smell—it's already making me strong."

"You wait." She laughed.

When she brought the food, Timothy began to eat ravenously. "Was there any coffee left over?" he asked.

Her eyes twinkled from the dishpan. "I knew you would want another cup, so I made enough the first time."

She brought the coffee and asked anxiously, "Do you really feel better?" Then she went back to the pan.

Timothy, his head bent over the poached eggs, heard a rustle at the door. At first he thought it was the rising wind, but as he turned his head, a woman came in, the hem of her long skirt muddy.

She was small and hatless, wet and dripping, one hand trying to brush rain from her hair and eyes. "Oh," she said, a burlap bag of groceries in her arms, and not noticing Timothy, who was seated almost behind the opened door, "what a nasty day! Have we had any customers?"

"One, Big Agnes," said the child, glancing at Timothy while Big Agnes pressed against the counter to remove the small sacks from the bag. She was scarcely taller than the child.

"Little Agnes, if business doesn't pick up, what will we do?"

Little Agnes giggled. "We can still eat, maybe. Where is your hat, Mother?"

"The wind blew it off," Big Agnes said, still placing the sacks on the counter. "The wind blew it into the avenue. Then a horse stepped on it and drove it a foot into the mud. My poor red feather!"

"We'll get you another hat."

"No, hats are too expensive. I'll use my kerchief, but I won't have any red to wear."

"But Big Agnes, when you go into the grocery stores, you must have a hat like a lady."

"But not now," said Big Agnes. "Oh, I wish the rain would stop. We'll never have anyone in today."

Little Agnes giggled. "We can eat more ourselves."

Timothy Baines, who had been thrown into a garbage can in an alley at birth, and had been named for the gentleman in whose can he was found, and had been brought up in the streets and alleys of New Orleans; Timothy Baines, who had been a decorated soldier of the war, and who had given his gentleman the coup de grace at North Fork Town and later killed a woman, hunched his shoulder to turn better and took the guitar from the top of the box.

He had seen only the profile of Big Agnes' face as she entered the shanty, but he knew. Well, he thought, his fingers trembling, this is it, it must be it, and it's now or never. But I know how I'll know what it is. And he had looked in every building on the waterfront but this one, and all the time it was within a stone's throw of the *Maizie Trout!*

He couldn't play guitar any better than he could a piano, and

275

much less one with a broken string. But in the round room and in his deserted classroom he had learned to pick out a tune with one finger, and he had toyed with mandolins and fiddles. He would take one string of the guitar, the shrill little E, and pick out the tune he wanted.

Slowly, the first notes sounded.

Big Agnes turned rigidly from the counter; perhaps, Timothy thought from somewhere back in his mind, she turned because she didn't know I was here.

His eyes on hers, which looked into his, he continued to pick the little E. She was trembling now, and it came to him like the rush of a great wave, trembling not because of the "Sparkling Spavinaw," but because of him.

She remembered.

Big Agnes took a step forward. "I didn't know if you would ever come back. I met the *Maizie Trout* for so long; then I stopped looking."

"I've never been back until now," Timothy said, rising.

"He can't afford to pay for his breakfast, Mother," Little Agnes whispered. "He's sick."

Timothy took a small hand; then he seized Big Agnes and kissed her.

"Ooooh!" said Little Agnes.

During the few moments while Timothy and Big Agnes were alone in the rain outside the shanty, and while Little Agnes waited on the second customer of the morning, a down-at-heel man who had taken the table with the chair, Agnes told Timothy that after the birth of her baby, by some unknown father, she could not bring the child up in the same life she had led.

"I'm not making excuses," she said, standing beside Timothy with his slicker draped over their heads, "but when my father and mother died, I came to Fort Smith. It was hard to find work then, and I took a little room on Second Street, but I never stayed on the Row. Now you know what I am, or was."

"You mean you've kept going at this little place?"

"Yes, and I'm proud of it."

Timothy kissed her while the rain beat down on the slicker. No, he thought, looking into her brown eyes, she wasn't as young as on that far-off day on the cobblestones, but neither was he. He was proud to be getting a little gray.

"Well," he said, "let's close up for today. There won't be many customers in, and we'll go to the avenue. I want to buy you something."

"What?" she said, her eyes still big in his.

"A ring, and yesterday while I looked for you, I found something pretty in the window of Batchelor's Department Store."

"Do you mean that little hat in the bustles?"

"That's exactly it."

"Timothy," she said, "you do remember! I don't know why I loved you so long ago. Maybe it was because you understood and didn't talk to me like other men."

"Maybe I did understand," said Timothy. "I've been batted around myself."

"Where did you learn my song?"

"From an old cowhand."

"I played it for many people."

"Shall we go to the avenue? I've a good horse that will keep us out of the mud, all of us. We're three featherweights."

She drew back in consternation. "I just thought, we can't go. People from the avenue who have helped me may come to eat today, and it would be so bad for them in the mud."

"Get Little Agnes ready," said Timothy in masculine pride, "and I'll get some slickers and paint a sign, 'Agnes—Closed Today,' and we'll drive it into the mud at the foot of the avenue."

When he returned from the *Maizie Trout* and helped mount Big Agnes and Little Agnes on the horse before and behind, Big Agnes said from her slicker, "But the signpost says 'Closed Today and Sunday.'"

"Sure," said Timothy. "Tomorrow's Sunday. When we go back to the *Maizie Trout* with two hats and a lot of clothes for two pretty girls, we're going to stay there for two days, and I'll do the cooking. I never was so hungry in my life."

On Sunday morning, a day clear and bright on the Arkansas, the river sparkling under a soft south breeze and a steamboat screeching its way downstream toward the mountain, Timothy said to Captain Keeter while the mother and daughter promenaded the dappled deck in their new hats and dresses, "Now we can get down to business."

"We'll get down to business," Keeter said, "but do you know what that poor child did last night? She had a stateroom to herself, but she'd never slept away from her mother. Agnes told me she knocked on her door at midnight."

"It's all touching," Timothy said, watching the feathered hats with the circular upturned brims and the elastic bands under the chins, and approving the new dresses which swept the bright deck, "but now, let's talk."

"Shoot," said Keeter. "Do you want a beer?"

"I'll have one," Timothy said. "I think my stomach is up to it."

"Then pull the chairs out, while I get it."

When they were settled in the chairs, Timothy spoke. "You told me the steamboat days on the Arkansas are finished."

Keeter nodded.

"You're wrong," Timothy said. "The steamers will never be finished as long as one can float. Now, don't look surprised. I've been thinking about this ever since I found Agnes. I'll tell you why I want to throw in with you." He shifted his hump in the chair to be more comfortable. Somehow, life on the rivers would be like waters of forgetfulness, and he had a new life now.

At Timothy's remark, Keeter grinned with satisfaction.

Timothy said, "We're going to make a showplace of the *Maizie Trout*. We'll knock out all the staterooms and build an apartment for me and Big and Little Agnes."

"I wouldn't mind having extra space myself," Keeter said, "but to tear things up now, after all that painting!"

"We'll keep the old galley for personal use, but the big change will be on deck. We'll take the cargo space beneath the superstructure and wall it waist high. At the back, we'll build a larger galley."

"What the devil!" said Keeter.

"I said we'd make a showplace out of the old girl, and we will. I can cook, Agnes can cook, and the kid can cook. We'll serve meals on this steamboat that won't be found this side of New Orleans. We'll put into what good towns are left downriver, or on the Mississippi; the *Maizie Trout* will be the last of the sternwheelers. We'll serve food and wine by music and colored lanterns. If people want to dance, they'll have the whole deck. You know," Timothy said seriously, bending forward, "someday people will begin to look for these old steamers. We'd just as well be first. Man, they'll be lined up on the banks waiting for us. You get the crew; I'll get the waiters. We'll share the profits."

"Your mind is spinning," Keeter said, taking his cap off and lighting his pipe to smoke furiously.

"The kid makes me think of one thing," Timothy said. "She's got to have schooling, so we'll pick a good town on the Mississippi, maybe down in Louisiana, where it's warm in winter; the rest of the year we'll be free to run up the river and the Arkansas and the Ohio, where people will be waiting for you at the landings, like in the old days."

Captain Keeter stood up. He looked beyond the cook shanty toward the landings and the mountain. Yes, the old days were gone; he had known it for years.

Timothy said, shifting himself in his chair again, "We'll place a flat bronze marker on deck where Jessup died. It's part of history."

"Yes." Keeter turned, the cottonwood leaves lisping. "Yes, it's part of history." He extended his hand. "It's part of history."

That evening Little Agnes and Timothy sat on the deck of the *Maizie Trout,* their fishing poles extended, their bare feet in the water.

The child still wore her new hat. "Mother says you will be married tomorrow."

"Would it please you?"

"I would love it. When did you meet Mother?"

"A long time ago, but I never got back."

The brown eyes looked into his.

"I was way down in Indian Territory." Timothy wondered about his eagles, if they had a cabin of their own somewhere, or lived at some rancher's desolate line camp in New Mexico or Arizona.

"And we'll stay on a steamboat the rest of our lives?"

"As long as you wish—or until some young man carries you off."

The child giggled.

"Big Agnes sure told you to get out of the galley in a hurry. I never saw her so happy. She was still wearing her hat too. She said she'd make a well man out of you."

"Yes, she told me to get out," Timothy said.

"She said you used to live almost in the Chickasaw nation."

"Yes," Timothy said, watching his unmoving cork.

"Mother said you used to live high up on a hill."

"Yes," Timothy said, still seeing Elfreda's farewell at Dorch's grave. "Someday I'll tell you about it."

The whistle of the *Maizie Trout* quavered. Keeter was testing his new engine and boilers, and tomorrow, after the wedding at the Le Flore, the steamboat would put out and strike for the Big River.

"I've got one!" the child screamed, pulling her line up, the feather on the hat jerking.

The fish slapped Timothy in the face, and he and Little Agnes sat there, hugging each other and laughing.